MADELEINE'S WAR

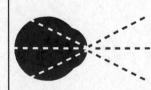

This Large Print Book carries the
Seal of Approval of N.A.V.H.

MADELEINE'S WAR

PETER WATSON

THORNDIKE PRESS
A part of Gale, Cengage Learning

GALE
CENGAGE Learning·

Farmington Hills, Mich • San Francisco • New York • Waterville, Maine
Meriden, Conn • Mason, Ohio • Chicago

GALE
CENGAGE Learning®

LIBRARY OF CONGRESS CATALOGING-IN-PUBLICATION DATA

Watson, Peter, 1943–
    Madeleine's war / by Peter Watson. — Large print edition.
    pages cm. — (Thorndike Press large print basic)
    ISBN 978-1-4104-8080-4 (hardcover) — ISBN 1-4104-8080-1 (hardcover)
    1. World War, 1939-1945—England—Fiction. 2. Large type books. I. Title.
PR6073.A875M33 2015b
823'.914—dc23   2015011550

Published in 2015 by arrangement with Nan A. Talese, an imprint of Knopf Doubleday Publishing Group, a division of Random House, LLC.

Printed in Mexico
1 2 3 4 5 6 7 19 18 17 16 15

For Coco, Tim, and Pip,
in memory of Nicola Hodgkinson

This story is based on a series of true events which took place on either side of D-Day in Britain and France in 1944.

■ ■ ■ ■ ■

MAY
SUSSEX

■ ■ ■ ■ ■

1

I remember that day so well — late May 1944, early evening. As Winston Churchill himself said in another context, it was both the end of the beginning, and the beginning of the end.

Southwater. A small Sussex village, made up of barely more than one street, with white-painted houses set back from the road, a pebble-faced church, a stone-built school, a pub — the Black Prince, which looked appetizing though we never had time to visit it — and a roped-off cricket field which bordered the road, where play sometimes stopped the traffic on match days, when the ball was hit beyond the boundary.

The airfield, which was our only reason for visiting Southwater, was well hidden, beyond the village, off the Chichester road. The lane by which it was approached wound round and dipped through a copse of beech trees — until you were again facing the village, but viewed from behind. The loamy field, flat on its northern reaches, and edged by a line of hawthorn, rolled away to give at its southern limit a fine view of the Sussex Downs, Pevensey in the distance, and beyond that, on a clear day, a very clear day . . . France itself.

There was a hangar of sorts at one end of the field. Just brick walls with a corrugated iron roof, and an abandoned concrete bunker, which had, in an earlier era of the war, stood ready to resist invasion.

Madeleine and I were lying on the grass, waiting. Waiting for the pilot and waiting for the moon. These were our last hours together, at least for now. She was wearing a blue dress with small white flowers printed across it, a dress made in the French style in our London factory, in keeping with her cover. There was a single row of pearls at her neck, and a leather shoulder bag lay on the grass beside her. She wore flat shoes. Her hair fluttered and flowed out behind her in the wind. Her gypsy hair, as I sometimes called it, her Botticelli hair, was her most distinctive feature — long, auburn, and unruly-curly, floating about her like the goddess in *The Birth of Venus*. She was forever pulling it away from her face, or gathering it up to let the back of her neck breathe.

She loved her hair, though she knew it was always going to be in the way. She was tall, but not too tall, and when she raised her arms to pull back her hair, whatever blouse or shirt

12

or frock she was wearing tightened over her breasts. Her skin was paper white, and her lips more creamy brown than red. In the early evening light, she stood out — she *shone* — like a stained-glass figure on a dim church wall.

Across the field, to our left, the roofs of Southwater mingled with the trees, soon to be lost in the gloom.

Madeleine leant across and kissed my cheek. She had a slender, wispy figure, like those Debenham's models pictured in the newspapers. She often held her lips slightly open, as if she were out of breath, or having second thoughts about saying something. Her eyes were the burnished brown of whisky (whisky is my main vice). When she was astonished, or amused, or aroused, her eyelashes settled on her cheeks like bird's feet on sand.

"Will you miss me?"

"Silly question. Let's go through your poem again."

She rolled back on the grass and shook her head. "No need. I haven't forgotten it." She squinted at the sky. "What time does the moon rise?"

I looked at my watch. "Half an hour, forty minutes."

"Why did we get here so early?"

"Regulations. Nothing last-minute. So your mind is settled before you go. So you don't

13

forget anything. You've got your instructions, sewn in as you were told?"

She picked up my hand and kissed it. Her lips were warm and wet. "I think you are more nervous than I am. And I'm the one going."

"Don't unstitch the instructions until you hear from us. Just in case you are caught and tortured . . . It's safer for you not to know things before you have to."

"You *are* nervous, aren't you?"

"I've been there — you know that. I know what it's like on the ground in France, how dangerous it is, what the risks are. I'm right to be nervous. It helps to be a little bit nervous — it stops you getting slack."

At that moment we heard a car.

We scrambled to our feet. The car emerged from the copse of trees in the lane, its headlights already blazing, and then the lights started bobbing and weaving as the car slowed and drove across the grass of the field. Although the colour had gone out of the day, I recognized the vehicle as a Morris, standard issue for the Royal Air Force.

We watched as the car was parked next to my Lagonda, the engine was switched off, and the driver got out. He came towards us. I recognized him.

"Jack!" I cried. "Matthew Hammond. Matt Hammond. Remember me? — Drucourt, forty-two."

He looked at me in the gathering gloom. He was a compact man, muscular and sinewy.

He held out his hand. "Of course, of course. How's the wound?"

"I'll live, but I've been grounded."

"Chest wound, wasn't it? Shrapnel."

"You've got a good memory."

"And?"

"I lost a lung, had to give up sabotage — and tobacco, of course, or that's what I told the quack. All the rest is working, though. For now at least. And you're still flying."

He smiled. "Shot down once, over Valençay. Managed to parachute to safety, then got away along a ratline." He nodded. "So here we are, still at war."

"Where's the rest of your squadron?"

"Five miles away. On a field four times as big as this one, with a concrete strip." He looked about him. "This is much better for what we are about to do tonight." Looking at Madeleine, he went on. "And this is tonight's mission?"

He and Madeleine shook hands.

"Hello," she said. "I'm —"

"Don't tell me," he said quickly. "It's safer for us all if I don't know." He looked at me. "It will take me half an hour to get ready. These Lysanders need TLC. By then the moon should be on the rise. Does that give you long enough?"

"Oh yes," I said. "We're ready now."

"I'll be as quick as I can." And he walked off towards the hangar.

"How long will the flight be, do you think?" said Madeleine.

I stroked her hair. "Le Gâvre is north of Nantes and inland from St. Nazaire — about five hundred and fifty miles direct but probably nearer to seven hundred with the route you will take. Close to four hours in the air, I'd say."

She looked up at me. The cleft in her chin formed a tiny shadow. "Do you really think the invasion will come from the Atlantic?"

"I don't know *where* the invasion will take place, or when. It will be soon, we know that, but exactly when . . ." I shook my head again. "You could be going to help the Resistance play their part when the invasion starts — or you could be a decoy. None of us knows."

"I hope I'm not a decoy," she sighed. "Not after all this training."

Her voice matched her height and figure — rich, deep, with that French-Canadian lilt she had picked up at school in Quebec.

"Being a decoy would be safer."

She shook her head vehemently. "Stop trying to reassure me! That's not what I want. Imagine life after the war and not having . . . not having been in any danger."

"Talking like that *is* a danger."

"You've been in danger, you've got *your* wound."

I let a pause go by. "You were right earlier — I *am* more nervous than you. If you are not on your toes the whole time . . . I messed up. I don't want that to happen to you." I gestured to Jack, now making noises in the hangar. "We've got half an hour. Let's go for a stroll over the field."

The dark had descended completely now and as we walked away from the hangar, the night closed in around us. I put my arm around Madeleine's shoulders and buried my face in her hair. The soft sweetness of her scent rose to meet me, the muskiness I had first breathed in Scotland weeks before when she was training in Ardlossan and I was part of the instructor course.

"I won't go on," I said as softly as I could, "but if the worst happens and you do get caught . . . If they can prove you are what you are, then they can execute you. They will probably torture you before —"

She stopped, disengaged herself from under my arm, turned and put her fingers to my lips. "We've been through all this, *hundreds* of times." She tapped her pocket. "I've got the pill we are all given." She kissed me. "I'll use it. I've told you before, I'm not sleepwalking here. I know what I'm doing and why. And you know why too. Stop treating me as if I'm — I don't need to say that again, either."

She looked up at me. "Just think. If I hadn't

injured my knee, all those years ago, I might have been a proper dancer by now, entertaining the troops somewhere, in Italy or the Middle East."

She had fallen, as a young member of the corps de ballet, and broken her patella.

"And we might never have met."

She kissed the tip of my nose. "You might have come to see me dance — hung around the stage door."

"I don't like queues." I grinned.

We walked on a bit, further into the field, arm in arm.

"I wonder what Leni's doing tonight?" Madeleine breathed. "Dinner à deux with Herr Hitler, or filming a night scene somewhere?"

Since Madeleine had discovered that the German film-maker had also begun adult life as a dancer, and then damaged her knee, she had followed Leni Riefenstahl's progress as she grew more famous and got closer and closer to Hitler. She was a walking archive of the details of Riefenstahl's life.

"Maybe she's *too* close to Hitler," I replied. "If Germany loses this war, she could end up in prison."

"Do you think so? I suppose she *is* the most well-known woman in the Third Reich. That's an achievement of sorts."

Off to our left, a full moon was rising, silvery, slightly mottled, like an old coin, rendering the sky about it a deep indigo.

"Is that the last full moon before the invasion?" she asked.

I nodded. "There's a good chance, I would say. Better than fifty-fifty."

I didn't tell her that I had sent more agents abroad in the past ten days than at any time previously. Tonight was unusual in that only Madeleine was going, but then I had had some say in that. If she had to go — and I knew she had to go, though it devastated me — I wanted her to myself at the last moments. The evening before I had seen off four, and five the night before that. Tomorrow three would be going. Anyone in the know could read the signs.

"And do you think . . ." Her voice caught. "Do you think it will be the last full moon I shall ever see?"

"Don't," I breathed. "Don't say that."

It was the only time I ever knew her to show any doubt about what she was doing.

"Time to go back, I think," she said in the same Quebecois tones. "Time for the Oak to fly."

"Just a second." I put my hand on her arm and with the other took a small package from my pocket. "This is for you."

She looked up at me, her lips slightly parted, in that way that she had.

"Matt," she said softly, her voice lingering on the last letters of my name. Her fingers

19

pulled at the tissue paper.

The paper fell open.

"Oh. Oh, yes! Of course, how like you. An acorn, a gold acorn." She held it in the palm of her hand. "It's beautiful, beautifully made — how lovely. I shall wear it always. No one will ever guess."

She stood on tiptoe and kissed my cheek.

"I found it in a shop near Hatton Garden and couldn't resist it. I thought . . . I thought . . . You know what I thought."

She pinned the brooch to her coat.

"I'm overwhelmed," she whispered. "Until this war ends, only you and I will know what this means. Our own wartime secret."

"If you get captured, throw it away. That's an order." I smiled.

"I don't think I have ever disobeyed you before, Colonel," she said. "But the Oak is not going anywhere without this acorn, not even if she gets captured."

She patted her hand over the brooch. "I already feel warm inside, just here."

She kissed my cheek again. "Let's go back now. Now I'm ready for anything. Ready for take-off."

As we approached the hangar, the bark of the Lysander's engine suddenly broke across the field as it erupted into life.

Madeleine picked up her shoulder bag and her other case, containing her change of clothing and her radio transmitter. The tone of the plane's engine rose and then fell, as Jack eased the Lysander out from under the hangar. He taxied a few yards forward, then stopped and killed the engine.

Silence closed in around us. How far from the war we seemed just then.

Jack got down from the plane and stepped across. He held something out to Madeleine.

"This is a map — once we get aloft, there'll be enough moonlight to read by. You can follow our route — west, more or less, to the Cherbourg peninsula, then south. Three hours and forty minutes if the wind holds steady."

Madeleine took the map.

"Now, let me see you into your parachute."

I stood and watched as he helped Madeleine fasten the straps in the correct configuration.

When it was fitted, she turned to me. She pulled her hair off her face again and kissed me on the cheek. "Don't wish me luck," she urged. "Don't say anything. Let these be my last words." Her voice fell to a murmur. *"Le chêne, je t'aime toujours."*

She brushed her lips across my cheek. A surge of desire rushed through my veins. How long before that would happen again?

"I love you. I love you always." She pressed a small packet into my hand. "Don't open it until I've taken off."

Turning quickly, she moved towards the plane.

Jack helped her up and in, stowed her bags, and lifted her made-in-France bicycle behind her. Then he hauled himself into the pilot's seat and all too quickly restarted the engine. In what seemed like no time the Lysander was taxiing towards the end of the field.

Madeleine didn't turn back, or wave. She had made her farewell in the way that she wanted. From now on she was Oak, Chêne in French, her code name.

The aircraft reached the far end of the field and turned. What had been a throaty growl from the engine was now a scream.

Then the plane lurched forward. For a few moments it bucked across undulations in the loam but then the grass leveled out, the aircraft's speed increased, and, as the plane came abreast of me, its wheels lifted clear of the ground. In the moonlight its shadow raced across the turf and disappeared. I waved but, in the dark, I couldn't make out either of the figures.

I watched as the Lysander banked, turning towards the moon. Its sound lessened but I continued watching as its silhouette grew smaller, etched sharp against the mottled silver disc in the black sky. I watched until the sound had disappeared, till the aircraft was no more than a smudge against the shiny expanse, then nothing at all.

■ ■ ■ ■

FEBRUARY

THREE MONTHS EARLIER
SCOTLAND

■ ■ ■ ■

2

Her hair, plastered to her face, hung down around the line of her jaw. Water dripped from her nose and her chin. Mascara smudges spread down her cheeks, like ink on blotting paper. The rope around her chest cut into the flesh on her arms. Her wet clothes steamed, even as she shivered in the night air. The brilliance of the arc lights bearing down on her seemed to bleach her already white skin. Behind was the dim outline of some farm buildings and, beyond them, in the distance, in the moonlight, the sea.

"Beim naechsten Mal lasse ich Sie länger unter Wasser!" shouted the man bending over her. "Next time, I'll leave you under the water for longer, do you understand?" he repeated in English. *"Beim naechsten Mal lasse ich Sie solange bis Sie tot sind.* Next time I'll leave you under until you are *dead!"*

He had all the insignia of a thug. It was not just the black uniform and the boots, the gloved hands that slapped the leather thong against his thigh in a regular rhythm, that were somehow chilling, as if distancing him from the proceedings. It was the bald head, the rimless spectacles, and the crimson birthmark snaking down one side of his face that really marked him for what he was: an ex-criminal-turned-tormenter. Men like him *relished* war.

"*Wie heissen Sie? Welcher Einheit gehören Sie an? Woher kommen Sie?* What is your name? What is your unit? Where have you come from? What is your target? I'm . . . losing . . . patience." He half sang the last sentence, as if to indicate he was enjoying his cruelty. Putting a gloved finger inside his collar, as if it itched, he reached forward with his other hand and lifted her chin. "Do you want to *die* of cold?"

She groaned. "Madeleine Dirac. I told you, I'm not German, I'm Canadian, and I'm part of a special —"

"No! No! *Nein!* We've been through all that. We watched you come in by plane, we saw you come in over the sea — we watched you parachute down, dropping conveniently into a restricted zone. The plane got away before we could get to you — *aber ihr Glück hat Sie verlassen.* But your luck ran out. Again I ask, What is your target?"

She shook her head viciously. Her wet hair, dank red ropes like a nest of vipers, flung beads of water across the light beams and into the dark. "I've told you already —"

"Enough! *Genug!*" He raised his head. "Hicks! Corbett!"

Out of the gloom beyond the arc lights, two other men appeared, both in the same black uniforms but without the trimmings of rank. They lifted her, still strapped to the chair, and carried her to a metal container which, in an earlier life, had been a sheep dip, several yards long, six feet wide and six deep.

"Now," said the man with the birthmark, stepping forward and peeling back his sleeve with a gloved finger to inspect his wristwatch. "It's getting late."

The two men manhandled Madeleine and the chair into the water. Her body disappeared. There was a thrashing in the sheep dip but the men held both the chair and the woman's form firmly below the surface.

The man with the birthmark waited. He was counting. When he had reached whatever limit he had set himself, he shouted, "Bring her up!"

The men hauled the woman and the chair from the sheep dip.

She was coughing, retching, crying, gasping for air. Her chest heaved, as water ran off her, her hair hung down before her eyes, some of it disappearing inside her mouth. She made a movement of her lips and coughed it out.

The man with the birthmark allowed her time to regain control of her breathing.

"Now," he said at length. "I'm not going to ask this again. *Welcher Einheit gehören* — What is your — ?"

"I don't speak German!" she suddenly screamed. "Are you stupid? I've told you. I'm a Canadian, from Trois Rivières. Three-*fucking*-Rivers. I was brought up in France and England. I'm a nurse. I flew up from Manchester, for pity's sake, in a Lysander —"

"Quiet," he growled. "That's enough. We've wasted enough time on you. You arrived in Britain by aircraft, illegally, in a restricted zone without any paperwork, and in plain clothes. If it was a Lysander, we'd have had notification it was coming — and we didn't. Whatever nationality you are — German, Austrian, Hungarian, Italian — it's all the same; the way you arrived makes you a spy and, under the rules of war, I am within my rights to have you shot. *Ich frage nochmal: was war Ihr Ziel?* I ask you again: What was your target?"

As he shouted and stared, the dance of the birthmark on his cheek made it look as though his face was on fire.

She looked at him. Her hair hung down, stuck to her skin. She blew it away from her mouth. "I — am — a — Canadian." There was another movement of her lips and this time she spat at him.

Slowly, deliberately, he raised his arm and flicked the spittle off his uniform with a gloved finger.

"Very well," he said. "You want to play it like that." Gesturing to the other men, he continued: "Take off her clothes, tie her up again, and put her against the wall over there. She'll be easier to bury and harder to identify later if she's naked." He nodded to the darkness beyond where the bright beams from the arc lights reached.

She struggled, or she tried to, but the men were too strong for her and, soon enough, she was naked and tied up again, but standing.

The man with the birthmark changed the angle of the arc lights so that they shone at full strength on the farm wall — a long windowless barn. In front of it, the ground was covered in dark, damp patches. Blood.

The men manoeuvred Madeleine in front of the wall. Feeling the stickiness of the blood on the soles of her bare feet, she looked down, and a whimper of despair leaked into the night air. She was thinking: How many others had been executed on this spot? And how recently? The two men disappeared beyond the range of the lights.

The thug with the flame on his face moved forward.

"Do you want a blindfold?"

29

She shook her head. She was near to tears. "You don't understand . . . I'm a —"

"No. *Halt! Genug!* Enough. You've had your chance. We're not brutes like you Nazis but we're not fools either. Fly into a restricted zone in plain clothes? . . . You were *asking* for trouble."

He took a pace back. The two other men had reappeared, this time with rifles. They stood on either side of him.

He took his pistol out of its holster and held it at his side.

"I ask you one last time: What did you come here to do? What — who — is your target?"

When she didn't immediately reply, he raised his pistol and took aim. The other men raised their rifles and did the same.

She was crying, but then she stopped. She shook her hair free of her face and stood up straight. Tears streamed down her cheeks but she looked them in the eye.

There was a long pause.

"Okay, give her a blanket," I shouted from beyond the reach of the lights.

A woman in a blue nurse's uniform ran from behind me out of the dark.

"Here you are, dear," she murmured, putting the blanket around Madeleine's shoulders. Madeleine collapsed into the woman's arms, and she was carried away.

The men in uniform lowered their rifles. One took out a packet of cigarettes and handed them around.

"She did well," said the man with the birth-mark.

"Nice tits," said one of the other men. "Oh, sorry, sir," he added, seeing me approach. "I didn't —"

"What are those?" I said, ignoring him. "Craven A? May I?"

As I savoured the cigarette — very much against doctor's orders — I watched as Madeleine Dirac was led away. She was clearly bewildered, as was only natural, but I was about to explain everything. First, though, she would be given a hot shower, dressed in her nurse's uniform, fortified with hot soup — and, if she wanted one, a cigarette.

Forty-five minutes later, Madeleine Dirac was shown into my office in the set of buildings that we in the organisation I worked for called "The Farm." It was true that it had once been a farm and it was still surrounded by three hundred acres of woodland, arable meadows, and rocky cliffs overlooking the shore of the North Sea. But it had other uses too.

"Office" is rather a grand word for what in fact was — or had been — a stable before the war, and still had one of those doors where the upper half spends much of its life open. Now, however, as the time was well past midnight, past 2:00 a.m. in fact, and it was still early February, both halves were firmly closed.

Maps, mainly of France, lined the walls, as well as various charts, showing when the full moons were due.

A small fireplace burned coal. There was a desk, with a telephone, a sofa, and two easy chairs. Madeleine Dirac sat in one, I sat in the other. Fresh coffee — not the usual wartime chicory substitute — brewed by my aide-de-camp, sat on the low table between us and a half-bottle of Scotch. We were alone.

Madeleine Dirac looked almost elegant in her tidy nurse's uniform and slightly prim black lace-up shoes. She had run her fingers through her hair, which was still wet and fell about her shoulders. But she hadn't put on any make-up and she looked pale.

"Are you tired?" I asked.

She moved her head from side to side, as if she couldn't make up her mind what to say. The edges of her hair sparkled in the firelight, making her look younger than she was.

"I'll sleep tonight, yes," she said, smothering a yawn with her hand. "But — but what on earth was going on out there? An hour ago I thought I was about to die. It was *not* a nice experience. What have I just been through?"

"Too tired for a whisky?" I leaned forward and lifted the bottle. "Maybe a little Scotch with your coffee? Might give you a lift."

"Good idea. My mother sometimes has

whisky in her tea. But I'm not letting you off the hook. What was — all *that*?"

"Oh, don't worry, you'll find out soon enough. That's why we're here now, in this room, alone. Certain things have to be settled tonight."

"What things? Why tonight? I'm lost."

Her voice was strangely intimate, yet deep and musical, with a Canadian lilt to it.

I poured the coffee, and the whisky, and handed them across.

I put more coal on the fire. Then I crossed the room, picked up a file from my desk, and sipped my whisky as I opened it.

"Madeleine Dirac, aged twenty-five. Born Trois Rivières. Three-Fucking-Rivers" — I looked up and smiled — "on April 20, 1919. Father: Didier Dirac, a dental technician from Louzac originally, in the Limoges region of France. Mother: Victoria Beale, a seamstress, from Chester. Educated at St. Mathilde's Ursuline Convent, Quebec City, and St. Hilaire Convent, Louzac, after your father decided he missed France. All correct so far?"

She nodded and sat further back in her chair.

"Father died 1933 in a shooting accident, after which your mother sold the failing dental technician's business. Eventually, you immigrated to England, where your mother had been born and grew up. Settled in London, though your mother subsequently

33

moved to Blakeney on the Norfolk coast. That was later, in 1938. From 1938 until 1942 you worked as a translator for a publisher. In 1942 you changed jobs, helping to train soldiers to speak French —"

"I wanted to do something more useful in the war. It doesn't sound like much the way you say it."

"Relax. I'm testing the file, not you . . . Last year, 1943, after approaching the commanding officer of the translation unit, you joined FANY, the First Aid Nursing Yeomanry. Is all *that* correct?"

"Yes, yes. I wanted to work for the war effort, do something . . . you know, *practical*. But all I got to be was a trainee nurse."

I nodded. "While you were training, I understand you saved the life of a mounted policeman. How did that come about?"

She pulled a face. "You *have* been digging. One afternoon, when we had some free time, a few of us nurses on the course went out together. We went to look at Whitehall — you know, Downing Street, Scotland Yard, Horse Guards Parade. While we were there, part of a barrage balloon that they keep flying over the government offices exploded with a bang and one of the policemen's horses was startled and reared up. The policeman fell to the ground, hit his head, and had a heart attack. I was nearby, so were the other nurses, and we knew what to do. That's all."

"But you took the lead."

"Someone had to."

"But why you?"

"I can be bossy. My mother says I used to be a bit of a tomboy."

"He came round, the policeman?"

"Oh yes, we were very close to him when it happened. His heart didn't stop for very long — seconds only."

I sipped my whisky. "FANY is not always what it seems. Sometimes it is *exactly* what it seems, but not always. That episode impressed your superiors. You were watched."

That got her attention. She sat forward. The shifting light from the flames of the fire flickered across her face "What do you mean? Watched by whom?"

I tapped my teeth with my whisky glass.

Despite her ordeal, and the late hour, there was a morning briskness about her.

"We needed to know how excitable you were. What your memory is like, what level of scientific and technological knowledge you are comfortable with, how well you fit in with others, whether you like to be a prima donna or are happy in the background, how fast you learn, whether your French is as good as it should be, given your background, whether you have an accent. All that took time."

She looked at me. She was thinking back, trying to remember being watched, wondering why she hadn't noticed. She closed her eyes. That was when I first noticed that her eyelashes settled on her cheeks like the marks of birds' feet on sand.

"Did you ever notice being watched?"

Would she answer honestly? That was important.

She shivered and gripped the skin under her chin with her forefinger and thumb. "Cree-py," she breathed, breaking the word into two. But she shook her head. "There was once, one time, we had some French people to look after in FANY, wounded soldiers, they said, who'd been evacuated from France. I was called in to interpret. But later I heard some of the so-called Frenchmen speaking English. So why then did they need an interpreter? But by then the emergency — if it *was* an emergency — was over."

"Yes, that was a test."

"Creepy twice over. What was I being tested *for*?"

"You are about to find out."

I refilled our whisky glasses. "From 1940 until the end of 1942 I worked in France, behind enemy lines. In 1942 I was injured — it wasn't the greatest moment of my life, I have to admit. I recovered, but it affected my mobility and I was invalided home. That, too, is another story. However, while I was in France I noticed something, two things, in fact. First, that although the French have an active and spirited Resistance, because the

36

country is occupied the Resistance workers are always being caught, and tortured, with the result that their lines of communication are penetrated by the Germans. Secondly, I noticed that the most important activity in the Resistance, from our point of view, the British point of view, is communication. Disparate Resistance units, and our sabotage circuits, have to communicate securely with each other and with us in London. But where communication is concerned, women — and not men — are the better couriers."

She was looking intently at me.

"Why? They are better couriers because all able-bodied men across the Channel should be working for the war effort, either in France or in German factories. They cannot move around unnoticed. But women can."

She was listening avidly now. Still no sign of tiredness — her gaze searched my face.

"And so, later in 1942, after I had drawn this to the attention of my army superiors, a decision was taken, at the very highest level — by Churchill himself — to authorize the training of women, to be dropped behind enemy lines, to act as couriers and, occasionally, as wireless operators in deepest France, *la France profonde*. Very occasionally, as explosives experts."

"Did you meet Churchill?"

"Just that once."

"What's he like?"

"Taller than I'd expected. He didn't say much, but he listened, asked the other people at the meeting if they had any arguments against the use of women —"

"And — ?"

"I can't go into details. Sorry."

"Don't worry about me. I'm not the sneaky kind. Why did the PM go with your plan? Are you a hero or something?"

"Not at all. I got a medal for the sabotage I carried out over there, before I was injured, but now I'm . . . Well, this is where we get to the meat of the matter."

She took her shoes off and pulled both her legs under her. "Okay."

"I'm inviting you to join something. It's not a something you can apply to join — you have to be invited. The number of agents in this something is few, because sabotage in France risks sparking reprisals from the Gestapo. In response to the blowing up of bridges or railways, for instance, the Nazis round up people at random and execute them, or take them off to labour camps in Germany. But some sabotage occurs, to keep up French morale and prepare them for the invasion, when it comes."

She yawned. "Don't worry," she said, blushing. "I'm not bored — really I'm not. It's just . . . you know, all that stuff, being underwater . . ."

"I know, I know. But we must get through

this tonight. You'll see why." I gave her a small reassuring smile.

"So. This something you're being invited to join . . . our main work is to drop agents, money, ammunition, and equipment — weapons — behind enemy lines, to support sabotage work, and to prepare for a general uprising in France when the invasion comes. The invasion will be soon now, though no one knows exactly when or where. Certainly not me."

Outside there was a rustle of wind that shook the window frames.

"Once we had decided that you were suitable, or at least not *un*suitable, we needed to test you, twice. The first test was relatively straightforward — a parachute drop. Many people — perhaps most people — are pretty hesitant about jumping out of an aircraft high in the sky, especially at night, so it makes sense for us not to waste time and money training people who will then balk at being dropped by a Lysander or a Hudson. You were sent to Manchester, therefore, to make two drops, the first without equipment, the second with equipment. You did well."

She nodded and a smile shaped her lips. "Don't sound so surprised. We women are not totally pointless." She let the last two letters stay on her tongue for a shade longer than necessary.

"I thought you were tired?"

"Not up here," she said, tapping her fore-head. "Haven't you noticed?"

"Maybe I should have let them shoot you."

"Why did you let them undress me? The whole thing was frightening enough without that. Did you or the others just want a peek?"

"The Gestapo's favourite interrogation techniques always include humiliation. We had to reproduce that as best we could. I have found stripping people is very effective. Now, shall we get back to the interview?"

She waved her empty glass.

I refilled both and leaned forward again.

"The second test involved the deception you've just been through. So far, we have found that the chances of one of our agents surviving six months in the field — I'm talk-ing about ninety-odd men, and two score women, in the organisation you are being asked to join — is about fifty-fifty. In other words, there is a high chance of your being captured. If you *are* captured, because you will be in plain clothes you will be classified as a spy — just as we played it in our little deception — and you can, under the rules of war, be legally executed. Before that, though, you will be interrogated and very possibly tortured, even though you are a woman."

For a moment her gaze turned inward.

"Our policy therefore is to train our agents to last out after capture for forty-eight hours, during which time everyone they know in their Resistance circuit disappears and hides or destroys incriminating evidence. This protects others who have not yet been caught. We give people several weeks of training in this unit I'm inviting you to join, but the hardest thing by far is to prepare people for interrogation and torture. If people *know* that interrogation is part of the training experience, they know it isn't real, they know they are not going to be hurt like the enemy will hurt them. There is always something phony about mock interrogations."

She gave a small nod of her head.

"You will probably have worked out what comes next. You were told that, having done two daylight drops in Manchester, we needed to see you in more realistic conditions — a long, cramped airplane journey, at night, like flying into France, with an equipment bag tied to your leg. What you didn't know is that you were deliberately dropped away from where you thought you would be landing and, as a result, you were 'captured' by the local military police. I say 'captured' in quotation marks, but the military police were genuine. You were told that you were being dropped near but not actually *in* a restricted area, and then you found out you were not where you were supposed to be."

She stared at me. Her eyes flickered in the firelight.

"In other words, so far as you were concerned, the situation was real. Very real. The aircraft from Manchester had flown north from Edinburgh over the North Sea and approached the coast from there. It was perfectly plausible for the local military police to mistake you for a German agent being dropped into a restricted zone, to gather intelligence or carry out sabotage."

I leaned forward and warmed my hands at the fire. "So . . . your interrogation *felt* real, the water torture *was* real, you were stripped naked — a *real* humiliation, as you have conceded — and, for a while at least, you really were confused, bewildered, and worried that you were going to be shot." I sat back. "Did you notice the blood on the ground in front of the wall, where you were standing?"

She shivered. "Are you kidding? It was cold and sticky and it *smelled.*"

"Cow's blood," I said. "Not what you were meant to think. A realistic touch, yes?"

"Di-a-bolical. And, I have to admit, brilliant." She shivered again and sank more whisky. Her skin was becoming a little flushed.

"Anyway, from our point of view, the deception worked. We saw how you behaved in a real, terrifying ordeal."

She held her whisky glass against her cheek. "I *was* frightened, yes, but I was angry too. Life doesn't happen like that, so I kept telling myself — except that, in a war, who is to say? All the usual rules are . . . no more. I kept telling myself that too. But it was all so *unfair,* it was all happening so quickly and before my war effort had begun. Then I got really bewildered when the man with the birthmark on his face pulled back his sleeve to look at his watch. I could have sworn it was a Graf Zeppelin. Did that mean he was a German in a British uniform, and a spy himself? On top of all that, I had nothing to tell them."

"No. You had nothing to give away. That is the most unusual part, from our point of view. We know now, from experience, with our own agents in the field, and German agents captured here in Britain, that the moment of capture itself is the critical time, the real trauma. That how people respond when they are first apprehended — a hand on the shoulder, a gun pointed at you, a door to a room forced open — is what counts. That moment, and the time immediately following it, is crucial . . . It tells us almost all we need to know about an agent. Who will crumble and give away secrets immediately, and who will hang on for forty-eight hours. Most people crumble immediately — not all, but most. And, as I say, we need people who can hold out for forty-eight hours."

I raised my glass to her. "You passed with flying colours. The fact that you spotted a German wristwatch in those circumstances is very impressive."

She set the empty whisky glass down on the table between us.

"May I take it then that I am being invited to join this something?"

I nodded.

"And what, exactly, *is* this club? What's it called?"

"You can't know that until you've agreed to join and signed the Official Secrets Act. But I can tell you that you'll be given the nominal rank of captain."

"And you are . . . ?"

"I'm a colonel, but we are informal — relaxed — about rank in the special services. We don't go in for stripes and badges on our arms. With us it's cunning that counts."

She warmed her hands at the fire. "And if I refuse?"

"You'll be sent back to FANY. We'll put it about that there's something odd about you, something fishy, that you failed the test you've just passed. You won't get any more war work, I can assure you of that."

She leaned forward, pressed her lips together.

"But you've been through all the tests. We haven't read anybody wrong yet. I'd offer a hundred to one that you won't say no."

"Fifty-fifty," she said softly. "Those are the odds of survival?"

I nodded. "And of being captured."

"You survived."

"Most of me. I lost a lung."

"How exactly?"

"Not tonight. It's getting on for three o'clock. Over another whisky, perhaps. It's time for your answer. I need an answer now. If it's no, you'll be sent away from here while it's still dark, in a closed van. You will never know, exactly, where this place is and you won't be able to find it — or us — again.

"In the field — if you decide to go — you'll have to get used to making swift decisions. In France it will always be late, usually somewhere remote, and there'll be no fire and probably no alcohol, but you'll always have to make up your mind in a flash. If you can't give me an answer this instant, you are no use to me."

She sat upright in her chair.

"I wish the odds were better. But how else will I ever find out how you lost your lung?"

45

3

There were six of us in the rail yard. Red brick buildings huddled off to one side, their slate roofs glistening in the drizzle. A disused mine lay at the end of the rails, its entrance overgrown with weeds and barred by rusting sheets of corrugated iron. This had been a busy acreage when the mine was open, and the one line that led away to civilization, and the rest of the rail network, beyond the low heather-covered mountains in the distance, split here into five or six subsidiary dead-end sidings. Old freight wagons had been shunted on to these branches and forgotten.

Weeds straggled between the ballast and the sleepers but the rails themselves were shiny steel rods. Invermore Siding had a new lease of life, at least for now. It was a secret part of the war effort.

I stood in front of a flatbed truck. Beside me stood my assistant, Duncan Kennaway. He was small, with fair hair, a deeply cleft chin, and a ruddy complexion that matched

the weave of his tweeds. The four recruits —
Ivan Wilde, Erich Langres, Katrine Howard,
and Madeleine — were wrapped up against
the weather — it was icy as well as drizzling
— but I had their full attention.

"I repeat what I told you yesterday. Now
that we have got to the practical part of the
course, we operate totally in French. We all
talk French, you all talk French, to me, to
each other, to the support staff. You don't
stop talking French until I tell you. Is that
clear?"

I looked at the others one by one.

"Oui, monsieur," said someone.

"*Bon.* Now," I went on in French, pointing
to the flatbed, "you've probably never seen a
rail wagon like this one." I turned and nodded. Across the dirty orange superstructure
was stencilled CAMIONS.

"Not in Scotland, anyway. That's because
it's French. It came here with the boat train
and was trapped in the UK at the time war
broke out. Now it's helping the war effort."

The cold wind gusted again. Loch Kishon
wasn't far away and there was little in the
way of hills between the rail yard and Loch
Hourn, the easternmost reach, hereabouts, of
the Atlantic Ocean.

I raised the tin I was holding. "This is
today's lesson. This tin looks like a perfectly
ordinary tin of motor oil, the kind you would
put in your Morris or your Wolseley any day

47

of the week. If you could afford a Morris or a Wolseley. But, as perhaps you are learning to expect by now, here at SC2 things are not always quite as they seem to be."

Madeleine and the others had been at Ardlossan Manse nearly two weeks now. After she had agreed to join the "club," and signed the Official Secrets Act, we had both grabbed a few hours' sleep. Early the following morning, we had transferred from The Farm to the headquarters building on the opposite coast of the Highlands. There she had joined the other recruits, who had arrived the day before, having been tested — and selected — earlier.

Ardlossan was ideal for its purposes. Nairn, where The Farm was, was on the east coast of Scotland, a location suited to the deception we had to create if recruits were to feel their interrogations as "real." If enemy agents were ever flown in from Germany, they would reach Scotland over the North Sea, not the Western Isles. But the western coast of Scotland was much more remote than the east coast. Ardlossan was as remote as only the west coast could be.

Had it been a person, Ardlossan Manse would have been red-headed and taciturn, like the stereotypical Scot. Three miles south of Ardnave, on McIntyre, one of the bleaker — if more beautiful — of Scotland's western peninsulas, there was a milky redness veined into the manse's stone façade. Its windows and doors were too small for the building's overall dimensions, giving it a forbidding look, closed in on itself against the weather, and the world.

In front of the manse a lawn ran down gently to a line of umbrella pines. Beyond them the rocks began, and beyond the rocks, depending on the tide, was half a mile or a mile and a half of sand, as white as a full moon and carved into huge snaky fingers by the grey-green inlets of Loch Hourn — when the waters were rising on Kyleakin they did so almost at walking pace. A mile offshore was Kiloran Bight, once part of the mainland, but now an uninhabited island — save for kittiwakes and gulls — and unremittingly barren, windswept. No trees, just gorse where the sparse shelter allowed. In the channel between the island and the mainland could be glimpsed occasional seals, their pelts pitch-black and shiny as oil, with heads like frogmen. In the night their barks punctuated your sleep and made you ask yourself if a submarine had just surfaced. The sound of the sea was always with us, a backdrop collapsing at intervals in a soft *shshsh*ing.

Ardlossan's strong point was its location, out of sight of any roads, at the end of a long drive and surrounded by bleak, bare hills and the sea. Its weak point was everything else — no heating in any of the rooms, except the great rooms which had fireplaces, too few bathrooms (that were, in any case, so far from the boilers that the hot water arrived tepid and brownish), leaks in the roof here and there, windows that rattled in the wind, and freezing flagstone floors in the halls down-stairs, making the house as emotionally cold as it was physically. Obviously, the War Office, or whoever owned the damned place, had got it on the cheap.

It was, as I explained to the recruits, the training establishment for SC2, Special Command Two, the specialist sabotage outfit created by Churchill at the beginning of the war to operate behind enemy lines. I was second in command of the French section of SC2, but because of my time in France, I was in charge at Ardlossan. My commanding officer remained at our headquarters in London. At Ardlossan, it was my job to teach the recruits "security" — how to survive in Nazi-occupied France, how to operate communications equipment, how to live off the land if needed, how to avoid standing out, how to spot when they were being followed, and how to lose the people tailing them when they were. How to survive — and resist — interrogation. Beyond that, my job was to instill in them initiative, self-reliance, cunning — and more cunning. I also taught a selection of sabotage techniques.

"Now," I said, moving to one side as Duncan eased out of the way. "Bend down here, near the axle. You need to see exactly how this works."

We all sank to our knees. In the damp it was dirty but there it was.

I pointed to the wheel of the wagon. "Look inside the wheel. You will see what I can best describe as a circular box, like a collar around the axle. See?"

They all craned forward.

"Can you see it?"

One by one they nodded.

I leaned forward again, stretched one arm through the spokes of the wheel, and passed my hand around the metal collar. "Somewhere here . . . there is a spigot, a sort of tap. Ah, I've found it. Major Kennaway, the tin, please."

Duncan passed me a tin, in effect a small bucket.

"I'm going to open the spigot and then you'll see the axle oil pour out, into the can." I took a small hammer from my pocket and tapped the spigot. After a few taps it swiveled, and oil began to drain into the bucket.

I fixed the recruits with a stare. "You need the bucket because you don't want the oil to pour on to the ground. That would give the game away that the axle has been tampered with. Carry the oil away with you to a place where the Nazis will never stumble across it." I sat back on my heels. "Now we wait for all

51

the oil to drain into the bucket. It should take no more than two or three minutes. Then we close the spigot."

I waited until the flow of oil slowed, then became intermittent, then just drops, then stopped.

Duncan took the bucket away as I tapped the spigot closed with the hammer.

I reached forward again. "Now, I need to find the depression where the oil is put *in.*" My fingers scratched around the collar. "Ah, here it is. All of you: feel here . . . Feel the depression where my hand is now."

One by one they reached forward and put their hands through the wheel to the collar.

"Can you feel it?" I asked.

Again, they nodded, one by one.

"Now I need some pliers to twist off the cap. Major?"

Duncan handed them to me.

The cap was fitted tight but, eventually, I managed to undo it.

"Now, with the cap open and the spigot closed, I pour the 'oil' — 'oil' in quotation marks — from this tin into the axle box."

They all watched. Soft rain pressed against my cheek as I poured in all of the contents of the tin.

Finally, I tightened the cap and stood up. Everyone else did the same.

I turned and waved across the yard. Straightaway, the small shunting locomotive started to trundle towards us, stopping when it reached the wagon. The driver got down, came round the back of the locomotive, and began fixing the wagon to the coupling.

"Okay," I said, "everyone on to the wagon. We're going for a short ride."

Duncan led the way, pulling the recruits on to the flatbed one at a time. The driver returned to his cabin.

He looked back at me, I waved again, and he eased the engine forward, with the wagon behind.

In the drizzle it was hardly a pleasant ride, especially as we picked up speed.

"Where are we going?" said Katrine Howard. She was tall and thin, with untidy hair. She had worked as a property manager at a theatre in Paris and knew all about wigs. That might come in handy one day.

"You'll see," I replied. "Not far."

I bent down and spoke quietly. "I've sent a message to one of our circuits in Paris. They are going to check up on your brother —"

"Oh, sir! That's wonderful! I'm so —"

"Wait till we get the answer," I said quickly. "Let's hope it's the answer we want."

Katrine had a brother who was mentally disabled. We had heard rumours that the Nazis had some pretty ugly policies regarding the mentally ill inside Germany itself, but we didn't know if that extended into France. Strictly speaking, it wasn't my job to involve

53

myself too much with the private lives of our recruits, but Katrine was clearly worried, which might affect her performance on the course. And in any case I could rationalise an inquiry on the grounds that it might throw light on what could become war crimes.

Our "train" passed a small loch, little more than a pond really. Then the line led over a stone bridge and a little hut by a switch.

"Hang on," I shouted above the wind and the hiss of rain that was generated by our movement. The wagon started to rock.

We passed another small bridge with a fast-flowing brown, peaty stream beneath it.

Madeleine was manoeuvreing herself across the wagon towards me. Her features were all but hidden beneath the many layers of clothing she was wearing. It was almost comical.

Suddenly the wagon began to buck more violently and a terrible screeching broke into the damp afternoon air. The wailing continued. There was a smell of burning of some kind, scorching. Then the engine slowed, the rocking of the wagon lessened, the screeching died down a few tones, smoke came from the bowels of the flatbed, and our little "train" juddered to a halt.

"Jesus!" hissed Madeleine. "What was all that?"

"I know!" cried Ivan Wilde. "I know!" Almost as wide as he was tall, Ivan Wilde had been a croupier in the casinos of Monte

Carlo before the war. He had very deft hands — all those card tricks, no doubt — which made him a very fast radio transmitter. And he had plenty of experience at working fast under pressure. His parents lived in Morocco.

"It's obvious. The wheels have seized up, haven't they? They stopped turning — that was the screaming sound we heard, and it's why the wagon was bucking like a demented bull." He looked at me triumphantly.

"Yes," I said, holding up the oil tin I had used earlier, so all could see it. "After I drained the collar of its oil, I replaced it with this, which isn't just oil: it contains carborundum powder, silicon carbide if there are any chemists among you. The powder does the damage, and pretty quickly as you can see." I pointed through the floor. "The ball bearings in the collar that we 'adulterated' will now be one big congealed mass of molten metal, like a massive dental filling; the axle and the wheel will be baking hot and this wagon won't be going anywhere without a new collar and bearings."

I held up the tin again. "It doesn't look much, does it? But, used secretly at night, a few of these cans will immobilize a train in a matter of minutes. When the invasion comes, once the Germans know where our forces are concentrated, all their units will converge in that direction. By then all of you will be in France. We will have dropped thousands of these tins for Resistance groups. Some will get lost, some will break open when they hit the ground. But enough will survive intact for you, wherever you are, to play your part in stopping Hitler getting his trains where he wants to send them. I don't need to stress how important it is that you get the hang of opening the collars, evacuating the oil — quietly and *without* leaving any telltale signs — and replacing it with these little beauties. All in a very few minutes, so you don't get caught."

I smiled at them. "So you are all going to remain here for the rest of the day, getting wetter still, and dirtier, and oilier, and opening and closing the collars that are still intact until you can do it in your sleep. There's no moon tonight, so I want you to stay here with Major Kennaway, and practice your skills in the dark. That's how you'll be doing it in France. Are you ready, Duncan?"

"Aye, sir," he said, jumping off the wagon and standing by one set of wheels.

Duncan Kennaway had served two tours of duty in France and was just as good at sabotage as I was. He had lost two of his brothers as pilots in the Battle of Britain and was now stationed at Ardlossan because his mother was twenty miles away and he was her only child left alive.

The others followed him down off the wagon.

"Come on then, Captain Wilde." Duncan almost sang the words in his Scottish-flavoured French. "You're the clever clogs who spotted what had happened, so you can go first. Kneel down here and feel for the spigot."

The rain was still easing down in a fine drizzle. I looked at my watch — it was nearly four. They would be at it for a good time yet; it was nearly dark already.

I put the empty oil can in the bag I was carrying, adjusted my tweed hat, and prepared to tramp back up to the sidings, to where we had left the Land Rovers. Duncan was going to run the show for the rest of the day, as I had administrative chores back at the manse.

Madeleine came up to me. "You're leaving us," she said.

I loved the French-Canadian lilt in her voice, its sing-song loamy quality.

"Uh-huh. Only for now. I'll see you in the mess later. We can have a drink in the bar after dinner, if you want."

Staff and recruits, all ranks, messed together at Ardlossan.

"I shall be shattered, like I have been every night so far," she replied, pushing a wisp of hair back under the brim of her hat. "But if I can stay awake — yes, I'd like that."

I marvelled at the raindrops that were caught on her eyelashes.

57

"Maybe tonight you could wear something a bit more . . . I mean a bit less . . . I mean, at the moment, you look like a Highland sheep." I grinned.

She pretended to be put out. "People with one lung ought to be very careful, you know. We agents in SC2 are trained to kill with our bare hands."

"Not yet you're not. We haven't got to that part."

I nodded towards Duncan. "Major Kennaway's itching to get on. And he's killed more than one person with his bare hands. Don't get on his wrong side."

She turned to Duncan, then turned back. "I'll go quietly, Colonel. For now. But be warned — sooner or later, I get on everyone's wrong side."

The evening had started in the way that all evenings started at Ardlossan — drinks in the bar, with its stable of stags' heads staring down at us, a few caps and lanyards festooning the more accessible antlers. Alongside the plentiful whisky there was beer and sherry but little else. Around the room, most of the young men belonging to the different sections — Holland, Greece, North Africa, among others — were making overtures to the few females present.

Dinners at Ardlossan were hardly romantic affairs, however. Tables seated eight or ten, so

58

were scarcely intimate. We always began with some sort of soup, always some sort of brown, followed by "white fish," as the cook — a lugubrious Glaswegian with a drinker's nose — called it, as though that conferred taste and delicacy on what was often a gooey mass, from which the bones, and any other attributes that might have given it flavour, had been removed.

With intimacy a non-starter, conversation at dinner was mostly "shop," about the technicalities of the job. General war talk was discouraged — we were surrounded by so much news, much of it grim, that dinner had become a sort of DMZ as far as fighting talk was concerned.

Drinks in the bar afterward were a different matter. There was a snooker table and a darts board, and by then whisky had been consumed over the white fish, and tongues had loosened. One of the very few perks of being stuck in the northern wilds of Scotland was that, amid all the other rationings — of meat, butter, milk, coffee, sugar — whisky was plentiful. We all knew how lucky we were and no one asked questions. For some reason our supply was a consignment of half-bottles, but nobody was about to complain. Scotch was Scotch.

Noise levels in the bar rose after dinner, collars were unbuttoned, the cigarette smoke grew thicker. The beginnings of a snooker competition were in progress and people gathered round the table.

Madeleine and I stood close to the fire. "After you left this afternoon, the rain got worse."

"You make it sound as though it was my fault."

"Hmm," she sniffed. "When I look back on my life, after this war is over, and if I survive, and if I have children, and they ask me what I did, I'll be able to say I changed the oil on some railway wagons." She leaned into me and our shoulders touched. She was wearing a blue dress, shiny, with matching earrings and a pair of high-heeled wedge shoes.

I was silent. Although I was several years older than Madeleine, I was not confident with women. We suffer our failures in life more than we enjoy our successes. Where women were concerned, I'd had rather more of the former than the latter.

"Move over, I need to stand by the fire. I was rained on all afternoon, thanks to you; the bathwater was more tepid than ever; and my bedroom faces north. If the world was flat I'd be able to see Iceland."

I moved so she could warm her legs.

"Major Kennaway said today, after you had abandoned us, that you'd saved his life. Is that true? How come?"

I shrugged. "It depends on how you look at it."

"That's what he said. Did you or didn't you?"

I paused. "His two brothers were killed in the Battle of Britain, within a month of each other — they were Spitfire pilots. He was in France, undercover. I was sent to find him and bring him home safely to his mother — he was the only son left."

I drank some whisky.

"I found where he was. Near Nancy, but he had been captured. The Germans were moving him east, by plane, where he would have been interrogated, tortured — and then . . . You can guess the rest. We managed to sabotage his plane — a little carborundum in the engine, so it seized up on the runway just before take-off. The runway was a good distance from the airport buildings but was close to some trees at the edge of the field. Three of us overwhelmed the pilot and the guard and snatched Duncan away, into the forest. It was dark and the Germans never found us."

"How did you know which plane he would be on?"

"The Resistance had people at the airfield."

"How did he get home?"

"We were both picked up by Lysander at the next full moon."

"Do we do that for everyone whose brothers have been killed?"

"No, not at all. But Duncan knew a lot

61

about SC2 — he devised some of our codes. We couldn't risk him revealing what he knew."

"So it wasn't really about his mother and his brothers?"

"That was an added bonus."

She was silent for a while as the flames flickered behind her. "That's not how Duncan sees it. He says you saved both his and his mother's life."

I smiled. "People in the field have to know that everything will be done to support them. That's why Duncan told you — to ink it into your mind." I gestured to her frock.

"I like your dress."

"All I have with me is two pairs of slacks, two blouses, two skirts, and this frock. It was the frock's turn." She gave a slight shiver. "I'm thawing out at last."

"When you've finished here, and move down to London, we shall fit you out in French-style clothes, with French labels, in French sizes — centimetres, not inches. Inches would be a giveaway."

"I can't wait. I'm tired of looking dowdy."

"Oh, I'm not sure French wartime styles are any better than ours. Don't get your hopes up."

"A girl's not going to be seen in Paris without . . . without showing a bit of . . . flair."

"How do you know you are going to Paris?"

She made a face. "Spoilsport! Bordeaux, then, or Lyon, or Louzac, for that matter. *All* French women are fashion-conscious."

"Louzac?"

"Where my father came from. Have you forgotten already?"

Madeleine looked up at me and smiled. Skin as smooth as eggshell, brown eyes as I said before, a brown-gold that reminded me of whisky (a lot of things remind me of whisky), and a furrow between her eyebrows, making it look as if she was always about to break out in a frown. But, after her hair, the fringes of which glinted in the light from the fire, it was her neck that caught the eye. It was long, curved, like that of a newborn foal. It carried her head like a swan's — the way she held herself she reminded me of a ballet dancer.

"I've never been to Paris," she said sadly. "I love the Paris scenes in that new film, *Casablanca,* where Bogart and Bergman begin their affair, driving around in an open-topped car before the Germans invade. But maybe I'll never go."

"Of course, you will. If you didn't have such eye-catching hair, you'd look a bit like Ingrid Bergman, so it's only fitting that you go. You'll love it, the cobblestones — especially when they are wet — the street lights, the smell of the Métro, the Grands Boulevards, with their chestnut trees, and the sidewalk cafés with their waiters in long black aprons, the way they wash their streets with running water that disappears into gutters. Not even the Germans can have ruined Paris."

"Are you always so nice about the Germans?"

"I can be, yes. Are all Germans Nazis, do you think? I don't."

She shrugged. "When I was a young girl, I wanted to be a dancer. I had a few lessons, got accepted by a dance school, then a small ballet troupe. I loved it but then I twisted my knee — badly — I tore all sorts of ligaments and muscles, and it never recovered completely. It ruined my hopes and I had to give up dance. I was heartbroken."

She moved further from the fire. "I'm telling you this because we are talking about Germans and I once read that Leni Riefenstahl started out as a dancer; then she too damaged her knee and had to give up. And look what happened to her — she turned to acting, then made those documentaries. Is she a Nazi, or not? They say she was — and maybe still is — Hitler's lover. She fascinates me."

"I wonder what the Germans think of us."

"I have no idea. Does anyone? I was once in love with a German." She sipped some whisky.

"You *were*? When? What was his name?"

"When I lived in Louzac, in 1933 — I was

fourteen. He was called Rolfe and I thought he was very dashing."

"And . . . ? Did he break your heart? Did you break his?"

She smiled, but before she could answer, Duncan Kennaway butted in. "Sir, the forecast for tomorrow is not good, not good at all. Instead of doing more fieldwork training, why don't we switch to codes?"

"And use the room overlooking the pines . . . ?" I asked, nodding. "Good idea — yes. Thanks, Duncan. Make sure the one-time pads are available, will you, please?"

"Sure. We've had a couple of messages from Roland Kemp in Paris, by the way. A list of current French phrases doing the rounds, and a list of collaborationist restaurants and cafés that our agents should steer clear of."

He handed over a few decoded telegrams.

"How's your mother?" I asked.

"As well as can be expected, sir. Arthritis doesn't go away."

"I can probably do without you tomorrow, if that helps."

"That's very kind, sir, but my mother is well looked after — and she'll bark at me if I turn up at home when she knows I should be here. A Presbyterian with arthritis is never easy-going and, to be frank, sir, I'm more frightened of her than I am of you."

I laughed and so did Madeleine.

"I'll leave you laughing, if I may, sir. I'm off

to bed now, so I'll wish you both goodnight."

He turned and was gone. All either of us could do was call out "Goodnight" to his back.

I looked at my watch. "It's —"

"Gone eleven, I know."

She turned and looked down at the coals in the fireplace. "And this fire's going out." She bent down and kicked some of the few remaining coals with her shoe. They flared into life, but it wouldn't last.

She turned back to me. "We were interrupted and I never finished telling you about Rolfe. Rolfe didn't break my heart, nor I his," she said softly. "He was a dog, my first pet, a German shepherd, who howled at the moon. He was a bit like you in one way — he looked ferocious, a bit knocked about, as if he'd been in a few fights, but he was really an old softie."

"I think you are about to get on my wrong side."

"Relax, Colonel. You'll know when that happens."

She swallowed some whisky and I watched as her throat moved. "Have you ever seen any of Riefenstahl's films?"

"I saw both of the well-known ones, the one about the Nazi Party rally, and the one about the Olympic Games."

"And?"

"The Nuremberg rally film was — well, it was impressive and scary all at the same time.

They say there were a million people who turned out for that occasion."

"She shot two hundred and fifty miles of film for the Olympic Games — isn't that a-ma-zing?"

I raised my glass to Madeleine. "You're impressive, too — knowing all those details."

I'd never met anyone quite like Madeleine before, a bundle of talents and surprises, who was as easy on the ear as she was on the eye, and who seemed to grow more beautiful by firelight, when flickering shadows moved over her skin like clouds on a hillside.

"Why does Riefenstahl fascinate you so much?"

She shrugged. "I like the way she breaks all the rules. When she started out as an actress, she toured with Max Reinhardt. He was the best director of his day, in 1920s Germany, but he was Jewish. It didn't matter then, not to her. But then she read *Mein Kampf,* Hitler's book, and she fell for him, intellectually and emotionally. She wrote to him, asking to meet him — and he agreed! Think of that. Now she makes Nazi Party propaganda, and that includes anti-Semitic propaganda."

"And you approve of *that*?"

"No, of course I don't. That's not what I mean. She's an adventuress, an opportunist — an opportunist with talent — oh yes. Nazi Germany is hardly a place where women are allowed to shine most of the time, but she *does,* she breaks all the rules."

"How come you know so much about her? You sound as if you want to be like her." I could quite believe that Madeleine had an ambition to match that of her German counterpart.

She inched away from the fire.

"I admire her from a distance. And it's not hard to find out things, if you know where to look. When I was in London with FANY, I would spend some of my spare time in Fleet Street. All the national newspapers there have libraries or archives, archives of their back copies, and they keep cuttings by category. They all have Leni Riefenstahl files. A little bit of rouge and lipstick gets a girl into places a man could never go." She smiled.

"Sounds like you're an adventuress in your own way."

Briefly she placed her hand on my arm. "I can't wait till you teach us how to kill with our bare hands. Then I can really get on your wrong side."

"You'd pick on someone who has only one lung?"

"You promised to tell me what happened."

I looked down. "As you say, the fire's dying. It's late and this room will be sub-zero any minute now. Why don't I tell you another time?"

She looked at me and drained her whisky.

"And in another place, perhaps. The beaches here go on for ever."

4

The main lecture room at Ardlossan — what in pleasanter and plusher days must have been the drawing room — boasted a high ceiling, sculpted into plasterwork lozenges, a stone fireplace with an enormous mantel at head height, a dado where the walls changed colour, from cream to white going up, and a row of French windows giving on to the lawns and the pines, and beyond them the rocks and the sea. When the weather was in the wrong place, as it was the following morning — as Duncan had predicted — the westerly rains hurled themselves against the panes of glass with a ferocious rasping sound. Every so often, I had to raise my voice.

In front of me the four recruits sat on plywood chairs. Ivan Wilde and Katrine Howard were both smoking. They had all been working since seven, including Madeleine. All recruits did an hour's training in wireless transmission every day between seven and eight, before breakfast. No one was allowed to be dropped into France until they could transmit forty words a minute by Morse code. So far, Madeleine had reached only thirty.

"One point of protocol, before we get going this morning. Rank is important in armies, generally speaking, but SC2 is a small outfit and an unconventional one. We live by our wits, our imagination, our *cunning*. That means we often break out of the strictly military way of doing things. As an example, we tend to be more informal than the more regular army units and that is reflected in the way we use first names. By now, you all know what the pecking order is here at Ardlossan. That doesn't mean there will be any relaxation of discipline, or professionalism, but it will make the business of day-to-day instruction less starchy. That's what we have found, anyway."

I held up a small booklet. "Now, this is what we call 'a one-time pad.' I'll come to what that means in just a minute but first I want to draw your attention to the fact that it is made not of paper but of silk."

I passed it around so they could run their fingers over the material.

"It may seem ridiculously extravagant of the War Office to sanction silk pads, but there is method in their madness. Can anyone work out what?"

I looked from one to the other.

"Easier to burn if we get captured?" said Erich Langres. Tall, lugubrious, and slow-moving, Erich had been a choirmaster in a Belgian·cathedral and came to us with a reputation as a brilliant organizer.

"Nice try, Erich, but paper burns faster than silk."

At his interview, I had found Erich to be very religious. I wasn't religious myself, but I knew that all the evidence we had in SC2 showed that religious people stood up to interrogation — even torture — better than non-religious people. That might be useful at some point. He had no family in Belgium, he had told us, but he was worried for his bishop, who had spoken out against the Nazis.

"Anyone else?"

"It doesn't deteriorate if it gets wet, like paper does."

"Absolutely true, Madeleine, and a good answer. But it's not the answer I want."

There were no other suggestions, so I carried on. "The one-time pad is the most secure form of coding there is. When you are dropped into France, these pads, separated into numbered pages, will be sewn into your clothing — around the hems of dresses for women, into the jacket pockets of men. Obviously, it's difficult to sew paper and in any case paper would crackle if you were searched. Being made of silk, the pages won't stand out if you are part of a routine body check, and you don't need to unpick any stitching until you are ready to transmit information. Our work is deception and these silk pads help. You will all be given your one-time pads in London after you leave here, and before you visit the factory where the French clothing is made up."

Rain beat insistently on the French windows.

"Now, what exactly is a one-time pad and why is it so secure? You can see that each page is stamped with a series of letters set out in a grid pattern, five along the top and seven deep. Those thirty-five positions correspond to twenty-five letters of the alphabet — we ignore 'Z' and use 'S' instead — and the ten digits from nought to nine. When you send a message, you simply write a series of numbers that corresponds to the position of the letters or the digits on the pad — and then you throw that page away, and use the next one, which is completely different, on the following occasion. We shall have an identical pad here in London and so deciphering your message is straightforward. But the code is different every time, and different for every agent. That makes it especially difficult to break. Clear so far?"

They all nodded.

"We do introduce a number of refinements. For instance, before you leave London you will be given two numbers to memorise. Let's say they are three and seven. The first means that, in any message, the first three numbers that you transmit are meaningless — just a random choice by you. It means that your message proper doesn't start until digit four.

"The second number — seven in this case — means that you will send your message in groups of seven digits, followed by a space. This is designed to delay decryption should your messages be intercepted — it avoids giving the enemy a clue to the message by the length of words. The words 'the' and 'a,' for instance, are normally easy to spot from their length, three letters and one letter, which means that four letters in total have been identified — 't,' 'h,' 'e,' and 'a.' Any questions?"

"Yes," said Erich Langres. "Am I right in assuming that we ignore the space between words?"

"Yes. Anything else?"

"What about punctuation?"

"Ignore that too. If, on very rare occasions, the punctuation makes all the difference in the world, spell it out — C-O-M-M-A — semicolon, and so on."

"Do we always have to transmit in English?" said Madeleine. On such a bleak day — dreich, as the Scots said — her hair was the most colourful thing in the room.

"No, you can use French if you prefer, but,

and this is important too, you must always keep your messages as short as possible, and never — but never — stay on air for more than twenty minutes. The Germans have direction finders and if you transmit for more than twenty minutes the chances are better than evens that they will be on to you."

I looked from one to the other — Ivan, Erich, Katrine, Madeleine.

"I want to dwell on this twenty-minute business a little while longer. As I understand it from Major Kennaway, Duncan, you are all doing well, improving your transmission speed up to the required level of forty words a minute. But don't forget you won't always have the comfort of Ardlossan as your place of transmission. One of the most difficult decisions you will have to make in the field is your choice of a location for sending messages. The transmitters are bulky. Do you leave them in one place, where they are well hidden perhaps, where you know the local routine and where transmission conditions are good? But, at the same time, that raises the risk that the direction finders may seek you out bit by bit, and also risks unreliable locals learning of your whereabouts. The Germans pay for information received."

I lit a cigarette of my own.

"But if you change locations a lot, to prevent the dangers of staying too long in one place, that can be risky too, precisely because the equipment is so bulky. Even though you will be given a transmitter that fits inside a battered French attaché case, if you have to open that case — at a roadblock, say — there is no disguising what it is. You will have to decide these things for yourself."

I took a long, satisfying pull on my cigarette. I wasn't supposed to smoke but . . . there is nothing like that feeling when the nicotine sinks down and spreads throughout your chest. Smoking, and whisky, had kept me going after the disasters that brought my time in France to an end. Now I couldn't smoke without thinking back.

"Also, although you'll be keeping your messages as short as possible, try to develop your own style, using particular words, or phrases. We call this your 'fist' and it's useful, in that a recognizable style or 'fist' is hard for others to copy or emulate. So if you do get captured and someone sends a message pretending to be you, if it doesn't have your 'fist' we'll know. Understood?"

One by one they nodded.

"Now, this is where it gets a bit more complicated. It is possible that one or more of you will be captured. If that is the case, it is — naturally — very bad news for you, but, at the same time, we need to know. The top brass back at SC2 headquarters need to know the exact picture. Therefore, each message that you send must include information by which you tell us that the information contained in your message is either genuine . . . or not genuine.

"Let me explain what I mean, by going back to the earlier example, of someone whose crucial numbers are three and seven — the first three letters are meaningless, the codes are sent in batches of seven. In this case, where the numbers are three and seven, we put them together, to arrive at ten.

"In this case, the agent would single out the tenth word in each of his or her messages for special treatment — misspelling. You make a deliberate spelling error. If the tenth word in your message is 'canal,' let's say, you spell it 'calan,' perhaps, or 'cnaal.' If the tenth word is 'explosion,' you make it 'epxlosion' or 'explosoin.'

"You will, in the course of your career in the field, probably make several spelling errors but you must always pay particular attention to the crucial word — the tenth in this case — and make sure it is misspelled. This is what we call the 'true check,' the check that confirms the message really is by you."

I paused, to let the information sink in.

"This is an important point. Never — but never — overlook it."

They were all quiet and very still. They all returned my gaze.

"Next, there is a second kind of check, what

we call the 'bluff check.' This is what you use if you are captured and yet are forced to send us a message while the Germans are standing over you. Then you need to send us a signal that your message is phony, that you have been captured and that what you say is being dictated to you by the Germans."

I got up and walked about a bit.

"This has to be subtle, not noticeable to the Germans, something that doesn't raise their suspicions, that deceives them effortlessly but effectively. What we have found works best is if you simply end your message with the phrase 'love to . . .' whoever it is. You must *never* add anything personal like that in your true messages, so that we will know, if you do say that, that you have been captured." I stood perfectly still. "Do you all understand? This, in the jargon, is, as I say, a 'bluff check.' "

I fixed every one with my stare.

"We, in the London office, will keep your nearest family members informed of what is happening to you, so long as it doesn't compromise general security. If you mention your feelings, or your family, or your feelings for your family, it will be taken as a bluff check, evidence that you have been captured. Am I being clear? This is important but I don't want to say it all over again."

"What if things happen to our families while we are in the field? It could happen?"

"Yes, it could, Ivan," I said. "It already *has* happened. If it's serious — if *we* judge it's serious — we shall pull you out, without telling you why until you get home. If we judge it's not serious, then . . . Well, I am afraid you won't be told. There will be no need to disturb you. That may not suit everyone but that's the rule we shall apply. Security is paramount."

I sat down again and leaned forward.

"Now, as the final thing, for today at least . . . The one-time pads are made of very fine silk and so they contain a good number of pages. But no one knows how busy they are going to be, so there's a good chance — about 70–30, I would say — that your pads will be used up. In other cases they may be lost or, if you are stopped at a checkpoint, it may be prudent to throw your one-time pad away. What then?"

Again, I looked from one eager face to another.

"We need a fallback, a fail-safe. And we've found that poetry is a good one."

"What?" said Erich.

"Poetry?" cried Madeleine.

"Yes, poetry — verse. Our agents learn three or four lines of poetry off by heart — it's much easier to remember if it rhymes. You take that with you into the field, in your head, not written down. You tell us what it is before you go, and it becomes the basis for

79

your last-resort coded messages. Obviously, the lines you remember have to include most of the letters of the alphabet. You can spell out numbers. It's less safe than a one-time pad, of course, but on the other hand some letters will be repeated so, using these codes, certain letters will have different values within any one message. There's a library of sorts next to the bar, and I'd like all of you to select a poem by the end of the week. Any questions about that?"

Ivan nodded. "I like the idea of Wordsworth and Keats helping to win the war."

"Maybe I'll use some Goethe," said Madeleine. "That way a German would be helping *us*."

"Brilliant," I said, smiling. Then I looked at Erich. "Erich, you look doubtful — what is it?"

He shook his head. "I've never been . . . poetry . . . I've never . . . Can you help me out?"

"It doesn't have to *be* poetry, Erich. It's just that most people find it easier to remember poetry because of the rhymes. That's all."

"I've memorized some of Churchill's speeches," Erich said. "How about them?"

"If they contain most letters of the alphabet and you really can remember them, then that's fine. But remember, if you survive in the field for any length of time, one of your messages may be for us to come and collect you, to rescue you from trouble. It would be — what shall I say? — it would be *unfortunate* if you couldn't remember your code, to send us that message."

Erich nodded. "Oh, I can remember the speeches, word for word. Would you like to hear one now — ?"

"No, Erich, we *wouldn't,*" said Katrine firmly. "Not unless you want to hear Madeleine on *Faust.*"

"Okay, okay," I said, grinning and doing my best to restore order. "Let me have your choices by Friday. I need them then because, every so often, from now on, I shall be asking you to recite your lines — just to make sure that you really have memorized them."

"Look at that," said Ivan, pointing.

We all looked across to the lawn where a slate had fallen from the roof.

"What are we looking at, Ivan?"

Who lets so fair a house fall to decay,
Which husbandry in honour might uphold,
Against the stormy gusts of winter's day?

He chuckled. "Shakespeare, of course. I *do* like poetry."

"I don't think I've ever seen the sea looking so peaceful." Madeleine sent a smooth, flattish pebble — one of many on the white sandy expanse — skidding off the tiny waves that fell at our feet. "It's hard to believe that if you sailed west from here, and kept going, that eventually you'd come to America. If the tide went out any further, you'd be able to walk it." She picked up another pebble. "We could run away from all this."

Today there was little wind, no rain, and precious few clouds. The sea was, for once, more green than grey.

Madeleine looked glorious, the deep auburn of her hair against the glitter of the sand and the sea. A light wind blew her hair across her cheeks and forehead and she kept pulling it away; she tilted her face up to the sun and closed her eyes. She looked as natural — and as wild — on that beach as the kittiwakes and the gulls.

I wanted to kiss her. More, I wanted to scoop her up off the sand and to feel the soft warmth of her body.

But I didn't know enough about Madeleine just yet to convince myself how much I liked her, and I was her commanding officer while we were in Scotland. That sounds formal, calculating, but Ardlossan was a small outfit. I had to be careful. I didn't *want* to be careful, but I knew I had to be.

I forced myself to be content just to be on the vast expanse of beach, alone, with her.

"This is the first real afternoon we've had off. The four of us, the recruits, I mean."

"That's not so odd, is it? You must have

worked out by now that nothing happens by accident here. You're watched at all times — 'observed' is perhaps a better word. We gave you absolutely no free time in the first two weeks — because we need to know how you are under pressure, how your judgment is affected, how your temper lasts out, how you behave when you're exhausted, whether your French accent or syntax or vocabulary slips. That's why you had everything thrown at you to begin with. As it happens, you all did rather well."

"We didn't finish our conversation the other night, when the fire went to sleep before we did. You were starting to tell me about your time in the field. Now, come on. Who *is* Matthew Hammond? I want all the details, good, bad, and gory. Nothing sanitized, please."

"The early bits are quickly told," I said. "Brought up in Plymouth, school in Taunton, but with every summer in France because my mother is French, from Delme in Lorraine. My father was a doctor, my mother was his medical secretary, and my sister is, of all things, a cellist with the West of England Orchestra, based in Bath. Or she was until she met and married an American movie producer and decamped to Los Angeles — she now plays with a symphony orchestra there.

"We were a typical doctor's family, I think. Lots of medical talk, openness about blood and other stuff that most people find gory, my father being called out at all hours. He was a good man, but he was really more interested in his work than his children — I rather think children bored him. He took it for granted that I would be a doctor and Alice — my sister — would be a nurse. When it turned out that neither of us was going down that road, he was disappointed; he felt let down and he turned away from us even more. He turned away from me especially — we were a typical family in that Alice was closer to our father and I was closer to our mother. At least I was. When my father died, she moved into a hotel in Malvern in the West Country. I see her a couple of times a year — not enough, I know."

The wind was strengthening. The colour was going out of the sea.

"My father had strong feelings — about music, medical research, healthy exercise — but he rarely showed his emotions, he thought that was crude. I think some of that rubbed off on me."

An ungainly seal hobbled ashore about a hundred yards away. Then it saw us and flopped back into the waves.

"I went straight from school into the army and from there, because I'm bilingual in French and English, I went into SC2, which I helped set up. So I've had a basic army training but no real regular army experience.

I did the first course here at Ardlossan that you are doing now.

"I was parachuted into France in November 1941, just a few days before Pearl Harbor. I was dropped into the Franche-Comté area, because I knew it. There are a number of canals between Besançon and Belfort and my job was to contact the local Resistance, help to arm and train them, and then blow up a series of bridges over the canals. This both blocked the canals and destroyed the roads, interrupting trade and military movement in two ways."

"You became an explosive expert?"

"Very expert at one stage, especially with incendiary devices. We had to be careful, though. If we blew up too many bridges, the Germans retaliated by shooting ten or twenty local villagers."

"So how did you figure that out?"

"We worked with the Resistance. Some villages, even then, had reputations for being collaborators' villages. We blew up the bridges near those villages and if they shot those villagers . . . Well, the Resistance weren't *too* bothered. But I don't want you to think it was all that clean and straightforward — it wasn't. I was mainly recruiting and training Resistance people and trying to patch things up between the communists and the Gaullists."

"Oh? You'll have to explain that."

"I will, in just a moment, but you'll be getting formal instruction on it very soon. And please, keep talking in French."

The wind gusted and blew strands of hair across Madeleine's face. She pulled them away. "Sorry."

I didn't say then what I might have said, that my first love affair, at age eighteen, had been a highly secret fling with the mother of my best friend at school, who had seduced me early one December evening when her husband and son — both choristers — had been rehearsing for the local carol concert. The affair had been consummated only a few times before she realised how dangerous her behaviour was. I had been hopelessly infatuated with her, and although I too knew that what we were doing was wrong and couldn't — shouldn't — last, it took a while to get over. More important, after that younger girls, young women my own age, were nowhere near as sexually experienced as Rob's mother was, nowhere near as exciting, and for a while that was a problem.

"France, as you know," I went on, "is a much more left-wing country than Britain. The Communist Party there is very strong. It has been very good for the Resistance, better in fact than anyone else. But of course by no means everyone is a communist, and many are against them. So patching things up was one of my jobs.

"I spent several months in and around Besançon. Most of my time was spent organising
airdrops of weapons and explosives — and
agents, of course. I set up four circuits in the
Lorraine area, which, being near Germany
itself, was more heavily populated with
Germans than some other areas of France."

"That must have been dangerous."

"At times, yes. I remember once, when we
were trying to blow up an oil dump, we ran
into a large convoy of lorries carrying armoured personnel carriers. They prevented
us getting to the canal bridge that we were
aiming for, so we hid in the lock-keeper's cottage. When we got there, there was a German
major and his French girlfriend, totally naked."

"What did you do?"

"He wasn't quite naked — he had his gun
with him. But I shot him, and the Resistance
leader shot the woman — not just because,
in his eyes, she was a traitor, but because he
knew her and she knew him, and she would
surely have betrayed us had we let her go. I
can't say I liked what we did, but it's the kind
of situation wars throw up."

I looked back the way we had come. We
were still alone on the beach.

"Anyway, the sound of our gunfire had
probably drawn attention to us, so we had to
get lost that night. We moved off into a nearby
forest, but we didn't know that the Germans,

suspecting it to be a Resistance hideaway, had mined the paths. One of the Resistance people stepped on a mine and was killed outright, there and then. I was a few yards behind and some shrapnel tore into me, into my chest. God, it was hot. Fortunately, one of the other Resistance people in our patrol was a doctor, and he looked after me. The shrapnel was locked in my rib cage, and though it didn't reach my heart, it had punctured my lung. The explosion meant we had to keep moving — and I was carried miles. Eventually, I was looked after in a Resistance field hospital, and the Germans, obviously, never found us. I took weeks to recover.

"I wasn't entirely idle. I gave classes in sabotage techniques from my hospital bed — actually a cave in a remote area. I gave English instruction — and I gave advice."

"How long did your wound hurt?"

"It still hurts sometimes, when I breathe."

She hesitated. "I hope I don't get injured or maimed. I think I'd rather be killed than disfigured."

"That's what we all think. I was lucky there, too. The shrapnel didn't spoil my good looks."

She looked up at me, her lips slightly parted.

"I've still got the piece of shrapnel if you want to see —"

"What's that?" Madeleine said quickly, in

almost a whisper. She pointed along the sand, to where a black something had been washed ashore.

Instinctively, we walked towards it.

As we came close we could see it wasn't black, but grey.

Madeleine stood over it. She kicked it, but gently, moving it with her foot. "It's . . . It looks like —"

"It's a life jacket," I said. "It got separated from its owner."

She looked up at me. "Do you think . . . ? Will the owner be —" she peered along the shore "— not so far away?"

"That depends," I said. "I hope they *were* separated some way off — the life jacket is German."

"It *is*? How do you know?"

I pointed. "The stencilled writing — there. See? It says SCHWIMMWESTE."

She looked out to sea. "And it looks so calm today. How did it get here, do you think?"

I shook my head. "Let's hope that whoever was wearing this was in a torpedoed U-boat that was sunk by our boys. Some of the crew got out, maybe, but there was a storm and . . . Well, this one didn't make it."

We stared down at the life jacket in silence.

"I know what you're thinking," I said after a while.

"Do you?"

"You're thinking that could be you, very soon."

"I'm not the morbid type." She nudged the life jacket again with her foot. "In fact, I was thinking about how lives end. This man, whoever he was, almost certainly died alone. Do you think that matters? Is it better to die at home, in your bed, surrounded by family — or doesn't it matter? Does it make any difference?"

She gestured at the life jacket. "I'll bet he was no older than I am. There could be a U-boat out there right now, looking at us with his periscope. Maybe they know about Ardlossan, what it's used for. Maybe they know all about SC2. Maybe that's what this life jacket really means."

"Unlikely. We're important to the invasion but not —"

"Maybe they think we know when and where the invasion will take place. Maybe they're about to attack — invade *us*!"

I laughed. "Don't let your imagination run wild like that when you are in France. Keep your mind on the ground."

She was suddenly serious. "You really *don't* know when the invasion will happen?"

"No, of course not. I should imagine not more than a few dozen people know that."

"Why, then, am I wasting my time with someone so low down the pecking order?"

"You tell me. You suggested walking on the beach."

She suddenly skipped away from me, along the sand. Then she stopped and turned back. "Tell me about the women in France. Were there lots? Did you have affairs? Was there someone special, who meant more than the others? Someone you still think about?"

I didn't say anything for a moment, thinking back. Madeleine had a way of . . . She wasn't forward exactly. But she certainly didn't like standing still.

"Do you believe people fall for types?" She looked up at me, her eyes big and round. "I mean, do people fall for the same kind of person over and over again — tall people, wild types, quiet souls?"

"You mean . . . How does it go? . . . Like men who always fall for women who remind them of their mothers? Is that what you're saying?" She looked at me and made her eyes appear rounder than ever.

"I don't mean that, no. Not exactly." I looked out to sea. No submarines as I could make out.

"Let's just say there was one woman who meant more than all the others. And the thing is — she had hair just like yours. Not the colour, but all curly and unruly and unmanageable. She was for ever doing . . . what you do with your hair, lifting it up, holding it off your neck."

"What was her name?"

"Celestine. Celestine Naucelle."

"Unusual, but pretty. Was she?"

"Yes, on both counts."

"What happened?"

I looked out to sea again. "I killed her."

I paused before turning back. "Not deliberately, not directly, of course. But I played a part."

We resumed walking along the beach.

"She was a doctor in a large hospital, an anaesthetist and therefore in demand during operations. She was the first one in her family to go to university and the first female doctor in the hospital where she worked. And she was secretly part of the Resistance, in which she had two roles. She helped with operations for anyone in the underground who was seriously injured during sabotage raids and who had to be treated in hideaways. And she stole medical supplies — drugs, bandages, surgical equipment, even German-made contraceptives. She helped keep the Resistance supplied with all that it needed.

"I met her when she was helping with an operation on an injured Resistance leader who I knew well. He had fractured his skull after falling from a train when a sabotage expedition went wrong. Had he died it would have been a disaster — he had so much information inside his head. He survived the operation but he was so badly knocked about that he was never going to be his old self again. So I was there to debrief him, find out all he knew, the minute he recovered consciousness.

"The operation was a success, but it took time for him to regain consciousness. I sat by his bed the whole time and Celestine looked in every so often. To begin with, I only knew her by her Resistance code name — *Méduse,* Jellyfish. It sounds so much nicer in French.

"Eventually, I was able to debrief him. By then Celestine — Méduse — and I had got to know each other and, after that, and when we could, when circumstances allowed, we started an affair. We started sleeping together. Because of her Resistance duties, she was anxious not to get pregnant. So we made a point of using the German-made contraceptives — we made endless bad jokes about it."

"How very adult. How did she die?"

I paused to light a cigarette. The sunlight on the sea glittered like a thousand splinters of broken glass.

"It happened after about six months, by which time we had spent a few weekends together in the mountains, and I had met her parents, and her brother, who was also in the Resistance. Then a big Nazi fish fell into our lap. His name was Möricke and he was the man in charge of the area, a *Gauleiter.* He was an exceptionally cruel man. In retaliation for a Resistance attack on a railway yard, he

93

had rounded up a group of children, twice the number of the German soldiers who had been killed in the attack, and had them shot, in front of their parents and families. You can imagine how popular he was.

"He was a keen rider but he had an accident and fell from his horse. He broke several ribs and injured his spine. The ribs were not the problem but the spine was. He had injured it in such a way that he couldn't be moved — at least not very far. He needed to be operated on quickly, and there was no German doctor on hand. A French replacement was found and Celestine was selected as the anaesthetist.

"This all happened in a rush. There was just time to call an emergency meeting of the local Resistance committee. Celestine was there, too, not because she was on the committee, as I was, but because she would be involved in the medical procedure. The committee discussed whether Colonel Möricke should die during the operation. Celestine was asked her opinion and she said she could manage to administer too much anaesthetic and that the excess wouldn't be noticed — Möricke would just 'die' during the operation."

Madeleine stopped and looked up at me.

I looked down at her. A breeze was getting up — the weather was definitely beginning to turn.

"She described exactly how she would do it. There were seven people on the Resistance committee, six French and me. Normally, I didn't have a vote on operational issues unless the other six were deadlocked. Which is what happened that time. Three thought it was too dangerous, that Celestine would be found out and executed and that she was too valuable to the Resistance to be put at risk. The other three said it was too good an opportunity to miss, getting rid of a monster, that such an opportunity would never come again, and that, if Celestine was confident herself of getting away with it, it was a risk worth taking, a risk we had to take."

I smoked my cigarette, hard.

"With the committee split fifty-fifty, all eyes turned to me. I asked Celestine to repeat, exactly, what she would do during the operation, and to explain again why the Germans wouldn't find out. She repeated what she had said before, in a very matter-of-fact type of way. Her calm was impressive."

I looked up at the seagulls overhead.

I glanced back to Madeleine. "There was one complicating factor that I haven't mentioned. One of the men on the Resistance committee, who had voted against Celestine killing Möricke, was a man who had been a lover of hers before I came along. That night he made an impassioned speech about us *not* putting Celestine's life at risk, arguing that she was more nervous than she was letting on. Then she made an equally impassioned speech about what a monster Möricke was, who thought nothing of killing children, and here was a chance to get rid of him. She knew her job, she said, and begged me to vote for the death of the German brute."

I took a deep breath.

"So that's what I did. I voted for Möricke to be killed."

We had reached an inlet in the beach, a finger of water that flooded inland for several hundred metres, so we turned and began the trudge back to Ardlossan Manse.

"That night Celestine and I went back to the cottage we used, made dinner, and drank maybe too much wine. At least she did, I drank whisky. During the dinner I became aware that she was in fact more nervous than she had shown during the meeting of the committee. We talked and talked and made love endlessly. Just in case, she said, she gave me a gift, a lighter, which she had had inscribed. It said —"

"Don't tell me!" cried Madeleine. "I don't want to know. That's personal, between you."

I looked at Madeleine, and smiled. I thought it was a good thing for her to say.

"Maybe that was a warning — the lighter, I mean; maybe I should have paid more attention. Maybe we made love too long, maybe it was her nerves. The long and short of it is that next day she botched the job. Möricke was dead even before the operation began. Celestine was arrested, an inquest was held, which showed that Möricke had three times the amount of anaesthetic in his blood that he should have had. There was a summary trial for murder, an abortive attempt to rescue her from prison, during which two Resistance men — one of them her brother — were killed, and, a day later, Celestine was shot."

Neither of us spoke for a while. The waves out at sea were getting larger and the tide was beginning to turn.

"Can you really be blamed?" said Madeleine softly. "From what you say, she seemed to know her mind and was confident enough. We all have to accept responsibility for what we do."

■ ■ ■ ■

MARCH

■ ■ ■ ■

5

At the back of the manse was a range of outbuildings, still in the same red-veined stone — mainly old stables and workshops. The windows fitted badly. Some of the old wooden stable hooks were still there, on the walls, no more than pegs really, along with a faint smell of hay, leather, and horse manure. On one especially wet and cold morning in early March, the recruits assembled there. I stood in front of them with Duncan Kennaway next to me.

"Duncan is running the show today. He's a bit of a whizz at certain forms of deception and tradecraft and he's going to introduce you to a few techniques and substances that might help you out in emergencies. After that . . . Well, we have a little treat lined up for you. Duncan?"

He was actually wearing his kilt today. Given the conditions, it must have been cold under all that tartan.

"Aye," he said, in his Scottish lilt. "Aye. I'm

going to start at the rough end and get easier. Well, slightly easier."

He held up a small glass jar. "This jar remains locked in a sturdy cupboard here at all times, and only Colonel Hammond — Matt — and I have a key. In it are small white pills, as you can see." He moved around the recruits, holding the jar in front of them.

"This is what potassium cyanide looks like close up. These are the famous suicide pills you have probably heard about. Swallow one of these and you're dead within seconds." He cleared his throat. "I mean it. Even a few milligrams of potassium cyanide are lethal for human beings. Swallow one of these and there is no way back. There is no antidote, and even if there were, there wouldn't be enough time to get hold of it and swallow it. You will each get one of these before you go to France, but we're showing them to you now so you have absolutely no doubt about how serious life is going to be when you get into the field. Have one last look before I put the bottle away."

Next he held up a small box. "This, believe it or not, is a camera. It fits into a pocket quite easily. See?

"You can only use this with someone in the Resistance who knows about cameras and can develop your pictures and send them on to us. The French won't have anything this small — our people have only just developed it. But if you come across unusual circumstances where your account of things might be doubted, a photograph sometimes does the trick. If you get anywhere near submarines, for instance, our people would love photos. Or enemy aircraft. Or simply photographing senior Nazi personnel — you never know what that may tell us. You should all be learning Wehrmacht and Gestapo insignia in any case. A camera like this one is invaluable. Or if you see what looks like large weapons on railway wagons — again, that can tell our intelligence people a lot. I'll be letting you play with this a little later on in the course."

He put down the camera and took up a tube. "Now, this looks like a tube of common toothpaste, but its chemical name is in fact cyanoacrylate. You don't need to remember that name, or the fact that the substance was invented only in 1942 and is still in the experimental stage.

"It was initially supposed to be a clear plastic, for the manufacture of protective gunsights, but as it was being developed, it emerged that it's much better as a sort of glue — a fantastically powerful glue. It sticks to everything and anything, and that is why it's in this tube. If you squeeze the tube, out comes a clear liquid, like clear toothpaste. But, and this is the point, within a few minutes — a very few minutes — this clear, soft, gooey mass hardens on contact with air.

If you press it between any substance — wood, ceramics, metals — they can't be separated."

He lifted some more things off the bench.

"Here is an old horseshoe that I found in one of the stables. And this is half of the slate that fell off the roof in the storm the other day — one is metal, the other a form of stone. Both very hard.

"I wipe their surfaces so they are as clean as possible . . . then I squeeze some of the glue on to either surface . . . like that. Immediately I've done it, I screw the top back on the tube, or else the glue inside will harden." He screwed the tube top firmly closed and laid it to one side. "I feel the glue with a finger tip — but very lightly. There are stories we've heard of people sticking their hands or fingers to tables or tools with this glue, and then not being able to separate them."

He grinned. "Aye, I'm not joking.

"Okay," he said after a few more moments, "The glue is beginning to set now so . . . I place the horseshoe on the slate and press it flat . . . like that. I keep up the pressure and wait for a couple of minutes. While we are waiting, try to think of the uses to which you might put this glue."

He looked around. No one said anything.

He picked up the horseshoe where there was no glue. The slate rose with it. He shook the slate. The horseshoe didn't budge. "Look," he said to Erich. "Pass this round, look at it closely. See, even the nail holes of the horseshoe, where the nails normally go . . . they are all filled with glue and it's rock solid."

Erich took it, examined it, and passed it to the others.

Duncan eventually took back the horseshoe and slate. "Now watch."

He dropped the slate on to the stone floor of the workshop. It shattered around the edges, but the part glued to the horseshoe remained stuck to it, intact.

"Now," he said, "think again . . . How might this glue be useful?"

"Repairing your shoes?" said Katrine.

Duncan nodded. "Yes, but I was hoping for something more related to the war effort."

A pause.

Then Ivan said, "Does it often happen that our wireless transmitters get damaged on being parachuted into the field?"

"Excellent!" said Duncan. "That's exactly the sort of problem you might have and when the glue could come in handy. Anything else?"

"Repairing torn tents?"

"Yes, good."

"Repairing weapons?"

"Unlikely, I would have thought."

"Except," said Madeleine slowly, in English, "as it hardens like that, you could squeeze some glue into the chamber of a revolver, say, and block it up."

Duncan nodded. "I hadn't thought of that — you're right. Keep speaking in French, please, Madeleine. Anyway, the point is — thinking creatively is good. Don't just think of the glue as glue — but in other ways too."

"Maybe you could repair broken binoculars with the glue," said Katrine.

"Good," said Duncan.

"Or the handle of a stirrup pump," said Ivan.

"Yes, again. Keep it up, in your own heads. Try to anticipate problems you might have."

He packed the glue away in his box of tools and took out some booklets. "Now, this is our final thing this morning — this is the treat that Matt referred to."

He handed the booklets round.

"This is all my own work — twenty pages on how to survive in the field, and how to live off the land if you have to go into hiding." He looked over at me and winked. "You have an hour to read this booklet and absorb its contents. Then we are going to drive each of you to a remote location about thirty miles from here. We'll come and pick you up two days from now, after you've spent two nights on the land on your own, surviving." He paused. "There's a full moon tomorrow, and the weather is supposed to be clear, so the exercise will also give you some experience of operating by moonlight — that might come in handy."

Silence.

"What?"

"You can't be serious."

"It's freezing out there."

I took over. "We know. And this is how it will be in the field. Something will happen when you're least expecting it, and you will have to make a run for it. With no belongings, just what you are standing up in."

"Matt!" said Madeleine. "*Sir!* I'm just wearing slacks and a shirt, and so is Katrine. We'll die of cold if you play this game. It's never this cold in France — we *are* in Scotland for heaven's sake. I grew up partly in Canada and it's almost as cold here as it is there."

I shook my head. "That's not strictly true. The French Alps and the Pyrenees can get very bleak. But yes, this is Scotland, so we will allow each of you to fetch one coat and one hat. That's all. You will all leave, each in a different vehicle, one hour and a half from now, having read that booklet, asked any questions of Duncan, and collected your hat and coat. You must be getting used to our tricks by now. And this *is* a military outfit, however informal — no more argument."

They all stared at us.

"Major Kennaway," I said softly. "Get out that camera again. Take their photo. Look at their faces — what a picture. They look horrified. Will they ever smile again?"

That evening, with Madeleine and the other recruits out in the field, Duncan and I had a quiet dinner together to discuss their progress and to explore whether any of them needed special attention.

"Katrine's the slowest at wireless transmission," he said, over yet more brown soup. "I think we should make her do an extra thirty minutes before supper every night, for the next week or so anyway."

"Good idea. Speed matters in the field. It might save her life. That reminds me, I must keep on at our people in Paris to chase up her brother, find out what the hell is going on."

"We haven't settled on Erich's poem yet, the one he needs as a fallback for his code."

"I thought he was going to use one of Churchill's speeches?"

Duncan shook his head. "He *said* he had memorised them, but when it came to it, he couldn't remember more than two or three lines — not enough to use all the letters of the alphabet, and in any case he remembered them patchily. We could never use them as a code because his words or word order might vary ever so slightly over time."

"So . . . ?"

"I have him in the library every evening. We're focusing on Keats and Dryden and

Wordsworth — short poems, short lines, strong rhymes. We'll get there."

"What else?"

"Madeleine. Two problems there." He stopped eating and sipped some beer. Strangely, being a Scot, he didn't like whisky. "First, she keeps lapsing into English — why is that, do you think? None of the others has that problem."

I sipped my own Scotch. "Good question. Her French is good, she's totally bilingual, so far as I can see. Is it something psychological?"

He shook his head. "I don't know — we've never had that type of difficulty before."

"So they've all got a weakness," I said. "Katrine's is her transmission speed, Erich's is his coding, Madeleine's is her lapsing into English. Nothing earth-shattering but they do need attention. What about Ivan — any problems there?"

Duncan nodded. He made a gesture, as if drinking beer or whisky.

"Do I need to have a word?"

"Better coming from you, sir. You're more tactful than I am."

"Maybe he's more nervous than he lets on. I've seen it before. I like him — leave it to me."

I went to help myself to more whisky, then had second thoughts.

"The two women are holding up well, don't

you think? They may not be as strong physically, but they are as robust in every other way."

"Good word: 'robust,' " replied Duncan. "That sums them up entirely."

"War is such a male thing, normally, but the difference in this war might just lie in our women having more of a role than theirs."

"And we trained them, some of them," said Duncan softly.

Neither of us spoke for a bit.

"You said there were two problems with Madeleine."

"I'm not sure the second thing is a problem yet," he said softly, "but it may be, down the line."

"Go on. What is it?"

He scratched his chin. "I think Erich's sweet on her."

I can't remember now whether I reddened when Duncan said that. But his remark certainly came as a shock. I know I swallowed hard before replying.

"Why do you say that?"

"They sit next to each other — very close — in the early mornings, when they are practicing their wireless transmission —"

"That's hardly —"

"Hold on! That's not all. They visit each other's rooms —"

"Yes, but . . . they're in the same class —"

He shook his head. "I know it doesn't

sound like much, but when you see them together —"

"I *do* see them together, in class."

"I mean when they are relaxing, after class, before dinner." He paused. "I can't put my finger on it, exactly, but . . . but there's an intimacy there, as if they are sharing some secret."

Now I shook my head. "Are you suggesting we take some sort of action? What can we do? They are not breaking any laws or regulations. I hadn't even noticed it. Are you sure you're not making this up?"

He shrugged and sipped his drink. "Maybe I am. But I don't think so."

"What, exactly, are you worried about?"

"I don't know. I just don't like it. Love affairs in small outfits like ours, in out-of-the-way places, can be very disruptive."

I swallowed hard again. "It doesn't sound to me like it's an affair. Not yet."

"And that's my point. You seem to get on well with her too. Can't you . . . can't you . . . say something?"

"Like what?"

"Warn her. Or warn them both. You're in charge."

"I'll sound like a headmaster."

"Which is what you are, in a way. At least tell them to wait till they get to London, where they can get lost in the big city."

I didn't say anything else. Duncan's news

had come out of the blue and I felt . . . I had to admit to myself that I hadn't seen this coming. Whatever "this" was.

Madeleine and Katrine Howard both stood in the manse bar with their backs to a roaring fire. Was it whisky they were holding in their glasses? I couldn't tell. Their hair was wet, Katrine's sticking closely to her scalp, Madeleine's heading off in all directions. Their bodies stopped the heat of the fire's flames from reaching the rest of the room.

I had my first Scotch of the evening in my hand as I approached them. It was about twenty minutes before dinner.

"You're back!" I said softly. "And both in one piece. I take it the experiment in living off the land didn't kill you?"

"It would take more than a few cold nights to do that," growled Madeleine.

"The men aren't back yet," said Katrine. "Maybe they had more of a problem than we did. Men are so hopeless at fending for themselves." She smiled sarcastically.

I looked about me. No, neither Erich nor Ivan was in the room.

"The exercise wasn't meant to kill you, just to —"

"Yes, what exactly *was* it meant to do?" said Madeleine. The loam had left her voice; her tone hinted that she was spoiling for a fight.

"Can you just step apart, slightly, please? So someone else can feel the fire."

Neither of them moved.

"I see. What went wrong?"

"Nothing went wrong. I dined on fried fish both nights," said Madeleine. "And Katrine here was just telling me she had rabbit both nights too."

"Delicious," said Katrine.

"Good," I said. "And how did you manage that?"

"I dammed a stream," said Madeleine. "At this time of year salmon smolt are leaving their spawning ground for the ocean. They congregated at the dam. I broke off a branch, to use as a fishing rod, and I used my hat, fixed to the branch by holes, as a net. I caught several smolt. Then I roasted them. Im-pecc-able."

"Enterprising," I said. "How did you start a fire?"

Madeleine eyed me. "When I went back for my coat and hat, I took some cigarettes and matches —"

"So you cheated!"

"I did not!"

"I said, Take nothing else, other than your hat and coat."

"And who are you to lay down the law? In the field, if we ever get there, we all know that lighting a fire is the most difficult thing to do in the wild — it's common sense, and it said so, in Duncan's booklet. And we all know that, if you are alone, a cigarette is at least a little bit of company. None of us is going to be separated from tobacco and matches for very long, and it's unrealistic of you to expect otherwise."

"I agree," said Katrine Howard before I could interject. "I didn't think of it like Madeleine did, but she's right. She gave me some of her matches and a few fags."

I edged nearer the fire as she moved. "How did you catch your rabbits?" I asked.

"I came across a broken gate, and used one of the planks as a shovel. I found a rabbit den and made a deep hole nearby in the peat, a trap, which I covered over with leaves. Two animals fell in during the night and couldn't get out. I skinned them and cooked them on a fire."

Before I could congratulate Katrine, there was a commotion behind me and I turned, to discover that Duncan had barged into the room. He ran towards me and then stopped. "We can't find Erich," he snapped. "He didn't make the rendezvous point at the time we agreed."

I put down my glass. "Were you supposed to pick him up at the same spot you dropped him off?"

Duncan nodded.

"Where was the rendezvous?"

"Where the Loch Loyne road meets the

track from Glen Fada."

I knew it. I nodded. "Very well, we'll take all three Land Rovers, plenty of lights, plenty of ropes, water, the medical box, climbing stuff — it should all be on standby."

"It is," said Duncan, beginning to leave the room. "I'll take one Land Rover, you take the second, Ivan can drive the third."

I turned back to Madeleine and Katrine. "Are you coming?"

"Of course, we are," said Madeleine, putting down her glass. "I'll get back into my slacks."

"Me too," said Katrine.

"It could be a long night," I called over my shoulder, as I left the room. "Bring some cigarettes."

Ten minutes later we were speeding down the drive of Ardlossan Manse. The beginning of Loch Loyne was about thirty minutes away, on a fast single-track road. We didn't expect to see any traffic — nor did we. We frightened a few rabbits and a solitary deer, but we saw no humans.

At the junction of the road and the track there was a patch of flat ground where we could park without blocking the road. Here we all got out.

Duncan had with him two men: one from the Cypriot section, the other I didn't recognize. Ivan had the Glaswegian cook with him, and I had Madeleine and Katrine — that made eight of us in all.

I looked about me. "This is where he was dropped?"

"Yes," said Duncan.

"Well," I said. "The land slopes away here, towards South Andvart. I'm sure he would have gone that way; it's much easier than turning inland and climbing. Do you agree, Duncan?"

Duncan was a local. He knew the area better than I did.

"Aye." He was handing round ropes and torches and bottles of water, taking what looked like flares out of his pocket. "I suggest we split up into three groups. If anyone finds him, light one of these flares — the others will then come looking for you." He handed one each to Ivan and to me.

"I'll stay in the middle," he said. Nodding to me, he went on, "You keep to the north, sir — depending on how long it takes, you'll eventually get to Loch Hourn."

I nodded.

To Ivan, he said, "You keep on the southern edge, and you'll come to Loch Morar eventually. It will be daylight before any of us reaches the sea, and if we don't find him . . ." He left the sentence unfinished.

"Leave the headlights on in the Land Rovers," I said. "That will help guide us back."

Without any more preamble, we set off. If

Erich had fallen and broken his leg, say, hypothermia would be an issue, so speed on our part was important.

My group started out. I was in the middle, Katrine on my right and Madeleine on my left. We were about twenty yards apart but we fanned out — so that we were soon separated from the other groups. The area we had to cover was large.

We had our torches, ropes around our waists, and bottles of water in our pockets. Every so often we called out, "Erich!," "Hello?," or "Can you hear me?"

The night closed in around us. Soon we were out of sight of the cars. The wind — more than a breeze — was cold. Occasionally we disturbed rabbits or hares, grouse and small deer. We always stopped and examined these locations, just in case Erich had fallen there. But he hadn't.

After an hour we came to some pines. We worked our way through those, shouting, with torches ablaze.

Nothing.

After that I suggested we spread out even more; we were now a hundred yards apart. There was no sign of the other groups.

The ground here was heather, broken by occasional trees, where we disturbed a range of birds. And the ground was steeper, and getting more so. I thought I heard running water in the distance.

We had been on the go for nearly two hours now. The moon was up — and visibility could have been worse. It would be midnight soon.

I saw a shape ahead of me. A cow? A deer? Erich? It suddenly lurched off into the darkness — a magnificent stag. Why on earth had it allowed us to get so close?

The sound of running water was definitely louder now, and the land was falling away quite sharply. I stopped briefly for a water break.

"Matt! Matt! Over here! Katrine, here, quick, I think I've found something!"

Screwing the top on my bottle, I hurried towards Madeleine, playing my torch ahead of me.

As I approached her, I noticed that she was coming towards me.

"What is it?" I said. "What have you found?"

"Stop here," she said urgently. "Let's wait for Katrine. The land falls away here quite quickly — it's dangerous."

"Yes, but —"

"Here's Katrine."

Katrine arrived, out of breath. "What is it?"

"Just stand here for a moment, and turn and look at where I shine my torch."

Madeleine turned and shone her torch in a slow sweep along the ground beyond where we stood.

"See, there's a cliff here, a vertical drop of

about a hundred feet. It must be the lip of a quarry wall — I nearly fell into it myself. There's no warning."

She held Katrine's elbow with her hand. "Now, inch forward, till you are standing on the very edge of the lip. Careful, Matt!"

We inched forward.

"Follow the beam of my torch as I shine it downwards. Try to move as little as possible . . . Do you see what I see?"

We looked down.

"A mass of rubble," said Katrine softly.

"Is that fresh earth?" I said.

"Yes!" said Madeleine. "That's what I thought too. I think Erich came this way, at night like we are doing, and slipped over the edge of the quarry. Say he fell down the quarry wall and started a small avalanche, a landslide. Maybe it covered him. Maybe he's buried underneath all that rubble."

"If he is," murmured Katrine, "is he still alive?"

"That depends," I said. "His head may be near the surface, but his legs may be trapped. He could have enough oxygen but not be able to move. We've got to go and see. But he may not be there at all."

I gripped both their arms. "Right," I said. "Let's all step back carefully from the edge. We don't want any more landslides."

"Shall we set off a flare?"

"No, not yet, Madeleine. We don't know

for sure that he's here. No point in stopping the others searching until we *are* sure."

"We need other men to go down into the quarry," Katrine protested.

"We need them to bring him up," I replied. "Especially if he's injured. But at the moment we don't know if he's down there."

"So what do you — ?"

"Look about you," I interjected. "There are no trees or rocks to fix a rope to. But I am a big man — biggish anyway. Katrine, you and I can hold the rope while Madeleine goes down, over the edge — she's the lightest."

I looked at Madeleine. "Think you can manage it?"

She hesitated, but then nodded.

"Are you sure?"

"I'm sure. I'll thread the rope under my thigh, which will take the strain. I was a nurse, remember — we do rudimentary physics, pulleys and all that, for patients who are badly hurt. Don't worry about me."

"Good. We won't descend here. If Erich *is* down there, we don't want another landslide."

We moved about thirty yards along the cliff. I unwound the ropes from around my waist, and from around Katrine's, and tied them together. Then I roped Katrine to me and we sat on the ground some ten yards back from the lip of the quarry, both of us gripping the heather groundcover.

Madeleine slipped the end of the rope under her belt, yanked it once or twice, to test how firm we were, and began to gently lower herself over the lip of the cliff.

"If he's there and alive, yank the rope twice," I said. "If he's dead, once, and if he's not there at all three times, and I won't set off any flares. Understood?"

"Yes."

The moonlight was still quite strong. I could see Madeleine clearly.

Then she disappeared and the tension on the rope increased. I dug my heels into the peat.

Katrine did the same.

The wind gusted. Clouds floated past the moon.

After three or four minutes, the line went slack. Madeleine had reached the floor of the quarry.

I looked at Katrine and she looked at me.

We waited.

We heard scrabbling in the landslide earth. From where we had stood it had been difficult to gauge the size of the slip.

The wind was getting up, larger gusts now, sending swooping sounds through the heather.

Then Madeleine's voice broke into the night air as she shouted.

"What did she say?" I asked Katrine.

She shook her head. "I couldn't hear either."

"What did you say?" I shouted across the quarry but my words too were caught up in the wind that was rushing in from the Atlantic.

Madeleine didn't reply.

Then the rope jerked, hard. Twice.

The smell of fried bacon leaked into the dining room. Duncan looked at me and grinned.

"I think we need an emergency more often."

I grinned back, and nodded.

We both looked across to the sideboard, where Craigie, the cook, had brought out a big tray with a mound of bacon rashers heaped on it.

All of us in the canteen rose, as one.

Bacon breakfasts were few and far between at Ardlossan, generally kept for bank holidays and other celebrations. Erich's rescue certainly counted as a celebration.

Where the bacon actually came from was a well-kept secret, by Craigie, but, as a line formed next to the tray, I said, to no one in particular, "Leave some for Erich. He's the man who's been through it."

"Where *is* Erich?" asked someone in the queue.

"Having a hot bath, with a whisky," replied Duncan. "He'll be down directly."

"What exactly happened to him?" said Ivan.

122

"How come he was in a landslide, and how come he survived?"

Duncan answered.

"As far as we can make out, in the depths of the night Erich came across an old truck. It was cold and he climbed into the cab for warmth. But the truck was on the lip of a quarry — it had been left there after a landslide had broken away part of the quarry cliff, and was too dangerous to move. The truck had been rusting there for years, abandoned, and the quarry was disused because its walls were unstable. There were warning signs all around, but in the dark Erich didn't see them. It would only have been a matter of time before the truck fell into the quarry all by itself."

Duncan reached for a plate on a side table. "Anyway, Erich's weight shifted the truck's balance."

The queue moved. We were a little nearer the bacon.

"As I say, there were signs all around the quarry, indicating the danger, but in the dark Erich simply didn't see them. Once installed in the cab of the truck, his weight shifted the balance — it tipped over into the quarry, falling down the cliff and causing a landslide."

"Nasty," said someone.

"Yes," said Duncan, "but although it was the truck that tipped Erich into the quarry in the first place, it was also the truck that saved his life."

"How come?"

"The windows of the cab were left closed when the truck was abandoned. When it fell, the landslide covered the cab with a mass of stones and rubble and soil but, being metal, the truck withstood the weight, prevented Erich from being crushed *and* ensured that he had plenty of oxygen — for a number of hours anyway. Madeleine saw the back of the truck sticking out of the rubble and heard him shouting."

"Where *is* the heroine of the hour?"

"She's having a bath, too."

"With Erich? She should have some reward," said someone, and the rest of the queue laughed.

It was more than three hours since Madeleine had yanked on the rope to indicate that she had found Erich and that he was still alive. I had set off a flare and then circumnavigated the quarry, with Katrine, using her torch and mine, until we found a section where there was a track down to the quarry floor.

After joining Madeleine, all three of us had shovelled the rubble away with our hands as best we could. In the cold night air we were soon sweating, but, after about an hour, the others had found us. It had taken all eight of us another hour and more to clear away the stones and soil and rubble. Some of the boulders were the size of two or three deer's heads.

Just as we were getting close to the cab of the truck, a sound filled the night air and Madeleine shouted, "Watch out!"

She turned, grabbed Katrine by the arms, and pulled her away. The smell of soil and dust filled my nostrils — another landslide had followed the first.

The night was dark but the moon was high. I rolled away from the noise just in time and stones and soil fell against my legs but no higher.

The rushing sound died as quickly as it had arisen.

I looked around. All the others were safe.

"Let's get a move on," I said. "Before there's a third."

We got Erich out and made it back to the Land Rovers without any further mishap. Since Madeleine and Katrine and I were particularly filthy after our exertions, and since Erich needed to be given plenty of space after his ordeal, my "team" climbed into the back of the vehicle, along with all the ropes and tools, where there were wooden benches over the wheels.

It wasn't exactly comfortable as the Land Rover began to buck on the winding road and, instinctively, I put my arm around Madeleine.

She responded by resting her head on my

shoulder.

Almost without thinking, I turned and buried my lips in her hair.

It smelled of mud.

Back at the manse, Erich, Madeleine, and I had gone straight into the bathrooms. Craigie had gone off, muttering about it being "time for a treat" — and so here we were, in the queue for a bacon breakfast.

"There she is!" shouted someone, as Madeleine entered the dining room, her wild hair still wet from the bath.

Everyone clapped. A few whistled.

"Well done!"

"You can rescue me any time, miss."

"Let her through. Come on, miss. You first. Craigie's done us proud."

Madeleine smiled and worked her way through the gap in the line that had opened up.

She took some bacon and what looked like artificial scrambled egg, and went to sit at a table near the fire. I didn't wait in line but went and sat with her. I was hungry but she needed company after the night she'd had.

As I was sitting down, however, Erich entered the room. He looked spick and span, in a clean white shirt and slacks, as though he'd had a good night's sleep in his bed. You would never guess what he'd been through. He came directly across to Madeleine and

126

me at the table and sat down next to Madeleine.

He held a packet in one hand. With the other, he reached for Madeleine's fingers and raised them to his lips.

As everyone in the room watched, he kissed the skin on her wrist.

"You saved my life," he said softly. "This is for you. None of us is allowed much, in the way of personal possessions, but it *is* silver."

He placed the packet he was holding on the table in front of Madeleine.

"No, Erich —" she began but he interrupted her.

"Take it," he said, softly but urgently. "Take it, please. A few hours ago I thought I was going to die. You must let me thank you — it's only right. In the next few weeks either of us, or both of us, could be killed. I have to thank you now.

"I can't tell you what went through my mind in that truck. I once got locked in the crypt of the cathedral where I worked in Belgium. It was an accident, when some workmen cleared up for the day. Later that night it poured with rain and the cellar where I was filled with several feet of water, rising all the time. Until I was rescued, I didn't know what was going to happen — the cellar was underground and the whole crypt could have filled with water. I was rescued after more than twenty-four hours but . . . small, underground, enclosed prisons are not . . . They are not my favourite places."

He gestured to the packet.

"Please open it."

Madeleine took back her hand and opened the package.

Inside was Erich's cigarette case, a small, elegant silver box that caught the sun shining in through the high windows.

"Erich," breathed Madeleine. "I can't —"

"Yes, you can," he said quickly. "I want you to have it. It's Belgian, so you can take it to France — it won't give you away. We'll all need cigarettes when we are in the field, and this will give you confidence, remind you of what you did here in Scotland, how you . . . Well, you know what you did. Whose life you saved."

All the others were watching.

I could sense that Madeleine thought the gift too much, the cigarette case too valuable for what she had done. But she also knew that to refuse it would not . . . would not suit the mood of the moment with everyone watching.

So she smiled, raised it to her lips, kissed it, and then kissed Erich on the cheek.

"Thank you," she said. "I shall treasure it, always."

6

We were back in the stables on the far side of the manse yard. Once again, Duncan was leading the show that morning, while I looked on. The four recruits sat on wooden benches or leaned against the stall walls. The smell of horse was as strong as ever.

Between Duncan and the recruits was a metal frame with clothing on hangers, all the clothing the same shade of grey.

"No prizes for guessing what these are," Duncan began. He took one hanger off the rail and held it up for everyone to see. "Wehrmacht uniforms, the genuine article captured by our people at some point in the recent past."

He took the uniform jacket off the hanger. "Uniform recognition is a routine but nonetheless vital part of your training. We've found that firsthand contact with the material itself is the most efficient and vivid way to rub in this part of the course."

He straightened his arms and shook the

jacket. "Come on, Katrine; you try it on first. This is a *Standartenführer*'s uniform, a colonel to you." He grinned. "See what it feels like to be promoted, Captain Howard."

Katrine stepped forward and slipped her arms into the sleeves of the jacket. It was, inevitably, far too big — her fingers just poked out at the end of the cuffs, and the two sides overlapped comically.

The others were laughing.

"Who's your tailor?" said Ivan. "So I can avoid him."

"You next," said Duncan to Erich.

He took another uniform from the rail. "This one is a *Rittmeister,* a company commander, with braid on its epaulettes — see? Erich, you try this one."

Erich got to his feet and put his arms into the jacket. He saluted Madeleine. Everyone laughed again.

Yes, Duncan was right. There *was* something between those two.

"Ivan, come on," said Duncan. Holding out another jacket he said, "This one has double plaiting of the braids on the epaulettes . . . It's a field commander's uniform, a *Stabsoffizier.*"

Ivan put the uniform on and began to do up the buttons.

"Err . . . no," he said quietly. "I think you'll find it's an *Oberstleutnant* uniform, a lieutenant colonel's jacket."

"What?" said Duncan, momentarily flummoxed. Then, "Oh!" he said. "You're right. My mistake. I'm confusing these two, Madeleine has the *Stabsoffizier* uniform. Well done, Ivan, thank you for correcting me. As you can see, it's easy to —"

Ivan shrugged. "When you are playing blackjack in a casino, and you have what we call a shoe, there are sometimes as many as four packs of cards in it. Sometimes, when they are shuffled the shuffling isn't always as complete as it might be, and for a while some cards are dealt in the same order as the time before. Some gamblers have amazing memories and can remember those sequences, or most of them. A good croupier has to do the same — otherwise the punters have an advantage for a while. You train your eye for detail, visual detail."

"So have you memorized all officers' insignia?"

"Yes. It's easy for me."

"And what else can you remember?"

"The layout and the letters of the one-time pads," said Ivan. "The geography of northern France — all the towns in the right order. There has to be a visual element — for example, I can remember the faces of all the card sharps who came through Monte."

Duncan turned to me. "That's a talent we may be able to use, sir."

I nodded. "We may need you in interroga-

131

tion, Ivan; I'll speak to my superiors about it. But let's get on now."

Duncan turned back to the class.

"Now, back to you, Madeleine. This one has green and yellow flashes at the collar — it's a field commander's uniform, an *Oberstarzt,* as Ivan has correctly pointed out."

Madeleine was no less swamped by her jacket than Katrine had been and the laughs started again.

"Enjoy yourselves," said Duncan, laughing himself. "But remember, this is not a game; you really do need to register these ranks — and you will be tested on it later, and you won't all have Ivan's memory. Now, take off the jackets you are wearing and try on some others. Remember, it's the flashes at the collar and the epaulettes that tell you the most."

The recruits milled around, taking off and putting on the various jackets.

"In the field, you also need to know," said Duncan, putting one jacket back on its hanger, "from the rank of the uniforms you see, what that rank implies for the number of troops that are likely to be in that particular area. It could be very important. For example, if you observe someone in a field officer's uniform, that is likely to mean —"

"Achtung! Achtung! Meine Damen und Herren. Achtung! Achtung!"

Duncan broke off, surprised.

We all turned to where the shouting was

coming from.

Madeleine was standing on a chair. She had buttoned up her uniform and put on a German military cap, one of a number we also had, and now she held under her nose the end of a small black comb — a perfect impression of Adolf Hitler's moustache.

We fell silent.

She raised her right arm.

"Liberty ist Stunk," she shouted.

"Freisprach ist Stunk."

Erich, the choirmaster, started humming a tune that I recognized but couldn't place.

The others also recognized what scene Madeleine was playing and they were laughing all over again and joining in.

"Wienerschnitzel und Sauerkraut!" cried Ivan.

"Baloney," replied Katrine solemnly. They redoubled the laughing.

Madeleine had caught Charlie Chaplin's "Great Dictator" perfectly. The film had been on show for a couple of years by then.

They all went on speaking the gobbledygook, gibberish German that Chaplin used in the film for a little while longer, and then they joined in with Erich in humming the same tune.

"What *is* that?" I asked.

"The Prelude from Wagner's *Lohengrin,*" said Erich. "Chaplin thought Wagner was just as *Stunk* as Hitler. That's why he chose it as the score."

133

Still laughing, Madeleine wound up the gibberish and got down off the chair.

Katrine went up to her and hugged her. "Brilliant," she said. "I'm glad you are on our side."

That night at dinner, we were all seated at the same table, as had become our habit. There was no talk of the course — everyone had had enough of shop talk throughout the day — and the conversation ranged over a wide selection of subjects — sport, theatre, the BBC's music coverage, American films, the weather inevitably.

I looked around me.

"Where's Madeleine?" I asked Katrine.

She shook her head, sheepishly I thought. "I don't know."

"And Duncan?"

She shook her head again.

I sipped my drink.

Just then there was a commotion at the other end of the room and the main double doors swung open.

From beyond the doors, out of sight, there was a weird kind of whirring sound, a sort of heavy breathing, and one or two moans. Then, all at once, a very plaintive version of "Happy Birthday" was struck up, and into the room marched Duncan, surrounded — that was the only word — by a set of bagpipes. He was blowing into the tube — I didn't

134

know its technical name — and squeezing the bag with his elbows. In no time the wailing sound filled the dining room, bouncing off the walls, disturbing the water in our drinking glasses, and even rattling the cutlery.

Behind him was . . . what can best be described as a cascade of sparks, falling from a plate held by Madeleine. She held the cake — for that is what must have been below the sparks — high in the air and she was singing "Happy Birthday to Ivan" at the top of her voice.

As they advanced through the room, everyone joined in, except for Ivan, who looked both pleased and embarrassed.

Duncan came to a stop right in front of Ivan, as Madeleine ran out of words. The sound of the bagpipes died — like an animal in pain — and he stood to one side as Madeleine laid the sparkling cake in front of Ivan.

He stared at the sparkles, and then at Madeleine.

"How did you know it was my birthday, and where did you get those . . . whatever they are?"

"This is an incendiary device we have tampered with," said Madeleine. "It's been neutered, sort of," she grinned, "by Duncan. As for your birthday, that's easy. You use the numerical version — twenty-one, three, fourteen — in your lock in the locker room. March 21, 1914 — so I worked out that you're exactly thirty today. It's a big birthday. Did you hope to get away with it?"

"No, no. I didn't think anyone would be interested. I'm touched."

"Craigie made the cake," Madeleine said. "Cut it carefully, there's a surprise inside."

Looking mystified, Ivan stood up and picked up a knife. He stuck it uncertainly into the middle of the cake, which by now had stopped fizzling. He cut until he recognised a resistance to the knife. Now he cut *around* the shape.

Next, he picked up a spoon.

We were all watching. Whatever was inside was going to be as big a surprise for us as for him. What on earth had Madeleine been up to?

He dug into the cake with the spoon. What he came up with was solid, a rectangle or oblong, about half an inch thick.

He smeared away the covering of cake, to reveal a paper wrapping.

He took that off.

Whatever was inside was carefully encased in waxed paper, entirely untouched by the treatment it had received.

"I know what this is," said Ivan. "It's a pack of cards. I can recognize cards a mile off."

"Well done," said Madeleine softly. "But what *sort* of cards?"

He undid the waxed paper wrapping. And took out the cards. He handled them expertly, as only he could, shuffling them in his fingers.

"There's something very special about these cards," said Madeleine. "See if you can spot what it is."

Ivan inspected the cards in his hands. "All the backs are the same, that's normal. Views of the highlands and islands, I suppose. Let me look at the faces."

He turned the cards over and fanned them out. We all looked on.

"They seem quite normal to me." He flicked the cards through his fingers as only a professional could do.

"All the royal cards look normal, the Jacks are a bit elaborate . . ." He carried on playing with the cards.

"Hold on, what's this? A blank face?" He looked at Madeleine. "Is this what you mean? A card with nothing on it?"

She nodded and smiled. "Yes, have you not heard of this?"

Ivan shook his head, clearly mystified.

Madeleine was delighted. "Craigie the cook told me. It's something every professional croupier should have — I found them in Drumlanrig. A proper Scottish pack of cards has no nine of diamonds —"

"Why on earth not? I don't get it," cried Ivan. "What's the point?"

"Well," said Madeleine, "there are several explanations but the best version, I think, is the one that says that, in the days of James

137

VI, the crown of Scotland was robbed of nine diamonds and, because no one owned up to the theft, the king made his subjects pay for the missing jewels out of their taxes. In that way, the nine of diamonds became known as the 'curse of Scotland,' and all Scottish playing cards from those days have no nine of diamonds, just a plain face. It's a nice touch, don't you think? I thought that, as a professional card player, you'd like a Scottish set of cards. As a memento of your time here."

Ivan took a step forward. I thought he was going to embrace Madeleine but he was clearly too shy. "Maddie, you are a treasure." He held up the cards. "That was — this is — a wonderful thought, a real memento of this place. I don't know how many sets of playing cards I have but this will go to the top of my list, never out of my sight for long. I . . . I only wish I had nine diamonds to give you."

Madeleine laughed. "There's a thought. But these are just playing cards, Ivan, hiding in a cake. You can take them to France and no one will know what they mean, just you and us."

Ivan looked at me.

"Do you give us any memento, after we finish the course? Any sign that we have been here?"

I shook my head. "Think about it. If you were found with something like that, in France, it could sign your death warrant."

He nodded. "I suppose you're right." He waved the pack of cards. "But this, this is something I shall always have with me. There's something imperfect about this pack. One card is missing. I like that. It tells us not to expect too much. In its way, it's comforting."

He turned back to Madeleine. "I don't know whether you intended to give me something comforting, but you did. You, above all, will be the person I remember from this course."

We stopped at the top of the hill. Ahead of us the tarmac sloped gently down the valley side to meet a small river. Off to the right stood a cluster of stone buildings with tall chimneys, like huge sticks of chalk. Blue smoke drifted from their tops.

"That's Benkillan," I said, pointing to the mountain opposite. As we looked, cloud shadows swept over the brown and purple shoulder.

"Let's rest for a while." I dismounted from my bicycle and Madeleine did the same.

It was about ten days after the recruits' experiment in living off the land and just a couple of days after Madeleine's wicked impression of Adolf Hitler and her rendering of "Happy Birthday" to Ivan. The recruits' progress along the course was steady. We had by now covered explosives, other sabotage techniques — how to immobilize vehicles, for instance — more radio transmission, using both one-time pads and their poetry codes, the principles of blowing up boats, should any of them be sent to harbours, the promised political instruction on the relationship between communists and Gaullists, as I had warned Madeleine, and the organisation of circuits for maximum security.

Now, in the later part of the course, the recruits had one afternoon free each week. This was the second excursion Madeleine and I had been on; we had only just discovered the bicycles in a shed in the rear courtyard.

We stood for a moment, watching the cloud shadows move across the hillsides, as the smoke from the chimneys rose in lazy curls.

"Are you ready to go?" I asked Madeleine. "We can free-wheel down the hill, almost as far as Gleneyre."

"Race you!" she squealed suddenly, remounting her bike and pedaling furiously. In no time she was twenty yards away.

I gave chase.

The clouds cleared, and although it wasn't a very warm day, the wind was slight, the view was magnificent — and the road was empty but for us. Sun glinted on the frame of Madeleine's bicycle.

The purple in the heather of Scotland always seemed to me an improbable colour for a plant and the great swathes of it on Ben-killan, across the valley, were iridescent today. A pity there was none in the parts of France our recruits were going to. Heather is a spongy covering to parachute in on.

My bicycle was picking up speed and I was gaining on Madeleine. I was a good bit heavier than she was, so gravity was on my side.

As I closed in on her I could see that she had taken her feet off the pedals and was holding her legs forward, so that the wind generated by her speed blew straight up her body — she obviously liked that sensation. She held her head back as the wind ran through her hair, redder than the rocks on Benkillan. Every so often she let out a *Whoop!* I have never seen anyone as happy as she was at that moment.

I braked and stayed behind. I liked the view exactly as it was. She was going away soon. It was a scene I wanted to savour — and re-member.

Just as our walks on the beach were not just walks on the beach, so a bicycle ride in the mountains was not just a bike ride. She had agreed to come when I had suggested it, so it was a step forward. There is always a moment, a stage, in any relationship, when behaviour comes before words. I didn't dare ask about her relationship with Erich and she didn't volunteer anything. But she was here

today and, so far as I could tell, she was loving it.

As was I.

There was a war on, somewhere, but we
had that road, and those mountainsides, to
ourselves and, for now, it was enough. She
was absorbed in what she was doing, absorbed in living. Her ability to do that was a
gift, a gift she was sharing with me.

I was as full with life on that bike ride as I
have ever been.

At the bottom of the valley the road flat-
tened out and Madeleine let her bike roll all
by itself until it stopped. I came alongside
and we both slipped off our saddles and stood
with our legs astride the machines.

"I won!" she cried triumphantly.

"You could have gone faster, if you'd made
yourself smaller. Less wind resistance."

"What? And miss all that wind rushing past
me — in my hair, making my eyes water? In
my mouth, up and along my thighs? That's
something you men never have, the pleasure
of riding a bike in a skirt." She grinned. "It's
quite sexy."

We leaned our bicycles against one another,
in a precarious arrangement and turned to
look at the site before us.

Madeleine twisted her head so her hair was
off her neck. "I know what this is. It's a circle
— a circle of standing stones. This is some
ancient cult site, isn't it? From thousands of

years ago."

I nodded. "It's called a cromlech. It's possibly an ancient observatory, from a time when the heavens were more active than they are now, when comets and asteroids were more common, and when interpreting the action of the heavens was the religious leaders' main work. There are a few of these in Scotland — usually in remote locations, like this one."

She looked around her. "Some of these stones are ten feet tall and more. Where do they come from, and how did they get them here?"

I leaned against one of the stones. Given their size they were quite solid.

"They come from about forty miles away. They must have been rolled here, on logs, I suspect, across the valleys. They could never have built carts strong enough to carry them, even after the wheel had been invented."

Madeleine passed the palm of her hand over the surface of one of the stones. "Are they carved like this, or are they naturally occurring?"

"I'm not an expert but I'm told that some of the surfaces are so smooth and regular they must have been cut. But with what, no one knows — as I understand it, smelting hadn't been invented then, so there were no metal tools."

Madeleine moved around, skipping now

and then, like a child, in and out of the arrangement of stones, running her hands over them, feeling the smooth patches, fingering the sharp ridges.

"Are there any carvings here? Or ancient paintings?"

"Look over here," I said, walking across to a large flat stone set into the ground. "See that?"

She followed me, and peered down.

I pointed. "A local historian showed these to me a year or so ago. Are these circles that have worn away, partly, or are they the letter 'C,' repeated one inside the other? Or, since they vary in thickness, do they show the various waxing and waning phases of the moon? See? No one really knows what they are supposed to represent."

Madeleine fell to her knees and, again, ran her fingers over the marks.

"Philippe would have loved this spot," she said softly in English. "A-may-zing."

"Philippe?" I said.

She looked up at me sharply, her eyes becoming larger and rounder. "What did you say? What did *I* say?"

"You said Philippe would have loved this spot."

She bit her lip. As she did so, our bicycles fell over.

Madeleine ran across and bent down and began to disentangle them.

"Come on," she said, holding the two sets of handlebars apart, "We've got that hill to climb. It will take all our breath. We can talk later."

And, without waiting for me, she leaned my bicycle against one of the standing stones, mounted hers, and set off back along the road we had come by.

Sometimes the most intimate conversations can take place in the most crowded places. That night was the snooker competition final and everyone turned up after dinner to watch the match. Besides the four players and the referee, all the kitchen staff were there, plus the recruits who would be dropped into other countries — Cyprus, Italy, Greece, and so on — and *their* instructors, even the drivers and the gardeners. There were getting on for forty people in that one room.

Madeleine and I sat on a settee near the fire. She had on her frock and had washed her hair. I couldn't be sure but I thought she had on more lipstick than usual.

"You don't want to watch the snooker?"

She shook her head. "Tell me, the people who worshipped at those standing stones — where did they live?"

"Nearby, I suppose. I told you — I'm not an expert."

"In what?"

"Flimsy houses that didn't last as well as

their temples. It was a time when people were more interested in their religious beliefs than in life on earth."

"You think so?"

"That's what the local historian told me."

She nodded. "What will happen to this house, once the war is over?"

I handed her some whisky. "It will eventually be sold, I should imagine."

She sipped some of the liquid and wiped her mouth with the back of her hand. "But will all go well? What if the invasion is a disaster?"

"That doesn't bear thinking about, but if it happens Ardlossan will continue to be used. I will continue giving courses. Continue taking people to see the standing stones."

A shout went up as someone made a good shot.

I glanced towards the noise. I noticed Erich looking our way.

"What time is it?" Madeleine asked. Her voice was especially loamy tonight.

I turned back to her. "Eleven forty-five."

"Too late for a walk — ?"

"Philippe, Madeleine. Who is — or was — Philippe?"

I sipped my whisky, and waited.

"Okay. 'Aye,' as Duncan would say. Here goes." She spoke as if to the fire. "As you know, my mother and I moved from France to Britain in November 1938. In March of the following year, when Hitler occupied Czechoslovakia, and when the French prime minister was given emergency powers for France to rearm, my mother decided on one last trip to Louzac, where we had been living before we moved. For a last look, she said, before the war, which she was certain would come. She didn't know when — or if — she would ever see Louzac again. She wanted to say goodbye to old friends. I went with her."

She held out her hand so she could feel the warmth of the flames.

"While I was in Louzac, I met Philippe Sompre. He was a geologist, though he also had an interest in archaeology. He was very good-looking, very funny, very charming — all the local girls thought the world of him. Some of them even sent *him* flowers, can you imagine that?"

She cleared her throat.

"But . . . *but* he had poor eyesight, very poor, so he had been turned down by the army. That had made him angry, and restless. Anyway, while my mother did her rounds, visiting all her old friends, Philippe and I went on long walks. There are a lot of little rivers and hills and caves near Louzac. The weather was unusually mild that March. I don't know whether it was because I was new, because I didn't live in Louzac, so I wasn't familiar to Philippe, but we seemed to get on. He confided in me."

147

More noise from the vicinity of the snooker table. She looked across. Was she looking for Erich?

"Being a geologist, in his spare time Philippe was making a map of all the caves in the area. He explained that France is very special when it comes to caves, that the rock formations favour them, and that ancient people lived there, often decorating them with art. Pictures of horses, cattle, foxes, and bears. It was his plan to map all the caves and then explore them, in the hope that he would discover a lot of ancient art and make his name."

She picked up the poker in the hearth and rearranged the logs in the fire.

"I was enchanted by all this. I loved it. He was so caught up in his own ideas, he was so convinced that he would one day make sensational discoveries, that it was hard not to be swept away. And I *was* swept away."

She set down the poker again.

"You may guess some of what happened, but not everything." She breathed out softly. "Visiting so many caves, just the two of us . . . it wasn't long before . . . Well, one day it stormed heavily; we were trapped in a cave for over an hour. You can guess that bit."

She pulled at the hem of her frock.

"So there I was, in France for just a few days, but I had met the most exciting man I had ever known until then — and I was in love. Oh yes, it was a real *coup de foudre,* an emotional thunderbolt to go with the storm outside the cave that day. And it was two-way. Philippe was as much in love with me as I was with him."

She frowned.

"Now we get to the difficult bit. I was, of course, in France for just a week, one over-all-too-quickly week, before my mother and I returned to London. With war looming, there was no chance we could stay. It was danger-ous to remain in France if you had some-where else to go, though I would have stayed and risked it, given what I felt for Philippe."

She fiddled with her necklace.

"So, one day, we spent a while in another cave, making love, and, after it was over, we talked. We decided that, if we were in love — and we *were* in love — we should get mar-ried. It wasn't absolutely certain then that there would be a war, but if there was to be, we wanted . . . we decided that, by being mar-ried, that would be the best way to cement what we felt for each other. It would help us hold up through the separation that a war, if it happened, would inevitably bring about."

She ran a finger reflectively round the rim of her glass.

"So that's what we did. The very next day, the day before my mother and I returned to London, Philippe and I took the train to Cognac, the nearest large town, and visited

149

the *mairie,* the town hall, where we were married. Marriages in France, as I'm sure you know, are civil affairs, not religious ones, so you don't have to arrange things with a priest — which was just as well in our case because I am a Protestant and Philippe is a Catholic. We celebrated in a bar, with some champagne, he took some photographs, and then we went back to Louzac. The next day my mother and I returned to London."

"So — ?"

"Hold on. I haven't finished — nowhere near. I never told my mother that Philippe and I were married, not then, but of course we did write to each other and were always hoping we could meet each other again. But then war was declared in September, and travel got very difficult, almost impossible for civilians. Philippe was smuggled to Britain in the summer of 1940, for a conference of Resistance leaders — he was one by then — and we met in Dover, where he was able to stay for two nights. Two glorious nights before he had to go back. He told me then that he had made a number of discoveries of ancient art in 'his' caves as he called them, and hoped to publish his results after the war. Things got even worse, of course, after the Germans established the coastal exclusion zone. Then we couldn't communicate at all."

"And have you heard — ?"

"Hold on! Let me tell you everything now,

and then we don't have to come back to it."

She leaned forward so she could feel the warmth of the fire on her face this time.

"The Free French, in London, under de Gaulle, had set up some underground channels of communication, and my mother, though English by birth, had also registered as being French living in London, because she'd been married to my father. So we were on the Free French books, so to speak. Anyway, one day in early 1941 — March or April, I think it was — a man arrived at our flat with two letters for me. One was from Philippe and one was from his mother."

She paused and closed her eyes, obviously thinking back. Her lush eyelashes lay on her cheeks.

"Philippe's letter was lovely. With France being occupied and the Resistance being set up, he came into his own. He couldn't be in the regular army, and that was just as well, with what was happening to French soldiers being sent east, but he could be in the Resistance. He knew where all those caves were, which were perfect hiding places for the Resistance, perfect storage places for food or explosives, and places where the injured could be looked after. He had found his métier and although it was dangerous I could tell he was loving it. It was a very loving letter, looking forward to the end of the war. He was certain the Germans would lose."

She closed her eyes again.

"His mother's letter was very different. She said that Philippe had eventually told her about our marriage. She said she thought we had been foolish as well as deceitful — foolish because he was a Catholic and I am Protestant. My mother is Protestant and insisted I be raised in her faith, the more so after my father died. But Philippe's mother wasn't writing just to admonish me or criticise me, but to give me the news that Philippe was dead."

Madeleine took a deep breath.

"He had become a senior figure in the local Resistance, she said, and a hero locally. His looks, his knowledge of the local terrain, the cave art he had discovered, showing how long the French had been in that land now occupied by invaders, all helped make him a local legend. But he had been betrayed. He had, his mother said, been shot in a prison yard at Cognac, the very town where we had been married. With the letter she had enclosed a photograph of me and Philippe that he had taken at our wedding but had not had time to have developed before I returned to London with my mother."

She looked at me.

"It was heartbreaking. I was a widow at twenty-two. That's when — that's really *why* — I decided to do something for the war effort. To have my own little revenge."

We were silent for a long time.

Eventually, I said, "None of this was in your file."

"I never talk about it. I didn't want people to think my war was only personal. I didn't mention it to you because I didn't want you to think . . . It's been three years now, Colonel, and I've adjusted." Her voice thinned a little. "It was glorious, but it only really lasted four days and I . . . I get emotional when I talk about it, like we are doing now, but really . . . I'm not going into France for Philippe any more. My motives are . . . I'm going because it's the right thing to do."

"You're full of surprises," I breathed after a moment. "I'll give you that."

Another moment of silence. She looked at me over the rim of her whisky glass as she drank. Her eyes grew rounder.

"Now what?"

She lowered her glass. "Erich's asked me out. He wants to take me to Fort William, for dinner."

I swallowed. "And what did you say?"

"I said I'd think about it." She tugged at the hem of her skirt again. "What do *you* think I should say?"

"It's not up to me, is it?"

"You've never asked me out. For dinner, I mean."

"I was working up to it. I thought I'd wait until we got to London. I'm your commanding officer at the moment. In London you'll come under someone else. In London we can be more discreet."

She regarded me, a slight smile spreading along her lips.

A burst of applause erupted across the room as the game was finished. Shouting, more applause, cries of "Well done!," "Congratulations!" Whistles. Glasses being banged on tables.

There was too much noise for either of us to be heard for a few moments.

Then she nodded and leaned forward.

"We are a small group in F Section. Just four recruits. If I turn Erich down, that could upset him, and upset the balance in the group in our final days."

I didn't say anything.

"I'm going to tell him yes, on that basis. It will be interesting to see Fort William anyway."

I couldn't read her expression.

Then she said, "All the same, I look forward to our dinner in London, Colonel."

"How is it that you don't like whisky, Duncan?"

He and I were sitting next to the fire in the snooker room, after dinner two nights later. It was late; almost everyone else had gone to bed. There were just two others playing darts. Madeleine was out with Erich in Fort William. They had not yet returned.

Duncan drained his beer glass. "I saw what it did to my father." He set his glass down on the low table near us. "My father was not a nice man when he drank. He hit us boys, he hit my mother. My elder brother stood up to him — and then they fought. That's why Callum went into the RAF early, to get away. My other brother couldn't wait to follow him as soon as he was eighteen."

"And what happened? What happened with you?"

I looked at my watch. It was just gone eleven. Where *were* they?

"My father fell ill with the drink — liver trouble. My two elder brothers were in training, to be pilots — if they passed their exams. I couldn't leave home like they did — that would have left my mother with no one. So I stayed on at school, and found that I was good at maths and liked it. Then, in the space of a few months, my father died of his illness, I was given a scholarship to Glasgow University, and my mother said I should go, that I had been tied to her apron strings for long enough. She went to live with her sister. At university I joined the army reserve in 1938, and just before war broke out I was invited to a code-breaking outfit near Prestwick in Ayrshire — they needed mathematicians, they said. From there I was taken into SC2 when it was created. The rest you know."

"Did your mother grieve much, or was she glad to be shut of your father? Did she never remarry?"

Still no sign of Madeleine and Erich.

Duncan shook his head. "No, she never remarried. In a funny way, despite his drinking binges, and the fights, I think she loved him. She was certainly very upset when he died. Then, when my brothers were killed, early on in the war, she was . . . Well, you know."

"Do you like living at home now?"

"I don't *dislike* it, but . . . when Siobhan and I get married I'll be moving out."

"And when is that likely to be?"

He stood up. "Can we talk about this some other time, Matt? I'm very tired and we've got to prepare our last little deception. We've got our work cut out, if we are to pull it off without anyone guessing."

I stood up, too. "Of course. And you're right. We can't lose our cunning this late in the course."

I picked up my half-empty half-bottle of whisky and followed Duncan out of the room.

The darts players had already gone.

I went to the front door of the manse, opened it, and stepped out into the night.

It was crisp, with a clear sky. No moon but countless stars. My breath escaped my mouth in tiny clouds that melted into nothing immediately. No sign of anyone arriving along

156

the drive.

I turned and went inside, closing the door behind me. I nodded to the sentry on duty. The manse was miles from anywhere, but it was still fully defended.

I climbed the stone stairs to my room. At the end of the corridor a window was open slightly. It made the light hanging from the ceiling sway but the open window kept the air circulating so that in our wing of the manse it didn't get stale.

I opened the door to my room. The light was on. Odd. I hadn't left it on.

Madeleine was lying on the bed. Wearing a raincoat and scarf.

I was both apprehensive and light-headed all at the same time.

She had taken one hell of a risk in coming here.

On the beaches near the manse, on our bicycle rides, in class, I had always been with Madeleine in public, or in a public place. I had long been aware of my growing feelings but hadn't allowed them to flood my system as I knew the dangers of incoming tides. But in the confined space of my room, with Madeleine stretched out on the bed, the fact that she had come straight from being with Erich to being with me . . . We were still at that stage where behaviour came before words, but her very presence here, now, was a bold extension of the code which, until then, we

157

had silently followed.

"Is that whisky in your hand?" she said softly. "Erich doesn't drink and I'm gasping."

I stepped across the room and handed her the bottle. She swung her legs off the bed and sat sideways on, holding the whisky.

"I didn't hear you come in. How long have you been back? Didn't Erich offer you a drink?"

"On grounds of security we had to pay off the taxi at the end of the drive. We walked the rest of the way —"

"Jesus! You must be rock-solid — it's freezing out there."

She grinned. "We didn't walk, we *marched*! But yes, the whisky will be a help." She drank from the neck of the bottle and wiped her lips with the back of her hand. "That's better."

"You look like someone in a western, drinking like that."

"Aren't you going to ask me how it went?"

"How did it go?"

She handed back the bottle. I sat on the edge of the bed, alongside her.

"There's not much to Fort William. All the buildings are like this place — windows too small for their walls."

"It's to keep the weather out. But that's not what I meant."

She unwound her scarf from round her neck. "I'm thawing out at last. I know it's not what you meant."

She unbuttoned her raincoat.

"Erich's very sweet — I'm not sure he's too used to women."

"Not all of us are."

She turned her head and eyed me.

"He spent the whole time talking about his family and his childhood."

"I've just had much the same sort of conversation with Duncan. Is that so terrible?"

"You didn't do that with me."

"Yes, but our first 'date' — not that you can call it that — was an interview just after you thought you were going to die. Not exactly a fair comparison."

"Are you always so fair-minded? You don't know what else happened."

"Do you mean he asked you to marry him?"

She chuckled. "I think . . . I think he likes me, yes. I think that if I gave him encouragement, he could fall for me, perhaps heavily. I don't think there have been many women in his life."

I drank some whisky. "So what are you saying?"

She paused, and took off her raincoat. "Would it shock you, would it change your mind about me, if I said I told him a lie?"

There was a short silence.

"I don't know the answer to that. What was the lie? Why was there a *need* to lie?"

"I told you before . . . that I went out with

Erich in the first place because he asked me and if I had refused him it would — it might — have upset the balance of our small group."

"Yeees?"

"I had to nip Erich's feelings in the bud. Before he got . . . well, before he let them run away with him."

I nodded. I knew exactly what she meant. "So what did you say?"

"I told him about Philippe. I told him the story I told you, about the caves, the storms, the way Philippe and I met, our *coup de foudre* marriage, how he went on to become a Resistance hero." She reached up and held her hair off her head for a moment. "But I didn't tell him Philippe is dead. I left the story, without telling any real whoppers, but so as to give Erich the impression that Philippe is still alive, and that I am a married woman. I said that I had volunteered for this job in the hope that I can soon be reunited with my husband. I think that let Erich down gently. Was it the right thing to do?"

I waited for a moment before saying, "I suppose so. How did he take it?"

"He was sad, I think. But I think he's been turned down by women before. It wasn't too much of a surprise, or too devastating. We'll be easy with each other the next time we meet. It won't disturb the group."

Again, I said nothing for a moment. Nothing she had said had calmed the fire burning just beneath my skin.

"Well, whichever way it went, you've had a more exciting night than I have. Brown soup with Duncan, a darts match, and the inevitable Scotch."

"Too bad," she whispered. "But the night's not over yet, is it? Or it doesn't need to be."

"Are we going to need more whisky at this point?"

"More spirit, certainly. You said you were waiting till London before asking me out. That would — sooner rather than later — probably have led to a situation very like the one we are in now. But the course here is over in two days. If I stay the night tonight, no one is going to know, not if I leave and go back to my room early in the morning. We can be as discreet here as in London."

We heard a seal bark out at sea.

"There you are," she said softly. "It feels right that we should make love here for the first time, with all the sand and the tides, and the seals and the heather, and the standing stones. Afterwards we can lie quietly and listen to the wind in the pines, and the call of the gulls. We won't have it for much longer and I've spent too many nights on my own in this place. You kissed my hair that night we were in the Land Rover, after we had rescued Erich. I liked it."

I half turned on the bed and leaned forward to kiss her.

161

"Why don't you turn out the light?" she murmured.

I got up and went over to the light switch.

The room wasn't in complete darkness. The bulb outside was swaying in the wind, so that the light that leaked under the door flickered as Madeleine stood up and began to undress.

7

I felt the sun on my neck as I gazed down at the four trainees spread-eagled on the grass. Spring had finally arrived at Ardlossan, at least for a few hours, and today's lesson was being held outdoors.

Ivan had taken off his tie, Katrine was wearing an Alice band, Erich was smoking, and Madeleine was wearing the frock I particularly liked. Duncan Kennaway lay flat on his back looking up at the blue sky. He, of course, had heard all I was about to say before.

"We don't often work you on Saturday mornings," I said, as the breeze gusted. "And this weekend is no exception, so I will keep what I have to say short."

I squinted as I looked down at them — the sun was in my eyes. "We are almost at the end of the course. We, on our side, have taught you almost everything we know about serving behind enemy lines in France. When you leave here, you will be sent to London, where you will pick up your clothes, clothes designed to fit in with whatever cover you are being given. You will receive your final orders, tailored explicitly to the region where you will be dropped, and the circuit you will join. You will also receive your instructions about the role you will be expected to play. We all know an invasion is coming but when, and where, is probably the greatest secret of the war. But that you will all play a part in that invasion is without doubt."

They all looked serious, apprehensive. Their real work was getting ever closer.

"We've worked you hard while you've been here. You expected that, I am sure. There's a war on and you are all anxious to play your part, which is as it should be. However, for the rest of today, Saturday, my colleagues and I will have a meeting, to go through the details about all the other people who will be following you here at Ardlossan." I smiled. "Another group, like you, who want to do their bit."

I rocked from one foot to the other as they took this in and, one by one, again nodded their assent.

"There is just one thing remaining. When you are sent overseas, dropped into France, you will be known not by your real names, but by code names. When you practice your transmissions from now on, you will use your code names only. So now is the time to

164

choose one."

I looked from one to the other again.

"Choose one that's simple, not more than two syllables — in English or in French translation — so you don't waste time in transmission, and choose something that is easy to remember but is in no way connected to you. Got it?"

I waited a moment. "When I was in France my code name was 'pasteur,' minister or pastor. You, Ivan, any ideas? We can do this bit of the lesson in English."

Ivan seemed puzzled and said, in French, "Is this a trick question, about being in English, I mean?"

I laughed. "No, not at all. It just makes sense to do this part in English. Off you go."

Ivan looked over his shoulder. "There's so much beach here, when the tide's out. How about *'sable'*?"

"Sand." I nodded. "Equally short in English and French — perfect. Katrine?"

"How about 'tide'?"

"*Marée.* Also good. Erich?"

"I like 'seal.' "

"*Phoque.* Excellent, but can no one break away from Ardlossan? How about you, Madeleine?"

She lifted her hair away from her neck. Her shirt tightened over her bosom. I noticed Erich looking too.

"All right, then," she said. " 'Oak,' how

165

about that? It is certainly short."

"*Chêne* in French — that's good, too. Okay. Why though, as a matter of interest?"

She shrugged. "There's a French proverb-cum-poem about the forest that someone once told me. There are several lines about trees, about the sycamore and the elm, and about the oak being the king of the forest. And there's one line I've never forgotten: 'Do not be afraid to go out on a limb . . . that's where the fruit is.' "

I smiled at her, thinking of our night together. Then, with an effort, I switched back to the others.

"From here on, your time at Ardlossan grows less strict. In fact, you can have the rest of today off. And, as it happens, there's a dance in Ardlossan town tonight, at the Drumlanrig Arms pub. People are coming from miles around — it should be . . . it should be like being a real person again. And you don't have to get up tomorrow — you can sleep in. The head of SC2, Colonel Patrick Manning, is arriving today, for the meeting I just referred to, and he'll be staying the night and for lunch tomorrow, so you will all get to meet him and ask him any questions you might have. And that's the end of the course. You are all free to leave immediately afterwards."

I held up a series of paper wallets. "These contain your rail tickets south, and the addresses in London where you will be staying, along with details of the nearest tube station and local bus routes. There is also a slip of paper with my phone number on it and a time when you will be asked to report to London headquarters. I will give them to you tomorrow."

I looked from one to the other. "Any questions?"

"Do we go to this dance tonight as couples?" said Erich, looking at Madeleine. "Or as individuals?"

"Neither," said Ivan swiftly. "We'll arrive as a four." He smiled. "After that it's every man for himself." His smile broadened into a grin.

"Any more *serious* questions?" I said, smiling also.

"Yes," said Katrine. "The obvious one. Where *are* the London headquarters?"

"Ah, well . . . You will be given the address — or *an* address — when you phone me, according to the schedule in these wallets. Obviously, there are certain procedures to be followed, to ensure we keep our headquarters secure. You'll learn about that as we go along."

I looked from one to the other again. "Any more questions?"

Madeleine, lying on the grass, raised herself on one elbow. "I've been meaning to ask this for days — you say we are members of SC2. Is there an SC1, or an SC3 and if so, what do they do?"

I looked at her, in her magnificent frock. That morning, before we had parted, we had agreed not to share a bed again, not while we were in Ardlossan. As we had lain awake in the early hours, listening to the night, it was enough, we agreed. An evening to treasure and remember. No point in risking the balance of our little group with the anonymity of London so close.

I pulled on my cigarette. "There's no SC3 but there *is* an SC1 — yes, of course. You will only find out what it is and what it does if you do well in SC2. One or two of you may be invited to join SC1 — that's all I can say."

"Are you in SC1?"

"I can't say any more, Madeleine. Don't press me, please."

I threw away my cigarette to indicate that the subject was closed. "So, enjoy the rest of your day off, have a good time at the Drumlanrig Arms tonight, and don't be late for lunch with the director tomorrow. One o'clock sharp. Now get out of my sight."

As it turned out, it had been overly optimistic to hold the final lunch of the course as a beach barbecue. The day had started out fine enough: blue sky, high birds, a wind that we told ourselves was merely "bracing." The tide was right and, if anyone caught any fish — as several were attempting to do, without success so far — that would set the seal on the last day of training.

But when it became clear that no immediate success was likely, I called the trainees together near the makeshift driftwood fire. In the past hour, the wind had got up, well beyond bracing, and most of us were wearing tweed jackets or waterproofs against the cold.

I stood near the fire as Duncan stoked the logs and turned the lamb chops. Their juices dropped from the metal grill, into the fire, sparking a crackling and spitting sound that was, in that cold, sunny air, extremely appetizing.

There was a crate of beer next to the fire, so I handed round some opened bottles. "Help yourself. There's plenty for everyone."

Ivan took a bottle and poured beer into the glasses held by Katrine and Madeleine. Then he began to pass round the metal plates, helped by Katrine.

Now the chops were done, Duncan lifted the metal grill, dug into them one by one with his long fork, and handed them to the recruits.

That's all there was — beer and chops — but, in the open air, with the smell of cooking so strong, it was enough.

A silent contentedness spread around the gathering as we munched away.

Wisps of sand were flying everywhere.

I let them finish their chops before going on.

I swigged some beer and wiped my lips.

"Now," I began, "as we enjoy this last lunch together, I have two announcements. The first is that Patrick Manning, the commander of SC2, isn't with us after all. He was called back to London overnight — because, as perhaps you have heard, there has been heavy bombing, by our forces, in France, at La Rochelle, Pau, Biarritz, and Bordeaux. He needs to check if any of our circuits have been affected."

Several of the trainees groaned.

"I know, I know," I said, smiling. "It's disappointing but the RAF probably didn't realize you were having your final lunch today and so didn't act according to the script. But you'll get used to disappointments like that before this war is over."

Duncan took the plates from the others. He knew, what I knew — that Patrick Manning had never been coming to Ardlossan and, in fact, did not exist. His supposed arrival was part of a final test for the recruits. Which I was about to reveal.

"Now," I said for the second time. "You all know that cunning is part of our business in SC2 — a large part, in fact. It is, if you like, our stock-in-trade."

I paused.

"It is now my job to fill you in on our latest

piece of chicanery. It took place yesterday and the targets were . . . Can anyone guess?"

I looked from Ivan to Erich, to Katrine to Madeleine.

"Well?"

Ivan shook his head. So did Erich. So did Katrine.

Swirls of sand rushed along the beach like ghosts.

Madeleine said, "Was it us? Were *we* the target?"

"Why do you say that?"

"You said 'targets,' plural. And before I started this course, you interrogated me, you interrogated me in a way that felt very real. What I mean is that the interrogation was a deception too, that was the only way it could be made to seem real, and it took place before the start of the course proper. It . . . it . . ." She faltered.

"Go on," I urged her. "What do you want to say?"

Everyone else was looking at her.

"It occurred to me that, if you could foist a deception on us *before* the course proper began, you could do the same after it had finished?"

"And we would do that because . . . ?"

"Because you wanted us off-guard. Maybe you wanted to see how we could handle drink, whether we stood out in the dance crowd. Whether we forgot to hide why we are here."

"Madeleine, you are half right," I said at length. "More than half right, in fact." I looked at her and smiled. "Well done. Last night's dance, or 'ceilidh' as it is called locally, was a put-up job. It was genuine enough in that all the Campbells and MacTaggarts *are* locals and have been attending dances like this hereabouts all their lives."

I sipped more beer. "But some of the people there last night were in fact *our* people, SC2 people, people you don't know and haven't seen before. They were there — and I make no apology for this — they were there to test you. To make you drunk, to flirt with you, to seduce you if necessary —"

I couldn't make out whether Madeleine was smiling or glowering.

"To seduce you if necessary — in order to test you to see how good you are at keeping secrets, how good or bad a security risk you are.

"I am afraid to say that one of you, at this very late stage, let the side down. One of you, after a few drinks, or very possibly after more than a few drinks, and after a few reels, went out for a walk between dances and let on to the person you were with that you were on some sort of secret course here at Ardlossan. You said you couldn't say too much about it, it was all top secret, but you did say that you would soon be going abroad. You didn't say where you were going, or when, but you said it would be soon. You showed off, peppering your conversation with French words."

I sipped my beer but there was sand in it. I turned the beer glass upside down and poured the remains of the liquid on to the beach.

"You didn't mention SC2 by name, you didn't give away any details of the training you have received here, and you didn't give away your code name, or the fact that we *have* code names."

Duncan was mechanically wiping the plates with a cloth. He knew what was coming.

"You gave away enough, though — enough for anyone with half a brain to realise that Ardlossan houses a secret military unit that is training people to operate in France in the near future. That is enough — more than enough — to make Ardlossan itself a target. If you had been talking to an enemy agent, he or she would have gained enough information that could be used to put Ardlossan out of business. He or she could even have chosen to kill one or more or all of us."

All eyes were on me.

Of course they were.

"Or . . . that enemy agent could have left Ardlossan alone but followed one of the trainees — or more than one if he or she had colleagues in the area — so that they would lead these enemy agents eventually to our headquarters in London. How much more damaging might that have been?"

I looked from Ivan, to Erich, to Katrine, to Madeleine.

"So, I am afraid . . . Captain Langres, that — at the last minute, the very last minute — you have failed this training course."

All the others turned to stare at Erich. He looked bewildered and devastated, downcast and sheepish. As well he might.

"I . . . I didn't . . ."

"Erich," I said. "Nora Heath, the woman you went for a walk with, and confided in, has done two tours in France and is now back in Britain on leave. She volunteered for last night's dance because she — like all the others — passionately wants to do all she can to help the war effort. Do you deny saying to her what I just said you said?"

"I . . . I . . . no." He paused. "I just thought —"

"No Erich, that's the point — you *didn't* think. Ardlossan might be four hundred miles from London, five hundred from the French coast, and six hundred from Paris, but that doesn't mean anything goes here. You have no idea how much of the war effort is concentrated here in Scotland. Neither do I, by the way, but what I do know is that there's just as much need for secrecy here as anywhere else."

174

Erich looked at me intently. "What . . . what is going to happen to me?"

"That's not up to me. When you agreed to join SC2, and to come on this course, you signed the Official Secrets Act. Which means that, technically at least, you have committed treason and for which the penalty can still be death."

Everyone gasped.

"But I don't expect that to happen in your case," I added quickly. "I should imagine that you will be kept in a secure holding centre until it is judged that the information you have is dated and no longer of use to the Germans — well after the invasion, I would think. But you'll certainly be kept incommunicado for a time, probably in solitary confinement, so there's no chance that what you know will pass to a wider circle.

"I'm sorry, Erich. But, by your carelessness, you put the lives of your colleagues around you — here on the beach — at risk. Or you might have done, had not Nora Heath been one of ours."

I raised my arm and everyone turned as two men, who were standing where the shore met the grass and the rocks, now started walking towards us.

"These men will take you to wherever you are going."

Erich looked at the men, then along the sand. For a brief moment he thought of making a run for it. But he quickly realised that would only make matters worse. He turned back to me.

"Whatever I did, I wanted to help in the war." He gestured to the others. "Like we all did."

"I know," I said. "And that's the tragedy — a tragedy for you, and for the rest of us, that we can't make use of your organisational talents, your excellent French, and your extraordinary memory." I waved my arm at Madeleine and the rest. "But I need the others to see the consequences of breaches of security, as well as you."

"Do we handcuff him, sir?" said one of the military police in English, addressing me.

I shook my head. "I don't think so. Not for now, anyway."

"Very well," said the MP. And to Erich, "This way, Captain Langres."

Erich held out his hand to Katrine. She shook it.

And Ivan.

And Madeleine. She made a half-movement to kiss his cheek but he backed away.

"You shouldn't have bothered to save my life," he said gruffly.

She didn't say anything.

He faced me.

"I only went with Nora because . . ."

He hesitated, then turned on his heel and, with the MPs either side of him, began his walk back across the beach to Ardlossan Manse.

Because what? Because Madeleine wouldn't go with him? Is that what he was going to say? Was he blaming me? How did he know?

■ ■ ■ ■ ■

APRIL
LONDON

■ ■ ■ ■ ■

8

Sunlight beat down on the red brick walls of the Wallace Collection, thankfully intact despite heavy bombing. The horse chestnut trees hereabouts were magnificent too, their leaves spreading thick hand-shaped patches of shade across the pavements. On the far side of the square, however, untidy mounds of rubble marked where a line of houses had once stood, Georgian beauties by the look of those left standing — but wounded — nearby. There was not the money — nor, just yet, the appetite — to start rebuilding.

Even so, it felt good to be back in London. Our offices, just off Baker Street, were a stone's throw from Manchester Square, and I often walked by it on my way to lunch. I usually lunched at a pub in Marylebone High Street called the Red Anchor, where I liked the beer and the Scotch eggs they served when eggs were available.

I turned from the square into George Street. You had to watch where you walked in

London in those days. Often there were craters next to the small ranges of stones and bricks. Some of them were six or eight feet deep, and if you fell into them you could do yourself serious damage. The craters had water in them too — you could even drown in them if you knocked yourself out in falling. The Blitz bombing had stopped, for now at least, and many of the more dangerous sites had been roped off — but not all.

I was meeting Madelcine at the Anchor. She had been in London a few days, since leaving Ardlossan, but I had had to tie up one or two loose ends and had arrived only that morning on the overnight sleeper. This would be our first meeting since Scotland, our first encounter in the vast, anonymous swathe of the capital.

I was a bit on edge. Would Madeleine have changed, now that she was back in the distractions and busyness of London? We'd only had one night of real intimacy — would that mood travel south as easily as we had done?

I turned north in to Marylebone High Street, a thoroughfare of shops mainly: grocers, hardware outlets, a famous shop selling model trains, and a pet shop with dogs and rabbits and chicks in the window, scrabbling around in the strips of newsprint with which the shopkeeper lined the floor. There was always a group of small children outside the pet shop and a few older boys hanging around the train shop window, where, occasionally, when the owner was in the mood, clockwork locomotives hurried round a figure of eight, under model bridges and signal gantries. I'd been a model train fanatic as a boy — the best of my collection being, ironically enough, an engine of the German make, Märklin. It was packed up now, in my flat near Lord's Cricket Ground, in a box and out of sight.

The Anchor had seen better days, but the level of devastation around it — there was a bomb site right next door — lent it an almost heroic quality. Still standing, it had been freshly painted by the brewery company, as if in celebration of this very fact. Its front was shiny black with gold trimmings. The Red Anchor sign was new too.

I pushed open the heavy glass door and went in. Andy, the daytime barman, was there as always, as was Barry, the landlord. Barry looked after three pubs for the brewery so he wasn't behind the counter all the time, as Andy was during the day. In the evenings, Barry employed a barmaid called Belinda.

I ordered my usual half-pint of bitter and sat at a table by the window. I had taken care to arrive a little early because I knew that Madeleine, like most women, hated to be alone in pubs — she said it sent out the wrong signals.

I looked about me. I recognized a few faces — two off-duty naval ratings, an official from the zoo nearby, a male nurse from Harley Street, and others I didn't know. No sign of any Scotch eggs today.

I opened my paper. In Portsmouth, the eight-day trial of a medium charged under the 1735 Witchcraft Act had just ended: she'd been given a nine-month jail sentence for tricking people who'd lost their sons in the war into believing they could contact them in her living room over a chemist's shop. The Poles had blown up a German troop train, killing hundreds — what reprisals would there be? I wondered. The German battleship *Tirpitz* had been attacked in a fjord in Norway.

"*There* you are."

I looked up. "My God!" I said. "I hardly recognise you. Make-up, a necklace, a new dress."

She was even more striking in London than in Ardlossan. The desire that I had been keeping caged broke free.

Madeleine, seemingly unaware of the dangerous effect she was having on me, smiled and sat down, giving me a peck on the cheek as she did so. "If you remember, I arrived in Scotland by Lysander — a *very* small plane." She looked down at herself. "This is a long way from being a new dress, though. But yes, it's one you haven't seen before. Do you like it?"

"If Hitler saw you, he'd have thrown over the Riefenstahl woman in no time."

She grinned. "I thought that if I'm going to be kitted out in genuine false French clothes, I'd better get some wear out of this frock before it's too late."

"If your hair were less wild," I said, standing up, "you'd look like Veronica Lake in *Sullivan's Travels*. What would you like to drink? I'm afraid the Scotch eggs I promised you haven't been laid yet."

"A very weak gin and tonic, please. And don't worry about the eggs. I can barely get into this frock as it is."

I was back in no time, putting her drink on the table between us.

"So," I said after a moment's silence. "I only got in this morning and I've just been catching up with paperwork, or trying to. How are you getting on?"

She pulled her French face. "Okay, I think. These political lessons we get, about the ins and outs of the French situation, are interesting, at this distance at least. It won't be nearly as much fun when I get into the field and have to take sides."

I chuckled. "Got it in one. That's something we can't teach you — how to manage the different warring parties *inside* France."

She smiled back.

"I probably shouldn't say this," I said, "but I'm going to anyway. I've missed you. I know it's been only a few days but —"

"Me too," she whispered, putting the tips of her fingers against my lips. "And . . ." She hesitated. "I probably shouldn't say this either but . . . in case it makes it any easier . . . my digs . . . well, they are just *awful*. For a start they are in Wembley — *Wembley*! That's miles away. Twelve stops on the Bakerloo Line and halfway to Montreal. And I have to share with another girl, and the bathroom is miles down the corridor, *and* the food is terrible. Are you going to take me away from all that? You said you would."

"Well," I said softly. "Although I missed you, I thought it wasn't necessarily a bad thing, us being apart for a few days. After the hothouse of Ardlossan, it gave us a breathing space, to see if —"

"Is this some kind of tease, or a joke?" She drank some gin and tonic and tugged the pearls at her neck. "You've got to take your chances in life, Colonel, and I, for one, didn't need three days apart to assess my feelings like some bloody accountant." She set down her glass on the table with a clatter. "Now, please don't send me back to Wembley. Remind me where your flat is?"

"Hamilton Place, off Chepstow Place. Lisson Grove."

"And do you have a double bed — or do we need to buy one?"

A couple of other customers, in some sort

of uniform, looked over at us.

"Keep your voice down," I whispered, blushing. "Yes, I have a double bed."

"Hallelujah!" she cried, but softly. "What's more, I have this afternoon off." She grinned.

"Well, I *don't,*" I replied quickly. "It's my first day back in the office. I can't just abandon all the paperwork I need to catch up with." I lowered my voice. "And there's new stuff coming in all the time. In fact, I'm not at all sure how early I can get away tonight."

"I'm flexible," she said, holding out her hand. "Give me the keys to your flat, and tell me the exact address. I can go back to Wembley this afternoon, collect my belongings, and move in with you. By the time you get home it will be like you're back in France — you will be living in occupied territory . . . my wash things, my underwear, my frocks . . . *everywhere.* You'll have been invaded." She grinned. "Now give me the keys."

I handed them over.

That simple gesture filled me with a feeling of warmth, too. All my time in London, I'd lived alone. Sharing my flat with Madeleine, sharing a bed . . .

"We haven't talked about Erich —"

She reached out and again put a finger to my lips. "Later. Plenty of time for that."

She sipped her gin and tonic.

"Any news of the date of the invasion? Are

you in on the secret yet?"

I shook my head.

"In that case, is there anything I should know about your flat? Does it have any bad habits? Does the door need kicking? Is the gas dangerous?"

"No, it's all fairly tame. But . . . you should know that I have a dog. I haven't mentioned it before because . . . because he's not as dashing as Rolfe. I picked him up this morning, from a friend he was staying with."

"Is he fierce? Does he know I've a specialist training in unarmed combat?"

"He's a West Highland terrier, very white and reasonably good-natured. He'll growl at you, bark a bit, then roll over to have his tummy tickled. Take him for a walk in Regent's Park and he'll fall for you like I have."

"So now there are *two* males in my life — that is very satisfactory." She smiled. "What's his name?"

"Zola."

"A French writer? Why?"

"Not quite. It was the code name of the surgeon in the Resistance who took out my lung, and saved my life."

She smiled and nodded, dropping my house keys into her bag. "Does he know he's had a dog named after him?"

I paused briefly. "No. He was arrested six months later and sent east. No one has heard from him since. He may be dead. It's my way of keeping him alive."

She looked at me, leaned forward, and kissed my cheek.

"You are a good man. Try not to be home *too* late. I'll take your mind off the Resistance."

The lift at Tewkesbury House, in Cathcart Place, was one of those rickety mahogany and glass affairs. It rose and fell unsteadily, encased in what seemed like a metal cage, with all its cables and pulleys on show, its operation accompanied by a whirring-wheezing sound that only underlined its advanced age. It did not inspire confidence.

So far as I was aware, the Ministry of War owned the entire building in Cathcart Place. Our offices lay entirely behind a set of frosted-glass double doors, on which were inscribed, in gold capitals, the words SOVER-EIGN SCIENTIFIC. Immediately inside the double doors were two desks, occupied by two women, Hattie and Freda, whose job it was to sound like receptionists while deter-ring casual visitors, should there be any, from enquiring further about the purpose of the company they served. Posters showing Sover-eign Scientific "products" lined the walls — telephones, radios, speedometers, pressure gauges of one kind or another. In other words, nothing of direct military use.

The fourth floor of Tewkesbury House,

which had its own second set of security doors, was given over entirely to the French section of SC2. The two floors beneath us housed the smaller Italian, Dutch, Scandinavian, Greek, and Cypriot sections. The ground floor was where the recruits received their lectures on politics and social matters, which were kept up-to-date by recent arrivals from the field. The top brass were housed, fittingly, on the top floor, the fifth.

On our fourth floor there was a large central typing pool, what seemed at times like an acre of grey metal desks, with black tops, where the clack of typewriters was as insistent as the roar of the sea at Ardlossan. The offices of the senior staff were down one side, giving on to Cathcart Place. Around the other edges were the cryptographers, telegraph rooms, logistics, finance, special ops (for unusual pieces of equipment), the forgery department, translation, weather, and transport. At any one time, between sixty and seventy people worked in our section.

It was a hybrid building, half red brick and solid as stone. Its echoing corridors made that part of Tewkesbury House seem like a courthouse without lawyers or police. The rest was 1930s brutal, under-windowed, with square, plain, box-like rooms, prefabricated walls, and windows that threatened to fall off their moorings when a strong wind swept up Baker Street.

My "office" — to use a word that was too grand for what was barely more than a cupboard — was run-down and badly in need of a lick of paint. It had just one window, looking out on to Cathcart Place, a dead-end lane that had once housed a collection of garages, ironmongers' yards, and warehouses but was now a line of bomb-ravaged rubble. The "office" had room — just — for a small wooden desk, which would not have been out of place in a country school; two chairs, one either side of the desk; a bookcase; a radiator; a metal filing cabinet; a coat hook on the back of the door; and framed photographs of exotic railway destinations — Prestatyn, Margate, and Truro — on the walls. The only signs of what I really did in the war effort were the pile of folders on the desk and the three telephones next to it.

I had half a secretary — Geraldine, always known simply as "G." — whom I shared with Toby Sheldrake, head of encryption/decryption. I was for ever irritated with G. — I felt sure she used the fact that she had two bosses to avoid both of us most of the time, by pretending to be with the other. Certainly, she was never nearby when I wanted her, or so it seemed.

As I walked along the marble-floored corridor that afternoon, my steps clattered like Wehrmacht jackboots on Friedrichstrasse. A tall man with a long lugubrious face and a length of lank hair hanging down over his forehead was just emerging from my office.

"Ah, Matt, there you are. Good." He stood to one side but followed me back in, closed the door behind him, and sat down on the chair reserved for visitors.

I hung my coat on the coat hook, sat down too, and gestured to the pile of folders on my desk. "Sir, this is how far behind I am with my paperwork, after my weeks in Ardlossan. Can it wait?"

He shook his head so that his spectacles caught the light. "No, I'm afraid it can't."

Hilary Armstrong, the *Honourable* Hilary Armstrong, as his father was a baronet, was the top man in F Section. He was my immediate boss, and at only one remove from the minister of war himself. In theory, that also made him just two away from Churchill.

Hilary was the perfect example of what our French colleagues called a *rosbif,* a "roast beef." He had ruddy cheeks, a moustache that bristled like a lavatory brush, and a voice with the longest vowels in history. He came from a "goooood" family of soldiers, who had served in every conflict since Waterloo. This made him a man of supreme self-confidence, intensely patriotic even by the standards of the time, who was never seen without his regimental tie, hand-cut suits, and brown brogues — he clearly did not depend on his wage packet as so many of us did. He was older than me but only just and until now had served the entire war behind a desk. So far as I was concerned, in this he had betrayed his family tradition, and, however talented an SC2 commander he was, I held it against him that he had not seen action in the field. I could not forgive him this, though in the office I had to disguise my true feelings. All the people we were sending into France and elsewhere were taking bigger risks with their lives than he was.

I looked at him now. He had rather droopy eyelids, half covering eyes that never gave anything away — they played the Whitehall poker game to perfection. He had boxed at school, he told me, and had once been cut over the eye. The scar that had formed afterwards had never quite gone away and he sometimes rubbed his thumb over it. He did that now.

"We've had a curious message from Trident."

I hunched forward on my chair. Trident, I knew, was the code name for Alex MacGibbon, our man in the Banquet circuit operating in the Rennes region of France. Current rumour, which is all it was at that stage, held that the invasion would occur in the Pas de Calais. But if it came in Normandy, which was another possibility, Rennes would be vital.

"Yes, sir," I said.

"Trident has sent a message to say that he needs one hundred thousand francs for sabotage activity and can we please drop it to him in the usual way."

I sat back in my chair. "And that is curious because . . . ?"

Hilary brushed his hair off his forehead. "Unlike you not to see what's what immediately. It's curious for two reasons. One, Trident's message, on this occasion, was sent in English, when usually he transmits in French. And secondly, there *is* no usual way of sending him money — we have never done it before. You know that."

I played with a ruler on my desk. Hilary was right. And I should have spotted it myself immediately. "What about his bluff checks?"

"Omitted. As were his true checks."

I was suddenly out of breath.

"He has been captured, then." My heart seemed to swell in my chest. Capture, for an agent like Trident — every agent, come to that — meant interrogation. Interrogation, eventually, meant torture; then deportation, imprisonment, and, finally, but not too far down the line, execution.

"May I see the transcript of his message?" I said.

Hilary handed across a slip of paper.

I cast my eye over it. The letters were set out in groups, as they were in the coded message. That was normal, so we could judge exactly what the agent was saying.

After I had assimilated the whole thing — which took a few moments — I said, "This was dictated by the Gestapo, and Trident is trying to tell us so."

Hilary took back the slip of paper and said, "That's one possibility. Or . . . *or* . . . he transmitted in a hurry and forgot the usual procedure."

"Is that likely?" I said. "He went through Ardlossan — I trained him myself." I shook my head firmly. "He's been captured, sir."

"Why didn't he use his bluff checks?"

"Because the Gestapo know about them." I leaned forward. "This is serious, sir. That circuit's been penetrated."

"You think so?" He didn't look convinced.

"Yes, and we certainly must assume so."

He scratched his chin. "If what you say is true, that's the third agent we have lost in the past month and a half."

"I know."

Hilary shifted in his seat. "We can't be *certain* he has been captured — the request *might* be genuine —"

"Hilary! Sir! — I can't believe you might think that!" I looked out of the window.

"Didn't you ever make mistakes in the field, under pressure? I know you think I have no hands-on experience but I'm trying to be understanding here —"

"Don't be," I said quickly. "You were ahead

of me to begin with, but I'm catching up. Trident's an experienced agent, sir, ten months in the field. He knows — or has learned — how to handle pressure, and he knows how important the correct procedure is. No, he's been captured all right."

I looked out of the window again. There were barrage balloons to the south, silver and sobering.

Hilary sat in front of me without speaking for a while, tapping the tips of his fingers on my desk. "Did he make a mistake, or was he betrayed? Will we ever know?"

I was thinking furiously. I looked at the calendar on my desk.

"It's April 13th," I said.

"What's the date got to do with anything?"

"I don't know whether Alex has been betrayed, or made a mistake. But . . . this may not be as bleak as it sounds."

"What do you mean? I'm going to have to write a bloody letter to his wife —"

"Not necessarily, sir."

He rubbed his moustache. "What? Are you going to tell me what's going on in that devious brain of yours?"

A smile crept across his lips but then disappeared.

"Can we afford one hundred thousand francs?" I leaned forward.

"You're not thinking of paying? I thought you thought — ?"

196

"I *said* 'Can we afford it?' "

He paused. "I can find it, yes. But —"

"If we send the money, the Gestapo will think we have been taken in — am I right?"

"Ye-e-es, I suppose so. But — ?"

"Think."

I took out my cigarettes.

"They will either take the money and spend it, disposing of Trident as they go along, as they would do anyway if we don't send the money. Or . . . they will be taken in, which may have consequences."

I took two cigarettes from my packet. "One, it may keep Trident alive for a little longer, giving him at least the chance to escape, though I don't hold out much hope of that."

I gave a cigarette to Hilary.

"Two, in due course, perhaps . . . they will send us other messages, with fresh instructions. Showing they haven't spotted that we have seen through their deception."

A light went on in Hilary's head. "Oh . . . I see — Yesss!" He lit a match and leaned forward.

I nodded, letting him light my cigarette too. "And . . . depending how high up you are in the food chain, sir, as the invasion draws near, we will be in a position to feed the Gestapo . . . whatever information it suits us to feed them."

He looked at me, having fully caught up. "That could well be worth a hundred thousand francs."

I nodded again, straightening my tie. "Exactly. And Trident will not have been captured for nothing."

He stood up. "I'm not at the top of the food chain, but I do know someone who is. A couple of people actually. They might just go for this."

He stood and turned to leave, but turned back. "The only people who have seen Trident's message are the person who was on duty, of course, and the decrypt analyst, Toby Sheldrake."

Toby was in charge of codes and communication, and the man with whom I shared G. He was next in the pecking order after Hilary and me.

"Let's keep it that way," he said. "We need to have a word with Toby and tell him to make sure all messages from Trident from now on are seen only by you, him, or me. And we'll assign only one cryptanalyst to handle his messages." He nodded. "You do it, Matt. It will attract less attention coming from you."

I tapped ash into an ashtray. "You're right."

He opened the door, nodded, and said, "Our role in the invasion may have just got more interesting, Colonel."

My flat was on the first floor of a white-painted, eighteenth-century terraced house, from where you could hear, if not see, the buses in Lisson Grove. There was a small flight of steps leading up to the front door and, inside, a graceful staircase of generous proportions that ended in a landing with two doors opposite one another.

Not having my key, I knocked. It felt strange having to knock on my own front door.

Beyond the door Zola started barking immediately. Could he tell it was me — from my smell perhaps? — or did he bark every time someone knocked on the door? I'd been away so long I couldn't remember.

Madeleine opened the door, and I gasped. She was wearing only a towel. Two towels in fact, one around her torso, and one — like a turban — around her head. She had washed her hair and taken a bath — her skin still had that ruddy-red hot-bath complexion and her hair, what I could see of it, was still wet. Its curls and ringlets sparkled in the light.

Zola looked up at me and wagged his tail, but not overmuch. He hadn't entirely forgiven me for deserting him when I had been in Ardlossan, and he obviously couldn't be certain how long I was going to be around this time. So he was circumspect with his affections.

I closed the front door behind me and bent down to stroke him. The hallway of my flat was hardly the best room — green wallpaper that I didn't like, but hadn't had the energy so far to change, a mirror, a coat rack, a photograph of the old waterfront at Marseilles, a small table against a wall, a jug with no flowers. Flowers were not my priority.

Madeleine looked up at me and then took off her towel.

"Remember this?" she said.

I ran my eyes over her naked skin, her breasts, the dark brown circles around her nipples, her stomach, her thighs, the wedge of hair at the base of her belly.

"It's been three days," I said in a whisper. "But it felt like forty days in the wilderness. Hang on. I'll help us to a drink."

She reached forward, took my hand, and placed it on her breast. "Feel my skin, how warm it is, how hot. You go into the bedroom and get undressed. I'll make the drinks."

"There's only whisky or gin," I said. "All we had in Scotland was whisky. Let's have gin for a change."

I went through into the bedroom. Zola followed.

I took off my clothes, and laid them on a chair. Zola jumped up and sat on them. He liked to do that and hadn't forgotten. I was touched. He usually slept there.

I got into bed, took off my watch, and put it on the bedside table. I looked around. The room seemed tidier than I remembered it, and the window was wide open. Noises —

traffic noises, church bells, a roar from an animal in the nearby zoo — rolled through into the room. They brought back the silence of Scotland.

Madeleine came in with the drinks.

"There's no ice," she said. "But I've run the tonic bottle under the tap. It should be cold enough."

She handed me a glass and sat on the bed, unselfconsciously naked. She unwrapped the towel around her head and pummeled her hair. It led off in all directions.

"How was your afternoon?"

I made a face and swallowed some gin.

"There are some things I can't tell you, Madeleine. I'm sorry."

I tapped my temple.

She ran her finger round the rim of her gin glass.

"I told you at Ardlossan, I'm not the sneaky type. Your secrets would be safe with me. But I won't pry, not about war matters anyway." She grinned and pulled the sheets down and touched the top of the line of scar tissue that began in the middle of my chest, below my throat. She ran her finger all the way down the line, to where it ended just above my belly button.

"I've never asked. Having only one lung, ought we — you know — ought we to be careful? Not be too energetic, I mean, not go at it the way that we did in Scotland?" She smiled, slightly ironically.

"I'm here now, aren't I? I've survived one bout with you. I'll risk another." I put my glass down by the side of the bed. I reached forward and held her shoulders.

She opened her lips and I pulled her towards me.

There was a small noise. When I looked, I could see that Zola had jumped off the pile of clothes he had been lying on and scampered into the other room.

9

One of my jobs as SC2 second in command was to take the night codes from our headquarters in Cathcart Place to Broadcasting House at the end of most working days. You could walk from where we were to "B.H." in Portland Place in a matter of minutes, but even so I was always accompanied by an armed bodyguard, in plain clothes, so as not to attract attention. I was instructed to vary my route as much as possible, in case I was being watched, but there were only a limited number of ways to cover such a short distance. I sometimes walked east straight along Wigmore Street, and turned left into Portland Place; sometimes I went through Manchester Square into Devonshire Place, and occasionally I wound my way through Upper Wimpole Street and Harley Street Mews. But it only ever took a few minutes.

The night codes at the BBC had by then become something of a national showpiece. They were read out — in a sombre voice —

after the *Ten O'Clock News,* and were required listening for most people even though they had no idea what the codes meant — the point being that they were deliberately weird and mysterious and, apart from anything else, were meant unfathomably to boost morale. The news reader might say such things as "Trafalgar Greets Lightning," or "Saturn Three Is Not Satisfied," or "Indian, Four, Black." Given that I was second in command at SC2, I knew what some of the messages meant — I had drafted them myself. But I didn't understand all of them, and in any case many of them were nonsense. In order to avoid the obvious giveaway that more codes would be sent out ahead of important military initiatives, complete fakes were used all the time to ensure that roughly the same amount of "messages" were sent out every evening.

People knew that the codes were necessary, or thought that they did, but that didn't stop us making fun of them. On bumping into someone you knew well but hadn't seen for a time, you might say, enigmatically, as you shook hands, "Pyramid Shadows Pharaoh." And they would reply, "Wasp Stings Frankfurt."

I had a pass to get me into Broadcasting House but by the time I had arrived in London, I was known to all the receptionists at the BBC, and even though I took out my pass and brandished it, they hardly glanced at it.

My destination, as always, was the third floor, the news department, and *its* deputy director, Alistair Prior. Alistair was a bouncy, round Yorkshireman who had started life as an engineer, and had been responsible for many of the broadcasting innovations that the BBC had introduced.

There was a lift in B.H., but I preferred the stairs and ran up them three at a time. My bodyguard, Tony, remained in reception on the ground floor. B.H. wasn't a security risk.

I reached the main corridor of the third floor and pushed through the double doors into the newsroom. Several of the reporters who looked up from their desks, and who recognized me, smiled or waved. I was the source of mild amusement to them, and they referred to me — to my face — as "Mystic Matt" because of my mysterious messages.

Alistair was bending over one of the desks as I came in. He turned, saw who it was, and straightened up. Smiling, he came over to me and held out his hand.

"Welcome back," he said. "I know better than to ask where you've been, but it's good to see you again. Your stand-in while you were away is a real misery-guts."

"Have a heart, Al. Jock's okay but his wife was killed in the Blitz and he's having a hard time getting over it." I looked around the newsroom and then back to Alistair. "I haven't been anywhere exciting," I said. "And I'm glad to be back in London."

He led the way into his office. I followed, closing the door behind me. Strictly speaking, the handover of the codes had to be done privately: my purpose in the BBC offices was, formally, a secret — but in the newsroom that had gone out of the window months ago.

Alistair and I sat down. I took out the envelope with the codes inside and he reached down into one of the drawers on his desk and took out a bottle of Laphroaig and two glasses. This, too, had become a ritual.

Alistair had an incongruous build. He was small but barrel-chested, his hair was thinning, and he had rather fleshy lips. But his features added up to a smiling face that was somehow more than the sum of its parts. I liked him. Some months before, his brother, who was with our forces in North Africa, had gone missing and I had used the SC2 network to establish that he had been injured — injured and not killed — and invalided to an American hospital base rather than a British one. That had set Alistair's mind at rest and our friendship had gone on from there, the Laphroaig sessions being one result of it. It was in the natural order of things that the codes had to be taken to Broadcasting House at the end of the working day, so we were hardly doing anything that might have been frowned on had our superiors known about it.

He raised his glass to me. "You missed a couple of good shows while you were away."

"Oh yes?"

"Yes, a new Rattigan, *No Medals* at the Vaudeville, with rave reviews for someone called Thora Hird. And we're going to get a new theatre on the South Bank after the war — assuming we win, of course. Oh, and yes, Ivor Novello went to jail and was released."

"He *was*? Why? What happened?" I was a great admirer of Ivor Novello's songs and Alistair knew it.

"He allowed a fan of his to claim petrol for him, as being of national importance, when in fact he was using it just to drive his Rolls to and from the theatre. He definitely used the petrol, and with rationing he should have asked questions. But he convinced the court he didn't know what the fan was up to. She was besotted by him, and did him a favour without his knowing about it, or asking for it. So he was imprisoned for not being careful enough, but released immediately because he didn't know she was behaving fraudulently. All right for some, eh?"

"What news of the invasion?" he said, adding the words without a pause, as if it was entirely natural — and perhaps hoping to surprise me into revealing something.

I shook my head and frowned. I didn't like

it that he had tried to bounce information out of me. It was out of character. I paused before saying, "What have you heard?"

He swallowed some whisky. "The feeling here is that it's going to be the Pas de Calais."

"Oh yes? Why do you say that?"

"We've had RAF pilots in here, for programmes, and while they have to be careful what they say on air, off air they say that when they fly back from the continent, the Pas de Calais area is the most heavily populated part — populated with German soldiers, guns and tanks, I mean. In other words, the Germans are expecting the invasion in the Calais area and they must know something we don't."

I sipped my whisky. "That could be it — but I don't know, I really don't."

"And if you knew you wouldn't tell me, right?"

I nodded. "Sorry. Is it *so* important for you to know right now?"

He grinned. "Yes and no. The actual place is neither here nor there." He checked himself. "But what I would dearly like to know is *when* the invasion is going to happen. For purely personal reasons."

I waited, giving no ground at all.

He sighed.

"Viv and I are finally getting married. She wants a big, formal, fancy, white wedding with all the trimmings, and she wants it quickly. She would be devastated if we chose a day and it happened to be the day."

I was relieved and relaxed into a smile. "That's wonderful news, Al. Viv must be delighted." Vivien was Alistair's long-term girlfriend, who had been agitating to get married for as long as I could remember.

He nodded. "She's pregnant, of course."

I made a face. "By accident or design?"

He flashed his eyes at me.

"I daren't ask. But it means we are getting married soon — that's why I want to know." He looked at me long and hard.

"I'm sorry, Al," I smiled, shaking my head. "Even if it means not being invited to the great day . . ."

He held up the envelope with the codes in it. "Nothing in here? You must know what some of these messages mean?"

"Some," I replied, nodding, "but by no means all. You'll just have to pick a day and hope for the best."

Alistair drank some more whisky and took the codes out of the envelope. He scrutinized them.

"*Fougère manque pré.* What does that mean?"

"Fern misses meadow."

"*Conducteur est cramoisi?*"

"Driver is crimson."

He shook his head. "This one's in English: 'Farm, Farewell, Fantasy.' Do you know what *any* of these mean?"

"I know what the last one means, but not the others. They may not mean anything."

He finished his whisky. "You're invited to the wedding anyway — I'll give you a date very soon. But . . . but, if you do learn something, and you are in a position to tell me . . . to help Viv really — it's her day after all . . ."

"I shall look forward to it," I said. "Whenever it is. But I'm not going to be able to help you, Al, you know that. Do you know *anything* about military affairs?"

"Not really. Not other than what I read in the papers."

"Did you know that attacking forces, on average, lose three times the number of men that defending forces lose? If the Germans do know where the invasion is going to take place, I don't think we have a chance. So I hope for our sakes that it's not the Pas de Calais."

I stood up. "Say hello to Viv for me, and tell her congratulations. Any idea what you want as a wedding present?"

"Of course." He stood up too, smiling. "The date of the invasion."

He came round his desk, and held out his hand. "Good to have you back. Sorry about what I did just now. It was a bit underhand of me. It won't happen again, I promise. See you tomorrow. How's *your* love life, by the way?"

"Looking up, as it happens."

"Good! Great. What's her name? Bring her to the wedding."

"Madeleine. I will . . . unless —"

"Unless what?"

I shook my head. "Nothing."

I opened the door to his office and hurried out. As I descended the steps of B.H., I told myself glumly to start preparing for an unpleasant change, a change as potentially big in my life as the wedding would be for Alistair. Bigger even. Madeleine had swept into my affections when I wasn't expecting it, and bowled me over. But by the time of Alistair's wedding, I might have seen her for the last time.

When you have lived your life on your own, as I had until the point when Madeleine moved in with me, and if you don't count a West Highland terrier as a person — which Zola would certainly have had views about — you get used to having things your own way. Apart from the needs of your job, you are a free agent — you get up when you want, go to bed when you want, do the washing up when you want, shave when you want, cook what and when you want, tidy up when you want, empty the ashtrays when you want . . . and all the rest.

When I got home from Broadcasting House that day, Madeleine was waiting for me. She had been to the hairdresser and her hair smelled differently. She took me straight to bed and Zola went without his walk, which was normally my first task on arriving home. He had to wait for nearly two hours and he was not pleased.

Like most of the trainees who had been through Ardlossan, Madeleine was given political instruction in the mornings after she had returned to London, but had the afternoons free. In SC2 we knew that the agents would be sent abroad soon enough, and so their afternoons were deliberately left for them to enjoy the time they had left as best they could. Madeleine, as I was to discover, as well as going to the hairdresser, had taken my flat under her wing.

As we lay on our backs on the bed early that evening, with Zola uttering the occasional whimper, because his walk had been overlooked, I raised myself on one elbow and reached for my cigarettes.

"What's happened to the table that used to be here?" I said. In our rush I hadn't noticed it had gone.

"I had a tidy up," said Madeleine, rolling over and kissing the back of my shoulder. "The bedside tables go better by the sofa in the drawing room, with lamps on them. Go and have a look."

I couldn't tell her that was something else — besides her hair — that she shared with Celestine, who had also been manically tidy. What I did say was, "I'm too exhausted to move. At least for now. Where are my cigarettes?"

"Over there, on the desk."

"That's no good, it's too far away. After a couple of hours' sex with you, I need reinforcements to hand. A cigarette after sex is one of life's great luxuries. You should know that."

"I've just moved the furniture around a bit, that's all. You'll see — you'll like it. I moved the table in the kitchen from the middle and placed it against the wall, I've moved the wireless to the side of the fireplace, so it's easier to keep warm while you're listening, and I've put the standard lamp by the sofa, so it's easier to see to read at night."

She let the last letter of that last word hang in the air.

"And you've moved the bedside tables."

"Yes, the drawing room was a little lacking in furniture. We can buy two new tables at the weekend."

"Can we? And do you have any more plans for my flat? Is the bed as you like it?"

She chuckled. "The bed's fine. Though I wonder what the people in the flat underneath make of all the noise."

I turned over and kissed her breast. "*You*

make most of the noise, so you'd better go down and apologise —"

"I do *not*! Take that back, or I'll never do . . . you know . . . again."

I sighed, got out of bed, retrieved my cigarettes from the desk, and lay back down again. I lit two cigarettes and passed one to her.

Zola whimpered again.

"I resumed one of my formal duties today, taking the night codes to the BBC."

"Oh yes? And . . . ?"

"I can't tell you much, but the invasion isn't far off. As a matter of fact, one of the codes tonight is about you."

"It was? It is?" She hoisted herself up on one elbow and looked at me. One of her breasts rested on my arm. "What did it say?"

"It told a certain circuit you are coming soon and asked them to recommend a landing site."

"Where am I going, and when?"

"I can't tell you either of those things yet. You know I can't tell you that. Not yet."

She was silent for a moment and straightened the bedclothes. "I can understand why you can't tell me *where* I'm going. I realize that might have some bearing on where the invasion might be. It's important that's kept secret. And I know the timing may be important too. But . . . *but,* Matt, aren't you being just a little bit inhuman? Here we are, making love, having sex . . . blotting out the rest of the world, the horrible world we are forced to live in. Don't you think . . . You now know how long we've got, how many days or weeks it is until . . . until it comes to an end, at least for a while. Don't you think I deserve to know that too?"

She reached out and tugged at my chin so that we were looking directly into each other's eyes. Her hair fell onto her shoulders. "Can you . . . Could you make love to me knowing how long we've got, when I don't? Could you make love to me knowing it's the last time, when I don't?"

"That's just it, I don't know how long you've got, I really don't. I agree that . . . if I knew that tonight would be the last time we could make love, and you didn't know, and I didn't tell you, that would be, as you say, inhuman. The invasion date and location is the biggest secret of the war, and I'm just as much in the dark as you."

She gripped my thigh with her fingers, digging them deep into my flesh. Then she slackened her grip and lay back on the bed, blowing cigarette smoke towards the ceiling.

"Do I believe you, Colonel?"

"You have to."

She turned to look at me. "This is the first time I have ever doubted anything you have said."

She turned her back to me and whispered,

over her shoulder, "It's a horrible feeling."

Later that evening we took Zola for his long-delayed walk. The north side of Regent's Park was only about six hundred yards away from the flat, but it had been closed for various military purposes, so we drifted south to the Marylebone road, then east, until we came to Harley Street and Devonshire Place.

Madeleine had on a navy-blue mac, one that made her look like an off-duty nurse. She had her arm in mine and I held on to Zola's leash. We stopped every so often so that he could explore lamp posts and trees and parked bicycles. We made slow progress, but it didn't matter.

It was a simple thing, Madeleine putting her arm in mine, but it was like having an electrical jolt in your side — or, better still, it was like having a fish on the end of a rod, that quivering, restless feeling of life itself. But, really, it felt better than words can say.

Traffic swept past us — omnibuses, army lorries, ambulances, taxis, the occasional out-of-date horse-drawn cart.

"I suppose, soon, those carts will disappear completely." Madeleine pointed at a sad, rather decrepit horse pulling a rag-and-bone cart, the driver sitting on the edge of the contraption with the reins slack in one hand, and a long, light whip in the other. "What else will disappear, once this war is over, do you think?"

She looked up at me and squeezed my arm. Another jolt.

"Newspapers," I said. "Radio will replace them, and maybe TV as well."

"TV?"

"Television. Don't you know what that is?"

She shook her head, so I explained and then went on. "Private medicine will go, too."

"It *will*? How do you mean?"

"After the war people won't stand for the divisions that existed before 1939."

"Oh yes? Why? Why not?"

I waited until we could cross the road at Devonshire Place. I had never seen so many taxis.

"There'll be big changes, once the fighting is over — you'll see. Everyone, from all walks of life, has given his or her all in this war. We can't go back to the way it was beforehand. People will want equal access to doctors and hospitals, equal access to schools, equal access to everything. And they'll deserve it."

She squeezed my arm again. "A politician as well as a demon lover — I'm impressed."

I stopped, turned towards her, and kissed the top of her head, savoured her smell. "You don't have to be a politician to see what's going on around you. Wars *do* that, shake things up — kill off bad old ideas and bring in new ones."

"What will happen to SC2 after the war?"

"We'll be disbanded, I suppose," I said. "MI6 don't like us: we're competition. They'll want us out of the way once peace returns."

"And people will never know we existed? Is that what's going to happen?"

"It's possible," I said, nodding. "If you have children, after the war is over, you can never tell them what you did."

She didn't say anything for a moment. We had turned off Marylebone Street into Harley Street, where the shadows were growing longer. Doctors here still wore their traditional uniform of striped trousers, black jackets, and waistcoats, and some had bowler hats. Taxis were setting them down and picking them up.

"Now," I said, breathing out and clearing my throat. "It's your birthday next week —"

"How did you know that?" she cried, turning to me.

"I saw your file, remember? At The Farm."

"Yes, it's true. I can't help it."

"I've got you a gift, but it has to be secret."

"Oh yes? I love secrets — when I know them."

"Yes. I've bought some petrol on the black market. I thought I could bring the Lagonda out of mothballs and take you to see your mother."

She squeezed my arm. "That's very sweet, Matt. But there's a problem."

"There is?"

"Yes. Knowing my birthday was coming up, I wrote to my mother, and she wrote back. She sent the letter to my digs and I only got it yesterday, when the girl who would have been my flatmate if I'd stayed in Wembley brought the letter into the political course."

I frowned. "And that's a problem because . . . ?"

"My mother lives in Blakeney, on the Norfolk coast — and she told me in her last letter that, from the Wash to the Bristol Channel — all around the southern coasts of England — only authorised personnel, and registered locals, are allowed within ten miles of the sea. It's a precaution so that any German spies stand out more clearly. And that means we can't visit her. She could come up to London, but we wouldn't need the Lagonda for that."

I felt angry with myself. "Yes, of course. I should have spotted that." I thought for a moment. "Or . . . we could meet your mother somewhere just outside the exclusion zone?"

She shook her head. "Would that work? It would be expensive, don't you think? Would local taxis have petrol for that — for something so trivial and not war-related? Rationing is tight."

I was silent, thinking.

"I know what would be a perfect birthday present." She squeezed my arm.

"What?"

"Why don't we visit *your* mother? She's nowhere near the coast, is she?"

"No, she's in Malvern. We *could* go there. Don't you want to see your own mother before you go abroad?"

"Yes, yes, I do, of course. But I think it will be easier if she takes a train and comes up to London."

"Are you sure? I thought . . . I thought my idea would be perfect for you, but I admit I had forgotten about the coastal exclusion zone."

She squeezed my arm again. "This way, we'll have the best of both worlds, and see both mothers." She bit her lip. "I'm sorry what I said earlier, about doubting you. I shouldn't have said it — I shouldn't even have thought it."

I took my turn in squeezing her arm. "You have no cause to doubt me — I promise."

We looked across the street, to where a young woman was wheeling a pram. A young boy was riding a three-wheeled bicycle alongside her. As we watched, he almost rode off the kerb into the road, and his mother pulled him back and slapped him across the neck, shouting, "Brian! If I've told you once, I've told you a hundred times — be-*have*!"

Madeleine winced and breathed, "If we . . . If you and I carry on the way we just did, in bed I mean, and I get pregnant . . . what then? Would you like children, Matt?"

220

I gave a throaty chuckle, but didn't answer her directly. "If you and I carry on the way we just did, as you put it, for much longer, it will be a miracle if you *don't* get pregnant in that time. Which would be good in a way, because we wouldn't send you out into the field if you were pregnant. But . . . and don't take this the wrong way . . . If it should emerge, when you're in France, that you *are* pregnant, we can always bring you home. In fact, we'd insist on it." I looked down at her. "You know the statistics as well as I do, Madeleine. The chances are evens that you won't last —"

"Don't keep saying that!" Madeleine dug her nails into my arm. "Of course I know the bloody *sta-tis-tics*! You don't forget your chances of dying."

We walked on for a few steps. Zola was straining at his lead. And he was panting, getting thirsty. At Park Crescent, we turned for home and crossed over the main road.

Madeleine squeezed my arm once more. "Forget the statistics, Matt. I will either survive or I won't. Answer my question — would you like children, a son maybe?"

"In theory, I'd like children," I said at length. Nodding across the road towards the young mother with the pram, I added, "I'm not sure I want *that* sort of children."

"You're not allowed to choose your children," she replied. "Whoever arrives, arrives."

"What about you?" I said.

"How do you know I haven't got some already?" she answered. "I'm old enough."

"That's true," I said. "But if you had, you would surely have mentioned him or her — or them — by now."

She paused. Then, "I'd like *your* children," she said softly. "I can't say that about every man I meet."

For much of my adult life, there'd been a war on. Before that, I'd been in the army preparing for a war that might happen. Children had not loomed large in my concerns. But now . . . could I see Madeleine as a mother, myself as a father?

"I think I could get used to the idea of a daughter, more easily than a son."

She chuckled. "Why do you say that?"

"I'm not sure. I have a sister. I think she's nicer than me. More responsible, she thinks of others more, remembers birthdays and things like that."

"Maybe I'll meet her one day, if I make it through."

"Yes, I'd like that. You'd get on with Alice, I think."

It hit me then. It had been hovering about for a while but it hit me that evening. That if Madeleine didn't make it through, my own life now was going to be . . . almost as badly damaged as hers would be. I would survive physically, yes, but . . . No, no point in going down that road until . . . unless it arrived.

We were passing Marylebone Station now, with its ornate glass and wrought-iron forecourt. Ahead of us the pavement was blocked. There were wooden barriers, painted red and white, two policemen, with dogs, a heap of rubble and a group of men looking into a crater in the ground. One of the policemen was moving towards us but I recognized the signs and knew what was happening, what had happened.

"Let's cross back over the road," I said quickly to Madeleine. "It's an unexploded bomb."

I led the way into the road, waving to the traffic so it slowed. "If they thought it was about to go off, we'd have been kept much further away. But we're safer on the other side of the road, even so. Come on."

The traffic lights in Lisson Grove had changed to red and we were able to scuttle across the wide expanse of tarmac. Madeleine picked up Zola and carried him.

"These men earn their wages. There must be unexploded bombs all over London." She set him down on the sidewalk again.

We walked quickly for a couple of hundred yards.

After a while we slowed. "I should think we are beyond the range of the bomb now," I murmured.

I reached across and held her hand. "That

was a good thing to say, that you would like my children. Look . . . I'm not very good at this sort of situation. I think I fell for you the first time I saw you, months ago, that night at The Farm. God knows when you fell for me . . . but it's only in the last few days that we have . . . that the slow burn caught fire. So I don't know . . . are you saying — with what's coming up, all the uncertainty — are you saying you want to get married . . . is that what's on your mind? You did it once before, after all."

She didn't reply straightaway.

She stopped, to let Zola inspect the base of a tree.

"It's crossed my mind, of course it has. And yes, it's what I did before. But not this time, Matt. I don't think so. Not because I don't . . . I like it just the way we are. We haven't known each other long — you're right there . . . Getting married wouldn't change anything. I thought it would with Philippe, but now I don't think so. We'll either survive the war or we won't. And our feelings will either survive or they won't — marriage won't change that, I don't think so anyway."

She looked up at me and smiled, her eyes growing rounder. "Look at what happened in *Casablanca* — their love survived but bigger events got in the way, and they both accepted that, and went their separate ways. Remember that famous line, when Bogart says, 'We'll always have Paris!' Who is to say the same won't happen to us, that events won't intervene? We'll always have Scotland — and now Lisson Grove." She laughed again. "It's not Paris, exactly, but it's just as much . . . It has been wonderful, Colonel." She squeezed my hand. "It still is."

I chuckled. "I like the idea of you as a mix of Ingrid Bergman and Leni Riefenstahl."

"Ah, I'd settle for that," she replied, smiling and holding her hair off her neck. "Yes, I'd settle for that."

"And if you *do* get pregnant?"

She paused for a moment. "There's no point in worrying about that unless and until it happens." She put her arm in mine again.

I kissed her on the head, smelling its new smell again.

It brought back the ride in the back of the Land Rover in Ardlossan, the night we had rescued Erich. When her hair had smelled of mud.

"When I'm in France, I'd like you to do me one favour."

"Name it."

"Can't you guess? You're supposed to be clever."

I thought for a moment.

A bus went by, advertising on its side the latest films.

"Oh yes. Of course. I've got it!"

"You *have*?"

"Yes. You want me to cut out and keep all the newspaper clippings on Leni Riefenstahl."

"I don't believe it! Yes, that's exactly right — you'll be busy, of course, but —"

"Don't worry," I said. "You can rely on me. While you're away in France, she will be the only other woman in my life."

10

Funny how no one — so far as I know — has written about cigarettes in wartime. Not only were they in short supply, most of the time, when we needed them most, but their quality was poor. The tobacco was thin and tasteless, the paper was thin and crumbled in your fingers, or on your lips, and the smell . . . the smell was . . . best forgotten.

As Hilary Armstrong sidled into my office the next morning clutching a leaf of crispy, wafer-thin paper of the type our code people used, I was just lighting the first cigarette of the working day.

He was, as usual, dressed as if he were going for lunch at some country hotel — a three-piece brown tweed suit, a thin gold chain leading from the buttonhole in his lapel to his upper breast pocket, a pale blue shirt, exquisitely ironed, regimental tie, and hand-sewn brogues that I can only describe as glowing with age, brown as beer. His socks, drawn taut over his slim ankles, were charcoal-grey. He settled into the chair across from my desk and laid the thin sheet of paper on my blotter.

"Those are quite some shoes, sir," I said. "Do you have a slave to shine them for you?"

He smiled a weak smile. He had something else on his mind.

"Alex MacGibbon — or the Gestapo behind him — wants a quantity of cigarettes dropped as soon as possible."

I picked up the slip of paper and read what was on it.

"Still no security codes — bluff or otherwise?"

He shook his head. "No."

"What do you want to do?" I pulled on my own cigarette, wincing slightly at the taste.

"I want to talk it over with you, first. Isn't that obvious? That's why I'm here. What's your reaction?"

"Tell me first — what do you hear from upstairs?"

He took back the piece of paper and folded it, leaving it on the desk between us.

"They are considering our plan . . . your plan, to use MacGibbon to spread misinformation, I mean." He tapped the paper with a long finger, his nails glowing like pearls. "But we need a prompt response to this message, if we are to continue to keep the Gestapo thinking they have duped us."

I pointed to it and nodded. "My guess

is . . . that it's a test."

"A test? Hmm. How is it a test? How do you mean?"

"There are no security codes. That's unnatural. We, here at headquarters, might have forgiven Trident one oversight, but not two or three — he's an experienced agent." I nodded as my conviction took hold. "So — you reply by reprimanding Trident for not following proper procedure and say you can't consider any requests unless they are made in the correct way. And tell him to stay off air as much as possible."

"That could frighten the Gestapo away."

"How? No, sir. The opposite. We played along the first time, putting the lack of codes down to naivety on Trident's part. We can't allow him to get away with it a second time — that would be unnatural and look suspicious. No, you reply to Trident tersely and tell him to shape up. Only if the Gestapo think we have been thoroughly taken in will we be able to use them down the line. That means acting suspiciously if MacGibbon breaks the rules. And I agree, sir — we must do it promptly."

Hilary picked up the slip of paper and slid it into his jacket pocket. "Trident's is not the only piece of news we've had today."

"Oh yes?"

"Yes. We've heard from Apple, Spencer Fullerton, who runs the Orchid circuit in Paris.

Apparently, the Gestapo headquarters are at 78 and 80 avenue Foch."

I whistled. "That's a very smart address — they must have oodles of power. Do we know who the commanding officer is?"

"I was coming to that. Yes. According to Fullerton — Apple — it's a certain Wolf Grundmann. You've heard of him?"

"I'll say. When I was in France he was known as the 'Butcher of Besançon.' He's very bright, very ruthless, and very ambitious. In 1941, at least, I was told he had Himmler's ear. If he's running Trident then MacGibbon is as good as dead — Grundmann shows no mercy.

"Our only hope — and it's not much of one — is that he is so ambitious that any plans we feed him will cloud his judgment, if they offer him the opportunity for advancement, and for promotion. What I mean is, he might just be the perfect target to mislead the Germans about the invasion."

I pointed to the ceiling. "Tell that to your people upstairs. Is Apple safe, by the way? Tell him to keep his distance — Grundmann is fiendishly clever and horribly cruel. Make sure the entire Orchid circuit knows that. In fact, we should warn all our agents in northern France not to take any risks where Grundmann is concerned. In Besançon he even had children executed — children as young as eleven — because they were being used as couriers, or he thought they were. No one can expect any mercy from him." I leaned forward, as a thought flashed into my head.

"Wait. On reflection, sir — I don't want to be a wet blanket — but there may be more to this than meets the eye."

"What do you mean — how *can* there be? Apple has given us a fantastic piece of information — *two* pieces, the Gestapo's address in Paris and the name of the commanding officer."

"Yes, but maybe that's just too fantastic. We are now playing for high stakes — very high stakes. We are dealing with the date and location of the invasion — possibly the most important piece of intelligence in the entire war, since the Americans joined in. We know the Gestapo have penetrated Trident. They hope, there, to lure us into revealing details about the invasion. What if they've done the same with Apple? What could reassure us more that Apple has *not* been penetrated than for him to provide us with such valuable information?"

I tapped more ash into the ashtray between us.

Hilary was frowning but I carried on.

"Knowing the address of the Gestapo in Paris is some help — yes; and so is knowing Grundmann's name. But, from their point of view, the Germans' point of view, it may be a price worth paying, a risk worth taking, if it buys them our trust — if it encourages us to drop our guard and reveal ahead of time . . . where the invasion will be."

Hilary was shaking his head. "I can't believe . . . I can't . . . surely . . ." He looked up as a thought struck him. "Say you're right, say Orchid has been penetrated like Banquet has . . . It's a terrible thing to say but, although it means Trident and Apple are sacrificed, we now have *two* ways, two avenues, to mislead the Germans. If the people above me buy it."

His eyes were glowing. If we could pull this off, he could see his knighthood down the line.

"Yes," he said softly. "Yes, I see it now. Two conduits filing misinformation — lies — is much more convincing than one. If we are right to be so skeptical, and if the Gestapo have penetrated two of our circuits, then, bleak as it sounded at first, they may actually have done us a favour."

Madeleine and I were two hours and more out of London, we had a tankful of black-market juice, the Lagonda was behaving itself, and we had the top down. Zola was in the small back seat, like a panjandrum, with the wind in his face, and we were on course to surprise my mother at lunchtime.

I was proud of my car and had asked Madeleine if she wanted to drive, but she had astonished me by saying she didn't know how.

"Something to teach you when you get back from France," I had replied.

The traffic was slow through Northleach. I knew that there was a major interchange at the far end, with the Stow-on-the-Wold–Cirencester road crossing our path. As we inched forward, the throaty growl of the engine cut into the morning air. If you owned one like I did, you could always tell a Lagonda by the thunder of its engine.

"How long will this traffic jam last?" said Madeleine.

"We're about two hundred yards shy of the crossroads, just beyond the curve of that bend. When we're through there, the road rises in a long, shallow hill, then descends to another small village, with a level-crossing. That's quite busy, so we may be held up there for a few minutes by the trains. But after that the road should be clear. Why?"

She closed her eyes. "I just love speed. No one's ever given me a birthday present like the stretch we did just now. Sixty miles an hour — for-mi-*dable*! Do you think that people will ever do a hundred miles an hour?"

"They already do on racetracks."

"Heaven! Maybe, after the war, when you get a new car, a couple of birthdays from now . . . a hundred miles an hour! Imagine!"

She reached over and squeezed my leg.

"Remember when we took that bicycle ride in Ardlossan, careering down the side of the mountain? All that wind in your hair, on your thighs . . . no one could do that before, could they — I mean, before we had bicycles or could drive in open-top cars at sixty miles an hour? One day they'll have music in cars and you'll be able to drive fast and listen to Mozart or Hank Snow."

"Who? Who's Hank Snow?"

"Hmm. Only one of Canada's greatest singers. Don't you know 'The Prisoner Cowboy'?"

"No, sorry."

"You *have* heard of Mozart?"

"Was he Canadian?"

I accelerated just a bit, as the traffic moved forward. Madeleine's hair was made for an open-topped car. On the fast, straight stretches of road it streamed out behind her, like flames. On the slower bends, when the eddies of wind came from all directions, it wrapped itself around her face. She peeled it away with her fingers, closing her eyes and holding her cheeks to the sun, her lips slightly parted. Black-market petrol wasn't given away, but that day it was worth every penny.

Speed and being in love are alike: the two most invigorating sensations there are.

The rumble of the car bounced off the façade of the houses lining the road. "Do you think so? I mean, do you really think they'll have music in cars?"

"Oh sure. There'll be car radios and even small gramophones for specially designed records."

"Is that such a good idea, do you think? Won't it be a distraction, unsafe?"

She put her hand on my thigh. "Is that a distraction?"

I reached down and removed it. "Yes."

"Where are we having lunch?"

"I don't know. Are you hungry already?"

She shook her head. "No, not yet. But isn't part of the pleasure of food thinking about it ahead of time?"

I smiled and looked across to her. "Up to a point. Thinking about it too much is a sure-fire way of getting fat very quickly."

She shook her head again and grinned. "I'm safe. I think about bed much more than I think about food."

Before I could reply, the traffic ahead moved and we reached the crossroads with the Stow–Cirencester road. A tractor turned off the Stow road in front of us, so we were very slow going up the hill that led out of Northleach. It was belching filthy exhaust, too, so we kept our distance and our mouths shut. At the top of the hill, however, the tractor turned off and we picked up speed going down the hill into the next village. Just before we reached it was the level crossing — with its gates beginning to close.

"Can you make it if you hurry?" said Madeleine softly.

"Are you kidding?" I started to brake.

"Look at her!" said Madeleine suddenly, urgently. "She's having a go."

I could see instantly what Madeleine meant. Coming towards us was a Land Rover pulling a horsebox. As I brought the Lagonda to a stop, twenty yards short of the slow-closing gates, we watched as the woman driving the Land Rover mounted the slightly raised section of the level crossing, where the rail lines were. In fact, from the way the horsebox was bobbing about, the crossing wasn't as level as it might have been. The Land Rover had almost reached the other side of the crossing but one of the gates was closing between the back of the Land Rover and the front of the horsebox, where the coupling was. The woman kept the Land Rover moving forward, but the gate also kept closing — till it hit the coupling and the front of the horsebox was pulled into it.

Both the gate and the Land Rover-and-horsebox stopped, jammed together. The other three gates carried on closing.

"Oh, my God," whispered Madeleine loudly. "Now what? The Land Rover is safe but the horsebox is trapped —"

"Stuck straddling the railway lines," I added, half to myself.

As we watched, the woman got down from

the Land Rover, slipped through the gap in the gates, and went to the back of the horse-box. She looked along the line, and then let down the back of the box and disappeared inside.

A few moments later we saw her back out of the box, pulling on some reins.

At first the horse wouldn't budge and she pulled harder.

She looked along the line again.

Suddenly, as she did so, the horse rushed forward — and knocked her over.

It panicked, and kicked out. The woman, getting up off the ground, was hit by one of the horse's hooves. She screamed and fell back down again, clutching her arm.

Still no sign or sound of a train but it couldn't be long.

"Look!" cried Madeleine.

We both had the same thought at the same time.

Blood was spurting from the woman's arm in an energetic arc.

We both scrambled to get out of the Lagonda, jumping over its low doors.

Madeleine looked across at me. "Give me your belt."

I had it off in no time. "You try to stop the bleeding, I'll try to stop the train."

I registered other people around but no one else appeared to be doing anything.

Madeleine reached the woman and knelt

next to her. She was screaming. Calmly Madeleine slapped the woman's face and then slipped my belt under her shoulder. She was going to make a tourniquet to stop the blood loss.

I slipped between the gates and looked along the line.

There was a train about a quarter of a mile away.

How long did it take a train to stop? If I ran towards the locomotive, would the driver see me? Given its speed, I had only seconds to run down the line — would it make any difference?

No.

Either the engine driver had seen the horsebox blocking the line, and was already braking, or he hadn't, and he was too close for any action on my part to make a difference.

The only difference I could make was with the creature in most danger.

The horse hadn't gone anywhere. Its halter rope, which the woman had dropped when she fell, had entangled itself in the hinges between the sloping lip at the back of the box, and the floor of the horsebox proper.

I grabbed the rope, freed it, and pulled at the horse's head.

The train sounded its whistle. I could hear its regular pounding sound quite clearly now.

I pulled the horse again.

It came towards me, then baulked.

Madeleine had led the woman back through the gap in the gates, all the while keeping a firm hold on the tourniquet. Seeing the difficulty I was having with the horse she held the gate further open with her free hand.

I pulled the horse again.

The train was now very close and the horse must have sensed it. Suddenly it rushed forward as it had done earlier.

I got out of the way, fast, and the horse rushed through the gap between the gates. The train hurtled past us, the driver using the whistle for all it was worth. We were enveloped in steam and soot. The steam was hot and the soot smelled. There was a mangling, cracking, wrenching sound, on top of which the locomotive's wheels screamed as they skidded and sparked as the driver tried to stop the train.

As the horse rushed by me, I managed to hold on to the halter, though it felt for a moment as though my shoulder was going to be yanked from its socket. The hold I had on the halter caused the horse to wheel round. It slipped on the road with its metal-shod hooves and lashed out with one of its legs. The leg missed Madeleine by a fraction, but a hoof came down full square on the nearside front mudguard of the Lagonda and ricocheted on to the nearside headlamp, that beautiful bulb of gleaming chrome.

The glass shattered, and the metal pod was

dented and knocked out so that it faced down, like a drunk man on a lamp post.

"Winston!" shouted the woman whose arm Madeleine was holding.

Amazingly — but a bit late in the day — the horse calmed down.

I took the opportunity to glance over my shoulder at the level crossing.

Half the horsebox was missing — lengths of splintered wood and twisted ribbons of metal lay all across and around the railway lines. The train was stationary at last, about a hundred yards further on, hissing and oozing steam, like an irritated dragon.

I looked at Madeleine. She was covered in blood.

She eyed me. "It's a good job you didn't tell your mother we were coming," she said, wiping some clots off her cheek. "She won't be disappointed that we didn't make it. She wouldn't have wanted to see you dressed like that."

Her eyes got larger and rounder as she grinned.

I looked down. My trousers were just sliding beyond my underpants.

"Close the door. I've had a pot of coffee made — want some?"

Hilary's office was bigger than mine — naturally, since he was the top dog. He had a window looking towards Baker Street, more elaborate wallpaper, *two* chairs for visitors to sit in, and a standard lamp for winter days. He also had a lavatory en suite and a door in one wall which gave directly on to his secretary's office, a secretary he had all to himself. There was a small lamp on his desk which he lit when the weather was gloomy, as it was now, giving the whole room an intimate glow. He had the same railway posters on the wall as I did.

I nodded and he poured the coffees from an enameled jug. From the smell that began to seep into the room, it was the real stuff, not the dreary chicory substitute that most of us had to put up with. I wasn't going to ask him where he got it. That might embarrass him.

"I shouldn't tell you this but I got it on the black market. Not bad, eh?"

"It's a long time since I tasted anything like this, sir. Are we celebrating?"

"Yes, sort of." He raised his eyes towards the ceiling. "We've got the go-ahead from upstairs. To start misleading the Gestapo, I mean." He nodded and smiled at the same time. "I've not been told any more than I knew before — not the date or the place of the invasion, except that it is soon. But I have been told where to send the next batch of agents. They are not to know anything, of course. They are to conduct sabotage wherever they are sent — sabotage is sabotage.

But upstairs has examined our code traffic and is as satisfied — as you are, and as I am — that some of our circuits have been compromised, *and* that that can be turned to our advantage. We can send fake messages about the invasion in code. Upstairs will do the coding, we send them to the compromised circuits."

He stood up, lifted the coffee jug again, and refilled both our cups.

"What I tell you now, here, in this office, goes no further — do you understand?"

I nodded. "Yes, of course."

"Not even Madeleine, Matt. She must know no more than she would be told if you and she were not . . . were not . . . you know what I mean."

"We are living together," I said. "At least we are for the next few weeks. Until she goes to France. But you have my word that I won't tell her any more than I am supposed to tell her. Is that sufficient? Does that do the trick?"

"Of course, of course," he said quickly. "I wish you weren't under one roof together, but I know you're not a security risk, Matt, so I trust you." He grinned slightly. "Although I can't say I approve of your tact or timing, I can't fault your taste. And it's a free country, and freedom is what we are fighting for.

"Here's what I've been told. In the next weeks we are going to drop quantities of sabotage equipment, invasion currency, and fake Wehrmacht uniforms into several areas of northern France, together with several tons of incendiaries and explosives. These will all be in the Amiens region — places like Rainneville, Saisseval, and Dommartin. These are near the river Somme, which, as you know, reaches the Channel in a big, marshy bay at St. Valery. Amiens is also a railhead, where lines from Rouen, Paris, and Reims converge. The town is very well defended — it basically governs the approaches to the Pas de Calais, and you can draw whatever conclusions you want from this plan, as no doubt the Germans will do, if they really have penetrated our circuits."

He pulled out a packet of cigarettes and offered me one. I took it and leaned forward with a lighted match.

"At the same time," he said, "we will send much the same, plus underwater explosives, to the Nantes region. That is also a railhead, governing the approaches to two bays on the Atlantic — the Bay de Bourgneuf, near Nantes itself, and the Breton and Antioche channels at La Rochelle. The first has landing beaches and La Rochelle has coastal forests. Again, I can't stop you from drawing your own conclusions about what this means. Obviously, it is partly designed to induce the Germans to spread their resources over two areas, but we won't know ahead of time if they have been taken in."

He squashed his cigarette stub, hardly smoked, in his coffee cup saucer.

"I want you to organise all this, Matt. We can't afford to let this overall plan be known about except for you and me. Not even Toby Sheldrake is to know — is that clear? I'm pulling rank here — don't let me down."

I nodded. "I understand, sir."

"Hmm," he said gruffly. "Here's the difficult part. We need to know, once and for all, whether our circuits have been penetrated by the Gestapo and, if so, which ones. The only way that upstairs can think of to do that is to send two people into the field — one in the Amiens region, the other in Nantes — *without* telling anyone they are coming —"

"What?"

"Think about it. If some of our circuits have been penetrated, then we can't be sure that we aren't in a clever game of bluff and double bluff. The Gestapo think we have been taken in; we think they are being taken in. Since so much is at stake, with the invasion, we have to at least *assume* that they suspect a double bluff. We must know, therefore, whether the Germans have been fooled, after we send the equipment into Amiens and Nantes. That means we need people on the ground, people who we can be one hundred per cent certain the Germans *don't* know about, who are acting as our eyes and ears. We have to send in some of our people — our best people — who will know about the circuits in Amiens and Nantes. But the circuits won't know about them."

"You mean they are going to be dropped in all by themselves, with no one to meet them, no local support, no one to offer them cover, food, or protection?"

He nodded. "That's about it."

He looked at me hard and breathed out. "That's exactly what I mean."

I delayed before adding, "That's almost certainly sending them to their deaths."

He adopted his poker face for a moment, but said, "It's imperative we know whether the Germans have been taken in. That comes first — there's no arguing with that."

"Who do you have in mind?"

"We may need to send more than two, depending on what happens to the first pair. But, in the first instance, Albert Rondin to Amiens . . . and Captain Dirac to Nantes."

I crushed out my own cigarette on the saucer between us. My insides were churning.

"Why her?"

"Come *on,* Matt. She's good, very good — that's enough. Her French is perfect, she's bright, innovative, resourceful. She was ranked the best of her group at Ardlossan — you know that. She's good-looking, so she's got more self-confidence than some of our other agents and that's always an important factor. She'll stand a better chance than the others of staying out of trouble and of doing the job for us."

He paused. "I chose her myself."

He stared at me. He didn't blink.

I don't know whether he was daring me to question his judgement. He sat very still.

I had told Madeleine that the odds of an agent's staying alive for six months in the field were fifty-fifty. In this new situation — a situation I had myself done so much to bring about — the odds were a good deal shorter.

But Hilary hadn't finished. "There's also the fact that, since you know Madeleine so well, if she were to get caught, and the Germans were to 'turn' her, she would almost certainly be able to let you know by some detail that would show she had been captured. That was also a factor in my decision."

"You told them upstairs about Madeleine and me?"

He sat up straight in his chair. "We live in a small, closed world, Matt. There's no way your . . . your affair with Madeleine could not be known about. The war comes first, you know that. I'm surprised that you're surprised."

He still didn't blink or move. "I don't want you challenging my authority on this, Matt. It's an important evolution in SC2's role. I want a united team under me. Is that clear?"

I shook my head but said nothing. Not

then. I took out my own cigarettes, handed him one, although I didn't feel like it. He did the honours with the matches.

"It was your idea in the first place, Matt, this double-bluff scheme, I mean."

"But it doesn't follow that Madeleine should —"

"Do you want special treatment for her? Would she want that herself?"

"No."

"She's good, Matt. I repeat: the best of her group. She speaks French as well as Rondin, who's from the Channel Islands, by the way; she's faster on the wireless transmitter and as a woman she'll be able to travel around more easily." His gaze was unflinching. "My decision is non-negotiable. The subject is closed."

I said nothing for a moment. I knew that I had to accept what he said.

But I didn't have to like it. Madeleine and I had been sharing my flat for only a few days, but those few days had seemed so natural, so *full,* so rich in different kinds of detail, so dense with promise and variety, a world away from living on my own. Even Zola liked it, I could tell.

For the briefest of moments, it occurred to me to try to stop Madeleine going. I wanted her all to myself. I wanted the flat-sharing to go on and on.

But I knew I couldn't do that. And I knew that Madeleine wouldn't want that either.

"What will her cover be? She'll have to meet up with the Resistance eventually."

"Upstairs have that worked out. She'll be a bookbinder, a member of the French Guild of Bookbinders, with a forged guild membership card — no one will bother to double-check that at all carefully. She'll say she's travelling around the second-hand bookshops of the country, offering to repair very old, very valuable books. It's the kind of area most Germans will know nothing about; it's dry and arcane and so it is unlikely anyone will bother her. And yes, she'll make contact with the Resistance eventually, but not until we know whether the Germans have been taken in — whether they have increased security in the Nantes area. She — and Rondin, of course — will have to stay underground and anonymous until after the invasion. Then it will be easier for them to 'emerge,' as many more people will come out of the woodwork, once the assault is under way."

"And how long will that be?"

He looked at me through the smoke of his cigarette. "I can't say, Matt. I can't say because I don't know — I swear. All I have been authorised to say — and this is something we can tell Rondin and Madeleine — is that it will be weeks, not months."

He leaned forward and lowered his voice. "Don't hold me to this — and I shall deny it if you ever repeat the conversation — but . . .

from something I heard upstairs — and no, I'm not going to say what or who it was — I got the impression that the invasion is not a matter of weeks rather than months away, but a matter of *days.*" He smiled thinly. "Look at it this way: Madeleine doesn't have to stay alive undercover for very long."

The red anchor was jumping. The place was crowded, standing room only — you had to fight your way to the bar, and cigarette smoke made the air blue. But no one seemed to mind. The piano made all the difference.

On Saturday nights the Anchor had music and people came in for a form of entertainment they couldn't get at home. They would stand with a glass of beer or a gin or a whisky in one hand, a cigarette in the other, and sing their hearts out. And the Anchor wasn't alone: as you walked up Marylebone High Street, or along Euston Road, or Oxford Street, or anywhere in the West End (and the East End too, for all I knew), as you approached the pubs you were welcomed by the sounds of singing.

I think the practice must have begun in the Blitz, in the very dark days, when people were frightened, when our losses were high, when an invasion the other way round seemed imminent, and they discovered it was a cheap and easy way to keep up their spirits.

The men sang just as lustily as the women

— everyone knew the words even if they couldn't keep exactly to the tune, and in any case no one minded. Being together was what counted and the pianist in the Anchor was rusty anyway. No one minded that either.

I usually enjoyed the sing-alongs but that night was tinged with an inevitable sadness. There were four of us — Katrine Howard, Ivan Wilde, Madeleine, and me. We had arrived too late to get a table so we all stood, leaning on the bar, where we didn't have to fight too hard for a drink. Ivan, as part French, part Moroccan, was the only one not too sure of the words, but he manfully did his best.

We bellowed out "A Nightingale Sang in Berkeley Square," "The White Cliffs of Dover," and the Andrews Sisters' "I'll Be With You in Apple Blossom Time." Singing at the top of your voice while inhaling cigarette smoke is thirsty work and the bar was under siege the whole time. Barry, the landlord, looked on with a satisfied eye.

Then the pianist took a break — it was difficult to play and drink and smoke all at once — and the four of us turned away from the piano and huddled together as best we could, surrounded by so many others.

"This happens every Saturday?" said Ivan.

I nodded. "It's London's equivalent of the Scottish ceilidh."

Ivan smiled. "But no test, eh?"

I grinned, shaking my head.

"No test," said Madeleine, "but a ceremony."

"Oh yes?" I looked down at her. Her hair sparkled in the overhead lights of the bar.

She lowered her voice to a whisper. "As we all know, Katrine and Ivan have got their orders, and are off to you-know-where in a couple of days. This is a farewell party."

"The last meeting of the 'Ardlossan Three,'" said Katrine, with a chuckle.

"And, as I am the one being left behind," Madeleine said, pulling a face, "I am the one presenting the farewell trophies."

We all looked at her.

She delved into her bag and took from it two slim packages in plain brown paper. She gave one each to Katrine and Ivan.

"What's this?" said Katrine.

"Maddie!" said Ivan. "I haven't got anything for you."

"Open them!" said Madeleine, softly urgent. "Pron-to! The pianist will be back any minute and we won't be able to hear ourselves speak."

Katrine handed her gin and tonic to me to hold, while Ivan found a spare space on the bar for his beer glass. They both tore at the paper.

Each had been given a slim book.

Katrine held it up in front of her. "Friedrich

Schiller, *La Demoiselle d'Orléans.* What's this?"

"Part of your disguise," said Madeleine. "Ca-mou-flage. It's a French translation of a German classic. In case you don't know, Schiller is, with Goethe, the greatest of the German classic writers, and this is one of his masterpieces, about that great French heroine, Joan of Arc."

She downed part of her own whisky and soda. "I found them at the back of a bookshop in the Charing Cross Road — they're second-hand, knocked about, and I've bought one for me, too." She helped herself to one of the cigarettes that Ivan was offering around.

Still speaking quietly, she went on, "My idea is this: say you or I get stopped at a roadblock and, for one reason or another, the Germans are suspicious. They go through our things, your things, my things . . . and what do they find? They find that we — you and me — are reading a German classic. In translation, yes, but the fact that the author is German might well make them more sympathetic to us, to you and me. In a tight situation, where they are trying to work out whether they believe us, believe our cover stories, a book like this might just make all the difference." She drank more gin. "It's a good story, I don't think the ploy is too obvious, the book isn't bulky . . . so — who knows? — it might save our lives."

Katrine looked from Madeleine to Ivan to me and said, "What do you think?"

"I think it's brilliant," I replied. "I wish I'd thought of it."

"And so do I," said Katrine, stepping forward and giving Madeleine a big hug and a kiss on the cheek. "But I want you to write in it, in French of course. Something personal and warm — that will be even more convincing, yes?"

"Me too," said Ivan. And he gave Madeleine a kiss and a hug as well. "I should have done that a long time ago," he said, blushing.

Madeleine smiled at him, took back the books, and manoeuvred herself to the bar, so she could write on something firm. She took out her fountain pen. "Anyone, any ideas?" She looked at us one by one.

Neither Katrine nor Ivan had any suggestions.

Then Ivan said, "How about 'Not all Germans are the enemy'?"

I looked at him sharply. "A bit obvious — no? Not personal enough."

He nodded. "Maybe. Yes, you're right."

Madeleine said, "How about 'If this makes you think of me every time you open it, I will be happy'? It sort of implies that the person who gave it was a German, or a lover of German culture. It might reinforce the message." She looked around. "You can always say it belonged to someone else before you owned it, so the dedication doesn't apply."

"Brilliantly ambiguous," said Katrine. "You always were the most inventive among us, Maddie, and you haven't lost your touch."

Madeleine started writing the inscriptions as the pianist returned.

He launched into "Long Ago and Far Away" and in no time the pub was again a riot of music and noise amid the smoke.

As I joined in, I asked myself whether I would see Katrine and Ivan again.

Madeleine's brilliant idea — and it *was* a brilliant idea — had just made their lives marginally safer. But only marginally. She herself was going into even more danger than they were. But I couldn't tell her that. Not yet.

MAY

11

The minute I got into the office in Tewkesbury House on the following Monday, I
sensed a change in atmosphere. I couldn't
put my finger on it exactly — but there was
an urgency about people, an intensity even,
and what I detected as a slight bounce in
everyone's step.

I entered my office none the wiser. My half-
secretary wasn't there, but she came in soon
afterwards.

"*There* you are. Good weekend?"

I turned and nodded. Was Geraldine implying I was late? I was *not* late and my weekend
was none of her business.

"What is it, G.?" I sat down at my desk and
examined the papers that had arrived that
morning.

"Meeting in the conference room, upstairs,
in . . ." She looked at her watch. "Twenty
minutes, at ten thirty."

I nodded. "Subject?"

"I haven't been told."

"But you know, don't you? I can sense it, I can feel it."

She looked at me for a moment, savouring the fact, relishing the moment that she knew something, something important, that I didn't. It was normally the other way round.

"Well?" I said.

"Robert Wingate has turned up. He wasn't shot — he escaped."

I looked up sharply. This was very good news. Wingate had been one of our best agents, operating south of Paris, and occasionally in Paris itself, but he had gone missing about six weeks before in mysterious circumstances and hadn't been heard from since. We had all assumed he was dead.

"Get me his file, will you?"

"I have it here." She handed across a buff manila folder. On the cover it said, simply, MAGPIE, Wingate's code name.

"Coffee?" I said. "Or what passes for coffee these days?"

"Coming up," she said, turning on her heel and disappearing through the door.

I spent twenty minutes leafing through Magpie's file and arrived in the conference room upstairs on the stroke of 10:30.

And there he was, Robert Wingate. About forty-five, with a slight stoop, due to some congenital spinal defect in his make-up, salt-and-pepper hair, lots of it, and heavily pock-marked skin. Hilary had thought that Magpie's stoop made him look *so* unathletic that no one in the Gestapo would give him a second glance. It also explained why he wasn't away in the army — he was so obviously unfit for combat. Hilary had been right, up to a point: Robert had worked undercover in France from early 1942 to the spring of 1944 without any problem.

We shook hands. "Welcome back, Robert," I said. "And well done for making it home. Which ratline did you use?"

"Good to see you, Matt," he said. "How's the lung?"

"I'll live, but go on . . . Tell me, how did you get out?"

"Hold on, Wingate. Don't throw that away on Colonel Hammond alone. We all want to hear what happened."

That was Hilary arriving, with our superior, Lieutenant General Frank Grieves, the overall head of SC2. Grieves was a tall man, with spiky hair and a moustache so bushy you could have brushed your shoes with it. He was in civilian clothes.

With him was Leslie Coates, Hilary's opposite number in the Balkans section; Preston Brodie, head of the Dutch section; and James Goldsworthy, of the African section. Such high-level gatherings were rare and, Magpie apart, I was the most junior member, there only because Wingate was himself from the French section, and I had helped train

259

him and sent him into the field.

We settled around the table.

"Where's Penny?" said Grieves.

"She's here," said Penelope Poole, sweeping into the room. "She's here."

Penny was Grieves's personal assistant and kept the minutes of such high-level meetings as were held. She was a handsome woman of about fifty, in a khaki-coloured frock that buttoned down the front. She had a pad and a pencil with her and an impressive pair of spectacles, which she put on as she sat down.

"Fire away," she said, setting the pad and pencil in front of her.

"Hold on," said Grieves. "We require minutes of this meeting but I remind you all that such meetings as these are top secret. You can't tell your spouses or lovers, if you have them, or your secretaries, who I sincerely hope are not the same person. With the invasion so close, there has to be a clamp down on all information. I don't know what Robert here is going to say, any more than you do, but before the meeting ends we'll discuss what use — if any — we're going to make of his information. After that, outside this room, you are all to watch your tongues. You are all senior enough for me not to have to say that twice, so I won't."

He turned to Magpie.

"Robert, you have the floor. What can you tell us?"

"Thank you, sir," said Wingate. "It's good to be back — I've had a few scrapes in the past weeks, I can tell you." He took off his jacket and loosened his tie. "I've got two main things to tell you, but, for the record, and to answer Matt's question, I got out via the Gustave ratline. That goes south, over the Alps, from Grenoble to Digne to Castellane to Grasse, and I was picked up at La Napoule, from where I was ferried to North Africa, and flown back here yesterday. All that the people in this room need to know is that that ratline works very well — everything is done at night, it is all very efficient and professional, and I was well fed. Morale is high — people know the invasion is not far off and they are all keen to convert from being a ratline to being active saboteurs."

"Who are they run by?" said Grieves.

"I don't know, sir. That's part of their professionalism. I only knew them by their code names and they only knew me as Magpie. I did know the name of the man who runs the César circuit south of Paris, near Auxerre, who passed me on to Grenoble — his name was Paul Dutuit, and he was — is — impressive. A big bear of a man whose circuit members do as he says without question. He makes things happen very quickly. They are standing by, waiting for instructions come the invasion. They have one of our agents among them, with a wireless transmitter. That person is a woman, code name Chain."

Grieves was nodding. "Good, good. All very useful. Especially that bit about morale. But you said you had two things to tell us. Is this the time to move on?"

"Yes, sir. Of course. Do you mind if I smoke? I haven't had an English cigarette in weeks."

Grieves fished out a packet of Craven A. "Have one of mine, if you like the brand, that is?"

"Perfect, sir. Thank you."

He lit his cigarette and took a few puffs. He exhaled.

"First, the thing is . . . the Gestapo have penetrated several of our circuits —"

"What?"

A collective shiver went round the room. Hilary and I exchanged glances.

"How do you know this?" Grieves was leaning forward. He knew what Hilary and I knew, of course, but he wasn't going to let on. Was this independent corroboration of what we suspected?

"In Paris, which is a big, messy place, there is, as you can imagine, a lot of gossip. We in SC2 operate circuits, with British agents and French Resistance members, as you all know, and the French, some of them, operate undercover, working for German officers. Some of the French even work at the Paris headquarters of the Gestapo, and of course they overhear things. They even see things. As I understand it, several British agents have been captured, some of them have been held prisoner in the Gestapo headquarters — which is in avenue Foch by the way. And . . . here's the most important point — some of them have been turned, or else forced to transmit wireless messages back to London, as if from agents in the field."

A short pause occurred while we all took this in. Penny's pencil, scribbling away, was the only sound.

"Do you know which agents have been captured or turned?" Grieves himself lit a cigarette.

"No, sir."

"Do you know how *many* have been turned?"

"No, sir."

Grieves nodded. "What was the other thing?"

"I met one of the French Resistance workers who doubles up as a cleaner in the Gestapo offices. According to her, one of our SC2 agents is a double agent. He — or she — has been turned, and is now working for the Germans. The main aim of this double agent is to find out — obviously enough — the timing and the location of the invasion."

Grieves leaned forward. "You don't have a name or a code name?"

"No, sir."

"Do you know when and where this 'turning' took place?"

"No, sir. But the conversation I had was a week before I left for Grenoble and I've been in the ratline for more than a month."

"You couldn't let us know this news any sooner?"

Wingate tipped ash into the ashtray on the table. "Oh no, sir. Transmitting from a ratline risks the direction finders locating a whole set-up. I couldn't endanger that."

Grieves nodded. "I understand."

He smoked his cigarette. "So this agent was turned at least five weeks ago — and very probably more than that."

"Yes."

"And tell us," said Grieves, "what happened to you? Why did you have to leave? You'd been doing so well."

Wingate nodded. "Actually, there's a story there, too, sir. At least I think there is." He finished his cigarette and crushed it out in the ashtray.

"Now that the invasion is getting close, French national politics are beginning to divide the Resistance groups. Some circuits are communist, some are Gaullist, and, basically, they hate each other and, when and if liberation comes, and elections eventually follow, they will be at each other's throats — you can bet on it. It's something to bear in mind in briefing recruits, if we're not doing it already."

"Do you hear that?" Grieves's gaze swept the room.

Hilary and the rest of us nodded.

"And what happened with you? Did you get caught in the crossfire between Gaullists and communists?"

"No, sir. I don't think they will turn on each other quite so nakedly while France is occupied — that would look too bad later. No, my case was because of a slightly older motive."

"What do you mean?"

"I think he means an affair of the heart," said Preston Brodie.

"Do you?" said Grieves. "Were you having an affair with — ?"

"No, sir, not me," said Wingate quickly. "But Colonel Brodie is right, indirectly at least. The Resistance operated a bar in a suburb of Paris, Le Léopard in rue de Nôtre Dame. It made sense — a bar is where people go to relax. They could meet apparent strangers and talk and swap information without it seeming odd. Unfortunately, the head barman, Didier Filbert, was two-timing two women and, when one of them was given the heave-ho, she got her own back — by denouncing Didier and his other *amour* to the Gestapo. It's not the first time it's happened, but it did mean that Didier would almost certainly be tortured, and who knew what he would divulge under pressure? He knew all about me and I had no choice but to assume he would give away my code name and whereabouts. Everyone who is captured knows they will be tortured and so they are told to try to hold out for forty-eight hours, to give other people a chance to disperse and/or escape. I assumed that's how long I had before they came for me."

Grieves nodded but was silent for a while.

"Very well," he said at length. "Thank you, Robert. I take it we're giving you some leave and that after that you'll come back in a different capacity — is that right?" He looked at Hilary.

"Yes, sir," said Hilary. "To begin with, he can brief our agents on the latest developments in manners, language, French ways of doing things."

Grieves nodded.

"Good. Now, that was all very useful, but since it is all about France, it means I need to talk to Hilary and Matt. If the rest of you would excuse us, please . . ."

The others got up and ambled towards the door.

"Do you want me to stay?" said Penny.

"You'd better," replied Grieves.

After the others had gone, and the door had been closed again, the general went on, addressing Hilary and me equally.

"Where does that leave us, do you think? Rondin and Dirac are due to go into the field at any moment — right? Does this change things for them? Matt?"

I shook my head. "Magpie's information is very useful, sir, very. It confirms what we thought, that some of our circuits have been penetrated, but Robert's information doesn't tell us just how wide the penetration is. It also tells us — so far as it goes — that the Gestapo isn't aware that we are aware of their penetration, if you see what I mean. But we still need to find out if they have been taken in by our deception regarding the invasion. That means Rondin and Dirac must go ahead as planned. But obviously no one outside this room must know, in case this double agent, if he or she exists, finds out."

Grieves tapped his fingers on the table. He shook his head. "They are going to be very exposed, aren't they? Rondin and Dirac, I mean."

"Yes," I said. "But, from what Magpie told us, it's more important than ever for us to know how the Gestapo and their fellow Germans are reacting. And if they've turned one of our agents, it also means that Rondin's and Dirac's missions are all the more important. But they must be warned of this extra risk."

Grieves nodded. "When will they be told? And when do they go?"

I looked at Hilary.

He looked at me. "The May moon is tomorrow." He transferred his gaze to Grieves. "I am going to brief Rondin later today, sir. Matt here will do the same with Dirac."

Grieves nodded his head. "Such brave people," he breathed. "Do they know how poor are the odds of their getting through this?"

Neither Hilary nor I answered.

Grieves stroked his chin with his hand. "But we do need to know if the Germans have been taken in. The PM will ask me. Eisenhower will want to know — it's natural. Even Stalin might want to know." He collected up his cigarettes and his matches. "And Magpie only confirms that the Resistance has been penetrated even more than we know." He stood up. "There's no alternative, I'm afraid. If it's any comfort to their families, I will ensure that Rondin and Dirac are decorated for their efforts."

He looked at Penny. "Don't put this in the minutes."

He turned back to us. "What empty words I've just spoken. If it were my child going on such a mission, and she or he were to be killed, *nothing* would be of any comfort."

For the briefest of moments, Myra Hess's fingers were stilled above the keyboard of the Steinway grand. No one in the room breathed. The noise of the traffic in Trafalgar Square seemed more distant than it was. Dust particles hovered in the sunbeams spilling on to the floor, waiting, like us.

Hess's lunchtime concerts in the National Gallery were reasonably safe affairs, now, in 1944 — London hadn't been bombed, by day or by night, for some months. But at the beginning of the war, and especially in the Blitz, when the Steinway and the audience had been removed to the basement of the gallery, for safety's sake, the legend was that Myra Hess would pause just before beginning her playing, in case the Luftwaffe should be overhead, as they had been on many occasions, ready to drown out her music.

She launched into a Bach prelude.

I had been several times before, but that day, after the meeting with Robert Wingate, was a first for Madeleine. As the music filled the hall — the first square gallery at the top of the entrance stairs, now devoid of pictures, of course, which had been hidden away somewhere safe, I hoped — she leaned into me and rested her hand on my thigh. She hadn't been feeling well earlier on but she seemed all right now. I didn't know whether the perfume I could smell was actual perfume or whatever she washed her hair with, but it had a freshness that the gallery lacked. After five years of war, London had a knocked-about, jaded, lived-in look and feel about it.

People were still cheerful, waiting for the invasion, but you could tell they were weary too, and would be grateful when the war was over.

I was particularly on edge. Today, Madeleine had been supposed to be seeing her mother for lunch but someone had phoned on Mrs. Dirac's behalf, to say she was ill in bed with the 'flu that was then going round, and had a temperature of 101 degrees. She would travel to London in a few days.

Madeleine had taken the news in her stride — 'flu was 'flu and a temperature of 101 needed watching.

But she didn't know what I knew. Not yet.

The music increased in tempo then, and one or two individuals in front of us began to nod their heads in time to the rhythm. Then it got too fast for anyone's neck muscles and, in a swooping climax, it ended.

We all applauded rapturously, and one or two whistled.

Miss Hess — who hadn't yet been made a dame, as she would be later — sipped some water from a glass on the piano. I remember that although it was May, and sunny, it was cold in the shade and she was wearing a fur coat that day — there was no heating in the National Gallery. As she prepared for her next piece, she blew on her fingers. Everyone laughed.

With her eyes closed, and a slight swaying

of her upper body, she started to play her last offering of the day, the one that had quickly become everyone's favourite: "Jesu, Joy of Man's Desiring."

I closed my eyes and let the lovely notes wash over me, clean and pure, the perfect antidote to what was going to happen later in the day. A succession of clear sounds, each one distinct, followed one another in what seemed an inevitable pattern, like water falling over rock.

I leaned against Madeleine and she leaned against me. Field Marshal Rommel was quoted in the papers that day as saying he didn't think an invasion in the north of France could work. Was he trying to put us off? Was he worried that it could work all too well? Did he know what he was talking about?

The music came to an end. The applause was, as always, enthusiastic, grateful but not overlong: people had jobs or families to go back to. There was a war on.

Madeleine and I joined the crowd spilling out into Trafalgar Square. Nothing much was said on the way down the steps — the soothing effect of the music still lingered.

As we emerged into the square — clear skies but for the barrage balloons over Whitehall — I took Madeleine's arm.

"Where are we going?" she said. "I'm hungry."

"Northumberland Avenue. Let's walk down

there to the river."

She stopped and looked at me. "No lunch? We could have the table I booked for me and my mother at —"

"Not just yet, no. We need to talk where we can't be overheard."

I led the way across the road at the traffic lights.

She struggled to keep up. "I don't know much about music, but that concert . . . There were two pieces by Bach, one by Brahms, one by Schubert, and one by Chopin. Am I right?"

"Yes. Well done."

"But . . . isn't that weird? I mean, don't you think it's odd?"

"All but one being Germans, you mean?"

"Yes. Yes, that's *exactly* what I mean."

I looked down at her. "We're fighting the Nazis. Those composers have been dead for years and most of the great music is German anyway."

"But even so . . . to me it was weird."

"I'm sorry if you didn't enjoy it."

"Oh, I *loved* it. I wish I'd been before; I wish I could go again. What was that first piece, the one that wasn't by a German?"

"One of Chopin's nocturnes."

She began to hum it.

We reached the Embankment and crossed to the riverside. Here we had a good view up and down the Thames. Plenty of barrage balloons here too.

We turned left, towards Waterloo Bridge and St. Paul's — standing there, defiant, so far unbombed. The pavement was wide here and we could talk safely without being overheard.

I stopped, leaned on the stone parapet and looked out at the water. The tide was quite high, the water a sludgy yellow.

Madeleine stood alongside me.

I took a gulp of river air. "Do you feel all right? Quite recovered from earlier? You and your mother would have made a fine picture at lunch — both ill."

"Oh, yes, I'm okay now, thanks. Don't fret. It was nothing."

I paused and took a deep breath. "You're leaving tomorrow night," I said. "There's a full moon and the weather forecast is good."

She let out a brief cry. "At last. I won't see my mother but . . . At last." She put her arm in mine and squeezed. "Something's just snapped inside me. My heart is pumping, as if it has suddenly changed gear." She swallowed. "Do hearts have gears?" She laughed. "I don't suppose they do." She kissed the shoulder of my jacket. "And where am I going?"

"Le Gâvre," I said. "That's north of Nantes and inland from St. Nazaire. You'll be dropped near the Fôret du Gâvre."

She nodded. "To do what?"

"Let's walk," I said, leading the way. I put my arm in hers; that would keep people away, I thought.

"There's good news, Madeleine, and not-so-good news."

She said nothing but kept looking forward.

I tried to sound both matter-of-fact and re-assuring, though whether I succeeded I still don't know. "Over the past few weeks, we think that some of our circuits in France have been penetrated by the Gestapo —"

"But that's —"

"Hold on. Hold on. In fact, we no longer *think* some circuits have been penetrated, we *know* they have. As a result, we've had to change tactics and box clever. Without letting on that we know the circuits have been infiltrated, we have been feeding the Germans false information about the whereabouts of the invasion."

"Double bluff." She looked up at me, searching my face for news. Her eyes grew rounder.

"Something like that. But our problem is, we don't know if they have been taken in. And this is where your mission counts — and counts big-time. You are going to be dropped at Le Gâvre with a transmitter and a bicycle."

I said nothing for a moment, letting her take in the information.

Her face, her lovely face, puckered into a frown. "I understand but . . . but how do you know whether my circuit hasn't also been penetrated?"

Spot on. Trust Madeleine.

I stopped and looked down at her. "That's the . . . that's the bit of news that's not . . . not so good." It was my turn to swallow, hard. "You won't be met, Madeleine. No one knows you're coming."

We drifted back over to the parapet and looked out again at the river.

A military band was marching down the Embankment. A few people were following it, but the noise of the instruments meant we couldn't be overheard.

"This afternoon you are going to be given your fake ID papers — you will be a repairer of antiquarian books — and the name of the circuit you are meant to join, and all their details, about who's who, who is in command, where he lives, what the passwords are, and so on. But your mission involves two aspects. First, we need evidence of military activity in the Nantes–St. Nazaire area — Nantes, Challans, Aizenay. I can't tell you where the invasion is going to be, because I don't know, I still don't know, but it won't be in Nantes. However, in our false messages to the Gestapo, via the circuits they have penetrated, Nantes is a location we have highlighted as one of two possibilities. We need to know from you what the status of the military build-up there is — are the Germans moving forces *into* the area, are they moving forces *out* of the area, or are things static? Have they been misled by our misinformation?"

I turned to watch the band go by. Several buses were caught up behind it, and some lorries.

"You might be able to decide this for yourself, but it's possible that you will need the help of the local circuit. And that's the second part of your mission. To find the people in the circuit and observe them *before* contacting them. The coded message that we sent out via the BBC news last night said your mission had been cancelled. A lie. If, when you have seen the lay of the land, you decide the Le Gâvre circuit *hasn't* been penetrated, then you can declare yourself to them. But — and this is all-important — if you think they *have* been compromised, then you have to continue acting on your own. Either way, you must let us know via your wireless transmitter."

Madeleine didn't say anything for a while.

Then, without looking at me, she murmured, "If the circuit *has* been penetrated, and I can't contact them, what happens next?"

I reached for my cigarettes.

"You have two choices. Later today we will give you details of a ratline in that part of France, by means of which you can escape, and come back home. Or . . . or you can stick

276

it out — if you can manage it — and wait for the invasion, then join the local uprising, helping with sabotage. Once the invasion has begun, lots of locals who are too scared to act now will come out of the woodwork, and it will be much safer for you."

I put my hand on her arm, two cigarettes in my fingers. "Madeleine, I can't hide from you the fact that this is now both a much more important, *and* a far more dangerous mission than we have ever discussed before. And I can't hide from you that I have no idea what the odds are of your surviving in the field, without the protection of a local circuit who know the ropes in the area where you will be operating. So . . . if you want to withdraw, you can. We can't force you, and a reluctant agent in the field is almost certainly worse than useless, and as good as dead."

Again I brushed her arm with my fingers, and held up a cigarette.

"I mean it."

She took the cigarette but hesitated for quite a while before nodding her head. "I know you mean it, Matt. And it's tempting. But we've been here before, we know that that's what wars do, throw up these impossible situations which no one in their right mind could ever contemplate at any other time. They make ordinary people do extraordinary things, in which they either succeed or don't succeed, and in which they either survive or don't survive."

She looked out at the river and bit her lip.

I held out my lighter and lit her cigarette, then my own.

"And if every ordinary person refused to go through with every extraordinary, impossible mission — what then? What would happen to us as a fighting force, as a people, and what would we — we as a generation, I mean — tell our children?"

She took hold of my hand.

"It's my time, Matt. As you say, I've been given something to do that's more dangerous than we thought, but even more important. The two go together. It's right. *For-mi-dable.*"

She squeezed my hand.

"I'm glad you told me here, by the river. This is a lovely sight, Parliament, all these bridges, the curve of the river, the Savoy." She smiled. "When I get back, you can take me to the Savoy for dinner — we can go dancing, have an American cocktail, and walk along here afterwards. Is that a date?"

I nodded and swallowed hard. "It's a date."

12

I waited in the meadow in Southwater until all sight and sound of Madeleine's Lysander had quite vanished. The field was flooded with moonlight, and I sat in the Lagonda and opened the package she had slipped into my hand just before she left. It was the silver cigarette case Erich Langres had given her at Ardlossan after she had rescued him.

As the dew came out, the grass began to smell, fresh and damp. She had been given an important duty in the war, more important than either of us had imagined when she had joined SC2. But it suited her ambitions exactly. She had gone abroad in the best possible frame of mind.

I was pleased for her but . . . how empty that field seemed now that she was gone. She'd be parachuting in on a field very like this one before the sun came up. With no one to meet her — alone, as I was now.

To take the edge off my gloom, I drove to the pub in the village, the Black Prince, the one I had never had time to visit before. I sat for a moment in the car park, filling my new silver cigarette case with smokes.

The bar was busy, so I ordered a whisky chaser and found myself a quiet corner.

There were some soldiers in the bar and they were discussing a film they had just seen, *The Spoilers,* with Marlene Dietrich and John Wayne.

One of the men was obviously a film maniac. "That was her one hundred and twenty-eighth film," he announced.

"Prove it," said someone else, not really interested.

"Colin, only people called Colin know that sort of thing," said a third.

"She was paid four hundred and fifty thousand dollars by Alexander Korda for her role in *Knight Without Armour,* which was made in London."

"Someone shoot him."

"Colin, get some beers in."

"While she was in London, the Nazis offered her oodles of money to go back to Germany. Know what she did?"

"Colin, *shut up*!"

"She took out American citizenship."

"You could do the same, Colin. You can leave now."

"I like knowing about beautiful women, don't you?" Colin would not be silenced.

"She's certainly beautiful," someone

chimed in. "That poster for *The Blue Angel,* with her wearing stockings and suspenders, and that song — what was it?"

" 'Falling in Love Again,' " said Colin quickly. "You know she nearly didn't get that role? There was someone else in the offing — you'll never guess who? Go on, guess. Anyone?"

"No, Colin, let's have some proper conversation now, not one quiz after another —"

"Go on, guess. It's someone you've all heard of. I promise I'll shut up afterwards."

"No, Colin."

"I haven't a clue."

"You've been told already — it's your turn to get in the drinks. That's much more important than some German actress's name."

"Do you all give in?" Colin's gaze swept the bar.

His eye fell on the barman. "How about you?"

The barman shrugged. "I only know the names of three German women — Dietrich, Eva Braun, and that film-maker, the one who did the Olympics; Lenny somebody."

Colin looked disappointed. "There you are," he said. "You're right, that's who it was, Leni Riefenstahl."

Well, well, well. Colin might be a pain but . . . did Madeleine know what I now knew? Suddenly, I felt warmer inside.

■ ■ ■ ■

JUNE

■ ■ ■ ■

13

I lay on my back in bed and looked up at the ceiling. The first light of the day had leaked into the room about twenty minutes before, and there were no more moving shadows. This early in the morning, the traffic in St. John's Wood Road was thin.

How boring the ceiling was in daylight. Since Madeleine had been gone, since she had flown away towards that mottled moon, I couldn't sleep.

I put my arm out to where she should have been. She was slender but she had left a vast, empty space of sheet and eiderdown in her absence. And a faint smell of her, now fading fast.

Madeleine had been dropped near Le Gâvre as planned, thanks to Jack. Or so she had said in her first transmissions, transmissions that were correctly encoded and contained no mistakes, other than the deliberate ones. So far as we could tell, it was her "fist," and her true and bluff checks were correct.

We didn't know exactly where she was, or how she was faring on a day-to-day basis because, quite rightly, she didn't waste time on air with extraneous details like that. But she had clearly bicycled her way towards St. Nazaire, from near to which she had sent us several reports — that the streets were awash with German troops, that more troops were still arriving, and that she had faced several roadblocks but had been let through all of them — no one was interested in a book-binder of antiquarian books, who read German authors in translation. She was proving just as adept as we had hoped. I couldn't ever relax while she was in the field but . . . but, so far, she was doing all right. More than all right — *"fan-tas-tique,"* as she might have said.

And, most important of all, she was confirming that the Germans, at the very least, were not pulling their troops out of the St. Nazaire area, rather the reverse. She reported that she had overheard a conversation in a baker's shop, to the effect that an order for a nearby German barracks in St. Nazaire had just been doubled, on account of more troops arriving. Exactly the kind of convincing detail we needed.

She couldn't get within ten kilometres — six miles — of the actual coast, she had told us: the Germans kept the coast fiercely guarded — they had a coastal exclusion zone like we did — but she had familiarised herself

286

with a large hospital in St. Nazaire as a good place to overhear gossip. And she had seen a submariner brought in for treatment after he had been caught up in a fight aboard his ship. St. Nazaire, we knew, was a submarine base, so that seemed to indicate that the subs — or U-boats as the Germans called them — were not being relocated: another piece of good news.

Rondin's reports showed much the same picture. Hilary had communicated this immediately to General Grieves, who had taken the information to Churchill and Eisenhower.

"With any luck," Hilary had said to me when he came back from the meeting, "our little plan — *your* plan — to convert the penetration of our circuits into a double bluff, seems to have worked a treat. Fingers crossed, eh? I got the impression from the mood of the meeting that the invasion is only days away now."

That had cheered me no end. It would be good to be having a go at the Germans, taking the fight *to* them, rather than merely soaking up punishment as we had been doing, in London anyway, for five long years. And I was pleased for Madeleine's sake. She had survived the first few very dangerous days of her time on the ground in France alone. More than survived — she had shone. Once the invasion had begun, her life would surely become much easier. She had told us that she didn't think the local circuit in St. Nazaire — code-named Crossbow — had been penetrated.

The ceiling above the bed wasn't getting any more interesting, so I decided to get up. I put on my dressing gown, a gesture which always excited Zola, who clearly couldn't tell the difference between a dressing gown and a raincoat and always optimistically concluded that we were going out for a walk. Instead, I went through into the kitchen and put on the kettle, to boil some water for tea. There were no eggs, but I had some bread, a few days old, and a small block of margarine. I could at least make some toast.

I lit the gas, cut the bread, and put a slice under the grill. There was a bit of Marmite left, to give a lift to the toast.

Zola, having worked out that we were not going for a walk just yet, flopped down on the kitchen floor. But he kept an eye on what I was up to. He knew he didn't get fed until later in the day, but . . .

I went into the bathroom to inspect the razor on my shaver. I hated shaving. I was just passing the ball of my thumb over the blade of the razor when the telephone rang.

I stopped breathing.

I put down the razor and looked at my watch: it was 5:40.

Early — very early — for a phone call.

Was someone ringing me with news of

Madeleine? If so, news at 5:40 could hardly be good news.

I hurried through the kitchen, switching off the kettle and the gas for the toast, and sat on the bed.

Did I need to prepare for life without Madeleine? I had only known her a matter of weeks.

An early morning bus accelerated in Grove End Road. I could recognize that engine sound effortlessly.

The telephone was still ringing.

I leaned forward and picked up the receiver.

"Yes? Matt Hammond."

"What are you doing? Are you awake?"

"Hilary? Yes, sir. I was just making breakfast."

"Forget it. I want you in here. Have something at your desk. Our troops went in overnight. The invasion's started. Normandy. Drop everything. Get into the office as quick as you can."

He rang off and the line went dead.

He was right. I had to get into the office, and pronto. No time for breakfast, no time to shave, no time to take Zola for a walk. That didn't pose the hygienic problems it might have done. Today was a Tuesday, and Mrs. Crosland came in on Tuesdays to clean and change the sheets. She would take Zola for a walk outside. I left her a note just to make sure.

As soon as I reached the office, I could see that everyone had been called in early. Hattie was already on reception but not yet Freda.

At the far side of the typing pool, Hilary had erected an easel and on it was a large map of the north of France. Others were gathered round him; and he was just starting to draw on the map. I dumped my bag on my desk and went to stand with the others.

Hilary nodded at me but didn't stop what he was doing.

"The prime minister is going to make a statement in Parliament later today, but this is my understanding of what is happening."

He pointed to the map and the lines he had drawn on it.

"There are five beaches, between here — Quinéville, in the west — and here — Cabourg, in the east. A fifty-mile stretch of beach, being attacked by the United States First Army, and the British Second Army. For those of you who know northern France — Normandy — the landings are either side of Bayeux, near Saint-Lô and Caen. Four thousand ships are involved. There are clear skies over the beaches — for now at any rate — but so far the Luftwaffe has not appeared.

"Now," he said, "I've told you what precious few details I know — the invasion is only hours old, after all. I will learn more later today and will pass it on as soon as I am told. Eventually, of course, the newspapers and the radio will be full of it. But our immediate job is to make sure that our agents in the field know what's happening. They may learn something in France, but it will be a time of rumour and counter-rumour, and we owe it to our people to ensure they get the unvarnished truth. We don't know, yet, whether the invasion is going to be a success, but we must at least tell them that it has started. So we need to prepare coded messages — short and to the point — for when they next check in."

He turned and pointed to Ernestine Ridley, Tina to everyone, a handsome older woman, an unflappable senior secretary with immaculate silver hair who was never seen without her cashmere kilt. "Tina here has the schedule of who checks in when, so I want the office manned non-stop from now on until everyone has been briefed. Colonel Hammond, Matt, can you see to it, please?"

"Of course," I said. "Tina, can you and I compare notes, please? Would you like to come to my office?"

She came up to me and, smiling, whispered, "We've all been in for a while and it's not even seven o'clock yet. Shall I pop out and get us a toasted sandwich, and a hot drink, and *then* come to your office?"

"Mr. Ridley is a lucky man, Tina. That's almost as good a prospect as the invasion itself."

"Mr. Ridley has been dead these past six

years, Matt. If you weren't so young, I might have my eye on you. See you in a min." She smiled and was gone.

I went back to my office, took off my jacket, and sat at my desk. I took out a list of agents who were still active in the field. On it there were 116 names. It was going to be a very long day.

I threw the paper bag the sandwich had come in into the wastepaper basket. "That really hit the spot, Tina. How much do I owe you?"

"Tuppence," she said. "Sorry the bread was so stale. The man in the shop said he hadn't yet had today's delivery." She grinned. "That's what comes of starting work so early."

I handed the money across. "Any sign in the shop that people know what's going on?"

She shook her head. "Business as usual, so far as I could see."

"I suppose the PM wants to make the announcement, and to Parliament first. Then all hell will break loose. Now, I have an alphabetical list of agents in the field, alphabetical by code. I need to convert that into an order of agents according to when they are due to contact us next. That means I need both their code names and their access codes. Hilary is preparing the tailored messages now."

"I think it might be better if we went back into the typing pool and pushed some desks together. It will be easier to spread out the papers and compare lists that way."

"Good idea," I replied.

We got up and went through to the typing pool, where more of the junior staff were beginning to arrive. We rearranged some desks so they formed a large rectangle and laid out the sheets of paper and set about what was, in effect, a massive coordination job.

"Now, let's see . . . We need to do some shuffling. I'll read out the names and the circuits, you tell me the times they are checking in, and then we can sort them into order. Ready?"

Tina nodded.

"Acorn. Erica Stanfield. Patron circuit, Melun."

"Three thirty to three forty-five," said Tina.

I made a note.

"Apple. Bettany Crace. Hawk circuit, Pontoise."

"Four fifteen to four thirty."

"Chain. Barbara Hapgood. César circuit, Auxerre."

"Five o'clock to five fifteen."

"Cloister. Vicky Webb. Spiral circuit, Rouen."

"Four forty-five to five o'clock."

And so it went on, tedious but vital. Those agents depended on our meticulous attention to detail — we couldn't let them down.

Eight o'clock came and went, then 9:00 a.m.; at 10:30 we had another break and went downstairs for more "coffee."

Still no sign in the café that anyone was aware of the invasion.

We were back at our desks at 11:00.

Twelve came and went and we were still at it. The first transmission we were expecting was at 2:00. We normally had no transmission in the mornings because, after all, agents had work to do.

At about a quarter past twelve, G. suddenly stood over me.

"This just came in. You might like to read it in the privacy of your own office."

I looked up, then at Tina, then back at G. "Is it from the field?"

"You could say that."

Odd form of words, I thought.

"Is it from Madeleine? From Oak?"

A firm shake of the head.

I took the slip of paper from her, but didn't return to my office. I read what was written right there in the typing pool. The clatter of keys was a backdrop we had learned to ignore. But I heard it now, preternaturally loud. Like the rattle of jackboots.

As I read the message, a slow, itchy sensation squirmed its way up the back of my neck.

+MANY·THANKS·LARGE·DELIVERIES·OF·ARMS·
AND·AMMUNITION·STOP·HAVE·GREATLY·APPRE-

CIATED·GOOD·TIPS·CONCERNING·YOUR·
INTENTIONS·AND·PLANS·STOP·WE·ARE·ALL·IN·
GOOD·HEALTH·HERE·IN·PARIS·BUT·ARE·
SIGNING·OFF·NOW·STOP=PARIS·GESTAPO·
STOP+

I looked up at G.

My mouth fell open.

"Has Hilary seen this?" I asked G.

"No. I thought I'd leave that to you."

"You're a real pal," I said, getting up.

I took the paper across the room and walked down the corridor. I knocked on Hilary's door and entered without waiting. He was on the phone.

He didn't like being interrupted unannounced. He glared at me, but reluctantly waved me to a seat, knowing I wouldn't barge in unless I had something important to discuss. I put the paper in front of him before sitting down.

He read it while listening to the conversation at the other end of the line. Then, "Sir, something's just come up. Can I ring you back — say fifteen minutes? Okay."

He put down the phone.

"Is this genuine, or a prank?"

"I think we have to assume it's genuine. They obviously know about what's happening in Normandy, and that their days in Paris are numbered."

"It could be someone playing silly buggers."

Just then there was a knock on the door and G. came in. She had another piece of paper with her. She just said one word before going out again. "More."

I took the paper.

+FROM·ALL·AT·HEXAGON·CIRCUIT·THANKS·FOR·
THE·MONEY·AND·THE·CIGARETTES·NOT·TO·
MENTION·THE·EXPLOSIVES·WHICH·HAVE·FOUND·
A·GOOD·HOME·STOP·ALL·YOUR·PEOPLE·ARE·
SAFE·SAFE·IN·OUR·HANDS·THAT·IS·AND·WILL·
BE·HEADING·EAST·WITH·US·STOP·SIGNING
·OFF=RENNES·GESTAPO·STOP+

I passed it to Hilary.

He hunched over it, running his fingers through his hair. "This is awful," he breathed. "We thought one or two circuits were penetrated — yes. But Paris is the French headquarters of the Gestapo; and we had no hint that the Rennes circuits were compromised. This is . . . this is a *catastrophe.* I must tell upstairs."

"And I must tell our agents, to keep clear of their circuits — unless of course it's too late. They must all disappear. Anyone in the Paris or Rennes ambit."

A thought struck me. "How is Rondin doing?"

Hilary nodded. "Fine. Good."

"Is he still independent?"

"I told him he could contact Proctor circuit

once the invasion had begun —"

"No! We must tell him to hold off, at least until he gets the go-ahead from us. And the same goes for Madeleine. She's nowhere near Paris, but all agents not yet integrated into the Resistance must hold off until we know how far this goes."

I stood up. "It looks as though Robert Wingate was right, and we have a mole somewhere in SC2."

Hilary shook his head. "That doesn't bear thinking about. We'll need to go back over transmission transcripts, to see when and how they first became . . . well, not kosher." He looked up. "I'll brief Grieves later today, and I'll cope with Rondin. This doesn't change your job — we must let every agent know the invasion has started. But you're right — tell them to steer clear of any circuits until we know more. And you'll see to Madeleine, right?"

I left him and returned to the typing pool, where, during the rest of that day, Tina Ridley and I briefed seventy-nine out of our total of one hundred and sixteen agents on the new situation. We were in the office until one the next morning.

By the time I went home that night, by taxi because the tube had stopped running, there were thirty-seven agents we hadn't heard from. One of them was Madeleine.

14

"It beggars belief," growled the honourable member for Stafford South, whose name I hadn't caught. "It beggars belief," he said again for those who hadn't heard him the first time. "It beggars belief that the Gestapo should have penetrated one of our most secret defence initiatives in this war — and got away with it for so long."

Cries of "Hear, Hear" and "Shame" were heard from both sides of the House of Commons. Some members stamped their feet.

"I call upon the secretary of state for war to dismiss the officer in command of this operation, and replace him with someone who can do the job properly, and I call upon you, Mr. Speaker, to lift the reporting restrictions on today's session of Parliament." The member for Stafford South was not a big man, but he did his best to seem substantial. "God knows, this failure does very little credit to our secret services, but we are not going to capitalize on the early successes of the brave invasion forces unless we learn to look disaster in the eye, recognize it as such, and then act promptly to eradicate the defects that have been identified."

He sat down.

Hilary turned to me and pulled a face. We were sitting in the gallery of the House, in the seats reserved for civil servants, looking down at the chamber.

It had been just over a week since the invasion. The assault was going well enough. Bayeux had been captured, despite fierce fighting in Normandy, and our troops were sixteen miles from Cherbourg. Major roads were being taken, lost, and retaken. It had emerged that the beach landings had been postponed by twenty-four hours at the last minute on account of the weather, which had since improved markedly.

That was all good news.

What was much less good news was that thirty-one of our agents in the field — fourteen women and seventeen men — had still not been heard from. We simply didn't know what had happened to them, but of course we feared the worst. It seemed that as many as nine circuits might have been penetrated by the Gestapo, before they advertised their breakthrough on D-Day. Seven of those circuits were in and around the Paris region, while the others stretched west, to Poitiers, Tours, and Nantes — barely thirty miles from

St. Nazaire and Crossbow, the circuit Madeleine had been preparing to contact the last time she had been in touch.

We *had* heard from Madeleine, but not in a way that settled my nerves.

The day after the invasion G. had brought me the decoded version of a message from Oak. It read:

```
+NRBH·TWO·BRIDGES·NEAR·LA·ROCHE·BER-
NARD·AND·CRAN·BOLWN·YESTERDAY·STOP·
RAILWAY·STATION·AT·REDON·HI
```

And then it just stopped.

It was a genuine message — her true check, the ninth word, was misspelled, as it should have been — but then it just stopped, in mid-sentence, mid-word. That didn't mean Madeleine had been captured, but it did mean that she had been interrupted in the middle of sending her message. But she might have escaped when she saw that her whereabouts had been discovered. She might have retreated, knowing that escape was more important than completing what she had to say — she could always do that later.

Except that she had not been in touch since her incomplete message, now over a week ago. And we hadn't had a chance to warn her to steer clear of *all* circuits.

I was beside myself with worry.

What am I saying? A week without any

contact, a week when the news was dominated by the fighting in France, when we were constantly hearing from agents in the field, moving around, facing new and perilous conditions, a week of German cruelties as their troops, under increasing pressure, took it out on the surrounding population, one massacre or outrage after another — people shot, tortured, and raped.

And still no word from Madeleine.

Nothing.

Day after day, every time I was in the office, every time the teleprinter clattered into life, I stood over the machine until the stuttering stopped, ripped off the paper myself, and took it to the decrypters, and waited there, holding my breath, while it was decoded, hoping that the message was from her.

It never was.

She was the best of her bunch, as I kept telling myself. She would surely have spotted if she was being followed, she would have sought out a place to transmit her messages that was safe, where she could see anyone approaching, where she had an escape route to hand.

She would know that we had received a truncated message from her. That we would know something sudden had occurred. That we — I — would be worried. So she would, as soon as she could, try to send us another message to say that she was all right. *If she could.*

But she hadn't.

On the other hand, she had almost certainly abandoned her transmitter, so how could she send us a message? She couldn't unless . . . unless she contacted the local circuit. But if she had done that, she had almost certainly walked into a trap. Because of the way she had abandoned her own message, we hadn't had a chance to alert her to the danger of contacting the local people.

If she had spotted that the local circuit had indeed been penetrated — as she was quite capable of doing — then she was alone in France, without the surrounding cloak of safety that a circuit would have provided, and without a transmitter and even, conceivably, without her bicycle, which she might have had to abandon.

She did have her cyanide pill with her. That was another source of worry.

Devastating as all this was, and wrecked as I privately felt, those weren't my only problems.

A couple of days before, Hilary came back from a meeting with his superiors, at which he was told that the *Daily News* had somehow got hold of the fact that many of our circuits had been penetrated by the Gestapo. *How* this information had escaped no one knew, though Hilary said that General Grieves privately suspected MI6, which had been suspicious of SC2 ever since its inauguration.

For the time being, under the fourteen-day rule, military censorship prevented this information from being made public at least for two weeks: the censor at the Ministry of Information was clearly worried about the effect the news might have on military and civilian morale.

But then the Opposition, which was of course represented in the wartime coalition cabinet, had called a debate in Parliament to discuss the matter. Despite it being wartime, and the government being a coalition, several days were still set aside for motions the Opposition wished to discuss.

Although Parliament debated security issues in secret in wartime, members who thought certain key issues should be made public could appeal to the Speaker to allow the press to print the proceedings without waiting the usual fourteen days.

"The member for Newcastle, Easington."

I didn't know his name either, but he was a tall, lanky individual with a mop of dark hair and rough skin. He was about fifty-five and a Labour Party member.

"Mr. Speaker," he said. "Mr. Speaker, I am astonished and saddened by what we have heard in this House today. For an organisation like SC2 to be penetrated . . . Well, such things, though regrettable, do happen in wartime. I fought in the Great War of 1914 to 1918 and that was known for *terrible* mistakes. So I am not going to stand here and condemn an organisation that, for all we know — and it is not our job to know — has done excellent work over the past four or five years."

He turned from addressing the Speaker, Douglas Clifton Brown, to the government front bench, where Anthony Eden, the secretary of state for war, was seated.

"But what I cannot forgive, and do *not* forgive, is the fact that no one — *no one* — spotted the penetration. This dereliction of duty, this appalling complacency, all the more abject since it took place in the dangerous run-up to the invasion, defies belief — as my learned colleague has just said."

He turned back to the Speaker.

"As you know, Mr. Speaker, this House is very divided on how much of our proceedings should be made public. Personally, I do not think you can make hard-and-fast rules about what the public mood will bear and what it will not. But I fall into the camp which holds that you cannot hide everything from our fellow citizens, who are sacrificing so much in this war. Had the invasion in France not gone so well — so well that His Majesty the King has been able to visit our troops in Normandy — then I am not so sure that it would have been a good idea to release information about German penetration of our secret services. But, since our forces are now, as I understand it, about to cut off the Cherbourg peninsula, I concur with the honourable member for Stafford South and urge you to lift reporting restriction on this debate."

Competing cries of "No! Rubbish!" and "Hear, hear!" spread around the chamber.

"Mr. Speaker, Mr. Speaker . . ." The member for Newcastle, Easington, remained standing and the noise died away. "I give two reasons for taking the view that I do. One, unless we are prepared to release the bad news with the good — as His Majesty's Government have done throughout the war — our propaganda loses its bite. The citizens of Britain expect to be treated as adults and this is no time to change that stance —"

"Hear, hear!"

"Secondly . . . secondly, Mr. Speaker, at the same time as we announce this failure publicly, the minister for war must also announce that heads have rolled. Only if heads roll, only if the relevant officials are shamed, only if someone bears responsibility for this fiasco, will performance improve in the future — and I remind honourable members of the House that although the invasion is going well for the moment, the war is a long way from being won."

The member for Newcastle, Easington,

drew himself up to his full height and buttoned his jacket. "So I say, Mr. Speaker, lift the reporting restriction on today's debate, but I also call upon the secretary of state for war to exercise the powers of his office and relieve of their duties those responsible for this shambles."

He sat down.

"Hear, hear!"

"The minister for war!"

The Speaker, Douglas Clifton Brown, was the MP for Hexham. He was difficult to make out under his copious wig of office, but from what I could see he looked terrified that he might soon have to make a decision.

The secretary of state for war, Anthony Eden, stood up. Good-looking, debonair, with a small, immaculate silver moustache, he oozed self-confidence.

"Mr. Speaker, as honourable members will have seen, I have listened to the debate today closely, following my opening statement. I have to say that I regret that members opposite have concentrated on the failures of SC2 which, after all, I did highlight in my opening remarks. At the same time, they have ignored and overlooked the fact that, thanks to some nimble thinking on the part of certain members of SC2, we were able to use the fact that some circuits had been penetrated by the Gestapo to mislead our enemies about where the invasion would take place. That is no small achievement, and I would like to pay tribute here to the men and women who have made the work of SC2 so profitable in the past. I . . . yes . . . ?"

Another member was standing up, and the minister for war, in parliamentary terms, "gave way," and sat down.

The man standing was small and fat and sweaty. I had no idea which constituency he represented.

"On a point of information, Mr. Speaker, the minister for war refers to 'men *and women*' of SC2. The fact that women were being used at all by SC2 is news to many of us. Can the secretary of state tell us why women were being used in such dangerous circumstances and how many of them, in total, have been used as agents in the field — and, as a result of Gestapo penetration, how many are missing?"

"Hear, hear!"

The minister of war was on his feet again.

"I am obliged to the member for Salford North," he said.

Parliamentary protocol always amused me. From the minister's tone of voice there was no love lost between him and the member for Salford North, but you would never be able to tell that from *Hansard,* the official report of proceedings in Parliament, when it was eventually published.

"Women have been used in SC2 since 1942 —"

"No!"

"Really?"

"Extraordinary!"

A ripple of excitement went around the House. This *was* news.

I was surprised. Had these politicians no idea about how the real world worked?

"Mr. Speaker. Mr. Speaker." Eden waited for the hubbub to die away. "Mr. Speaker, they are used for the simple reason that, in France, all men, all males between the ages of sixteen and fifty-five, must either work in war-related industries, or in the fighting forces on the enemy's side. They are forcibly sent by the Germans to Germany, again to work in war-related industries. It follows, therefore, that women find it easier to act as couriers, as wireless transmitters, even as sabotage agents. They don't stand out."

He looked directly at the member for Salford North.

"To answer the honourable member's specific point, Mr. Speaker, there are, at this moment, exactly thirty-seven women agents in SC2, three of whom have been killed and fourteen of whom are missing."

There was a silence in the chamber. The honourable members did not know how to digest this news.

"One other point, Mr. Speaker. I agree with

the member for Newcastle, Easington, that the penetration of SC2 by the Gestapo was a catastrophe, an unacceptable disaster. But I also reiterate that the situation was, to an extent, turned around. Thanks to the swift thinking of several senior people in the French section of SC2 command, some of our penetrated circuits were used, as I have said, to send false information to the Germans about where, exactly, the invasion would take place. We have evidence that, as a result of this misinformation, many German troops were kept in areas of France well away from Normandy — on the Atlantic coast, for instance — and were therefore not on hand to help repel our forces. To an extent, we managed to turn a catastrophe into partial victory."

Other members were getting restive, and he went quickly on.

"I conclude by saying this, Mr. Speaker. His Majesty's Government will not oppose the lifting of restrictions on the reporting of today's debate. I agree — the government agrees — we should stand ready to live with the bad news as well as the good, provided we don't *wallow* in the bad. But in this case the press should note the successes of SC2 as well as its failures. I do assure the House that, but for the misinformation we were able to feed the Gestapo over the past weeks, via those penetrated circuits, the Resistance by the Germans in and around the beaches of Normandy would have been far stiffer."

In the press gallery the reporters were preparing to leave. This was a rare day for them, with the fourteen-day rule lifted.

"So there need be no vote tonight, Mr. Speaker, but I have one other thing to add."

The reporters sat down again.

"I can report to the House that General Frank Grieves, the co-opted member of the war cabinet, who has had responsibility for SC2, is being relieved of his post. He is to be replaced by Lieutenant General Christopher Crichton, with immediate effect."

That night I did something I had never done before. I don't mean that I took a whisky to bed, along with all that day's newspapers, in an effort to catch up on the invasion news, and tire myself out in the process so that I could sleep. And I don't mean that I helped myself to another whisky, and several cigarettes, when sleep wouldn't come. I was still smoking too much.

I mean that I invited Zola on to the bed, in Madeleine's place, so that it didn't seem so empty.

He was missing her, too — I could tell. He made a show of sniffing the places where she used to leave her shoes, her bag, her wash things in the bathroom.

I lay on my back and rested my hand on

his fur, feeling the beat of his heart and hearing the sound of his breathing. He had never been allowed on the bed before and couldn't believe his luck.

From time to time, now, when I lit a cigarette, I took two out of my cigarette case without thinking. That had been my habit before she left, lighting two cigarettes at the same time. When I did that, and realised what I had done, my tonsils seemed to swell in my throat, I swallowed, and my stomach formed itself into a solid something.

The invasion news was good, up to a point. There was still fierce fighting inland from the beaches where the troops had landed, but when you looked at the map, the narrow strip of land which the Allies had captured was such a very small part of France and a good way — hundreds of miles — from where Madeleine was. Or had been when she had sent her last interrupted message.

I held the newspaper map in front of me and stroked Zola. What was happening in France away from the fighting? Understandably, perhaps, the papers had nothing to say about that. Had there been any uprisings among the French? Our own agents might have kept us informed, some of the time, but their job now — those who hadn't been compromised — was to help with sabotage, to keep as many German forces as possible from converging on Normandy.

From all that, I could conclude nothing about Madeleine's fate.

I put down the paper.

It had been several days now since we had heard from her. Other agents had reported in during that time, though by no means all. It began to seem that quite a few of them had been rounded up as news of the invasion spread. Maybe the Gestapo had been keeping them under surveillance, in case they revealed details of the invasion plans. But once our troops had landed, there had been no point in leaving them in place.

Had that happened to Madeleine? She had seemed to be doing so well, but perhaps she had been spotted days before and was discreetly followed. And then . . . ? Had she used her cyanide pill?

There is nothing worse than not knowing. On the other hand, no news is . . . not the worst news.

Zola turned his head and licked my hand.

I took my hand away.

I didn't feel like playing.

■ ■ ■ ■

AUGUST

■ ■ ■ ■

15

The window in my office was as ugly as a window could be. The glass panes were held in place by stark strips of flat metal welded together in oblongs. There were no curtains and just one pane, hinged at the top, which opened to let in air. It did, however, have a wide sill and that is where Zola found it comfortable to perch himself.

Since I had allowed him on to the bed at home, I had taken to bringing Zola into the office. No one seemed to mind — in fact, he quickly made friends with everyone — and I couldn't bring myself to leave him in Hamilton Place. We had still heard nothing from Madeleine, and it was now more than ten weeks since her interrupted message.

I had the Lagonda back after its kicking, but no will to use it and no petrol for it anyway. I'd persuaded my doctor to give me some sleeping pills and I was probably still drinking more whisky than was good for me. I wasn't going to pieces — nothing like that,

I'm not the type — but I missed Madeleine and feared for her. I spent as little time in the flat as possible. I went to the theatre or cinema most nights just to keep my mind off her. I had also bought her one or two pieces of jewellery to spoil her with if and when she reappeared, and to cheer myself up.

Madeleine had got the better of me in Scotland. She was able and a quick thinker. Maybe she had broken off in mid-message to escape and had contacted the ratline that ran down the Atlantic coast. Could that mean she was, even now, on her way back home? If so, she wouldn't be able to make contact and her journey would take time. That part of France was still under German control — that too could explain her silence.

But we were now well on into August. If she *had* found a ratline she should be home sometime very soon. And I couldn't get the thought of that suicide pill out of my mind.

I studied the progress of the invading forces with keen interest. The German retreat had at last begun. Having taken Caen and the Cherbourg peninsula, our forces had pressed south, past Rennes towards Nantes. For a short time they were very close to where Madeleine had been, but now, heading east, they were only sixty miles from Paris. Eisenhower had felt confident enough to transfer his headquarters from the south of England to France.

None of us had liked the flying bombs that had suddenly materialised over London, and the hurried evacuation of women and children that had followed. We had all relished the news of the attempt on Hitler's life. Maybe there would be other attempts before long, one of which would be more successful.

I had an added interest in the progress down the Atlantic coast, of course, but that was stalled for the moment while the push on Paris went ahead. We were still getting messages from circuits in the east of France that hadn't been penetrated, but the situation on the ground appeared chaotic at best. There were isolated pockets of German resistance — in Brest, for instance, the westernmost tip of the Brittany coast — that were cut off from other German forces. The Allies left the German outposts where they were, since they could do little damage and fighting them would have risked lives unnecessarily and held up the main thrust.

The Atlantic coast was simply not a priority any more.

In the wake of D-Day we were — thankfully — busier than ever in SC2. Our duties were now slightly different in that —

The door to my office opened and G. put her ahead around the edge.

"Meeting upstairs, *now*. And before you ask: I don't know what it's about. Shall I look after Zola?"

317

Hearing his name, he perked up.

"Come on," G. said, patting her thigh. He leapt down from the windowsill and followed her.

"Tart!" I said softly, smiling.

Upstairs, in the conference room, Hilary was already there, along with Christopher Crichton, his — our — new boss. The hand-over that had been announced in Parliament had only just occurred — the invasion had occupied every moment of everyone's time.

Penny was in the room already, together with all the other section heads.

Everyone sat down.

Crichton was a tall man with a long neck and long fingers, some of them stained brown from the cigarettes he smoked constantly. He lit one now and didn't offer them round. He was in uniform with a shiny Sam Browne leather belt cutting diagonally across his chest.

Arranging his cigarette packet and an ashtray neatly in front of him, he sniffed and tapped some ash from his cigarette into the ashtray.

"This morning I attended a war cabinet meeting," he said without preliminaries and looking around without smiling. "Bad news, I am afraid." He cleared his throat and looked at Hilary. "Following the debate — or should I say debacle — in the House of Commons the other week, Hilary here and I had worked

318

out a plan that was designed to do two things. It was decided, firstly, that someone from here — someone senior — should go to France, find out about everything that has happened to our agents, and if possible discover one or more of them alive, and so go some way towards rescuing SC2's reputation."

He looked at me.

"You, Matt. It was you we were going to send."

This was news. It had crossed my mind, after the fiasco of the Gestapo's penetration of SC2 had been revealed, that I might be dismissed, and maybe Hilary too. We had played some part in reversing the setback but . . . the army is a curious animal and you never could predict quite what would happen, who would take the rap.

I returned Crichton's gaze.

"But not now?"

He nodded, finishing his cigarette.

"No. It turns out that we have as many opponents among our Allies as among our enemies. MI6 say they have had enough of our antics and 'games,' as they put it, and, as the older, more established service, they have petitioned the cabinet to support their view that they have enough experienced people on the ground in France to do what we were going to do. And, they say, they are more used to operating undercover than we are —"

As I went to interrupt, he waved me down. "*And,* in addition to them, the foreign secretary said that he had been approached by de Gaulle's people — de Gaulle in person, I should say — more or less demanding that SC2 be banned from France. De Gaulle is about to move to France himself and he has his own agenda, as you know. But in this case, what with MI6 making the fuss they are making, the French argument fell on fertile ground." He grunted. "Ground is the right word, I'm afraid. We've been grounded."

"But . . . but . . ." I stumbled. "Are we just going to leave our agents to their own devices, make no attempt to rescue them, or even find out what happened to them? What will Parliament make of *that*?"

"You're not listening, Matt," said Hilary briskly from across the table. "*We* are not going looking, but MI6 *is.*"

"You really think that's going to happen?" I cried. "They don't know our people, they have no idea how they behave or operate, how they think. It . . . it's madness!"

Crichton fixed me with a look. "All of what you say is true, Matt, or true enough . . . but it's beside the point." He sighed. "Since D-Day the war has moved on. Remember that speech of Churchill's, in November forty-two, about the battle in North Africa not being the beginning of the end, but the end of the beginning?"

He didn't wait for the answer.

"D-Day was the beginning of the end, and people — people everywhere but especially in Whitehall — are starting to think about life after the war, and are positioning themselves accordingly. What this manoeuvre of MI6 is all about is controlling the memory of the war, so that when the story comes to be told, MI6 wears all the haloes and SC2 is remembered as . . . well, as the ugly also-ran."

He took out a handkerchief and wiped his lips with it.

"I am afraid I didn't see it coming. I'm too new in this job; I was too busy familiarizing myself with the details here, to play politics. MI6 took advantage of that, to come up with this flanker. That's how cabinet works, sometimes."

He half turned to Penny but still addressed the table, "Don't put this in the minutes, but SC2 has been well and truly fucked."

St. George's church in Whitfield Street looked very pretty. There were so many flowers they almost obscured the altar, flowers being one of the few things that weren't rationed. Sunshine sliced in through the stained-glass window of the south transept, throwing bright red and purple patches on to the stone floor. The stained glass reminded me of Madeleine, the way she stood out, whatever the company. The organ was playing softly a tune I didn't recognise, though it sounded like Bach.

I had a good seat, about three pews back, on the groom's side. Alistair Prior was already in his place, in what looked like a brand-new light grey suit — not a completely perfect fit but then a lot of tailors were fighting in France. He had a large white carnation with green trimmings in his buttonhole. He waved to me as I sat down.

The timing had worked out well for him. We were now at D-Day plus two and a half months. Being pregnant had not suited Viv, so Alistair had told me; she had been ill for a few weeks early on and the wedding had been postponed twice.

But here we all were at last, minutes away from their tying the knot. I was pleased for them, of course, but Alistair's marriage brought home my anxiety for Madeleine.

The music changed, increasing in tempo. Guests were now streaming in. Although I was in a pew near the front, I was seated at the end of the row, away from the main aisle, so I felt fairly safe in taking out my newspaper, to kill time. In any case there was news that I wanted to reread. I opened my copy of *The Times* to page 4, where the war news was concentrated.

A second invasion, in the south of France, between Marseilles and Nice, had begun a few days before. I wanted to check on progress. And Toulouse had been liberated by partisans, with other risings taking place in the Massif Central.

"That news is several days old, you know."

I looked up and to my left.

A small, pudgy man had sat down next to me. He was wearing a sports jacket, with a multicoloured sweater under it, a dark blue shirt, and corduroy trousers, dark green. He didn't look as though he had changed for the wedding.

Seeing me eyeing his clothes, he said, "I came straight from the office — I work with Alistair at the BBC and I'm on shift. I could get away only at the last minute."

I nodded.

He went on. "I recognise you — you're Mystic Matt, right?" He smiled.

"Guilty."

He held out his hand. "Martin Vallois. I work in the French news section of the Beeb."

We shook hands.

I tapped the paper. "I suppose it takes correspondents a little while to find a phone, to phone their copy through."

He nodded. "Yes, transmitters are too bulky to carry around. And in any case, it's not always clear what is happening." He pointed to the paper. "Even partisans exaggerate. Toulouse isn't completely taken yet, not from what I hear."

"What else do you hear that's not in the

papers yet?"

The organ music changed again.

The bride's mother arrived. She kissed Alistair and sat down.

"The Germans are withdrawing east, mainly via Dijon, before our troops in the north meet up with our troops from the south and cut them off. And there are three pockets of strong resistance on the coast —"

"You mean the Atlantic coast?"

He nodded. "The Germans had — still have — three U-boat bases, at Brest, St. Nazaire, and La Pallice, that's near La Rochelle. They are holding out at all three places. The Allies can't get in and the Germans can't get out. They may still be planning a U-boat offensive."

Just then, the organ music changed again, and everyone stood up.

The bride had arrived.

Vivien came into view, resplendent in her white dress, its train held up by two page boys in powder-green.

I felt a slight twinge as I saw her draw level with Alistair. The music had faded, the vicar was speaking, welcoming us and inviting us to witness Vivien and Alistair's joining in holy matrimony.

Then we were launched into the first hymn. I joined in absently.

In the normal course of things, I enjoyed a good singsong but not just then. What Martin Vallois had told me occupied my mind.

It was now getting on for thirteen weeks since Madeleine had been heard from — I was obsessive about that sort of detail. It wasn't quite out of the question for her still to turn up, but Vallois had raised a new possibility.

When she had last been heard from, she was near St. Nazaire. What if she had been captured by Germans and held there, only for St. Nazaire to be cut off, isolated by the Allies? If that had happened, she couldn't have been taken back to Germany to be executed. The small garrison of Germans in St. Nazaire might be keeping her alive, as part of the bargaining that would surely take place later in the war, when they would have to surrender.

Or was that wishful thinking? It was improbable but . . .

When I had entered the church my hopes for Madeleine had been fading. Indeed, I had been planning to pray for her during the service. But now, all of a sudden, and thanks to Martin Vallois, I had new cause for optimism. It was a long shot, but it was something, though at the same time it unsettled me. Was I doing enough for Madeleine? Was it enough just to sit in London behind a desk?

The service ended and we all straggled slowly out of the church, held up by the bridal party, which was keen to pose for photos. When I eventually reached the top step, outside the main door, and was looking down on Alistair and Viv, both of them covered in a dusting of confetti, I suddenly noticed G. on the edge of the pavement. Odd. What was she doing here? She didn't know either the bride or the groom, so far as I was aware.

As I thought this, she saw me, her face lit up, and she beckoned me towards her. There was an urgency in her manner. I fought my way through the crush and crossed to where she was standing.

"G.! What — ?"

"Am I glad I found you! I thought you might have taken the rest of the afternoon off."

"Why? You know better than that —"

"Message from Hilary. You are wanted at Number Ten at eight o'clock tomorrow morning."

"Number Ten? You mean — ?"

"Yes, of course that's what I bloody well mean. Eight o'clock sharp, that's what Hilary said. Downing Street."

16

I had only been in Downing Street once before this and my second visit was a very brief one. As I arrived, at two minutes to eight o'clock on the following morning, the door miraculously opened to let me in. In the hall was Hilary standing next to a man with one arm, the sleeve of his naval jacket pinned back more or less to where his elbow should have been.

"Good, good," said Hilary quietly, in that way of his. "Bang on time, Matt, excellent." He was in his usual three-piece tweed suit, striped tie, and shiny beer-brown brogues.

He turned to the man beside him and said, "Okay, we can go. Lead the way." He turned to me, smiling, and said, "Frank here lost his arm at Dunkirk. But all the rest of him is in full working order."

Frank stepped forward, the main door was opened, and out we went, back into Downing Street. The morning was sunny and fresh.

We turned right and headed west, down a

flight of stone steps at the St. James's Park end of the street, and Hilary slowed his stride so that I drew level. "The PM's in his war office, the bunker below ground. Ever been?"

"No. I didn't know there *was* a bunker. Where is it?"

"You'll see. Not far. It's reassuring in its way, but it's not that deep. I'm not sure it would survive a direct hit."

At the foot of the steps we turned left, along the edge of the park until we came to King Charles Street, running between what I did know was the Home Office building, and the building housing both the Foreign Office and the Treasury. That street also ended in a flight of steps.

"Do these steps have a name?"

"Buggered if I know," growled Hilary.

"King Charles Steps, sir," said Frank. "Here we are."

I suddenly saw what he meant. Set into the wall at the foot of the Foreign Office building was a small door. It was a sooty black, hardly different from the dirty stones with which the Foreign Office walls were faced. There were no markings, and it was wholly inconspicuous.

Like the Downing Street door, it opened as we approached — seemingly all by itself — and we went straight in. A woman with raven-black hair immediately closed and locked it behind us.

We showed her our passes.

"Sign in, please," she said, scrutinising each one carefully. "You are expected."

To Frank, she said, "Take them down to conference room E, that's —"

"I remember," said Frank. "Third on the right round the bend — am I right?"

"Show-off!" she murmured, but she was smiling.

We descended some stairs. Not many, maybe fifteen; so we weren't all that deep. Hilary was right — this bunker would not survive a direct hit.

At the foot of the stairs we turned left. The bunker, I noticed, was built of large breeze blocks, painted over in that universal wartime khaki-green colour. Someone must have made a fortune out of that grey-green paint.

Frank led the way.

The bunker was busy. People were coming towards us, secretarial types, men in uniforms with lots of medals and/or gold braid, including younger men who must have had some special skill — like languages — to save them from being at the front. Off to our right we passed a variety of small rooms, teleprinters coughing out scrolls of paper, people hunched over what had to be coded messages, deciphering one after the other. We passed a cramped bedroom with a narrow single bed; on the open door were the two letters: "PM."

At the end of the corridor we turned left

into a wider passageway. Along its ceiling was a huge, square metal tube running its length and painted matt black. It must have carried air either into or out of the bunker. I was already beginning to feel the heat of being down there.

At last we turned in to a room set with tables and chairs. The walls were made of the same breeze blocks, painted the same grey-green as everywhere else. There were no windows, of course, and no pictures; just a grille where, presumably, the fresh air was led into the room from the great black metal tube in the corridor.

"Take a seat, gents, I'll tell them you've arrived," Frank said, and went out.

"Can we smoke in here?" I whispered to Hilary.

"I don't know. I shouldn't think so. I wouldn't risk it. Don't want to get off on the wrong foot."

"What wrong foot? What's going on, Hilary? There hasn't been time to ask."

He shook his head. "I don't know. All I know is that yesterday afternoon I got a phone call telling me to be at Downing Street at eight this morning, and to bring you with me, without fail. That's all — I was told nothing more. Then, when I got to Number Ten, about three minutes before you did, I was told we were coming on here. And that's all — aha!"

He broke off as two men filled the doorway. One was tall and thin, with silver-grey hair. The other wasn't quite so tall, but was still bulkily built, with a cigar wedged in his mouth.

I leapt to my feet and so did Hilary.

The bulky man was Winston Churchill himself.

He stepped forward and held out his hand.

The PM took the cigar from his mouth.

"Sorry to drag you down into this hellhole but it's a busy day today." He put his hand on the shoulder of the man standing next to him. "Colonel Hathaway will explain what all the cloak-and-dagger is about but I wanted to meet you and to ask you one question."

I looked at him.

He waved his cigar. "You have only one lung but you go on smoking. No problems?"

"Not so far, sir," I said.

"In that case, do you want one of these?" He fished in his jacket pocket and took out a cigar.

"Well, I . . ."

"Go on, take it. For good luck in France." He chuckled.

"France?" I said.

"Hathaway will reveal all," he countered, still smiling and preparing to leave. "Hilary, you come with me, will you?"

The prime minister gave me a small nod and led Hilary out into the corridor, closing the door firmly behind him. I could see that Frank was stationed right outside.

The thin, silver-haired man held out his hand and as I shook it, he said, "Rupert Hathaway. I'm the PM's 'fixer,' his *consigliere,* as the Mafia say." He grinned.

He sat down on one of the upright chairs and put a manila folder on the table. I could see that stencilled across it were the words TOP SECRET.

He nodded to the cigar. "Quite a memento, eh? I don't have one and I have *two* lungs." He smiled. "Right. Down to business and my first task is to remind you that you've signed the Official Secrets Act. Whatever comes out of this meeting, what went on here can never be revealed. I mean that. Am I coming over crystal clear?"

"Yes, yes, of course."

He unbuttoned his jacket, crossed his legs, and sat back. "Good. In a minute I am going to tell you one of the biggest secrets of the war but first some background. The PM — he won't mind me saying this behind his back — is a bit of a cowboy. He likes daring, innovative schemes, and some of the things SC2 have done have caught his imagination. He also likes people who have 'the nous' — his words — to turn adversity into an opportunity. So he was impressed by your scheme — when you found out that some of the SC2 circuits had been penetrated — to feed the Germans false information about D-Day. He thought that showed his kind of 'low cunning' — his words again.

"Then there was all that hoo-ha in Parliament about SC2 using women agents, followed by MI6 moving in and taking over."

I made a face but said nothing.

"The PM wasn't too happy about that himself — after all, he authorised the use of women as agents in the first place and he still can't see what's wrong with it. But he didn't want our agencies squabbling at such an important time of the war, with the invasion just beginning, and he had his mind on that, so he let it ride.

"Now, however, the situation has changed, something has cropped up, something we must put a stop to. We think you are the man for the job. It means going to France. Immediately, I mean — sooner than that, in fact. Just as soon as we can set up your cover."

I still said nothing. But Madeleine flashed into my mind.

"One general question before I go on. Do you know much about science, physics in particular?"

I shook my head. "I understand electricity well enough, and magnetism, osmosis, all that kind of thing, and I've heard about electrons and neutrons and Albert Einstein and Arnold Rutherford, but that's about it —"

"Ernest Rutherford," he said. "Ernest. Not

Arnold."

"There you are," I said. "That's how much I know."

He nodded. "You know more than most. It probably won't matter. Now, let's get down to it." He cleared his throat. "The nasty part.

"The war will go on for several months yet, maybe longer, maybe longer in the Pacific than here in Europe. We, on our side, are pretty sure of winning now, but nothing is certain and we want to conserve as many lives as we can. And we can't yet be sure what shape the peace will take. All these factors come into what I am about to tell you — the greatest secret, I can't stress that enough.

"For several months now, in the New Mexico desert, in the United States, Allied scientists — American, British, Canadian, Danish, and one Frenchman — have been working together on a new kind of bomb. It's called an atomic bomb, and it works — if it does work, it hasn't been tested yet — it works by splitting an atom of radioactive uranium, releasing untold amounts of energy. These split other atoms in a geometric progression, a larger and ever more powerful chain reaction. So much energy is released, I am told, that one bomb — one single bomb, one explosion — can destroy an entire city, killing tens of thousands of people and mortally wounding as many again from radioactive burns that still kill but more slowly, causing cancers and other diseases."

He looked at me. There was total silence all around.

"We are, of course, hoping that we do not have to use this bomb, we are hoping that when we tell the Germans or the Japanese that we *have* this weapon — that they will see sense, avoid needless killing, and surrender. But we can't be sure.

"That's the basic scenario. Here's where you come in. As I said, one of the scientists in New Mexico is French. He has a particular speciality, which I won't go into, since you don't need to know and it will only confuse matters, but his role in the project, while vital, is now coming to an end. Since the invasion has started and parts of France are now liberated, he — quite naturally — wants to return home as soon as he can and to join in the fighting. He wants to see some action at home."

He uncrossed and recrossed his legs.

"Here's the difficulty. This man — his name is Daniel Legros — is well-known among his fellow French physicists, and is especially close to one man — François Perrault — whose name you may know. Have you heard of *him*?"

I shook my head. "Sorry."

"It doesn't matter — in fact, it might even help, given what I'm about to say. What you do need to know is that, just before the war, when he was professor of physics at Belfort University, in the east of France, Perrault won the Nobel Prize for physics. He is a brilliant man, and was the first person to demonstrate the rate at which uranium decays. You don't need to know what that means either."

Hathaway rubbed his chin.

"Legros was able to take part in the New Mexico business — it's called the Manhattan Project, in case you ever hear it referred to, though even that name of course is top secret — he could take part in the project because, when France fell in 1940, he happened to be at the Cavendish Laboratory in Cambridge here in Britain, and so he simply stayed. Perrault, however, was in France. And that's what makes this so awkward. He was in France and he was very brave. He abandoned his laboratory work at Belfort immediately and went underground, helping to organise the Resistance. He has been very successful, has never been caught, has helped with a lot of sabotage, and is a specialist in intelligence and communications. He is now in Paris as one of the ex-leader-heroes of the Resistance. He may go into politics when the war is over."

He leaned forward and put the palms of his hands on the table.

"Now we get to the real meat, the killer fact." He fiddled with a gold ring on his little finger. "François Perrault is a communist, a very fervent, dedicated communist. In the

1930s he visited the Soviet Union several times and made many contacts there, and some close friends.

"Step back again. It's already clear that Stalin and his generals will almost certainly meet our forces somewhere in Germany. After the war, then, even if we win, Europe is going to be divided — into American- or British-style democracies, in the western part, and Soviet-ruled communist countries in the east. This will be the new reality, the new division, the new shape of Europe, after the war. Obviously, it won't be a stable situation — although the war will be over, rivalries, possibly very deadly rivalries, will almost certainly continue. Hitler will be out of the way, we hope, in some jail somewhere, if he doesn't get killed or kill himself, but we'll still have Stalin to contend with, and he is just as murderous as Hitler, maybe even more so. You'll be aware of all these stories coming out about Stalin's so-called purges — thousands of people killed in Russia because their faces didn't fit?"

I nodded.

"The logic of the situation, therefore, is that Stalin must not learn about the Manhattan Project. He must not know about the bomb until we are so far ahead, until we have built so many of these bombs, that he will never be able to catch up and will have to do as he is told."

He opened the file in front of him and took out two photographs.

"It is a foregone conclusion that when Legros" — and he placed a finger on one of the photographs — "gets to Paris, the first thing he will do is tell what he knows to Perrault." He pointed to the other photograph. "And, before long, Perrault, with his sympathies, will tell the Russians. That must not happen." Hathaway looked at me directly. "I'll repeat what I said: That. Must. Not. Happen. Legros or Perrault, or both, must be killed before they meet."

He turned the photographs round and pushed them across the table until they were right in front of me.

"It's not a pretty situation, I can't disguise that. Both men are French, our allies. Neither has done anything wrong — in fact, Legros has worked hard on the weapon that may win the war at the very end. Perrault is a Resistance hero, a Nobel Prize winner. But . . . but circumstances have changed. We can't afford to take any risks."

"Can't he be . . . Can't Legros be dealt with while he's in America? Wouldn't that be easier, less messy?"

"I was coming to that. And the answer is yes. We're trying. Or we shall be trying soon — this plan has only just got the go-ahead. But it's not the sort of thing we want coming out after the war is over, and in any case killing Legros is easier said than done — because we have to make it look like an accident and the New Mexico outfit, the Manhattan Project, is so close-knit that we can't approach someone *inside* the compound. Because if we do and we approach the *wrong* person, and they refuse, they might well tell Legros. Then the whole plan would be scuppered. Once he leaves the compound, he will almost certainly go straight to a port or an airport and there'll be precious little chance to make something look like an accident at the last moment.

"We can't have him arrested in America, because the French authorities there don't know about the Manhattan Project and if they made a fuss that would draw attention to his presence in North America. We don't want that, in case it alerts the Russians. If Legros were angered by his arrest, he might even divulge something about the Manhattan Project itself.

"We're still going to try to kill him in America, or aboard the liner he sails on, but we need you in France, standing by, as backup. In a way it's fortunate from our point of view that there was such a fuss over those women agents, and that MI6 stuck its oar into SC2's affairs. We'll be able to announce that the PM has intervened, that MI6 is back in its box, and that you have been selected to go to France to seek out what agents you can, women in particular. It's good cover.

"We'll brief the press that you are an SC2 hero, with a Military Cross, but also with only one lung, the result of a war injury. That will create sympathy for a hero, who is only engaged in a mopping-up activity, nothing 'aggressive,' so to speak. It will square it with de Gaulle's people, too."

He played again with the ring on his little finger.

"I also gather you have a special interest in one particular agent . . ." He tailed off.

I remained silent.

"So, until we contact you, to tell you either that Legros met with an accident in America, or that he did *not* meet with an accident, you are free to pursue both SC2 projects — doing your best to discover the fate of all the agents, and that of your own more personal interest. But then, if we fail with Legros and he makes it to France, it's all down to you. By then you must have located Perrault and prepared a plan, or you will have found out where Legros is expected to surface. Legros will be harder to locate and kill than Perrault, because he'll be on the move, but his death won't arouse as much attention. You'll find it easier to escape if you kill Legros than if you kill Perrault. In either case you must make it look like an accident, so there's no damage to our relations with the French.

"That's it."

When I didn't say anything for a time, he

went on: "I understand you have killed three people. Is that correct?"

I nodded.

"May I ask how you killed them?"

"Two I shot, the other I garrotted."

He raised one eyebrow.

"I'm impressed." He nodded to himself. "So . . . how can I say this . . . killing, killing at close range, is not a problem for you?"

"I . . . I had thought — hoped — I'd seen the back of it. They were desperate times."

"I hope I've shown that we're *still* in desperate times."

I breathed out heavily. "But there's something . . . almost *theoretical* about all this, isn't there? You can't be certain that Legros will tell Perrault or that Perrault will tell the Russians. Maybe Legros is an anticommunist."

"Maybe. But we can't take that risk. We understand that several of the physicists in the Manhattan Project think the information should be shared with the Russians. One of them travelled all the way to Downing Street to bend Winston's ear. The PM told him to stop interfering!"

He shook his head. "No, both Legros and Perrault are scientists, and long-standing colleagues. When they meet, they are bound to talk physics, uranium, plutonium, atomic bombs. Our calculation is that the great secret will change hands. A lot of wartime

341

activity is about calculation — you know that."

It's not every day you are asked to kill someone, still less an ally. Until then, I hadn't really looked beyond the end of the war, but if what Hathaway said was right, the end of war was only the beginning of something else, almost as bad.

Quite apart from that, could Hathaway be trusted? Was the Manhattan Project for real? Was there some other reason — too secret for me to be let in on — for Perrault's assassination? Was I being roped into something that I would regret?

But if I couldn't trust the prime minister, who *could* I trust?

And at the same time, it would mean I could go to France, and that was where Madeleine was, alive or dead.

All of a sudden my insides had settled. I was more comfortable in my skin. I was going to be *doing* something at last.

"And if I get caught?"

"You know the answer to that, too. You are on your own. It was a personal vendetta, as a result of what happened earlier in the war. You went beyond your remit, your girlfriend or wife was killed in France, perhaps by the Resistance — we'll work something out. The real reason cannot surface. We'll give you written authority, signed by the PM, to say you are looking for agents. That will give you access everywhere, and be one hell of a memento after the war."

"If I say no?"

He nodded again. "I would understand. But I — we — calculate you won't say no. Someone you love is missing. You hate sitting here, being unable to go looking. This is your chance. We are offering you a deal, a quid pro quo. A momentous job in the war, the opportunity to have an important effect on the post-war world, and a chance to settle something personal. If you agree, you won't hear from us again until the Legros mission in the United States or aboard ship either succeeds or it fails. You will receive an anonymous secret telegram saying either that 'the wedding has been called off,' or else 'the wedding goes ahead.' "

He didn't say anything else for a moment. Then, "What's it to be?"

I remembered asking Madeleine much the same question at her interview for SC2 in The Farm. In war, all the important decisions have to be taken quickly.

I rolled the PM's cigar near my ear, then under my nose.

"I'll take this with me," I said, holding it up before slipping it into my pocket. "If I succeed with Legros or Perrault, I'll send you a brief message: 'Havana smoking.' How's that?"

"I think it's melodramatic." He paused. "The PM will *love* it."

17

I had never seen so much shingle. There was more shingle in Blakeney than there was sand in Ardlossan. It rode high out of the water, a grey-yellow North Sea, and disappeared east and west as if it would go on for ever. This was not a romantic seascape — far from it. It was much too bleak to be romantic.

I didn't know Blakeney and I didn't know north Norfolk or East Anglia. And I doubted I would be coming back any time soon. I had twenty-four hours before I left for France, just enough for a swift dash to see Madeleine's mother, in case she could tell me anything about her daughter that I didn't know and might help find her. It was a long time since we'd had word from Oak and a mother's inside knowledge might make all the difference.

The train from King's Cross had stopped an interminable number of times — Hitchin, Baldock, Cambridge, Ely, Downham Market, and all the rest — arriving at King's Lynn more than three hours after its whistles and steam had seen us off. I used Mr. Churchill's letter for the first time to get me inside the coastal exclusion zone. It worked perfectly.

I had found Madeleine's mother's cottage easily enough. The taxi that I shared with another rail passenger belonged to a firm, the King's Men, with a small office in the harbour town. We had stopped there and simply asked if they knew where Mrs. Dirac lived. They did.

The only problem: she wasn't in. I hadn't been able to alert her to my arrival: I knew from Madeleine that she didn't have a phone and letters to and from Blakeney would have taken too much time. I had been waiting now for more than two hours and it was coming up for three o'clock. The last train back to London left King's Lynn at 7:13 but I had made a reservation at the Blakeney pub, the Three Crowns, in case I had to stay the night.

I was sitting now on a small wooden bench on the harbour jetty, watching the fishermen coming in. Most of them already had their catch packed up in long, thin fish boxes by the time they arrived home and simply winched the boxes ashore. The fish would be down in London by midnight, where they would land a pretty penny. The fishermen would have made even better money in wartime but for the fact that they couldn't go too far out to sea because of the threat of enemy submarines.

Across the jetty was a small, green-painted caravan with a flap in one side, selling tea and cakes and sandwiches, and I thought a mug of tea would not go amiss. The wind wasn't letting up.

I got to my feet and started across the jetty. Another fishing smack was chugging down the small channel-amid-mudflats that Blakeney was at low tide. As I did so, I noticed another taxi coming down the gentle hill of the High Street. It pulled round and stopped outside the white-painted cottage that I knew belonged to Mrs. Dirac.

I watched as the solitary figure in the back seat leaned forward, presumably to pay, and the figure waited, presumably for change or a receipt. Then the driver's door opened and the taxi man went round to the back of the car, taking out what looked like a large briefcase. A small woman got out of the rear passenger door. It was not obvious, at that distance, that this was Madeleine's mother. Their physical resemblance was slight to non-existent: different hair colour, a different build — Victoria Dirac was chunkier than her daughter — and she had a different way of moving. The taxi man handed her the briefcase, closed the boot of the car, and returned to the driver's seat. Mrs. Dirac took a key from her handbag, waved the taxi driver goodbye, and let herself into her cottage.

I decided to have some tea anyway. I wouldn't like it if, the minute I got home after a trip, someone knocked on the door. We might well get off on the wrong foot.

So I bought a tea and a digestive biscuit, and went back to my bench, keeping an eye on the cottage in case Mrs. D. decided to go out again straightaway.

After about a quarter of an hour I crossed the jetty and knocked on her door.

There was a short delay, and then she opened it. Unlike Madeleine, she had dark hair, cut short, vivid blue eyes. She was wearing a tweed skirt with a cream silk shirt. She looked very smart and businesslike, very composed.

"Yes?" she said.

"Mrs. Dirac, I'm Matthew Hammond, Matt Hammond — does that name mean anything to you?"

She looked puzzled for a moment, but then her face broke into a smile, followed by a frown. "Yes, yes, it took me a moment — not expecting . . . You haven't got bad news, have you?"

"No, no!" I said quickly. "No, that's not why I'm here."

She closed her eyes and covered them with her fingers. Dropping her hand and opening her eyes, she said, "Thank the Lord for that. I thought . . . You know what I thought."

I nodded. "Of course. It's natural. I'm sorry

if I startled you."

"If you don't have bad news, do you have *good* news? Have you come all this way from London specially?"

"Might we go inside, Mrs. Dirac? Somewhere we can sit and talk."

"Yes, of course. Silly of me. Please come in."

The front door opened directly into the living room, which was pleasant enough, with airy windows, two sofas, a wireless, a big mirror on one wall, and a fireplace with several photographs of Madeleine, her mother, an older man whom I took to be her father, and a younger man about whom I didn't want to think too much right now. A small pile of what looked like sheet music was stacked on an upright piano.

Hearing us, a dog came through from another room — a spaniel. He, or she, came up to me and sniffed my trousers.

"Wellington!" said Mrs. Dirac. "Behave!"

She looked at me and smiled. "Don't mind him. He has a general's name but he's harmless."

I stroked the dog and he jumped up on to a sofa.

I sat down next to him and Mrs. Dirac sat in a cane chair opposite me.

"May I offer you something? I'm forgetting my manners — I've only just got in after a day at a client's house in Cromer. I make and fit curtains — that's what I was doing all day. Have you been waiting long?"

"It doesn't matter at all how long I've been waiting, but I'm glad we're here now. And I don't need anything except your permission to smoke."

"Yes, let's have a cigarette?" she replied. "Have you got enough for me?"

I took out my cigarette case and opened it. She reached forward.

As she took a cigarette I said, "Madeleine gave me this."

She let me light her cigarette before saying, "So you are more than her boss?"

"She didn't tell you?"

She shook her head.

I paused for a moment. I wasn't sure what to make of what she had just said. And I couldn't make out her mood. Was she anxious that I was there? She seemed calm.

"The reason I am here, Mrs. Dirac, is that — and I don't want you to be unduly alarmed — is that we haven't heard from Madeleine since a couple of days after the invasion in June —"

She looked up sharply, holding her tongue between her lips. It was an expression that still gave nothing away.

"The last we heard was when she broke off in the middle of a transmission. It's obviously not the best news we could have, but it may not mean the worst, not by any means. If we, in the office, in the government, felt that, I wouldn't be here."

She rearranged some books on the low wooden table between us. She looked straight at me. Her gaze was steady. "Go on."

"Madeleine was scheduled to make contact with a local Resistance circuit in a certain part of France. At least — she was if she felt that circuit was safe. Some of our circuits, as you may have read, were penetrated by the Germans.

"If she *did* contact the circuit and made a mistake . . . if she judged the circuit hadn't been penetrated when in fact it had . . . then most likely she would have been captured. However, if she decided the circuit *wasn't* safe, then she had two choices. She could either remain in France, until the Germans eventually started to withdraw, then join the Resistance in a rebellion, *or* she could make contact with one of the ratlines — the escape routes — and eventually be ferried safely home. Moving along a ratline can take anything up to three or four months depending on the exact route and the German presence in the areas which the lines pass through. And that's provided she didn't get injured, or ill. Once you are in a ratline there is no communication, because communication is a weak point and we need the ratlines very badly."

She nodded. "It's been close to three

351

months now since D-Day. And didn't I read that the Germans have begun their withdrawal?"

"Yes, but we haven't given up hope. And Madeleine is not the only one who hasn't been in touch — thirteen others are missing." I didn't intend to mention that all our agents were equipped with suicide pills.

She closed her eyes again, and then opened them. I still couldn't read her mood. She *must* be anxious but . . . maybe she could sit on her feelings.

"What is it you want from me?"

"I want you to tell me about Madeleine and her time in France. What were her habits? In the chaos of invasion, what might she have done, where might she have gone? If she was injured, how would she have reacted? If you were me, and had to go looking for her, where would you look, where would you start?"

She leaned forward, crushed out the remains of her cigarette in the ashtray, and stood up.

"I think this calls for a drink, yes? Whisky suit you?"

I nodded. "Perfect."

"I'll put Wellington in the garden. Then we can concentrate."

She picked up the dog and went through into another room. I heard a door open and close as she let the spaniel outside. Then there was the sound of a tap running. Did she find comfort in action? She came back with a tray, a cut-glass decanter of whisky, two glasses, and a jug of water.

She sat down again and poured the whiskies.

"Water?"

"Yes, please. About half and half."

We raised our glasses to one another and for a moment enjoyed what the whisky had to offer.

"I can think of two things, Colonel Hammond; two places she might go, if she got the chance. One is the Convent of St. Hilaire in the northern part of the Limoges region. Madeleine was never going to be a nun, but she went to school there, and she loved it and made some good friends. Some of them *will* have become nuns, and Madeleine would know she would receive sanctuary there and they would hide her if it were necessary. She mentioned it to me."

She sipped her whisky and a thought struck her. "How did she move around? Did she have a car?"

I shook my head. "A bicycle."

"And where was she dropped — I take it she *was* parachuted in?"

"Yes," I said, "but I am not allowed to tell you where."

She just looked at me, tapping her teeth with her whisky glass.

"Le Gâvre," I whispered. "Now forget it, please."

Ever so slightly, she smiled. "That's not *so* far from St. Hilaire. Bicyclable in a day or two, I should say."

"You said two things."

She nodded.

"Did she tell you about her marriage?"

"To Philippe, you mean? Yes, she did. I found it a weird story — I couldn't quite believe it, but I understand he was killed, carrying out Resistance work."

"Yes, he was. It was tragic but I am sure Madeleine, happy as she might be with you, might want to visit his family home, his grave even — if there is one."

She pulled at the sleeves of her shirt.

"Madeleine was eighteen when she fell in love with Philippe. It was her first time and she was eighteen. You're never . . . In my experience one is never quite in love again like you are the first time, in your teenage years, when you are so innocent. Madeleine has what you might call 'unfinished business' over Philippe, so she may well have risked a lot to go and wind it up."

"She had the rest of her life to wind it up."

Mrs. Dirac shrugged. "Yes, of course. But that's not how people think, is it? She was *there,* or near there. That's all it would have taken. Believe me, I know my daughter."

I let a long silence go by, sipping my whisky.

I wasn't sure I bought all of what Mrs. Dirac said. The Madeleine I knew was anything but sentimental, and from what she'd told me, her affair and marriage to Philippe had damped down as quickly as it had caught fire.

But I couldn't afford to ignore her advice. I couldn't remember exactly where Madeleine had met Philippe — I mean the town from where they explored the caves and where they got married. But I did remember it was on the west side of France, south from Le Gâvre and St. Nazaire. I suppose she might just have thought it worthwhile to return to that part of her past, as her mother said. It was something to bear in mind.

I drained my whisky glass and looked at my watch. It wasn't yet five thirty.

"If I walk round to the taxi office, how likely am I to get someone to take me to King's Lynn?"

She pressed her lips together. "I can't say, but it's a short walk to the office. What time is your train?"

"The last one's at seven thirteen."

"You should do it easily, but if you can't get a taxi you can stay here if you wish."

"Thank you. But I took the precaution of booking a room at the pub. I couldn't be certain when you would be home."

She nodded. "Well, let's walk to the taxi office together. They know me so they might put themselves out when they wouldn't for a stranger. It was Jeannie Slater from the taxi firm who rang Madeleine to say I was ill on the day we were supposed to have lunch."

As it happened, there was no problem getting a taxi, and I made the train at King's Lynn easily enough.

As I was preparing to leave Mrs. Dirac's front room, I admired the photographs on her mantelpiece.

"Was Madeleine a tomboy? She looks like one."

"Oh yes. She could run faster than most boys her age, she was quite a clever fighter, and she was even admitted to a boys' gang." She smiled. "That was unheard of where we lived."

I buttoned up my coat. I could tell from the noise whistling down the chimney that the wind was as strong as ever. "And she gets on famously with dogs, too." I told Mrs. D. about the love affair between Madeleine and Zola.

"That's my daughter," she said as I finished. "She had a dog of her own after we moved here from France, but it drowned when it got swept out to sea in a storm."

"And who's that?" I said as nonchalantly as I could, nodding at the photo on the mantelpiece.

"Philippe, of course."

When I said nothing, she went on, "I didn't really know him, their relationship was so short, but he *was* my son-in-law and a French Resistance hero. And he nearly gave me a grandchild."

I looked at her sharply. "Nearly?"

She nodded. "Didn't Madeleine tell you? When she came home from France with me, after our few days in Louzac, and after their secret marriage, she was pregnant —"

"What!"

"Yes. And when her dog was swept overboard, she jumped in, to try to save it. But she couldn't . . . and on top of everything, in the exertion she lost the baby."

I didn't know what to say.

Then I did. "She told me about Rolfe, her German shepherd who howled at the moon. That was in Louzac, right?"

She nodded. "He had to be put down. But we got another when we came here."

Again, I didn't know what to say. This was all news to me.

"I'm not sure I should have told you," Mrs. Dirac said. "She never talked about it herself. When Philippe was smuggled to England in 1940 they spent a day or so together in Dover —"

"Yes, she told me that."

Mrs. Dirac took her house keys from off the mantelpiece. "She explained to Philippe what had happened and they tried hard, while he was in Dover, to make a baby all over again. But that time it didn't work. She knew

Philippe might get killed and she wanted . . . she wanted something of his to live on, should that happen. When we heard that he had been killed . . . it was devastating."

I was standing by the piano. I picked up the top sheet of music and opened it. As I did so, a photograph fell out and landed on the floor. I stooped and picked it up. I showed it to Mrs. Dirac.

"That's Madeleine and me in Berlin," she said, taking the photo from me.

"When was that?"

"Nineteen thirty-six, I think." She pointed to the sheet music. "That is her favourite Schubert song. Madeleine has a good singing voice and at school she won a prize, a holiday to a place that enabled you to expand your interest in your winning subject. She chose Berlin, to hear some Schubert sung professionally. I went with her, paying for myself, of course."

I replaced the sheet music on the piano.

"Madeleine speaks German?"

"No! Not really. She had to learn the German words of the Schubert songs, so she could sing them with the appropriate feeling, but that was all. She can't speak proper German."

Mrs. Dirac walked past me, opened the front door, and turned back. "We were talking about Philippe's death. I told her that the grief would pass and that she would meet someone else and that when she did she mustn't be always comparing him to Philippe. I hope she doesn't do that with you."

"I . . . I've never been aware of it. We seemed to have — we *do* have — a straightforward, clean relationship." I smiled. "And as I say, she seems to love my dog as much as I do. The three of us were — are — content."

"Then find her, Colonel Hammond. Find her, and give me the grandchild I never had."

I easily got the train. The 7:13 from King's Lynn was very crowded and got into King's Cross rather late. I flopped into bed with a drink and that day's newspapers, as was now my routine. Zola was in bed alongside me. I still valued his warmth and the other signs of life that he brought with him — the sound of his panting, his doggy smell, the mild thud of his tail when he wagged it. He now accepted his place on the bed as his natural right. This would be my last night with him, for a while at least.

Of course, the whole Blakeney encounter had been turning over in my mind. Most of all, of course, I didn't know what to make of the fact that Madeleine had never mentioned her pregnancy. Or her interest in Schubert lieder. Was that odd? Or was I being too — what was the word? — inquisitive? paranoid? She had never mentioned her trip to Berlin either — was *that* odd?

I don't know what I would have made of these thoughts and ruminations had a small item in that day's newspaper not caught my eye. It was a short report on page 6 of *The Times* to the effect that the day before a man had been arrested on suspicion of being a German spy, in Cromer.

I read that article twice, three times. A man had been arrested in Cromer, on suspicion of being a German spy, because, when asked the way to Sheringham, the very next village, by an off-duty RAF pilot, on leave from a nearby base, he had appeared nonplussed. Since the exclusion zone had been in force for months or even years by then, and only locals and accredited military personnel were allowed in Cromer, for a local not to know where Sheringham was . . . It was unthinkable. The police were called, and it was found that his identification papers were fake.

And, of course, that was the day before Mrs. Dirac had been in Cromer.

According to what she had told me, she had been fitting someone's curtains, but . . . that could just have been flimflam. Armed with the new information that Mrs. Dirac and Madeleine had been in Berlin in 1936, and that Madeleine had kept quiet about her taste for Schubert, on top of which Mrs. Dirac hadn't seemed especially anxious about the fate of her daughter, was this a . . . a new possibility? Was a new understanding of Madeleine coming into view? Had Mrs. Dirac been in Cromer to . . . to do what exactly? To see what she could find out about the arrested man? To report back to . . . to whom? If she *had* been in Cromer to make a rendezvous, would she have told me that's where she had been?

I didn't want to follow that line of thought, but I knew I had no choice. The thoughts wouldn't go away all by themselves.

I checked in the other papers. Yes, they all had the same story, about the arrest of a German spy in Cromer, though with no more details.

But there could be no doubt about the fact of the arrest and its reason.

To see more clearly I put out the light. I reached over to the bedside table and gripped what was left of my whisky. It was going to be a long night.

I searched my memory. For a few moments my mind was vague, blank, but then I suddenly started to piece together what might, at some point, become a picture.

I recalled that, at Ardlossan, when we had discussed using poetry as the basis of our fallback codes, Madeleine had mentioned using Goethe. Was that odd, or too obvious if she was a . . . not what she seemed?

Then there was the fact that she kept lapsing into English, rather than keeping to French as recruits were meant to do. Did that mean anything? Was it a sign that language was her weak point?

Was I making sense?

Zola scratched himself, vigorously. I scolded him and he stopped.

Had Madeleine shown an unusual interest in the German *Schwimmweste* we had happened across on the beach at Ardlossan? I had thought nothing of it at the time; her curiosity seemed only normal, but was it? Had it worried her unduly, that her fate might be much the same? Had it made her realise how exposed she was?

I heard an all-night bus pull away from the stop on the corner of Lisson Grove.

Madeleine had asked me many times about the date and place of the invasion. Was that natural curiosity, or something more? I hadn't, until now, felt that she had been unduly inquisitive, but then, if she was more than she seemed, she would be trained in dissimulation. I could read little into her behaviour on that score.

Or from her inquiries into SC2, what it was, whether there was an SC1. She had asked more questions than any of the other recruits, but that might only mean the rest were not unduly curious. She *had* shown more interest than any of the others but . . . I could conclude nothing concrete from her behaviour.

There *was* the fact that she was Protestant,

not Catholic. I wasn't too clued up on my French history, but there was, I knew, a Protestant tradition in France — the Huguenots — so it was entirely possible she was exactly what she said she was.

I swallowed some whisky.

On the other hand, if there was more to her than I knew, if she had stronger German links than she had let on, she might find it safer to keep to the faith she was raised in than to pretend to be Catholic.

I listened to the night. It was becoming a habit.

She didn't drive, or so she said. Could I read anything into that? Her mother had asked how she moved around France. Did that imply Madeleine *could* drive?

Early on she had said that, sooner or later, she got on everybody's wrong side. In the land of paranoia into which I was sinking, even that could be made to seem suspicious.

She had impersonated Hitler, or rather Charlie Chaplin's Hitler, when we had been inspecting German officers' uniforms, and she had spoken German — but a very rudimentary nonsense German that we all understood. She had given Katrine and Ivan a French translation of a German classic. It had been a French translation, yes, but she had known that — what was his name? — Friedrich Schiller — was a respected playwright. Was there anything in that?

Was there anything in her obsession with the Riefenstahl woman? Would a real German spy admit to such an obsession? Or was it bluff and double bluff?

Was there anything in the fact that her mother had cancelled lunch in London? Did they not want me to see them together, just in case I . . . what?

Were they a team? That's what the Cromer business suggested, if it suggested anything. A mother-and-daughter team — if they *were* mother and daughter, of course. The lack of physical resemblance between them didn't confirm anything, but it didn't support their story either. The photos on the mantelpiece could have been a deliberate decoy.

Where was I going with all this?

Then there was, of course, Madeleine's last message. Was it genuine? Had she really been cut off in mid-transmission, and been forced to escape? Or was that more dissimulation, a clever gambit to cover her tracks as she went back to her masters in Paris or Berlin?

I drank more whisky.

How had her mother behaved when I told her that her daughter was missing? She had been distraught, sort of, but had she been *very* upset?

I couldn't be sure, but I didn't think so.

So what did she know?

And Madeleine hadn't told her "mother" about me . . . Was that because I meant so little to her, was just one part of her plan, her trap, her deception? Is that why she had given me Erich's cigarette case — because it meant nothing to her?

I didn't know what to think.

Then there was Philippe. Had he ever existed, or was he just a concoction of Madeleine and her mother, to root them artificially in a specific part of France, and to add to their credibility?

The whisky was finished. The darkness was deep. It had begun to rain — the swish of car tyres on the surface of St. John's Wood Road told me as much, as did the spattering sound on the windows. I found that vaguely comforting, as I always did when it rained at night. I don't know why.

What I *did* know — and I am not proud of saying this — was that I had to avoid making up my mind, at least for the time being.

If I decided that Madeleine was . . . well, more than she seemed, I had to tell Hilary and he would have to tell his superiors. That might stop me going to France, might stop me having the chance to look for her. My mission might easily be aborted.

It wasn't too difficult to rationalise, of course. I had no concrete evidence that Madeleine was not exactly what she said she was. Just an old photograph, with a seemingly innocent explanation; and a coincidence about her mother's being in Cromer on the day after a German spy had been arrested there.

On top of which I had now been given an important assignment, far more important than Madeleine's relationship — or non-relationship — with me, and what else she might or might not be. No doubt Hathaway and the prime minister could replace me, but my withdrawal — whatever the reason — wouldn't be a popular move. There wouldn't be much time to find a substitute to stop Legros briefing Perrault. And the prime minister had given me one of his cigars.

I put the empty whisky glass on the bedside table, and laid my other hand on Zola's back. He woke up, turned his head, and started licking my hand.

No, I told myself, I had to keep my thoughts private for the moment, until I had more to go on.

Given more time, had I not been scheduled to travel to France the very next day, I could have checked out Madeleine's story — her past history — a bit more thoroughly than our people had been able to do before she arrived at The Farm. As it was, I had no choice but to take what I knew, and didn't know, or half knew, to France with me, and see what happened.

I turned on to my side and tried to sleep. Doubt is an awful snake of an emotion. Once it has you in its grip, it won't let go. It spoils everything.

I'd never had this kind of feeling with Celestine.

■ ■ ■ ■

PARIS
SEPTEMBER

■ ■ ■ ■

18

The American Jeep parked out side the Café Volnay, on the corner of the avenue Masson and the rue de Faubourg St. Honoré, was surrounded by a gang of boys, and one or two young girls, admiring the vehicle's spare design and pointing to what looked like a couple of rusting bullet marks disfiguring one of its high mudguards.

Three GIs — the Jeep's crew — were taking a break at the café's small marble-topped tables, drinking beer with their coffee and handing out cigarettes to anyone who cared to ask, including some of the boys who were barely in their teens.

The avenue Masson was a wide boulevard of horse chestnut trees, off which the rue de Faubourg St. Honoré cut its busy way towards the Elysée Palace in the far distance. Armed with my impressive letter of authority signed by Churchill and a few SC2 bits and pieces provided by Duncan Kennaway, I had set up my headquarters around the corner from the Volnay, in a disused school, the École Lavoisier, in the rue de Troyes. This had been carried out with the aid of Roland Kemp, code name Badger, who had run the Tablet circuit out of Paris for the past three years — one of the very few not to be compromised. In Ardlossan Roland had kept us in touch with the latest developments in French underground life.

We in SC2 had urged Badger and his circuit to find us some premises as soon as possible, so that no other Allied agency could get its hands on them. The war was a long way from being over.

The Volnay was not the nearest café to the *école,* but according to Badger it had formed part of the Resistance during the occupation and so was now used by circuit members out of a sense of loyalty. Not irrelevant either was the fact that, having been part of the Resistance, the Volnay now had a better-than-average supply of foodstuffs — its links to the black market were well established and lunch there, which is what Roland and I were now beginning, was more interesting than elsewhere.

We were sitting outside under an awning. It had rained not long before but had stopped for now.

"Patrice," said Roland when the waiter appeared. *"Bonjour. Ça va?"* How are you?

Patrice shrugged in the way that only

French people — and French waiters at that — can, but then a smile spread across his face as Roland held out a pack of Camels. Roland liked to roll his own cigarettes when he could, but, as he had told me, the French were short of tobacco and our supplies always made useful gifts, to ease the way with the locals. Patrice took a Camel, lit it with Roland's shiny lighter, and settled it in between his lips as if he had gone the entire war without a smoke.

In those early days of the liberation, in our part of Paris at least, restaurants didn't have menus. There was so little food, even at the Volnay, that you just took what was on offer — there was rarely a choice.

"What have you got for us today?" said Roland in French.

"Quiche," said Patrice, "or there's quiche. Quiche with spinach."

"No meat?"

Patrice shook his head. Ash that had formed on the end of his cigarette fell on to his white jacket. He brushed it off, leaving a smudge. "There's egg in the quiche, I assume."

"Quiche it is, then," said Roland. "And I think we've got some of that Bandol white left over in our bottle from yesterday. We'll have that."

Patrice nodded and disappeared.

The GIs were paying for their coffees and preparing to leave.

It was amazing how quickly life had moved on since the liberation. De Gaulle had arrived back at the end of August, barely three weeks ago now. To begin with, the Americans had been welcomed with open arms, and that was still mainly true. But some things — like the liberation currency with which I could see the three GIs in front of us were paying — did not go down at all well with some Parisians. De Gaulle liked to pretend that it had been the French who had liberated Paris, as if the Americans and British (and Canadians and Poles) had had no hand in it, and some Parisians felt the same way. The liberation currency reminded them of the reality — the part played by other Allied soldiers.

Still, the money was accepted: the soldiers knew their rights, and had risked their lives in getting to the avenue Masson. They weren't about to stand for any nonsense.

Roland I and watched them get back into their Jeep, offering yet more Camels to the boys and girls gathered around the vehicle, and then they zoomed off to L'Étoile and the Arc de Triomphe.

As we watched the GIs go, the wine arrived. The Volnay operated a very sensible system of charging customers only for the wine they drank. If you were regulars, as Roland was, and I was becoming — it was my third day in France — any wine left over in a bottle had your name scribbled on the label. The bottle was then left on the back shelf of the bar for when you next appeared. It also encouraged customers to come back.

Roland poured two glasses and passed one to me. We toasted each other.

I was just acquiring a taste for wine. In the UK I had always drunk beer or whisky, but Roland had insisted on introducing me to wine and I was trying to like it.

We sipped our drinks for a few minutes in silence.

The horse chestnut trees in the avenue Masson were now bearing fruit, bright brown conkers, shiny as a Sam Browne belt. Shiny as whisky. I remembered reading how, in World War One, many of the chestnut trees in Paris had been cut down to burn as fuel. At least that hadn't happened this time round.

Still without definite news of Madeleine, one way or the other, I hadn't given up hope completely. The British and American armies at least — being fighting organisations, used to the chaos of war *and* the requirements of post-battle life — had special departments to help track down missing persons. But the Resistance, especially now, with only half of the country liberated, and the other half not, was more interested in taking the fight to the Germans — settling a few old scores, and sorting out their own post-war positions — than in tidying up. In the same way, ratlines were being disbanded, and they were not at all bothered about telling anyone else. The situation was half orderly and half chaotic.

I searched the faces of everyone on the pavements of Paris, just in case. During my three days in the newly liberated capital so far, I had bought her another small bracelet, this time from Cartier, as a gift for when we met. And as a show of optimism.

I had never had the chance to buy Celestine any jewellery and I wasn't going to make that mistake again.

"Now," said Roland, setting his glass down on the table before us. "I have a couple of pieces of news today, but before I tell you what I know, can we just get some basic figures agreed? Things have been moving so fast in the past few days that I need to clear my head if I am to set things straight."

"Sure," I said. "Go ahead."

"Right, well. Am I correct in saying that there are, just now, September 1944, some fifty-seven circuits in France, thirty-two in what was until very recently the occupied zone, and twenty-five in what was Vichy France?"

"That's correct. With six circuits in Paris itself."

He nodded, reached forward again, took up his glass, and sipped some wine. "Well, the first thing I have to tell you is that, according to what I have been able to gather now that

376

the Germans have retreated very nearly to Aachen, out of the thirty-two circuits in the occupied zone, nine were penetrated, four of them in Paris. So far as we can make out, the penetration began in Paris, with the Boxer, Carpenter, Ladder, and Anchor circuits."

I nodded my agreement. "The only ones not penetrated in Paris were yours, Tablet, and Flagon, near Versailles — am I right?"

"Correct," he said. "Then the penetration spread east to Cobbler around Reims, and west to Starling near Chartres, Mountain near Le Mans, and Crossbow, inland from St. Nazaire."

It was my turn to nod.

"That fits — more or less — with what we know in Cathcart Place. How many people have we lost?"

"I'll come to that. You, I understand, are particularly interested in women agents — right?"

"Yes."

Roland took a piece of paper from his pocket and put it on the table in front of me. "This is just a set of numbers if anyone finds it, but I know what the numbers refer to. Look."

He pointed to a column of figures, taking out a cigarette from his pack as he did so.

"This top figure, two hundred and seven, is the total number of people in the nine penetrated circuits. Of that total, one hundred and sixteen are your people — our people — and the rest are locals. A few of these may have got away, but the great majority will have been captured, interrogated, and then either executed or shipped east to the camps. Most likely they would have been executed there too."

He pointed to the next figure down and lit his cigarette.

"This figure, forty-one, is your figure — I mean it comes from your people in London. It's the number of agents in all circuits, in all of France, on D-Day, still unaccounted for. Of that number, twenty-seven are men and fourteen are women."

He looked at me. "We haven't heard from any of them."

"Do we know if any of them have been executed yet? Do we know anything for certain in any individual case?"

"I'm working on that. One of the Parisians, Claudine Petit, who worked in the Gestapo headquarters, is now in prison at La Santé — that's the big maximum-security penitentiary in the south of the city. You have an appointment there tomorrow afternoon. It's in her interest to talk — otherwise, as a collaborator, all sorts of things may happen to her — so I'm hopeful she will be able to shed light on some of those agents who passed through Avenue Foch. And we know from the prison cells *within* Avenue Foch that captured agents were brought there for interrogation.

"The other possibility is Justine Coude-hard. She was a member of the Boxer circuit but was away on Resistance business when the penetration first happened, and she was alerted and stayed undercover. She is a very brave woman, a communist but a sensible one, able to put France before her beliefs when it matters, and she is known to have killed two collaborators. Her character is not in doubt, even if her politics are.

"She also happens to be — Well, let's just say that you and I have both seen plainer women. She has a shape like Veronica Lake. I was thinking that she might work with you, as your assistant, so to speak. She is a native Parisienne, she knows the country, the Resistance underground — she might be very useful when you are interrogating people. She can help you grasp whether what they are saying is plausible, whether it fits with what she knows about the way the Resistance — and the Gestapo — work and worked — Aah! Here's the quiche."

We sat back as it was served.

Roland held up the empty bottle of Bandol.

"Bring us another of these, Patrice, please."

"Any more Camels?" Patrice asked, bluntly.

"Sure." Roland took out his packet and shook one free.

Patrice nodded his thanks. "If I forget to

put the next bottle on the bill, don't make a fuss, okay? You know what Madame Cabris can be like."

Roland put his finger to his lips, looked at me, and winked. "That's Paris today, quid pro quo all round." After Patrice had ambled back inside the café, Roland leaned forward. "That's a first," he whispered. "He must like the look of your ugly mug."

We tucked in. The pastry was good, the spinach less so. But, after a few glasses of wine, it is amazing how things like that matter less and less. As the French say, "Only the first bottle is expensive."

The Hotel Séranon, where I had billeted myself, was in the rue de Beaufort, two or three streets away from the avenue Masson and the École Lavoisier, south towards the River Seine. The hotel was small and quiet, with a central courtyard that was a riot of flowers and one or two small trees. There were a couple of other British army types, like me, and the management only accepted commissioned officers, all of which made for an agreeable and fairly calm environment. I had two rooms, right next to the washrooms, on the second floor, overlooking the courtyard.

I could have stayed nearer the school had I preferred. But I wasn't sure I wanted to live too near the shop, so to speak. If I was to kill

Perrault, and get away with it, my anonymity might be crucial. I had to keep myself to myself.

On top of that, having been in France in 1941 and 1942, I had made my own contacts, people I hadn't seen since then and who might very well be dead by now, but who — if they were not — could possibly help me in my search for Madeleine. Especially as Madeleine might not be . . . what everyone else thought she was.

That evening, after my lunch with Roland, I put the finishing touches to the list of half a dozen French people with whom I had worked back in 1942, and who I remembered as being Paris-based or Paris-connected.

As I saw it, I had two routes to take. The very fact that the Gestapo headquarters in Paris had five prison cells, in the basement, as Roland had told me, was proof enough that captured agents were brought there and, presumably, interrogated in the first hours and days after their capture, while the information they possessed was still fresh. And we knew from our own experience, as I had explained to Madeleine and many others at Ardlossan, that if captives are going to "crack," they do so early on, in the first few days after capture. Presumably, people spent a few days in the Paris prison cells before being shipped onward to the east. But I'd have to check that out.

My second route was west, towards Nantes and the Atlantic coast. I knew about the Crossbow circuit, which Madeleine had been about to join. Crossbow would certainly have had links to the ratline which I had heard went down the Atlantic coast through Fontenay, La Rochelle, Cognac, Bordeaux, and on into northern Spain near Bayonne. If Madeleine *had* got on to the ratline, and travelled some way along it, before being captured, or injured, it would be difficult for me to follow her path *and* fulfill my other obligations. France was a big country — Bordeaux, say, was more than five hundred kilometres from Paris.

If she had been captured and was being held in the German enclaves of St. Nazaire or La Rochelle, then I was stymied. Presumably, there was no way into or out of those redoubts, not yet, anyway.

And there was always the chance she had used her pill. Or that she was — I had to say it — a German spy, who was now back with her masters in Berlin.

I took an early bath. You could never be sure in those days that hotels would have enough hot water for all their guests, so an early hot tub was safer than a later one. I put on a fresh shirt and socks and underwear and went out on to the street, staying away from the wide thoroughfares and keeping to the narrow backstreets that Paris does so well.

In the rue Leroux I found a bar-cum-bistro where I sat outside to begin with, for a pre-dinner drink. A previous occupant of the table had left a newspaper on his chair and I picked it up. Newspapers had sprung up like mushrooms in the wake of the liberation. There was still a paper shortage and the print quality left a lot to be desired, and left a lot of printer's ink on your fingers, but it was still good to have free newspapers again in the French capital.

In those first days in Paris I had to pinch myself several times. Ahead of me — it was as certain as anything — lay a series of very unpleasant and possibly dangerous duties. I would, I was sure, discover that several colleagues whom I knew well had been executed. Among that number Madeleine might well be included. Or I would discover that she was . . . a German agent. And on top of it all, I had to murder an ally.

But for now, here I was in beautiful Paris, enjoying an aperitif and anticipating dinner in civilized surroundings. In a curious upside-down wartime way, for the moment I felt *lucky.*

I looked about me, to remind myself one more time how beautiful Paris was. I ordered an experimental glass of red wine and settled down to read the paper. It was called *Limoges Matin,* a provincial rag that I didn't know, and no doubt it wouldn't last very long. Also, this copy that had been left on the seat where I was sitting was torn and incomplete; some pages were missing. But it was all I had.

About eight o'clock I left my seat outside, as it was getting chilly, and went inside to have dinner. There wasn't much choice but there *was* chicken, so I didn't delay, ordering that and a half-bottle of red wine.

With all the time I had, and with newsprint being in such short supply, and since a lot of the paper I had was missing, I read everything, all the subjects that I might not read usually, like the chess column, the bridge column (I played bridge badly), even the sports pages, accounts of teams I didn't know.

And then I saw something that made me . . . that made me hunch forward and move the paper into a better light so that I could be doubly certain of what I was reading.

It was an archaeological report, from Chabanais on the Vienne River in the wider Limoges area, between Bordeaux and St. Nazaire. It said that a major discovery had been made there, in a cave — the discovery of a painting of an ancient wild animal, an ancient form of ox, now extinct. The discovery showed, said the report, that ancient people had lived in that part of France for nearly thirty thousand years and confirmed that this was the earliest form of human habitation in all of Europe. The discoveries had been made, according to the journalist

384

who wrote the article, by a team of five people led by — I turned the page and . . . nothing. The next page was missing. Whoever had left the paper on the seat outside had taken the rest of the paper with him, or her. As Madeleine might have said, "Bug-ger!"

I needed to get that paper. I had to get another copy and find out exactly who had made the discovery.

When I looked at the front of the paper, however, I discovered that it was already three days old. Newsagents would already have returned or burned or destroyed what they had left over.

I looked at the masthead. Yes, the editorial offices were in Limoges.

I looked at the top of the article itself. No journalist's name.

But I would get there, I told myself.

Chabanais, I remembered, was near Louzac, which I now recalled was where Madeleine came from, or had said that she came from, and where she had lived with her mother, after her father had died and before they moved to Britain.

And Louzac was where her husband had made a speciality of caves and the ancient art inside them. Philippe had always hoped to make a major discovery in the area and now someone had. But it couldn't be him. How could it? If he had ever existed, he was dead.

19

La Santé prison, towards the southern edges of Paris, was a brick monster of a building. It was formed of five huge brown-black fingers. Each finger was five stories high, laid out in a line and formed of old bricks, overlooking narrow exercise yards where the sun hardly ever reached. Looking up, I could see that the windows were pitifully small, as if the architect had decided — or been instructed — to offer as little pleasure or hope as the materials would allow. Despite being so massive, the whole ensemble, within huge, fat walls, felt somehow constricting.

"Follow me," said Justine Coudehard. "I know the way."

We had passed by the main gate and shown our identity papers and, as far as I could see, we were now headed for a set of double doors at the foot of one of the brick fingers.

I was content to let her lead.

I already thought of her as Justine, although we had only met earlier that morning.

She had a mass of thick, flame-coloured hair and freckle-spattered skin. Her eyebrows formed a curved, rust-tinted "V," like a bird seen in the sky at a distance.

As for the rest of her . . . Well, Roland Kemp was right: she was tall, athletic-looking, with a long stretch of body between her hips and her bust. She moved with the slow, loping, languid grace of a gazelle or a giraffe, her feet treading the ground as if she didn't want to disturb the insect life.

We had met for breakfast, at the Café Volnay, with Roland. He had explained why I was in Paris. She had agreed immediately to offer what help she could. This trip to La Santé, to see Claudine Petit, was our first foray together.

We had travelled on the Métro, line 6, as far as the Place de St. Jacques, carrying our bicycles on the train, then ridden to the prison. During the ride, the heavens had opened but we had come prepared: both of us had raincoats and hats. The rain had stopped now. We had left our headgear with the bicycles at the entrance gate of the prison.

We reached a set of double doors at the end of the building we had been directed to at the main gate, and Justine knocked. There was a delay, the sound of a chain rattling, keys turning in locks, and then the door opened. Justine handed over our documentation. A tall, thin, entirely bald man scrutinised it, wrote something down in a book inside the door, and then we were admitted.

Ahead of us was another double door, then we were through into the main part of the cell block. A huge corridor lay before us: five rows of cell doors, one row above the other, with netting stretched across the block at every other level and from one balcony to another, to prevent suicides.

Before I could adjust to the scale of the prison cells, to the fact that there were so *many* of them, I was overwhelmed by the smell of the place, ingrained into the very fabric of the building.

We were led off to a small side room. It was clearly not the policy to let visitors get any closer to the realities of prison life.

We were shown into a small square room, with brick walls painted a dirty green, with an electric light, covered with a metal grille, set into the ceiling. There was a small square metal table, and four chairs. The table had a shallow depression in it at one corner, which I presumed was meant to serve as an ashtray.

Justine and I were left alone in the room, as the man went out, locking the door behind him. No doubt he would bring the woman we had come to see.

"Tell me about this Claudine woman. What exactly did she do?"

Justine wound her hair into a ponytail, using an elastic band she kept around her wrist.

"We're not exactly sure," she said. "She certainly worked at the Gestapo headquarters in avenue Foch. She said she was a cleaner and that she did it because she needed the money. But she's a little too educated to have been just a cleaner. So the question arises, What else might she have done? Did she sleep with any Germans, for instance?"

"How . . . ?"

"How do we know? Is that what you are asking?"

I nodded.

She shook her head vigorously, as if she was trying to get the prison smell out of her hair. "There are others who worked in the same building. Some are in this prison, some in other prisons — some are still free. We have a team looking into all these people who were or may have been collaborators, checking one story against another. If we find any inconsistencies . . . Well, that's where it gets interesting."

"Isn't it all very chaotic?"

She shook her head. "Less than you would think. The Germans were very methodical, but we in the Resistance have been keeping our eyes on rumoured collaborators, large and small, for some time. There's going to be quite a bit of score-settling in the weeks and months ahead. That's why I'll be interested to see what this Claudine woman says."

There was some sort of banging outside,

metal on metal, and for a few moments her voice was almost drowned out.

"She knows that if she fails to help us, then she is at risk, so I'm hopeful our visit today won't be wasted."

"You sound as though you know her."

"I know her type." Justine shrugged. "Don't forget, I know a lot of people who were collaborators. Claudine is safer in prison now than she would be out on the street. On the street she might have her head shaved. *Épuration,* it's called."

We heard footsteps outside; a key turned in the lock and the door opened.

Claudine Petit came in.

She looked frightened. She was a small woman, as befitted her name, with short dark hair, like a basin or a helmet over her head. She had tiny dark suspicious eyes that were never still in their sockets. Her face was drawn, thin, and bird-like. She wore a smock, its sleeves cut off well above the elbow.

She looked at me rather than Justine, and so I waved her to a seat.

She sat on the edge of it and leaned forward, nervous now. Her eyes jerked around from side to side without stopping.

We waited while the guard left us, and again locked the door behind him.

I waited some more, without saying anything. That would unnerve her.

Then I nodded to Justine.

"We know that you worked in the headquarters of the Gestapo," she said. "In avenue Foch. When did you start?"

"Why? Why do you want to know? Who are you?" She had a small voice, a small person's voice, high-pitched, almost a whine.

Justine nodded at me. "Special Command Two, from England. They sent agents into France, undercover, many women agents, to help us. It doesn't matter who I am. Many agents were betrayed and this man is here to try to find them, or what happened to them. How long were you at Avenue Foch?"

Claudine Petit was shaking her head. "I . . . I don't know anything —"

"Answer the question! How long were you at Avenue Foch? We'll get to what you know, or don't know, when we get to it." Justine slapped the table with her open palm. "Answer the fucking question!"

Claudine Petit held her hand to her throat. "The end of forty-two, November."

"That's better." Justine left her hand on the table between us, her fingers splayed. "And what did you do? What was your job?"

"I was a cleaner."

"Cleaning what?"

"The offices, the bathrooms, the kitchen."

"The bedrooms?"

Claudine Petit nodded.

"The cells?"

She hesitated. Then she nodded.

"And you worked there until . . . when, exactly?"

Claudine hesitated again, clearly calculating where this was going, where her best interests lay. Should she come clean with all that she knew, or feign ignorance? But she didn't know what we knew already, and that was her problem. She wanted us to trust her, she wanted us to be on her side, but she wasn't sure how to make that happen.

Justine was insistent. "When was the last time you worked at Avenue Foch? It's important that we know."

"Until . . . until the end of July."

Justine nodded. "That fits with what we know already. It will be better for you if you tell us the truth. If you do, then . . . we can tell the Resistance you are being helpful. Am I making myself understood?" She withdrew her hand from the table.

Claudine Petit nodded. She looked at me. She was uncomfortable with my silence. But then I spoke.

"Very well. Remember this, when you answer the next questions. Quite a few Germans have been captured already, here in Paris and in towns to the east. So we know certain things from them, from the horse's mouth, so to speak. Not everything, but enough, perhaps."

Justine leaned forward, paused, then growled, "When you cleaned the cells, did you see the inmates?"

Claudine Petit nodded and said, quietly, "Sometimes."

"What does that mean, 'sometimes'?"

"Sometimes not all the cells were full, sometimes the people who had been captured had been taken for interrogation in the interrogation room, and we were asked to clean the cells while they were away."

"And at other times?"

"We cleaned the cells while they were in the exercise yard. They had an hour's exercise every morning. We sometimes saw them being taken in or out of the cells."

"How many cells were there?"

"Five."

"Were they usually full?"

"Not always, no. People came and went."

"How long did people stay? How long, on average?"

Claudine Petit shrugged. "A few days. Up to two weeks. Never more."

"Then what happened to them?"

"They were shipped east."

"You know that for certain?"

Another shrug. "I was a cleaner, for pity's sake, a *French* cleaner. No one *told* us anything. It's what I heard, overheard, it's what the rumour was. Where else would they have gone?"

Justine leaned forward. "This is important. Was anyone *killed* in Avenue Foch?"

Claudine Petit shook her head. "I don't think so, no. Not that I heard. But I was only there in the mornings."

"Okay, okay." Justine picked up my cigarette case and opened it. She took out two cigarettes, put them both in her mouth and lit them. Then she gave one to me.

"Now, think . . . Have you any idea how many people, how many agents — captured people — passed through those cells while you were there?"

Claudine hesitated, but she was clearly thinking.

At this, Justine reached over, took a cigarette from my case, and laid it on the table in front of Claudine.

Claudine snatched at it, and I offered my matches.

"There were usually one or two prisoners in the cells. They were rarely full until the early part of this year; then they began to fill up."

"So," said Justine, "if we say the average stay was about a week, and if we say there were three prisoners at any one time, that makes three a week — that part's easy. Three a week for, say, thirty weeks, makes ninety overall — would that be about right?"

Claudine picked tobacco from her tongue. "That sounds a lot. I wouldn't have said that many. Half that maybe —" She shook her head. "That's just this year, of course."

Justine nodded. "How many were French and how many other nationalities?"

Another shake of Claudine's head. "Everyone spoke French. A few were obviously foreigners, to judge by their accents, but some foreigners spoke French without an accent. I noticed that."

Justine pulled her chair closer to the table. "Now we get to the real details, Claudine. This is where you can really earn your freedom. We need names."

Claudine, who had been visibly relaxing under the influence of the cigarette, suddenly became tense again. I noticed that the skin on her upper lip was damp.

"Names? I —"

"Who employed you?"

"I . . . I . . ."

"*Who* employed you?"

Claudine cleared her throat. "A man called Major Himmelweit."

"And he was . . . ?"

"He was . . . He ran all the domestic side, the support staff."

"And he reported to . . . ?"

"I don't know."

"Yes, you do. Think."

A pause. The cigarette was finished.

Justine held her hand over the pack.

"I think the deputy director at Avenue Foch was a Colonel Springer."

"There you are, you see. Your memory is

fine. Have another Camel."

Claudine grabbed at the pack greedily.

I spoke, keeping my tone gruff. "We know that the man in charge at Avenue Foch was Brigadier Wolf Grundmann, but who — and think carefully now — was the chief interrogator, who was the chief, the most active man on the payroll? Who was the *real* power in Gestapo headquarters?"

Claudine shook her head. "That was way beyond me. I was a cleaner."

Justine leaned forward again. "You were a cleaner who worked there for more than eighteen months. A cleaner with an education — oh, yes, we know about that. The Germans learned that they could trust you. You were a piece of the furniture. At times they would have talked in front of you as if you weren't there. This isn't the most difficult question we are going to ask you, Claudine, but I repeat: Who was the real power?"

Claudine savoured her cigarette. "I don't know for certain — you understand? But what I heard was that a Colonel Kolbe handled the interrogations. Everyone was a little scared of him because, they said — the other Germans, I mean — they said that he was very close to Grundmann, who in turn was a favourite of Himmler and had a direct line to Berlin. I was told that he did all the interrogations and authorised the . . . you know, the beatings and the other — the other things that went on."

"Did you personally witness any beatings?"

"No, of course not. The Germans never let the French near the interrogation room, not while there was anyone in it, but I was told by others, who worked different hours from me, that they heard the screams of the prisoners and sometimes had to clean away blood."

Justine leaned forward again. "Did you ever hear screams or clean away blood yourself?"

Claudine shook her head. "I never heard screams, no, but I did once — no, twice — see blood on the floor of the interrogation room. And I once had to clean it up from the floor of the exercise yard."

"People were tortured in the exercise yard?"

Claudine took a long pull on her cigarette. "No. I think . . . I think in that case that someone tried to escape, jumped from a cell window at night and didn't realise how far the drop was. I think he killed himself."

"Did that happen just once?"

"I think so. But others did escape."

"Yes. Let's come to that."

Justine's hand closed over the cigarette packet again.

"Tell us about the escapes."

Claudine hesitated. "There were two escapes that I know about, or I was told about. The first was when a man and a woman escaped from the exercise yard. There had been a delivery that day — I was never told what the delivery was — but it seems that someone, perhaps someone in the Resistance posing as a workman, left the yard gate open and the man and woman spotted it, and simply walked out of the gate into Paris and disappeared."

"And who were these people?"

"I don't have any names but I was told later, or I overheard, that they arrived on different days. The man worked in Paris, the woman was from somewhere to the west."

"Can you describe them?"

Claudine closed her eyes. "I can see them better this way. The man was tall and thin with a lot of blond hair — he looked German, but he was English. She was tall too, not as tall as him though, and she was a blonde. Cropped, straw-coloured hair."

I let out the breath I had been holding. Not Madeleine.

"And the other escape?"

Claudine nodded. "Oh, that was very different. He was ill, or he pretended to be, and a doctor was called. He overwhelmed the doctor, stabbed him with a needle to his heart, and knocked out the male nurse. Then he put on the male nurse's white coat and walked down the main stairs of the building and out by the front door. It was very audacious, I couldn't believe it when I was told. He was very daring."

"What did the Gestapo do?"

"I don't know, but I never saw the male nurse again."

"And do you have a name for us this time?"

Claudine nodded. "Someone heard the Gestapo call him Rollo. It's not a French name, is it?"

Justine looked at me.

I nodded. "Rollo Southrop. Part of Archive circuit, near Pontoise."

So Rollo had escaped, I told myself. And he hadn't yet arrived back in Britain, so far as I knew.

Justine was huddling forward again on her chair, leaning into the table.

"Now, this is the most important part, Claudine. More names. Names of prisoners, of captured agents, who passed through Gestapo headquarters."

"But I told you . . . there were — I can't remember —"

"That's not how it works." Justine nodded to me, as I reached into my briefcase. "We have a list here, which we are going to read out to you, slowly. If you remember the name, if it's a name that you recognise as having been through Avenue Foch, say so. This is very important because we are going to try to trace some of these people, whether they are dead or alive — do you understand?"

Claudine nodded.

"Do you have a family, Claudine?" said Justine.

"Yes, of course. My father is dead, but my mother and sisters are alive. One sister is married with two children."

"They will be worried about you now, yes?"

Claudine nodded. "Very much."

"So you will understand why we need to trace the whereabouts of all these agents. Their families need to know what happened to them."

Claudine nodded again.

"One other thing before we begin," said Justine. "Of all the agents held in the cells at Avenue Foch, how many were men and how many were women?"

"Oh, far more men, of course. I only saw — what? — about a dozen women in all my time in the building."

"They were brave, those women, yes? They weren't just cleaners."

It had the intended effect. Claudine blushed.

"We are going to start with the women's names," said Justine. "Some of the names are real names, some are code names. Just tell us whether you remember any of them. I'll give you another cigarette when we are finished. Ready?"

Claudine nodded.

Justine looked at me.

I had the papers in front of me and began

to read slowly.

I wasn't sure just how much we could rely on Claudine Petit's memory. A great deal depended on the results.

I began with the women's names, as Justine had said. Out of the first nine proper names, Claudine recognized three.

I tried to keep my voice steady when I reached "Madeleine Dirac."

Claudine shook her head.

I breathed out noisily again, and relaxed.

I got to the end of the list of proper names and then started on the code names. Just the code names of the women whose proper names she hadn't recognised.

"Brasero?" Brazier.

"No."

"Hérisson?" Hedgehog.

"Yes."

"Rossignol?" Nightingale.

"No."

I took a deep breath and held my voice steady.

"Chêne?" Oak.

I looked at her hard, trying to see if her body language gave away her answer before she said anything.

I couldn't read her.

Claudine nodded. "Yes — oh yes."

My chest bucked.

Madeleine had been captured. She hadn't committed suicide, or been held captive on the Atlantic coast — she had been through Avenue Foch and shipped east. That surely meant she was dead.

Justine had noticed my reaction — she stared at me, wiping her lips with her tongue. But I had to get a hold of myself. This meant at least that Madeleine wasn't — hadn't been — a German plant, and in any case I wasn't the only person to have lost someone in this war. Also, I hadn't finished with Claudine Petit.

We went through the men's names, during which I learned that Ivan Wilde, who had been on the Ardlossan course with Madeleine, had also been through Avenue Foch and then sent east. So he, too, was dead.

Briefly images of the wide stretches of sand at Ardlossan flooded my mind.

"Okay," I said. "That's the names finished with."

I looked across to Justine. "Would you mind waiting outside for a moment? There are one or two confidential things I need to discuss with Madame Petit."

Justine frowned. "Are you sure? I thought —"

"Yes, I'm certain. I won't be long."

Still frowning, not liking this one bit, she scraped back her chair, got to her feet, knocked on the door, and, when it was unlocked, left the room.

I offered Claudine Petit another cigarette

and allowed her a moment to smoke it.

"When I was in London, a few weeks ago, we heard from one of our agents who had escaped that you had told someone that you thought there was a double agent in Avenue Foch, a British agent who was also a German agent. Is that right? Do you know who the double agent was?"

She was enjoying her cigarette and was relaxing. She talked more easily now. Maybe it was because Justine was out of the room.

"Well, I think what I actually said must have got garbled in crossing the Channel." She examined her fingernails. "What I actually told some of the Resistance people I know was that, one day, I was sitting in the café of the Gestapo headquarters with Jaquine Varennes. She was a widow whose husband had been German. He died before war broke out, but that meant Jaquine spoke some German — though she never let on to the Gestapo because it might come in handy at some point. Anyway, she told me she had overheard two of the Gestapo people talking about a mole. Or, to be more accurate, they had used the word 'mole.' What she didn't know was whether they were referring to a German mole inside the British security services, or to a British agent whose code name was Mole. Her German wasn't perfect, and she only overheard the conversation, so of course she couldn't risk showing any interest."

Claudine herself risked a smile. "She could hardly ask them to repeat what they had said."

I nodded. "You and I are speaking French, Madame Petit, and you used the French word, *taupe,* for what we in English call a mole. Can you remember what the German is for 'mole'?"

"No. Because I didn't hear it, Jaquine did."

"It's easy for me to check whether any of our agents were code-named Mole, but even so I'd like to talk to Madame Varennes personally. Do you know where she is?"

She squashed out the remains of her cigarette in the depression in the table.

"Not precisely, no. After the Gestapo left Paris, she went south, to near Dijon where her son was in the Resistance. I haven't heard from her since."

"Who would know where she is?"

"I can't help you, I am afraid."

I waited for a few moments in case she changed her mind or remembered something else.

But all she offered was "Please tell the Resistance how helpful I've been. I didn't sleep with a single German. I want to get out of here and I don't want my head shaved."

The smoke was so thick you could have bottled it. The many candles didn't help — they made the shadows that moved across

404

the dance floor, in slow time to the music, as fuzzy as the reedy saxophone sounds on the edge of dissonance. The curvature of the ceiling, originally an arch beneath a railway embankment near the Seine, held in the sound as it did the smoke which rose, kissed the brickwork — and then hung there. Waiters in long black aprons swiveled their hips between the tables, trays held high on splayed fingertips, bottles and glasses balanced miraculously as they angled and swerved this way and that. Beneath the saxophone sounds, and the smoke, the urgent hubbub of voices — clotted with Gitanes and Gauloises — lay like a sediment.

La Pleine Lune — the Full Moon — had been a secret nightclub during the occupation, Justine told me, its entrance a small shed between the lines of a raised railway track that led from La Villette to Clignancourt. While the Germans had been in town, the club had opened only after midnight and, as it was nowhere near anywhere else, the noise it generated had attracted no attention. Now that the Germans had gone, a new entrance had been opened up, directly on the street. The club's name referred to the need for a full moon for supplies to be dropped to the Resistance.

It had been Justine's idea to come to the club the evening after we had stopped off at La Santé. Although she hadn't appreciated being excluded from the last part of the interview, she could see the mood I was in, that I had received the news about Madeleine like a kick from a horse. Anyone could. For me it was as if La Santé extended right across the city, now a grey, concrete barrenness that had entirely lost its charm, had lost every advantage — a place that had it in for me.

But Justine had forced me to come, found us some seats and a table, and sat me down. She had ordered some wine and filled my glass for me.

"Isn't there any whisky?" I had growled ungraciously.

"Later," she had said. "You can get drunk later. We need to talk first."

"I don't feel like talking," I said. "I feel like . . . butchering a few Germans."

She smiled. "There's a queue for that. You'll have to take your place at the back." She looked around her. "Everyone in this club would like to butcher Germans." After a pause, she added. "It might not be as bad as you think."

I was sitting slumped on a hard stool. I reached out, took hold of my wine glass, and brought it to my lips. It was red and tasted . . . not bad.

"On the other hand, it might be every bit as disastrous as I think." I looked at Justine. "You know better than I do that . . . all our agents who were captured were shipped east, after being interrogated — they were removed to Germany and the prisoner-of-war camps. All of our agents were in civilian clothes, acting behind enemy lines, as spies. The rules of war — not that the Nazis adhere to many rules of war — allow for spies to be shot."

She held her cigarette between long fingers. "Yes, I know. But that doesn't mean they actually *were* shot, or not yet. Our troops are making rapid headway. They may get to the camps before . . . before some of the agents are killed."

I shook my head and gave her a grim smile. "We are talking of what in overall terms is a small number of people. Well under a hundred. How long does it take to murder that number?" I shook my head again. "Being captured as a spy is the same as being executed. There are just a few days between the one and the other.

"Why don't they play something more cheerful?" I growled again. "They've all just been liberated, for pity's sake."

She made one of those French faces, a pout but where the corners of her mouth turned down at the same time. "*Ouf.* Now we are free to say what we like, happy or sad. Maybe, like you, the saxophone player has lost someone — or thinks that he has."

I didn't say anything immediately. We Allies were not quite as bloodthirsty as the Nazis — we didn't invariably execute the German spies we captured. So far as the British government was concerned, it was our policy rather to try to "turn" spies, a process that had become easier, not more difficult, as it had become obvious to many that the war was going against Germany, and being "turned" offered more of a future once the war was over. But the losers in any conflict are usually more vicious than the victors. So I couldn't harbour any doubts about Madeleine's fate.

"Let's change the subject," I said eventually, gripping the stem of my wine glass. "How are you communists going to get on with de Gaulle when the war is over?"

She made another French face. "How did you know I was a communist?"

"Roland told me."

"Are *you* a communist?"

I shook my head.

"Does it worry you that I am?"

Now I made a face. "Too early to say. At the moment, I'm more worried about having only Gitanes and Gauloises to smoke. My throat feels like scorched earth."

"Well, I don't mind your *not* being a communist." She smiled. "And, to answer your question, we will get on — how do you say in English? — 'like houses on fire.' I am being ironic, Englishman! De Gaulle thinks he won the war all by himself, without the Americans, without the British, without the Canadians.

He thinks he has a divine right to govern France, simply because he didn't give in —"

"Doesn't he have a point?"

She leaned forward and placed a finger on the table between us. "*Non!* De Gaulle was in London, hundreds of miles away, or in North Africa, even farther away. Who do you think was here, in this club, in the city, in the country? Who do you think organised the Resistance, the sabotage, the ratlines? *We* did, the communists. More than anyone else, anyway. Nothing could have happened without us — *nothing,* do you understand, Englishman? Our explosives people were the best — still are. We have our own code system — very sophisticated. And we — we communists — have assassinated more Germans than anyone else. We have *earned* our position."

The saxophone fell silent. A rustle of applause swept around the club. Dancers left the floor and, temporarily, the room — the thick fug — was lighter, less striated by shadow.

"De Gaulle was in exile. That means he was able to celebrate his return. You communists stayed and never went anywhere, so you weren't able to do what he did. Whether you like him or not, he knows how to put on a show, and he knows when a show is necessary."

She shrugged. "De Gaulle divides people.

He will divide the country."

"You think?"

"Of course. Look at your Mr. Churchill — he hates de Gaulle. So too does Mr. Roosevelt. De Gaulle cannot lead France."

"I wouldn't bet on it."

She eyed me. "Let us change the subject again, Mr. Hammond, or we shall argue. We have to work together, so we should not argue, no?"

I nodded. "What shall we talk about now?"

"Must I always call you Mr. Hammond, Englishman? Or Colonel Hammond?"

I smiled. "Matt will do."

"In the Bible, the apostle Matthew was a tax collector, no?"

"Yes."

"And his father was a tax collector, too."

"Yes. Is this the change of subject?"

"Why not? What does your father do, Matt?"

"He was a doctor."

"Was? He is no longer alive?"

"No, he was killed in the great polio epidemic of 1933 when I was twenty-one."

"No! My father, too! The same year."

"Really?"

"Really." She tugged the elastic band free of her hair and it fell down onto her shoulders. She wound the band around her wrist. "He wasn't a doctor, of course, but a schoolteacher."

I hesitated. This was turning into a bizarre — even macabre — exchange. But she meant well, and it took my mind off Madeleine.

Not quite.

The band had started up again, but this time it was a piano playing, a bass and some drums. Dancers reoccupied the floor.

Justine shook her head. "I don't believe it. My father was part of an experiment with a new vaccine. It killed him." She paused. "How much do doctors really know?"

I didn't know what to say. Then I did.

"That calls for some whisky, don't you think?"

"You don't like the wine?"

I shrugged. "You grew up with wine, Justine, I'm sure, just as you grew up with Gitanes. I grew up with mild English cigarettes and with Scotch. We've been drinking French all evening. Now it's my turn."

"Okay," she said, catching the eye of the black-aproned waiter and waving to him.

He came over and she ordered two whiskies.

"And your mother, Matt, did she remarry?"

I nodded. "About three years after my father died."

"And do you like him, your stepfather? Are you friends?"

I shrugged again. I preferred the piano to the saxophone. But the dancers obviously didn't. They had all left the floor again.

"I didn't have much to do with him. I think

411

my mother was more content having a man around than not having one. Then she was widowed for a second time and lives now in a small hotel. But she is content, I think. Mostly. Why do you ask?"

Another French face. I was coming to like it.

"Because I *hate* my mother's second husband. He is a businessman, a capitalist. My mother had a child with him and they spend much more time with his child than with me. I was always older, of course, but he is a very selfish man, very — how do you say? — very right wing, quite unlike my father, who was a teacher and very gentle, always helping others."

"Is that why you are a communist?"

"That's one reason, maybe, but there are many others. I —"

"No," I said, chuckling, to defuse the tension, "We've changed the subject, remember?"

She was about to launch into some sort of lecture, or harangue, or . . . I don't know what, but instead she sat back, allowed herself to laugh, and then visibly relaxed.

On cue, the whiskies arrived. I mixed water with mine, offered her some, which she declined, and then let the firewater slip down my throat.

"That's better."

She sniffed her drink, then sipped it. Then

took a longer sip.

"It's not as subtle as wine, is it?"

"Maybe that's its point. It gives you a kick, not a kiss."

She pushed her glass across the table.

"You have mine."

I pushed my wine glass in the opposite direction.

"This is like a dance, a dance of drinks."

She poured the wine from my wine glass into hers. She lifted it to her lips, drank, and lowered it back to the table. Her eyes never left mine.

"Would you like to dance, Matt?"

I hid behind my whisky glass for a moment.

Then I shook my head. "Not just yet, Justine. Not until . . . I need to find out about Madeleine."

"What do you mean?"

"Her exact fate — where her body is buried. And the others, of course."

"But how can we do that? If she's been taken east . . . ?"

"I'm not totally sure, but I can think of somewhere to start. We need a list of all the Germans working in Avenue Foch. Then we compare that with the lists that the Allied forward forces circulate of all officers captured, together with details of where they are being held. If we find names that match, we track them down and interrogate them."

Justine looked at me doubtfully.

413

"Yes, you're right to look skeptical —
needles and haystacks come to mind. But it's
the best I can do at this stage. I do have
credentials granting me universal access
anywhere." I explained about my Churchill
letters.

"I wasn't looking skeptical," she said softly,
when I had finished. "I was thinking. Hmm.
Throughout the war, the communists have
kept lists too — lists of Resistance people, of
Germans in any particular area, and lists of
collaborators, so that, when the war is finally
over, we know who the criminals really were,
on both sides. Our comrades will be keeping
up that practice in the east of the country,
near the German border. So . . . if any of the
Avenue Foch people did move on to the east,
and then stayed for a while, we'll have
records. I may be able to help — that's what
I was thinking."

"That gives us two bites at the haystack. We
could make a start tomorrow, if that's all right
with you?"

"Of course, of course." She turned her
head. "The music has changed again. Would
you like to dance to this?"

"No, no. It's good of you to try to cheer me
up, Justine, but dancing is beyond me at the
moment." I raised my glass. "Instead, a toast."

"Oh yes?"

"Yes." I swallowed some whisky. "Let's
hope first, that, for France's sake, the com-

munists and de Gaulle kiss and make up." I
paused when, again, she looked doubtful.
"And second, that I find at least one of my
female agents alive."

20

"Sir, there's someone to see you." Roland put his head round the door. He was in khaki shirtsleeves with braided braces, almost white. His tie was tucked into his shirt. His moustache was as pert as ever. He looked both relaxed *and* tidy. I envied him; I couldn't relax.

"Who is it?"

Roland looked at the card in his hand. "A Colonel Antoine Picard."

"What does he want?"

"He said to say that it was to do with your meeting with Claudine Petit."

I looked up sharply, but didn't immediately say anything. Nobody other than Roland, Justine, and myself was supposed to know about that.

"Tell him I'll be with him as soon as I can."

The École Lavoisier had been a small private primary school before the war; so it was a large house rather than a specially designed building like the larger lycées. The ground floor was given over to a reception area and a cafeteria and library, but the real work was done on the first floor where Roland, two secretaries, and two transmission officers worked. They occupied a large room with a bay window, and I had my office directly off that, at the rear. There still was a faint smell of chalk dust everywhere.

I had one thing to do before I could see this Picard man, and I had to do it myself.

I hung the DO NOT DISTURB sign on my door, banged it shut, so that everyone knew it was closed, and took out from the locked drawer in my desk the master list of agents that Tina Ridley and I had compiled on D-Day, setting out agents' code names alphabetically. If there *was* a double agent in France, then obviously I couldn't trust anyone, not even the SC2 staff.

I ran my finger down the list of code names.

No one was called Mole, or Taupe.

That settled that.

There *was* a double agent in SC2.

God forbid that MI6 should ever find out.

I put the list away, took the sign off my door, and shouted, to no one in particular, "Ask Colonel Picard to come up."

I was just putting my jacket on a coat hanger when he arrived.

He was a good-looking man, with a strong head and bushy hair, but he was inclining slightly to fat and his lips were fleshy.

417

"Colonel Hammond?" He had a warm voice and said my name in a self-confident, warm way, announcing in those two simple words that he spoke excellent English.

"Please sit down," I said, as soon as we had shaken hands. *Voulez-vous un café?*

"Bien sûr. Merci."

"Roland!" I shouted. "Have two coffees brought in, please."

"Co-ming *up*!" Roland answered in a sing-song voice.

I looked at Picard's card, which Roland had left on my desk. I held the card up. "This just says your name and rank. May I know more?" I spoke in French.

He answered in perfect English, and with a smile. "Yes, of course. I am second secretary to General Charles de Gaulle."

In the act of sitting down, I collapsed into my seat.

"And this is a . . . courtesy visit?"

He smiled again. "You can call it that if you like."

"What I mean is, I'm surprised you are here, in the offices of SC2. I thought the general doesn't approve of us. Have you come to try to send us away?"

Another smile. "No, not at all. Yes, it was true that — at one stage — the general was less than happy that SC2 was *expanding* its presence on French soil, rather than reducing it after the invasion, but we are on to a new phase of the war now, and I am here to help you."

"Oh yes? How?"

He took out an expensive-looking silver cigarette case and held it open for me to help myself. "You visited Claudine Petit in La Santé prison."

I looked up, automatically checking that my office door was closed.

I leaned forward and took a cigarette.

"How did you know about that? The meeting was supposed to be secret."

He tapped his cigarette on the lid of his case.

"You went with Justine Coudehard."

"Yes." No point in denying what was true. I lit a match and leaned forward, to light his cigarette.

"Coudehard is a communist."

"Yes, I know. I'm not a communist but . . . Well, she is being very useful."

He smoked his cigarette. "You are an experienced man, Colonel, so you will know that, in France — ah!"

He sat back as Colette, one of the secretaries, came in with the coffees.

She served them and went back out again, closing the door behind her.

We sipped our coffees, miming toasts to each other.

"You were saying . . ."

He nodded, placing his cigarette in the

ashtray on the desk. "As an experienced officer, you will know that the Resistance in France has always been divided into factions, and that the two largest and most powerful factions have been the communists and the Gaullists. So far, you have liaised on this project only with the communists."

"Yes, I did know there were — are — two factions, as you put it. But with General de Gaulle being . . . being so anti-SC2, I didn't think it worth approaching his people — your people."

He eyed me. "In this case, as it happens, we can be very helpful, and our interests coincide." He swallowed some coffee, put the cup back in the saucer, and pushed both of them to one side. He picked up his cigarette again.

"Let me explain. We know about your visit to Claudine Petit because we, the Gaullists, have our people inside the prison, inside the prison administration, of course. The communists are not the only ones with access.

"We know not only that you met Claudine Petit but *why* you met her and . . . and we also know what she told you."

He glanced out of the window briefly.

"You are looking for your agents — in particular your women agents — who passed through Avenue Foch, and you want to track them down, and find out their fates, dead or alive."

"Yes," I said. "And Madame Petit was able to help us some of the way."

He looked at me and tapped ash into the ashtray between us. "The information I have is, strictly speaking, top secret — I will explain why. But can I trust you, Colonel Hammond? Will you keep secret what I am going to say, even from Justine Coudehard? Especially from her?"

"It is difficult for me to offer any guarantees in advance. But if you are going to give me valuable information, then I *can* say that I will do my best to honour what you ask of me."

He nodded and thought for a moment. "Very well. I accept your answer. It's not ideal but what *is* in war?"

He smiled and leaned forward.

"We, the Gaullists, had someone in Avenue Foch. The communists do not know this — we never told them."

Where was this going?

He sat back again. "Let me explain. The weak aspect of Avenue Foch — from the Germans' point of view, I mean — was the food. They knew — and accepted — that French food was, is, better, much, much better than German food. They were in Paris, the culinary capital of the world, and they were in a privileged part of the army; they saw no reason why they should stint themselves."

I admired the fact that he could use an English word like "stint." What was the French for "stint"? I didn't know. Was there one? French has far fewer words than English.

"The Gestapo chose as their chef a well-known Frenchman, Gaston LeFèvre, from Lyon — where else? And Gaston, on our instructions, chose as his pastry chef a certain Monique Brèger. When I say 'our' instructions, I mean the Gaullist Resistance movement — again, we never told the communists.

"Now I get to the really secret part. Monique was exceptionally beautiful. She was sent into Avenue Foch with explicit instructions — explicit but obviously top secret — to try to sleep with a senior member of the Gestapo and in that way maybe find out whatever secrets they had — in particular what they knew about the Resistance. It was not — how shall I say? — a very savoury assignment, to use a culinary term. But you can see why . . . why we sanctioned it. It took a while — she was recruited to Avenue Foch in 1941 but she didn't get into Ulrich Kolbe's bed until 1943."

"Ulrich Kolbe! That's impressive."

He nodded. "And I haven't finished."

"Kolbe really fell for Monique — I'm not exaggerating. He took her on holidays when he had leave, to Switzerland, the south of France, the Atlantic coast."

"And did she . . . did she do as she was

instructed? Or did they turn her?"

"Good question — I can see you are an experienced officer. But no. She performed superbly. She found out a great deal about Gestapo plans, what they knew about the Resistance, your agents in SC2, MI6, morale in the United States. Monique was, in fact, pure gold. And she was wily. Every so often, she didn't tell us about some particular plan, where she could have prevented something or other. So Kolbe and his colleagues never suspected they had a mole. Or perhaps a snake would be a better word."

"And are you going to let me meet her? Does she have information that we would find useful? Is that why you're here?"

He nodded. "But I haven't quite got to the end of the story yet. You'll see.

"During the occupation, everyone had to collaborate with the Germans to some extent. That's how it worked — the Nazis had the power and enjoyed using it. If a baker was told to improve his bread, there was no argument. If a prostitute was told she was charging too much, she had to lower her prices. But there was a limit and everyone knew it. Some people, however — some of my countrymen and -women, I am sorry to say — went further, much further than the minimum, and openly embraced collaboration. 'Collabo,' it's called, as you may know. They derived power from it, made money from it, ate better, dressed better, travelled more than others. In Monique's case, of course, it was her *duty* to do all this. She was where she was to provide information and, in quite a few cases, she saved lives. We have it all documented and, when the war is over, and the chaos is ended and the time comes, we shall publish a full account."

He wiped his face with his well-manicured hand.

"But of course, to *be* a secret, her role could not be known outside the circle of a very few people. Everyone else thought she was a collaborator — that was the *point.*"

He shook his head.

"In early August, when it became clear after the invasion that the Gestapo would have to leave Paris, Kolbe told Monique that their affair was over, he was being withdrawn to Germany and . . . Well, she had to seek other employment. We had always anticipated this, of course — it was the good news we were all waiting for."

He shifted in his seat.

"What we didn't anticipate, what we had never expected, was the speed with which the *épuration* took place."

I nodded. "*Épuration sauvage.* I suppose that would be 'wild purification' in English, or something like that."

" 'Wild' is right. The women especially, and the women of Paris in particular, took it into their heads to 'cleanse' any female who had slept, or was *believed* to have slept, with a Nazi. *Collaboration horizontale* it was called — it's still called that, in fact. Dozens of women, hundreds perhaps, have been attacked in the past weeks.

"Perhaps you know this, perhaps you don't. Usually, a group of women will single out a collaborator, or someone rumoured to be a collaborator, surround her, overwhelm her, pin her down — and then shave her head. This is intended as a humiliation and it is certainly felt as such by those it has been done to. They are shunned, shops refuse to serve them, children shout at them in the street, or spit at them, no one will sit next to them on the Métro — if they have the guts to *go* on the Métro."

"Claudine Petit was worried it might happen to her."

He nodded. "And with good reason. It happened to Monique —"

"Oh no!"

"Yes. Only . . . that's what I wanted to tell you: it didn't stop at head shaving."

I looked at him.

"I don't know what it was with Monique. Maybe it was because the Gestapo were especially vilified, maybe it was because she had all those high-profile holidays with Kolbe, maybe it was because Kolbe himself was hated so much, or maybe it was because she was so beautiful."

He squashed out his second cigarette.

"She had acid thrown in her face —"

"What?"

He pressed his lips together.

"Yes. She is disfigured — and blind in one eye. You can imagine what it has done to her psychology, her social self-confidence."

A long silence passed.

Eventually, I said, "You're here. You must think she has information to give us. Has she agreed to see me?"

He nodded. "The attack has made her unwilling to go out on the street, and she can't have a normal social life. But it has only made her more determined to go on doing her duty where she can. When the story comes out, she will not be an outcast, but a heroine. If she can help you, as well as us, so much the better."

"Why haven't you published her story already?"

"Because of the war, what else? Other women have been attacked. Stopping the *épuration* itself takes priority for the moment. But we'll get there."

He crossed his legs and sat back. "There's one other thing. Monique is living in a safe house, an address no one knows. I will tell you, but *no one* else must know. Not your people here, and certainly not Justine and the communists. They don't know what the real situation is, and they must *not* know. If they found out they would make political capital out of it. She couldn't bear that."

"I understand."

He slid his cigarette case back in his pocket. "So you must go to see Monique alone, without Justine — I insist. Your French is quite good enough; you've a bit of an accent, but otherwise you sound bilingual to me."

"Thank you. And no, I won't take Justine and I won't let anyone follow me."

"Good. All I ask is that, if anything comes of the information she gives you, please tell us and we will publish it when the time comes. It will also help Monique's reputation, that she helped you British as well as the Resistance." He eyed me. "Do we have a deal?"

I nodded. "Of course. I'm grateful you came to see me and if I can ever return the favour, I'll do my best."

He ran his tongue around his lips. "I think the general was a bit too sensitive about SC2. But he knows how badly damaged France has been by collaboration. It's important to him — to us — that we play a big part in our own liberation. Vichy will stay with us as a stain for a while. De Gaulle — whatever you think of him — is our best hope of overcoming that."

I moved my head in a non-committal way. This wasn't my fight.

I stood up and so did he.

We shook hands. "I hope we shall meet again," I said, and he smiled.

I opened the door for him to leave.

Standing right outside the door was Justine.

21

The rue Morand was certainly quiet. Just behind the Gare de l'Est, near the Canal Saint-Martin, it was a narrow thoroughfare of workshops, garages, one or two studios, and — I noticed — a wholesale fur warehouse. Dogs and cats lurked in the rubble, some of which, it seemed to me, predated the war. It was not a part of Paris you would visit by choice. Antoine Picard's people had selected this location well, although I doubted whether Monique Brèger agreed.

Even so, I had arrived via three changes of train on the Métro, just to make sure no one was following me. With Justine's interest in Antoine Picard I was taking no chances.

I was as certain as I could be that I had not been followed. The only person who got off with me at the Riquet Métro station was an old woman who had been already in the carriage when I boarded at Port de la Villette.

The number that I wanted was 46 rue Morand. I found the even numbers and crossed the street, to the side with the odd numbers. Not every garage or warehouse displayed its number prominently, but enough did for me to register my progress. Number 46, I judged, would be more or less opposite numbers 43 to 49, and so it proved. I kept walking but noted that 46 was a tyre warehouse with three or four floors above it.

I walked on and went round the block, where I saw a café. I stopped for a coffee, to give myself a further chance to spot if anyone was behind. The only person in sight was loading bicycles on to a van.

I approached number 46 at a good pace, stopped suddenly, pressed the bell, and looked about me.

There was no one near. No one else had stopped suddenly, and no one was looking my way.

I waited, I heard footsteps, and then the door opened slightly.

"Madame Brèger?" I whispered slightly. "You are expecting me. Colonel Picard sent me. My name is Juno."

It was the name Picard and I had settled on during a brief telephone conversation when he had confirmed the date and time of the meeting. Juno was the code name of one of the British beaches at Normandy on D-Day.

The door opened, but the woman turned before I could say hello or shake her hand,

and retreated up some steep stairs.

At the top of the stairs she led the way into a long room, darkened by heavy lace curtains drawn across the windows. Two lamps with glass shades were twin pools of light throwing deep shadow everywhere else.

She sat in a low easy chair, just beyond the range of the lights.

The only other chair was on the far side of a dead fireplace. From there, as I sat down, I could make out her face, but not clearly.

Her left eye was grey-silver. A crimson patch, like a large leaf, lay over the same side of her face, extending as far down as her jaw. Above her forehead, a patch of hair was missing, presumably where the acid had killed the follicles. Part of her nose was red, her lower lip was distended, and the flesh on her neck under her chin was . . . It had the texture and consistency of dead leaves.

Despite all this, I could still see that, once upon a time, she had been very beautiful. The right half of her face proved it.

"Thank you for seeing me," I said as softly as I could.

"I hope I can help you," she replied.

Her voice was deeper than I had expected. And it was a self-confident voice. She might have been victimised, that voice said, and she might still be in hiding, for what others might still do to her, if they found her, but she knew what she had achieved, and nothing could take that away from her.

"Shall we start?" I said.

"You're busier than I am; you set the pace. Just one question."

"Go on."

"Where did you learn your French? It's very good but you have a slight accent — I can't place it."

I smiled. "I learned my French first in Switzerland, then I spent two years in the early part of the war in and around Lorraine. Can you understand me all right?"

"Oh yes, it's not that. Your syntax is near perfect, but your accent is . . . Well, I haven't heard that kind of accent before. That's all. Don't worry about it."

I said nothing for a moment.

"What shall I call you? Madame Brèger? Monique?"

"We are on the same side, yes? You are not a communist? Antoine said you were not a communist."

"No, I am not."

"Then call me Monique. You are . . . ?"

"Matthew, Matt. Matt Hammond."

"Matthew. Mathieu, my father's name. Ask your questions, Mathieu."

I got out a pad and a pen, and my folder.

"As I expect Colonel Picard told you, I work for SC2. I'm second in command of the French section, which will wind down soon, if the war goes as well as we expect it

432

to. We sent a number of agents into France, as you know, but forty-one are still missing; twenty-seven men and fourteen women. My job is to find out what happened to them, the women in particular. We fear that most of those who are missing have been captured, interrogated, and shipped east by the Germans, where they will have been executed. But we can't be certain in all cases."

I opened my folder.

"I interviewed a Claudine Petit in La Santé prison. She was a cleaner in the Gestapo headquarters in avenue Foch, and she recognised some of the names, but not all. If I could read out the names of the missing — their proper names and their code names — perhaps you could search your memory and tell me if any of these people did come through Gestapo headquarters in Paris and, if so, if you have any idea of what happened to them."

She nodded. "I can do better than that, Mathieu." She reached out to the table at her side and picked up a notebook. She held the notebook in front of her, smiling.

"I kept notes when I could," she whispered. "I knew it might matter someday. I don't have to rely on my memory."

I nodded, slightly incredulous — but marvelling at her efficiency. "Very well —"

"Before you go on," she said, "Did this Claudine Petit explain the difference between

433

Ravensbruck and Pforzheim?"

I frowned. "No, no — she never mentioned it. I don't know what you mean. What *do* you mean?"

Monique opened the book and leafed through the pages. Not finding what she was looking for, she closed it again.

"I would say that close to fifty agents came through Avenue Foch over the final few months. The Gestapo, as you must know by now, had penetrated several of your circuits —"

"Yes, we did find out about that, eventually, a bit late in the day but yes, I know what happened."

She nodded.

"People were kept in Avenue Foch for only a few days and then divided into two groups —"

"Oh yes?" This was news to me.

"Agents who the Gestapo thought were more important, or who resisted interrogation in Paris, who had information still *in* them, so to speak, were sent to Ravensbruck — that's a camp north of Berlin. There, as I understand it, they underwent more intensive interrogation techniques, more sophisticated torture methods, in fact, before being executed after however long their torture lasted, two or three weeks, or occasionally more, as I overheard it."

I was scribbling notes. "And the other group?"

"The other group consisted of people who, the Gestapo judged, didn't have any more secrets in them, so there was no point in interrogating them further. They were sent to a camp at Pforzheim — just across the Franco-German border. There, they were executed straightaway. The Gestapo thought it was safer to execute them on German soil — had they done it in Paris, word might have leaked out, the Resistance might have got involved, the graves might have become shrines. It was a straightforward bureaucratic decision."

She opened her notebook again.

"So, let me find the names I recorded and, if I can, I will tell you who was sent where."

While she flipped through the pages, I said, "I have proper names and code names. What do you have?"

She rubbed her blind eye with a finger. "I have some proper names but mostly code names — that's how they were referred to in Avenue Foch. I think the Gestapo preferred code names because it depersonalised things, and made execution easier — ah! Here we are."

She laid the opened notebook on her lap and smoothed down the pages with her fingers.

Her fingers were as beautiful as the rest of

her had once been.

"I'll read the proper names first. Just say 'Ravensbruck,' 'Pforzheim,' or 'no,' if you don't recognise a name or know what his or her fate was. Okay?"

"Bien sûr."

I started with the men's names this time. Out of twenty-seven, Monique had twenty in her written lists; twelve had been sent to Ravensbruck, eight to Pforzheim. The others she didn't know about.

When I switched to code names, the number she had notes about rose to twenty-three, of which fifteen had gone to Ravensbruck and eight to Pforzheim.

Then I came to the fourteen women.

I read their proper names in random order.

Of the first thirteen, she recognized eight, five of whom were sent to Ravensbruck and three to Pforzheim.

The last name I read out was Madeleine Dirac.

Monique looked down her records, a finger scoring down the page.

After a moment, she said, "No record."

The skin on the back of my neck was damp.

I now knew the probable fate of eight of the fourteen women, so I just read out the six code names that fitted the women whom she had not recognised, just in case.

"Marée." This was Katrine Howard, who had been with Madeleine in Ardlossan, who

Madeleine had given the Schiller book to, in the Red Anchor.

"Ravensbruck."

Poor Katrine. I swallowed hard.

"Rossignol."

"Ah yes. Ravensbruck."

"Poisson."

"Ravensbruck."

"Boulanger."

Pause. "No record."

"Maître."

"I didn't catch that — say it again, please."

"Maître."

"Yes! Pforzheim."

Slight pause.

"Chêne."

"Again?"

"Chêne."

"Hmm." Her finger slid down the page.

Turned to the next one.

And the next one.

"Ah! Yes. Pforzheim."

I wrote down what I was told and then pretended to go on scribbling as I did my best to assimilate the news.

I was breathless. I wanted to be sick.

This was terrible, terrible. Madeleine *had* been captured, just as Claudine Petit had said, but . . . but she had not resisted interrogation as fiercely as I thought she would, and had been sent to Germany to be executed immediately.

She wasn't a German spy — she was dead.

I tried to swallow, half retched, and felt the burning taste of vomit in my throat.

She had been dead for weeks.

I finished my scribbling and closed my book.

"You have been most helpful, Monique."

She grunted. "You don't look as though you've been helped. You look as though you badly need a drink." She stood up. "I know it's barely four o'clock in the afternoon, but would you like a drink? A stiff drink, I mean. A proper drink. Have I just confirmed that you have lost some dear colleagues?"

I put my notes back in my briefcase, nodding.

"Then let's drown our sorrows in a Ricard, yes?"

"I'd prefer a Scotch."

"Then Scotch it shall be."

She crossed the room to a sideboard with some glass decanters on it. With the disfigured side of her face turned away from me, in profile she looked normal, intact, beautiful.

She poured herself a Ricard, added water, turning it cloudy white, and emptied a generous helping of Scotch into a tumbler. Then she came directly across to me.

She was ready for me to see her close up.

I stood up and took the glass from her.

We toasted each other.

"To wartime bravery," I said. "Colonel Picard has told me what happened. I am very sorry."

She shrugged. "You spend years fighting the enemy and then your so-called friends do you the most damage." She looked up at me. "I was beautiful once."

"I can see that," I said.

"You were close to these colleagues you lost?"

"Yes. One in particular."

"A lover?"

I nodded.

"The one you kept for last, who was sent to Pforzheim?"

"Yes. Was it obvious?"

She smiled and gestured to the chair I had been sitting in.

"Sit down again, please, Mathieu."

I did as she asked, and she sat back again in her seat, nursing her Ricard.

She opened her book, leafed through it, turned the pages until she came to what she was looking for.

"Here we are." She sipped her drink, placed the glass on the table next to her chair and looked across to me. "On June 12, the Gestapo in Paris got word that two of the people on their way to Pforzheim, a man and a woman, had escaped." She held her finger steady on the page. "They were part of a group of five, but I don't know who it was exactly who escaped. I don't have their names or their code names. We never found out because the Gestapo had to retreat, like everyone else, and my relationship with Ulrich Kolbe came to an abrupt end. But it could be that . . . You realize what I am saying?"

I did indeed, and suddenly the day brightened, even in that darkened room.

"It's something," I said. I gulped my whisky. "A lifeline. Thank you."

She nodded and sipped her Ricard again.

I had got what I had come for, but I couldn't just leave.

"One other thing, Monique. While you were with Kolbe, or in Avenue Foch, did you ever hear, or overhear, any references to a double agent, someone who ostensibly worked for SC2 but in fact was a German agent? Did anyone ever mention or refer to a 'mole' or a spy?"

"N-n-no, but . . . now that you mention it, there must have been one."

"What do you mean? I don't understand."

"Well, I'm guessing, of course. But about a year ago Ulrich suddenly acquired an English cigarette lighter. I noticed it on the dresser in the bedroom we used in his flat. He took it away from me and I never saw it again."

"Couldn't he have bought it on the black market, or stolen it from one of the captured agents?"

"I don't think he would have stolen it, even from a captured agent. He was a remarkably upright man in some ways. He was a Nazi, of course, but I don't think he would have stooped to petty theft. And he wouldn't have bought it on the black market — he despised that, and, being the Gestapo, he didn't go short. He didn't need the black market."

She sipped her Ricard again. "For a time I wondered where he got that lighter, and who from, but I didn't dare ask him, and I must admit I had forgotten it until you mentioned it just now. He was fond of the lighter — at least he was till I noticed it was English, when he removed it — because, I think, it represented a big secret in the war. I'm piecing this together — since you asked your question about a double agent. It's the best I can do."

I nodded, writing down what she was saying.

That took a while. I tried my whisky, then I said softly, "And what was it like? Being with Kolbe, I mean. Leading a double life of such . . . intimacy? Was he good to you, gentle, generous, considerate? Did he have a family? All wartime experiences are unusual, but yours . . . yours was unique."

She sat back in her chair and again put her glass on the table next to it.

"That will be a big question for me, after the war. Before the war, before the Nazis came, the Germans were the most civilized people on the planet — the best culture, the best science, some of the best theologians even. Ulrich — I still think of him as Ulrich — was part of that civilization. He kept his brutality quite separate, he never brought it into the bedroom. He was never rough with me, he loved the fact that I was a pastry chef, and took a great deal of interest in my work. He had a wife and two sons back in Germany. He liked me well enough, but he missed his family."

"Did he never suspect you?"

"If he did, he never made anything of it. I . . . I shouldn't say this, perhaps, but . . . Well, I am very skilled at making love. He had power and he enjoyed spoiling me, because he *could.* And he made it easy for me. Sometimes I feel that those women who did this to my face" — and she pointed to the crimson mark on her cheek — "had a case. I *did* live well."

"But you —"

"Yes, I did. I took risks, I got information, information that saved lives . . . but in order to stay where I was I had to let some intelligence go by without any action on my part. If I had leaked *everything* I would have given myself away. So it cut both ways. I saved lives, I let some people die. It couldn't be helped."

She picked up her glass and drained it.

She pointed to her face again. "I have this

442

but I am *alive.* Can you say that about your dear friend?"

Later that night I lay in bed in the Hotel Séranon, accompanied by what I had left of the whisky I had brought from London, three of that day's newspapers, and the map of Europe I had also brought with me.

I was aware that I had, so far, done precious little about locating François Perrault, and would have to act soon, but that night the accounts in the newspapers were especially vivid about the pace of the war. The maps printed in the papers showed that our forces had taken Châtel and Lunéville, near Nancy, and that fierce fighting had broken out at Nijmegen. So some of our troops were quite a way east. At the same time, the Germans in Calais were still holding out, as they were at Brest. Most of northern France, Belgium, and parts of southern Holland were in our hands, but there *were* those worrying outposts.

Looking at the map, I could see that Lunéville — our forward-most point — was just under a hundred miles from Pforzheim, a few miles into Germany. At the moment, our forces were making headway at anything from seven to twelve miles a day, so even on the most favourable scenario we were more than a week away from reaching Pforzheim and that was —

Suddenly, from down below, came the sound of a door being opened quickly, and banging against the wall of the hall. Voices could be heard immediately, laughing, accompanied by the sound of more banging. I looked at my watch: 1:35 a.m.

Then I heard footsteps on the stairs, and more voices. Laughter, drunken laughter from the noise level.

I knew what was happening. This was the third night in a row of these late-night noises. An American jazz band, touring with the U.S. troops, had been billeted in the hotel and they liked to party when they weren't playing — staying out late, drinking, and joining in late-night jam sessions, in whatever club they found themselves.

The Hotel Séranon, once a quiet haven, was one no longer.

I tried to concentrate on my map.

If Madeleine *had* been the woman who escaped on her way to Pforzheim, she could, of course, be anywhere now. And there was no guarantee that, if and when the Allies reached there, and I was allowed into the prison, its records would tell me who had (and therefore who had not) been executed. At the same time, it was the best chance I had. Possibly, as Justine had said, not everyone there had been killed.

Maybe Madeleine was alive *in* Pforzheim.

Maybe that's why she hadn't been heard from.

More voices in the corridor outside, then the sound of a bath running. This had happened for three nights also. Why was it that American jazz musicians liked to take baths in the middle of the night? And did they have to tell each other about it, at the tops of their voices?

I heard a door open.

"Hey, you! Keep the noise down, will you? It's half past fucking one in the morning." I recognized the voice of one of the other British officers billeted at the hotel.

"Okay, okay," said a voice, in reply. "I'm just taking a bath, for Christ's sake."

"Well, do it with your mouth shut. Got it?"

"Sure, sure," said the voice.

But, at that hour, even the sound of the water running was loud enough.

The voice in the bath started singing.

"Shut the fuck *up*!" shouted the British officer. "Or I'll shoot you!"

"Scary," said the voice. But he shut up.

I finished my cigarette, drained the whisky glass, and put the newspapers and map on the floor. I put out the light and lay on my back.

Pforzheim was a long shot, a very long shot. But someone had escaped on the way there.

"*Voilà, mon cher,* I promised to show you

445

someone famous. Unless I am mistaken, that is Mr. 'Emingway over there — *no*?"

The lighting in the bar of the Ritz Hotel didn't actually *aid* anyone's sight at the best of times and, given the late hour we had arrived, and the smoke that thickened the atmosphere, visibility was far from ideal.

I peered across the room. The famous Ritz bar didn't seem to have suffered at all during the occupation. The crystal chandeliers glistened discreetly, the red-and-gold wallpaper absorbed the light and then returned it, the deep green carpet was as lush as spring wheat, and the small tables, with their paler green tablecloths, boasted diminutive candles that barely helped you distinguish one drink from another.

We had come on here after another jazz and whisky session at La Pleine Lune.

"It could be Hemingway," I replied softly.

The man in question was tall, and of muscular build, with a round face ringed with a grey beard. I had heard that a lot of literary types — journalists and authors — had flooded into Paris in the wake of the liberation. A lot of the better-heeled ones stayed at the Ritz — the Parisians sarcastically called it "Ritzkreig."

"Who's that with him?" I added.

"Gertrude Stein?"

"Better not stare," I said. "Let's leave them to their privacy, whoever they are."

"You don't believe it's Hemingway?" This time she pronounced the "H."

"It's hard to tell at this distance and in this light," I replied. "And besides, have you never noticed that when you see someone famous in the flesh, they never look *exactly* like their picture in the paper? It's close enough — we'll pretend it's him."

"I shall go and ask." She made to lift herself out of her seat, but I leaned forward and put my hand on her arm. "Leave them be, Justine. Let them enjoy their drinks. Sit down."

She sat down with a pout and a moue all at the same time.

"Why were you so keen to come here anyway?" I said after a pause. "The drinks are three times the price of those in the Lune."

She didn't say anything for a moment. Then, "You have been . . . how shall I say, how do you British put it? . . . 'off colours' these past few days. Ever since Colonel Picard visited you. What did he say? What did he tell you, this Gaullist? I see you are thinking thoughts, thoughts that you don't share with me, that you hardly ever smile, that you never look at me directly. You work in a mechanical way, you don't joke with people, you don't gossip, you certainly don't flirt. You are not happy and you are not much fun. I thought seeing some famous people would give you — how do you say? — an elevation, a lift. Maybe we would have something to talk about. Maybe you would smile."

She leaned forward and picked up her drink. "I was wrong."

She sat back again.

I took my time, sipping my Scotch slowly. At Ritz prices I couldn't afford to go any quicker.

"Do you have a husband, Justine, a boyfriend, a lover?"

"I am not married but of course I have a lover."

"Is he here in Paris?"

"No. He is in the east. He leads a union in Nancy."

"Do you miss him?"

She nodded. "Of course. But the war goes on. I know we cannot be together, not for now."

"But you love him?"

A smaller nod this time. "But he loves me more, I think."

I turned that over in my mind. An interesting answer — on the cold side, but practical. No doubt they were both members of the Communist Party, though I didn't want to get into that. It didn't *sound* like a great love match.

I weighed carefully what I could say. "A week ago, you were there — in La Santé prison — when I found out that *my* lover, Madeleine Dirac, code name Oak, had been captured and therefore almost certainly killed. That is why I am as I am. That is why I have been so . . . so *silent* this past week. Part of me is hoping, keeping alive a ridiculous hope that my Madeleine is one of the few — the very few — agents who have been captured but not executed. The other part of me is grieving. I'm sorry but I can't help it."

She leaned in to me so that I could smell the soap she washed with. Her skin, even that close, was unblemished.

"What is it you miss most? Her beauty? Her skin? Her body? Her talk? Making love? Waking up together?"

"All of that, of course, all of that. And —"

"Yes?"

"This will sound mad, but we have a dog, a West Highland terrier —"

"*Alors.* At last you are smiling."

It was true. I had noticed that myself.

"Sometimes, when we are making love, and not wanting to be left out, Zola — that's the dog — jumps on the bed, to keep us company. That always has us in stitches."

"Stitches? What is that, stitches?"

"It's slang for making us laugh helplessly. If I thought . . . if I thought I would never have that again —" I shook my head. "I can't imagine not having it again."

"Where is this Zola now?"

"He is staying with my secretary. They too have fallen in love."

She let a long pause go by.

I felt awkward but didn't know what more to say.

"So you are not just a colonel clearing up after a messy war, but something else as well. I should have guessed that something very personal was troubling you."

"It's more than that," I said. And I explained about Madeleine's affair with Philippe in the Limoges area, and the incomplete newspaper cutting I had encountered in the café on my first night in Paris.

"That part is easily settled," she replied. "Old newspapers are by law deposited in the Bibliothèque Nationale. It is in the rue de Richelieu and we can go whenever you want."

That was something, a glimmer of a way forward. Maybe.

She looked at me, smiled, and leaned closer still. "And there's something else, yes? Now you are worried that because you are grieving it will interfere with your ability to do your job?"

"That's one of my worries, yes."

"And the other worries?"

"I can't tell you everything, Justine. You must know that." But of course the ambiguity had got to me — not knowing what happened to Madeleine when she suddenly stopped transmitting; was she captured, had she been taken to one of the areas where the Germans were cut off, had she got trapped

450

in a ratline, or had she really been sent east, as Claudine Petit seemed to indicate? I felt out of breath just listing the possibilities that underlay the ambiguities facing me. "Why don't you tell me something, Justine? Tell me about the Communist Party."

"Why? No. You are not really interested."

"Do you have meetings? You must do."

She looked at me and shrugged. "Of course we have meetings; we are communists. Everything is discussed before we act. Because we discuss everything, and vote on it, we have good discipline. Unlike the Gaullists, who have to do what he says."

I didn't want to get into that.

"Tell me about *your* leaders. What type of people are — ?"

"Not tonight, Englishman." She nodded, lowered her voice again, and looked directly at me. She leaned forward and put her hand on my arm. "Would you like to sleep in my flat tonight?"

"What?"

"Don't worry. I don't mean would you like to sleep *with me.* What I mean is that I am sure the Hotel Séranon is very plain, very sparse, very cold emotionally. You yourself said the jazz people make a lot of noise late at night and stop you sleeping."

She took hold of her wine glass. "I have a spare bedroom. There are lots of flowers and photographs everywhere. The whole place smells of woman — there are books all over the chairs and tables, newspapers. It's untidy, but lived into — I think I mean 'lived in.' " She smiled. "I have wine, Pernod — we can buy some whisky, I can lend you a dressing gown — don't ask whose — and I have a radio tuned to the BBC."

I was weighing up her offer when she added, "And I share my flat with someone you will find irresistible. He's called Max."

"Oh? And why is Max so irresistible? Isn't your boyfriend jealous?"

She smiled and squeezed my hand again. "No, not at all. You see, Max is a Cairn — almost a West Highland terrier."

22

I'll say one thing for Justine: she was a good psychologist. I loosened up a lot after I moved into her flat.

It was amazing what a difference flowers and photographs and Max, Justine's Cairn terrier, made. But I was never going to get rid of that solid mass lodged near my heart, which kept me awake into the small hours, however comfortable the bed in which I slept. It woke me early however late I had dropped off.

What most preoccupied me, of course, was exactly *how* I was going to find out whether it was Madeleine who had escaped on her way to Pforzheim. Until I knew, one way or the other, I had put my visit to the Bibliothèque Nationale indefinitely on hold. No point in tempting fate. But I had at last begun to give some thought to my interim report and my little — or not-so-little — deal with Rupert Hathaway.

I knew, for instance, that my target had to

be François Perrault. Hard as it might be to kill him and get away with it, he was here in Paris, or so I had been told. Daniel Legros was miles away and would, most likely, only turn up at the last minute before meeting Perrault. No time at all to make any kind of plan.

The window of Justine's spare room looked out on to the slate roofs of Paris, and when it rained, which it did a lot that month, the slates glistened during the day against the metallic grey of the clouds, and glinted in the amber lights of the city at night, like the scales on a giant goldfish.

Justine's flat was only two stops on the Métro from the École Lavoisier — at a pinch, we could have walked.

We fell fairly quickly into a routine. Since I was always awake early, and since I have always been an early-morning person, I saw to breakfast. I put the kettle on, hurried downstairs to the bakery on the corner, bought four croissants still hot from the oven, stepped across to the newsagent's for that day's paper, and returned in time to make hot coffee — black market, of course. Having prepared everything, I left for the *école* before Justine, while she read the paper (after me) and cleared up. Everybody in the office found out soon enough that I had moved in with Justine and I didn't bother to correct any wrong impressions that news might have created. No one said anything, not even Roland. Even so, I thought it looked better if we arrived at the office separately. I don't know why it felt better — it just did.

Normally, my first task when I arrived at the *école* was to read the telegrams that had come in from London. Cathcart Place sent us a digest every morning of what our forces had accomplished the day before. That day I read that there had been an airborne invasion of Holland. Metz had been surrounded and was expected to fall at any minute, twenty thousand Germans had surrendered at Orléans, Boulogne had finally fallen, but Calais was still holding out. Some of our forces were already *in* Germany now, near Aachen and Trier.

The two decrypters in the office were female, and British. The three secretaries were French, and every day by noon, they prepared a summary of developments inside France, taken from the newspapers. All in all, we did our best to keep up to speed.

Roland Kemp was a taciturn man, a graduate of Cambridge University, where he had read German and French. Before the war he had studied in Dresden but had left in 1936, he told me, when the Nuremburg rallies had begun, and returned to Cambridge to do a second degree, this time in mathematics. He had been co-opted into SC2 on its inception in 1940: he was excellent at breaking codes.

He wasn't married, and I didn't know much more about him than that.

After I had been living in Justine's apartment for about a week, we had a breakthrough with Ida Cooper, code name Flame, or Flamme. A cipher from London told us she had not been captured, as we had thought, but had managed to take a ratline all the way down the Atlantic coast of France to Portugal, where, knowing the invasion was imminent, she had lain low. Once she had heard news of D-Day, she had quietly made arrangements to board a ship heading north. She had now reached Southampton safely. That meant only thirteen women now needed accounting for. I was pleased, of course. But, in my darker moments, I wondered whether, if Ida had at last surfaced, did that not mean that Madeleine should have turned up by now, too? If she had escaped?

I never quite finished those thoughts.

I was sitting at my desk, rereading the decoded report about Ida/Flame, and having these gloomy ruminations, when Roland knocked on my door and barged in, without waiting for an answer.

I looked up.

"Guess what?" he said.

"Hitler's surrendered."

"However did you pass the officer's exam, sir?"

We both grinned.

"I give up then," I said. "What is it?"

He laid a piece of paper on my desk.

"Ulrich Kolbe has been captured. He's in Saarburg Prison. The intelligence exchange system works — he was captured at the weekend."

Over Roland's shoulder, I could see Justine lurking. She had obviously been given this intelligence before I had.

"That's fantastic news!" I breathed.

This changed things, or it might do. As a high-ranking officer, and if I could persuade him to play ball, Kolbe should know where Madeleine — where all our agents — had been sent. If I could get to him, that should settle things, one way or the other, about the fate of the SC2 agents. Then I could concentrate on Hathaway's problem.

"Today is — what? — Tuesday," I added, thinking hard. I read the slip of paper he had put on my desk. "There's nothing to stop us leaving tomorrow, is there?"

"None at all," he said. "Well, that's not quite true. First I need to get you a vehicle and some juice."

"How soon will you know?"

He shrugged. "An hour. No more than two."

I nodded. "We have maps?"

"We wouldn't be much of an army without them, would we?"

"I mean a map with the front lines marked

on it. According to what I have read, our front line is around Trier — that's no more than twenty miles beyond Saarburg."

I reached for the phone on my desk. "I'd better check that we can, in fact, get out there."

Roland got up and went into the outer room to set up the vehicle and petrol.

I had the latest Expeditionary Forces staff sheet in front of me, several pages thick and bang up-to-date. In it were the current numbers of the British and American general staff. I called Tactical Liaison. When a voice answered, I explained who I was, where I was, and what I wanted to do.

"I need to get to Saarburg Prison immediately, to interview a captured officer, who was at one time the chief interrogator of the Gestapo in Paris. In connection with possible war crimes."

I wasn't sure of the army protocol in these circumstances. The man at the other end of the line had no way of knowing that I was who I said I was, and there was no system of identifying codes — who could keep track, or hold them in his head, with a war on? He either had to believe me or not.

"Hold on," he said, and the line went dead.

After a moment he was back on. "What rank is this prisoner?"

"*Standartenführer.* A colonel to us."

"And you say he was head of the Gestapo

458

in Paris?"

"Yes. Well, chief interrogator."

"Hold on."

The line went dead again.

There was a longer delay this time.

But then he was back.

"I can't tell you where the front is today, not over the phone. But I can tell you that Metz has fallen at last, and I can tell you that you will need a pass to go beyond Sierck-les-Bains, that's the Franco-German border. Even then you will only be allowed through to Saarburg in an armoured Jeep or Land Rover. And you should know that the area has not yet been de-mined, though that may happen by the weekend. If all that doesn't put you off, and you've already tasted all that Paris has to offer, and you've got the right paperwork, you can be our guest."

"Thank you, Colonel," I said and hung up.

"Roland!" I bellowed.

He came running to the door. "Sir?"

"I've checked with Reims. We are only allowed into Germany itself if we have an armoured Land Rover. Does that pose us problems?"

Roland sucked his teeth. "It might — they're not ten-a-penny. Let me see what I can do."

He disappeared again.

"Justine!"

She appeared in the doorway.

"Yes, Colonel."

"Two questions," I said.

She nodded.

"Have you travelled much in the east of the country recently?"

She shook her head. "No, but Gilles has." Gilles was her boyfriend.

"What's it like?"

She gave me one of her French looks.

"What do you think it's like? There's a war on. The roads are choked with military hardware; there are roadblocks every so often; every so often the roads have been bombed or shelled and haven't been repaired, so you have to drive into a field to get round the holes, or take small lanes, where you spend half your time backing up to allow something bigger to go by."

"So what sort of speed can we hope to achieve, assuming I can get the right sort of armoured vehicle in the first place?"

"Twenty to twenty-five kilometers an hour, at the very most."

"Somewhere between twelve and fifteen miles an hour. That's what I thought."

I turned and inspected the map on the wall behind me.

"Reims is directly on our route, and a hundred miles away. Say seven or eight hours motoring. We can spend our first night there." I pointed. "Reims to Metz is about the same distance, so that's our second night. Agreed?"

She nodded.

"Metz to Saarburg is about fifty miles, but we have to cross the border that day, and we're much nearer the front. That may well be another day's motoring.

"Today is Tuesday. If we get the right kind of Land Rover and can leave tomorrow, we should be in Saarburg by Friday night. Meaning we can see Ulrich Kolbe on Saturday —"

"You're in luck, sir," said Roland, barging back in.

Justine and I turned to face him.

"All available armoured Land Rovers and Jeeps are being shipped east — makes sense when you think about it; that's where the fighting is. You can take one, carry out whatever you have to do, then drop it off in Metz, at the transport depot. You can get a train back from there."

I looked at Justine.

"If Roland will babysit Max," she said, "we can leave whenever you like."

We both looked at Roland.

"I will, I will, of course I will." He grinned. "But only on condition that you don't tell anyone what I spent the war doing."

"G.? Is that you? This is Matt, in Paris. These phones are . . . It sounds like a gale on the line. Can you hear me?"

Another whooshing sound swept along the wires.

"I can hear you, just. How's Paris? Do you want Hilary?"

"In a moment, yes. Paris . . . Well, I'm learning to drink wine," I lied.

"Hmm," she grunted. "I'll stick to gin, thank you very much."

"How's Zola?"

"Behaving himself beautifully. He's with me now. Here, I'll put the phone next to him. Say something."

"Zola!" I cried, feeling foolish. "Zola! It's me — do you recognise your master's voice? Say something: bark or growl."

There was a rapid barking, then G. was back on the line.

"That confused him totally. What a shock — he didn't know *where* the noise was coming from. He's quite upset. I don't think we'll do *that* again."

"He's not usually so nervous. You're not overfeeding him, I hope."

"I am *not*! I probably look after him better than you do. I give him a bath every week."

I grinned into the receiver. "I'll bet that goes down well."

G. grunted again. "He likes it well enough, once it's all over. Now, enough of that. I'll put you through to Hilary before the gales on the line make it impossible to hear you."

There was a short pause, during which the whooshes and gales came and went more than once.

Then, "Matt? Matt? Is that you?"

"Yes, Hilary, here I am."

"Good, I can hear you. How's Paris?"

"Rainy, a bit battered, but still beautiful."

"Lucky bugger. How are you getting on?"

I told him about my meetings with Claudine Petit and Monique Brèger, and my upcoming visit to Ulrich Kolbe. "After that I should be able to compile my interim report."

"Well, that's something. How about — you know — your own mission?"

"Not good. Not good at all. Looks like she was sent east, to the camps. And that means —"

"I know what it means, Matt. What a bugger — I'm so sorry. But you can grieve later. That sounds harsh, but we mustn't lose sight of the wider reason you are in France. And I'm sorry to have to press you, but I do need that interim report. Despite the prime minister's intervention, MI6 haven't totally gone away — they're still a headache. They've been at this game longer than we have, and they've got one or two new MPs in their pockets, making trouble. Do you hear? You've got to put Madeleine to one side. I must insist."

"Okay, okay. I'll do all I can to act quickly after I've been to Saarburg at the weekend."

"Good. Good. I'll look out for your report."

"And how are you, Hilary? How's Crichton?"

"Crichton's okay, not so different from

Grieves. And MI6 is not our only headache — I've got a blinder, had it for a week. But I'll live."

We rang off.

I felt pretty glum. It looked as though I'd lost Madeleine. Foolishly, I wondered whether Zola would even know me when I did get home. How long is a dog's memory?

Justine reached up and, with both hands, pulled back her mane of rust-red hair and shaped it into a ponytail. The music at the Lune was different tonight — guitars and a double bass, softer, easier on the ears. Suggestive.

She was drinking wine, as usual; I had gone straight to the whisky. And — a first — we had eaten dinner in the club. Chicken was the staple in those days, if you could get it, and chicken it was that night.

We had spent dinner discussing the upcoming trip to Reims and points east. Justine had told me that, as soon as the trip was over, and assuming we got more or less what we wanted, she might stop off for a night in Nancy on the way back, to see Gilles.

"Is Gilles a communist, like you?"

"Yes, of course."

I nodded. "I read those pamphlets you gave me."

"And?"

"Those three secretaries in the office — the

three French girls. Are any of *them* communists?"

"Why do you ask? What has it got to do with the pamphlets I gave you?"

I tapped the back of her hand, resting on the table. "Don't be touchy. It's just that their résumé of the newspapers that they prepare every day never has anything in it about the dispute between the Gaullists and the communists. There must be *something* in the papers from time to time — yet they never include it."

"They are told to include only news directly related to military affairs."

"Oh? On whose orders?"

"Roland's, I think."

I nodded. "I'm going to have the briefing changed. We need some understanding of French politics. Not a lot, but some."

"I'm sure Roland — and the women — will do what you want."

"And what *is* the latest on the Gaullist-communist tussle? What's going to happen?"

"De Gaulle is still giving himself airs and graces, laying down the law, making proposals as if he is already president of France. Didn't Antoine Picard tell you any of this? If he didn't, what did he tell you?"

I said nothing.

After a pause she went on. "The party is having a conference in seven days' time to consider — and vote on — what de Gaulle proposes."

"Who actually runs the party now?"

"There is a steering committee of five — they will organize the meeting."

I sipped some whisky. "Who are the five?"

"Oh, you wouldn't know them."

"Really? I was here in forty-one and forty-two, remember. I met a lot of Resistance people, some of them communists. Try me."

Sipping her wine, she put the glass back on the table.

"Jules Pilany?"

I shook my head.

"Francine Adelbert?"

"No."

"Daniel Longchamp?"

"No."

"François Perrault?"

I swallowed hard but managed to say "No." But then, as Justine's brow puckered into a small frown, I added, "Hold on . . . Wasn't there a . . . Wasn't there a François Perrault who . . . Yes, didn't he win the Nobel Prize . . . for something . . . something scientific, before the war?"

She smiled. "Yes, well done. François is a most distinguished party member, who gave up his career for the Resistance. He has a lot of following in the party —"

"And who is the fifth member of the committee?" I didn't want us to dwell too much on Perrault.

466

"Oh," she said, temporarily wrong-footed. "Oh, it's . . . it's . . . Luc Lippens, who —"

"Ah!" I breathed, "*There* you are, I know Luc, or I did. Wasn't he based in Alsace at one time?"

She nodded, smiling still more. "Yes, yes he was. Well done again. You've got a good memory."

"Well, well. Where *is* this meeting of yours? Maybe I'll come along and say hello to Luc. If I'm allowed in, of course."

She swallowed some wine. "Oh, I can get you into the meeting. That's not a problem, though it might be boring for you. It's in the Théâtre Stendhal at rue Pierre au Larde."

It was my turn to nod. Today had been a good day. Two steps forward and none back.

■ ■ ■ ■

OCTOBER

■ ■ ■ ■

23

Saarburg Prison was vast, certainly in comparison with La Santé. Long rows of low, brick-built, single-storey huts with corrugated iron roofs, all surrounded by a high brick wall and, beyond that, a barbed-wire fence patrolled by guards with dogs.

The room where Justine and I were now waiting looked like some kind of classroom. Long wooden tables, long wooden benches, a blackboard at one end, fixed to the wall. A window with a metal mesh on both the outside and the inside. The same smell of chalk in the air that we had in the École Lavoisier.

Justine stood up and rubbed the backs of her thighs. "I need to stretch my legs. Three more days in that bloody Land Rover and I might never walk again."

I nodded. "I know how you feel."

Gilles had not exaggerated. The roads in northeastern France could scarcely bear the traffic on them. There was military traffic of all kinds, not just Jeeps and Land Rovers but armoured personnel carriers, endless lines of green-grey army trucks, troop transporters, tank carriers, engineering trucks with cranes, supply trucks, ammunition trucks, ambulances, military police Jeeps. There were also some ordinary cars, *hundreds* of bicycles, a handful of very slow tractors, and a few horse-drawn carts, holding everything up. Many of the roads were narrow, especially when they passed through small towns and villages. All along, at intervals, the roads had been bombed or shelled and not yet fully repaired, and we had to wait in line to carefully negotiate our way around the rubble. In a few places, the road was half closed and the two-way traffic alternated under the supervision of soldiers or the police.

Aircraft flew overhead, keeping low. In addition to everything else, there was the noise.

And then there were the checkpoints, on the outskirts of all the major cities and some of the towns. Mostly, people were just waved through — as we were — but not everyone, and so narrow were the roads that when someone was stopped everyone behind had to stop too.

We had in fact averaged no more than twelve miles an hour on each of the days we had travelled. Paris to Reims was eight hours in the saddle, Reims to Metz much the same, and yesterday, the fifty miles from Metz to

Saarburg, across the border, had taken another six and a half hours. In both Reims and Metz, we had eaten in the hotels we had found — we were too exhausted to go out in search of any entertainment. And in Saarburg, so far as we could see, our hotel had the only restaurant in town that was open for business.

"After *that* journey, I'm rather pleased we are returning by train —"

The door flew open, and there stood Standartenführer Ulrich Kolbe.

Almost six feet tall, barrel-chested, with close-cropped but glistening silver hair, brown eyes — his softest feature. Chin thrust out, badly in need of a shave, grey uniform trousers, loose brown knitted sweater that had seen better days.

I thought: We had all seen better days.

Here was the man who might have interrogated Madeleine. Who might have tortured her, or given the order for her to be harmed. And who might well have issued the order to have her sent east, to her death. What he had done — if he had done it — was not directed at me personally, but it didn't matter. The effect was the same. If I couldn't hate Kolbe, who *could* I hate?

He took one pace forward and stopped, just inside the door. His two armed guards remained outside.

"You are Colonel Hammond, really?" he

473

said in English.

I nodded.

"Do we shake hands?" He smiled.

I didn't say anything. Why was he smiling? What did he have to smile about?

"It was nothing personal, Colonel. It was the war."

I wasn't getting into that. This was my show, our show. He was the prisoner.

"This is Lieutenant Colonel Justine Coudehard," I said, giving her a rank she didn't have but which might just help intimidate him. "Do you want to do this in French or English? My German's no good."

"My French is better than my English," he replied, nodding at Justine. "What is it you want?"

"Sit down and I'll tell you. Cigarette?"

As he sat down, Justine closed the door.

We sat around the end of one long table, he and I on the benches, Justine on what seemed to be the teacher's chair.

I waited a few moments, so he could enjoy his cigarette. It had begun to rain outside — autumn was here.

"Where are you from, Standartenführer? Where did you grow up?"

"Weimar. Do you know Germany? Does that mean anything to you?"

"Goethe, Schiller, Herder. I go that far."

He nodded. "That's something."

"Have your family been told you have been

captured?"

"I don't know. The war is moving so fast."

"What family do you have? A wife — ?"

"And two boys, eight and six."

"Still in Weimar?"

"No, Berlin now."

"Address?"

"Fifteen Schliemannplatz."

I made a careful note, implying I would help get word to them if he played ball.

"How long were you in Paris, at Avenue Foch?"

He didn't reply.

"We have information that you were chief interrogator there. Is that true?"

He didn't move. Then he nodded briefly.

"When exactly did you first start impersonating one of our agents, sending back messages to us?"

"That's operational detail. The rules of war say I don't have to answer. Why should I tell you? Why should I tell you anything?"

"Cigarettes," I replied, smiling.

He just kept looking at me.

"All right then." I tapped my fingers on the table. "Later in this interview, we may move on to war crimes. If we bring charges and you are found guilty, you could hang. If, however, you are cooperative, helpful . . . Well, it could make a difference to what we recommend for you. It could make a difference between life and death."

"So you think Germany will lose this war?"

"The British are about to take Aachen. Calais has finally fallen, with five thousand German prisoners captured. In Germany itself sixteen-year-olds have just been called up. Goebbels made a speech on the radio the other day saying that — and I quote — 'every German house is now a fortress.' Three thousand bombers hit Berlin two nights ago — more than ever before — and the Luftwaffe has disappeared. It's just a matter of time, Standartenführer — months, not years. You are an officer, an educated man. You must know that what I say is true."

"I know we have some secret weapons that could make all the difference."

"Is that what you've been told? Do you *believe* what you are saying, or are we playing a game?"

He was coming to the end of his cigarette. I let the packet lie on the table between us.

"Let's forget about when you penetrated our network, at least for now. I am interested in the fate of our agents in F Section; all of them, but especially the women. You can help me there. You are not putting the future of the Reich at risk by telling us what you know. And I can get word to your family, via the Red Cross, that you are alive and well, without mentioning" — deliberately I paused — "Monique Brèger."

His head jerked back and he glared at me.

476

Justine was looking at me too. This was a name she didn't know. What was I playing at?

Kolbe scratched his chin. He had gone days without a shave and his stubble was clearly irritating him.

I broke the silence. "Let me ask you a general question."

I hunched forward over the table and spoke quietly.

"When you captured one of our people and brought them back to Avenue Foch, how long did you keep them there?"

He took his time answering. But then, "Two or three days usually. Some up to a week."

"Did you torture them?"

He eyed me levelly. "We roughed them up, yes. That's how I'd put it. We knew that their circuits would have been alerted when they were captured and disappeared from circulation, so unless we got information quickly, we would be too late. Also, we knew that people who are going to crack do so sooner rather than later. Avenue Foch was a kind of forward station, a first line of attack, so to speak. If they didn't crack straightaway, we didn't keep at them; we sent them east where the interrogators had more time, more space, and more . . . equipment. Paris wasn't the place for that."

I nodded.

Justine was taking notes now.

"When you say you 'sent them east,' what

exactly did that entail? What did that mean?"

"You must understand that all your agents — your British agents, I mean — were operating in plain clothes, as *spies*. They had a different status from, say, the French who worked for and with them. The Frenchies were Resistance people and, in some cases that we thought were suitable, we tried to 'turn' them, persuade them to work for us. But for the British agents, being sent east meant one of two things. Those who were interrogated and revealed nothing were sent to Ravensbruck. That's a prison camp north of Berlin where, as I understand it, they would be interrogated more intensely and then executed by firing squad, whether they revealed anything or not. Usually, they were kept in the camp for a week or two before the end came. Anyway, not long."

I didn't say anything. I knew most of what he was telling me, but confirmation was always useful and you never knew what extra detail he might provide and how important that detail might be.

"And those who weren't sent to Ravensbruck?"

"Those who weren't sent to Ravensbruck, who cracked early and told us what they knew, whatever it was, were sent to Pforzheim — that's not far from Karlsruhe, and only just across the border, if you know your German geography." He leaned forward and laid one arm on the table. "We were entirely within our rights to execute those agents, and of course we could have done it in Paris if we had wanted to. But if we'd done that, their graves might have become known, and could have formed the focus of Resistance activity, or bad propaganda, one way or the other. So they were taken into Germany itself, somewhere remote, near Pforzheim, and executed and buried immediately in unmarked graves. That was the policy laid down by Himmler in Berlin."

For a moment, we all sat still, each of us looking at the other, as this news sank in. It squared exactly with what Monique Brèger had told me.

Kolbe was so matter-of-fact. And, in a way, he was right. Our agents *were* spies, and the rules of war *did* allow for them to be executed if captured, as I had told Madeleine and the others at Ardlossan several times. Moreover, these events had taken place at a time when it was becoming clear that Germany would most likely lose the war. What did we expect?

Then I said, "If I mention some names to you — real names and code names — might you recall some of the people who passed through Paris?"

He bit his lip but gave a small smile. "I can try, yes. I'll play that game."

I looked at Justine, who reached down into her briefcase and took out a folder. She passed the document to me and I opened it, laying out the sheets of paper between us on the table.

"I'll start with proper names. Just say Ravensbruck or Pforzheim, or 'No,' if they mean nothing to you."

I gave him another cigarette. I went through the same routine as with Claudine Petit and Monique Brèger. When I read out the full names of the women, Kolbe knew the fates of all but four of them, including the fact that Katrine Howard had been sent to Ravensbruck.

I took a deep breath and said, "Madeleine Dirac."

He paused for a moment, then shook his head firmly. "No."

My hands were clammy and I wiped them on my trousers before reaching for the paper with the code names on it.

Rossignol and Poisson, he confirmed, had both been sent to Ravensbruck.

"Maître" had been sent to Pforzheim.

"Chêne."

A pause. Kolbe went to say something, chewed his cheek, then just said, simply, "Pforzheim."

I tried not to show my feelings. Pforzheim meant a quicker death than at Ravensbruck, but that was little comfort. Again, it confirmed what Monique had said.

"Tell me," I said, struggling to be as matter-of-fact as I could, "tell me, once these agents had left your office in Paris, did you ever hear from them again? I don't mean from them personally, obviously, but was any information about them, later, ever relayed back to you? Or, did they simply vanish eastwards, and that was that?"

He nodded. "Normally, they vanished, and that was that, as you put it. Except, as I remember, on two occasions."

"Oh yes?" My pulse quickened, all of its own accord. "And they were?"

"Let me think. The first time must have been in . . . I would say . . . April of this year . . . yes, that's right . . . We had just begun our penetration of your circuits and were intercepting messages from two or three of them. We got word from Ravensbruck that one of the agents there, under — what shall I say? — under their more . . . *sophisticated,* more persuasive interrogation techniques, had indicated that your people back in London suspected you had a double agent among you — in SC2, I mean. That one of your senior agents was in fact one of ours, and was leaking intelligence to us. Our people in Ravensbruck, of course, had no idea of what the true situation was — the true situation on our side, I mean — but they just reported their findings to us, as they occurred."

"And? What *was* the true situation?"

He smiled. "You were there, Colonel. Did *you* have suspicions?"

I swallowed. "I am asking the questions, Standartenführer Kolbe. You are in no position to question me. Did this person ever give you an English lighter?"

He looked at me hard. Was he concealing a reaction? But all he did was shrug. "Then I can't remember what the answer is. It was months ago. There've been a lot of . . . developments in between."

He sat back.

"Very well. Have it your way. I hope this double agent, if he or she exists, will be as loyal to you as you are to him or her, when he or she gets caught." I looked out at the rain for a moment. "So, what was the other occasion when you heard back from points further east? Can you remember that?"

"Oh yes. There's no need to be sarcastic. That was very different — I'm not giving anything away here that you couldn't find out elsewhere, given time."

The sound of the rain on the roof didn't quite drown out Justine's scribbling in her notebook.

"We got word from Pforzheim that, on the way there, two of the agents — a man and a woman — had escaped, escaped and disappeared."

Finally.

The escape was confirmed. All Monique

Brèger's information was confirmed.

The skin on my neck was damp.

"When was this? And do you know who they were?"

"Of course I know. We were very angry in Avenue Foch — spitting blood — that these people had been allowed to get away. It was bad for morale, just after the invasion, and they could have been fed back into the Resistance, knowing what they knew about the layout of our headquarters, our procedures . . . They would have been well placed to carry out serious sabotage. We kept it from Himmler — he would have had someone shot."

"And . . . as I say, when was this?"

"About the time of the invasion or just after — June or thereabouts. I remember thinking it was an especially fortunate time to escape, just as eastern France and western Germany would be beginning to . . . Power would be shifting, people would be on the move in greater numbers than before. The chaos would be worse than ever."

It was my turn to nod. "Now," I said, as calmly as I could. "Tell me . . . Can you remember the names of the people who escaped?"

He thought for a moment.

I held my breath.

"I can't remember their real names, but I can remember their code names — yes, because they were so distinctive."

I looked at Justine, then back to Kolbe.

"Okay, go on."

Time seemed to slow. I breathed in but didn't breathe out.

"The man was called Reynard, Fox; and she was called Nonne, Nun."

I was silent. The air in my lungs slipped out slowly but then my throat closed up. The skin under my chin was damp, damp and cold. Nun, Nonne, was nothing like Oak, or Chêne. There was no possibility of a mistake. The names were just too dissimilar.

I lit a cigarette. I tried to stop my hands from shaking. My throat was still closed up, but I gulped at my cigarette — I had to *do* something.

Madeleine had been in Pforzheim since the middle of June at least, ten and more weeks ago. Which meant she was dead, had been dead for weeks by now. The fact that two of our agents had escaped would have made it more likely, not less, that those who did reach Pforzheim would be quickly killed. The Gestapo would have made it clear they would not tolerate any more agents being allowed to escape.

It was all over. My pulse thundered in my ears. Madeleine wasn't a German spy, but that was small consolation. I had come to the end of the road.

But I could grieve later, I told myself, as

Hilary had said. I wasn't unusual in this war in losing someone close to me, closest to me. I could examine my feelings later. My pulse almost drummed out these thoughts.

I closed the file that was still in front of me.

"That just about wraps it up," I managed to say, handing him the rest of the cigarette pack. "These are American; I hope you don't mind."

He took the pack and pocketed it. Then he leaned back.

"You are a civilized man, Colonel Hammond."

I didn't say anything else.

He patted his pocket. "I don't mean the cigarettes, though I thank you for these anyway. When I refused to tell you something a moment ago, you didn't lose your temper, or shout and scream. Or not very much. You left me my dignity."

I still didn't say anything. I hadn't meant to leave him his dignity, but what he had told me had left me momentarily speechless.

"May I take it that you will tell the Swiss Red Cross to relay the news to my wife that I have been captured but am safe? And may I take it that . . . that you won't mention Monique?"

I nodded again. "Enough damage has already been done." I explained about the acid throwing.

He almost choked on his cigarette, coughing and heaving.

"You're sure?"

"I've seen her." I described the crimson mark on her face, the damaged follicles.

Justine stared at me again as I told the story.

Kolbe squashed out his cigarette, looking chastened and shocked. "And you don't blame me?"

I looked at Justine and back to Kolbe.

"Monique Brèger doesn't blame you."

I half wished I hadn't said that. I wasn't there to comfort him.

He stared at me, wiping his lips with his tongue, but he didn't speak for quite a while.

We heard the guard dogs bark outside.

Then he nodded.

"This is a big moment, Colonel Hammond. My father was in the First World War and was on the western front in 1914 when, at Christmastime, as I am sure you know, the troops fraternised. He always remembered it as . . . as . . . the most natural episode of his war. By luck he had a lot in common with the English soldier he met. He had more in common with that man, he used to say, than with his superior officers."

He wiped his lips with his tongue again.

"This is my moment, Colonel, my moment to show I am not just a soldier, as you have just shown me you are not vindictive merely because we are on different sides."

I am not sure he had summed me up correctly, but I still said nothing. It is sometimes the best way in interrogation.

He leaned forward and lowered his voice.

"So . . . Colonel Hammond, I will tell you something that I would not have told you had you lost your temper, or maybe even tortured me, or not been so understanding about Monique Brèger. Something for nothing — isn't that what you say? Well . . . I will tell you that we *did* have an agent high up in your organisation. In fact, we had *two*."

Justine put her hand to her mouth. She knew the French agents better than I did. Was he about to deliver a great shock?

Then he shook his head. "But I will not tell you their names — you will have to work that out for yourself."

I shrugged irritably. "If you won't give me names, how can I know whether you are telling the truth?"

He leaned forward again.

"Do you know what the truth is, Colonel Hammond? I won't tell you the names of these persons for two reasons. One, I will not betray the Reich, any more than I have done already. But second, these persons, whoever they may be, may not have been double agents. Yes, they betrayed some of your secrets, they knew all about your training methods, but who is to say if they did not betray some of our secrets too? These persons may simply have been working to survive, by

487

making themselves indispensable to you, and indispensable to us at the same time. It can — and does — happen, in a war. You will have to identify these persons and then decide if they are double agents, or double double agents. I wish you luck in finding their names."

I stood up. "And I wish *you* luck, Standartenführer Kolbe. Germany is going to lose this war, and I think you'll need rather more luck than I will."

He shrugged again and wiped his lips on the back of his hand.

At that moment he seemed more self-possessed than I did.

If what he had just told me was true, there were two moles inside SC2, not one.

If MI6 found out, they would have a field day.

And there was another — even more disturbing — possibility. If Madeleine was one of the two moles inside SC2, had Kolbe and his Nazi colleagues deliberately protected her, pretending that Chêne, Oak, had been sent to the camps and executed, when in fact she had been sent back safely to Berlin? All Kolbe's talk about double double agents could be flimflam.

Madeleine was dead. Or . . . she wasn't. And if she wasn't . . . I had been made a fool of.

24

There had been a derailing of the Métro while I had been away, and on my first morning back in Paris I had to walk to work. At several places along the way I noticed what I should perhaps have noticed before — bunches of flowers laid against buildings, against kiosks, against railings, at the entrance to small parks. I asked people who were standing over them, and looking at cards that accompanied the flowers, what they meant. I should have guessed. They were sites where Resistance heroes had been killed, or arrested before being taken away and never seen again.

Looking through the digest of newspapers that Colette and the other secretaries still put together, I registered that at St. Nazaire and La Rochelle the Germans were still holding out. That might have interested me more at one point, but not now.

I also read that General Patton had had a narrow escape, when a shell had landed near him but failed to explode. Now *there* was someone with luck.

On my desk, I found a mound of telegrams, mostly about personnel: people who had turned up; people who had worked for SC2 and whose bodies had been found in various regions of France; details of new recruits in the pipeline. Based on this information, and as soon as I could get my head around the figures, I now had enough material to compile my interim report. That should keep them quiet in Cathcart Place, and in Parliament, too.

In fact, one of my telegrams was from G., with news of Zola:

+ALL·WELL·WITH·Z·THOUGH·HE·IS·OFF·HIS·FOOD
+STOP+IS·HE·MISSING·YOU—OR·MADELEINE?
+LOVE=GERALDINE+STOP+

I stuffed that telegram in my pocket. Soon I'd have to tell G. the news about Madeleine. But not yet. And not all of it. I was still digesting what I could tell to whom — and when.

There was another telegram, this time from Hilary:

+NEED·AMMO·FOR·PARLIAMENT·URGENT+STOP
+PLEASE·SHOW·PROOF·OF·LIFE=HILARY+
STOP+

Yes, yes, I said to myself tetchily. I'll get on

it. It was all very well for Hilary to say — as he had said, the last time we spoke — that I should "grieve later," but grief isn't like that. Grief is an ocean where the waves obey their own rhythm, their own tide, where we are just thrown about to stay afloat as best we can. Where there is in fact no guarantee that we will keep our heads above water. Surely he knew that, damn him.

I reached for my typewriter and angrily took it out on the keys.

HILARY, JUST BACK FROM SAARBURG PRISON.
INTERIM REPORT IN 24 HOURS. REGARDS=
MATT

Someone else could key it into the telegraph machine.

I got up and went through into the outer room.

"Right," I said to Roland, trying to calm down. "Fill me in on what's been happening since I've been gone."

He rubbed ink from his fingers with a wet paper napkin. "Well, there's been quite a bit of activity in southern and central France. An uprising in Clermont-Ferrand, led by the Resistance, with some SC2 help, and around Dijon. The Germans are making a run for it near Besançon. Three of our male agents were in hiding north of Marseilles, but are safe now, one body has been found dead in the Pyrenees, one woman is in hospital in Clermont-Ferrand — Nancy Pargetter. She's still alive but I'm told she's dying — from typhus."

He threw the napkin into a waste bin. "Typhus is a problem in prisons, by the way. Be careful if you have to do any more prison-visiting."

I nodded, trying hard not to let my anger with Hilary pass over to Roland. "Do I smell burning?"

He leaned forward and looked into the waste bin. "You're right!" he said sharply. "Christ, a cigarette stub has set the napkin on fire."

He got up and put his entire foot into the wastebasket and stamped the flames out.

"Now," I said, "I've seen some of the telegrams, but I haven't collated them — have you?"

He nodded. "I've started. By my calculations, we can now account for ninety-four out of one hundred and sixteen agents. That means twenty-five are dead or still missing. Out of that ninety-four, sixty-seven are dead, and twenty-seven are alive, either here in France or back in Britain. Of the twenty-seven survivors, fourteen are women. Of the twenty-five still missing, thirteen are women."

"Okay, I have more information about the women. I found out at Saarburg that seven women were sent from here in Paris to a camp north of Berlin — that's the Ravensbruck I referred to, where they have almost certainly been executed. Here are their names." I handed him a piece of paper.

"On that list, also, are five women who were sent to the other camp, Pforzheim. One escaped on the way there — code name Nonne, or Nun — but the others will have been executed. That makes eleven names in all, to add to the ninety-four, meaning we now know the fate of one hundred and five agents out of the one hundred and sixteen, and that only three of those unaccounted for are women."

"What's all this in percentage terms?" said Roland. "Parliament will want to know things like that."

"You're right," I said as I felt a nudge against my leg.

I looked down. During Justine's absence in Nancy, I had brought Max with me into the office just as I had with Zola in London. Max was looking up and panting.

I smiled at Roland. "He needs to be taken outside for a moment. Will you do it while I work out these percentages?"

"Sure," he said, grinning.

The figures didn't take long. Overall, 65.5 per cent of agents had been killed, while 44 per cent of the women agents had been killed; and while 11.7 per cent of agents were unaccounted for overall, 10.7 per cent of the women were unaccounted for. So women had not, as we had feared, fared especially badly. Though the risks they had taken had equalled the risks taken by the men, their fates were broadly similar. That would stand up well in Parliament.

I was just laying out the figures neatly on a sheet of paper when Roland came back from taking Max for his stroll. I showed them to him. "This will form the basis of my interim report."

He looked at them. "Respectable figures, I would say. The women performed well, without being exposed to disproportionate risk."

"My thoughts entirely," I replied. "Did Max behave himself?"

"Oh yes," said Roland. "Nothing to complain of there. Oh, and this arrived for you, just as I was coming back into the building."

He handed me a small brown envelope, the kind that contained telegrams, with TOP SECRET stencilled at the top right-hand corner.

I felt a weight settle on my shoulders, and for a change it had nothing to do with Madeleine. Who was sending me telegrams other than through our normal transmission office? Who knew I was here in Paris, in this very office?

There was only one answer: Rupert Hathaway.

It was good timing in a way. I was about to

file my interim report and I was as certain as could be that Madeleine was dead.

"I'd better open this in my office," I said to Roland.

He nodded.

I took Max with me, closed the door firmly, and ripped open the flap.

There was a thin, crisp sheet of paper inside.

Holding my breath, I rapidly scanned the contents.

+THE·WEDDING·GOES·AHEAD·AS·PLANNED+
STOP+

I went to bed early that night. The weather had turned colder, the temperature had dropped faster than those bombs we were raining on Berlin, and I let Max clamber aboard. He lay against my legs, adding his warmth to what I generated myself.

Not that I slept. How could I, knowing that Madeleine at best was dead and at worst was a German spy? On top of that, I now had to kill a man. A man I didn't know, a man who, to all intents and purposes, had never done anyone any harm, who in fact was a force for good, certainly in his scientific and Resistance life. Yes, I had killed people before, both at a distance with a gun, and close up, in hand-to-hand fighting. But that was at a different stage of the war, and the people I had killed were very definitely the enemy. This man was an ally.

That wasn't quite true, of course, not if you accepted that, as Prime Minister Churchill himself had suggested to me, the post-war world was going to be so different from the world we all knew before.

But the world didn't *feel* very different, not to me anyway. Not yet.

How was I going to steel myself to kill François Perrault? And, arguably more to the point, how was I going to do it in such a way that it would seem like an accident? How long did I have? If Hathaway's telegram had reached me within a few hours of being sent, then Daniel Legros had just set sail to cross the Atlantic, and would be at sea for four or five days. I had to assume Hathaway's people had reasons for not killing Legros while he was at sea. Add a day travelling from Le Havre to Paris — no more because he would want to contact Perrault at the earliest opportunity. All of which meant I had less than a week to carry out what I had to carry out.

The Communist Party meeting was the day after tomorrow. Then I would lay eyes on Perrault at last. That's all I wanted to do. Justine would no doubt want to introduce me, but if at all possible I wanted to avoid that. I would find what I needed to do easier — or at least less disturbing — if I kept my distance beforehand.

I must have dropped off. For all of a sudden I awoke with a jolt as the bed mattress lurched and a body rolled in beside me.

"God, it's cold," said Justine hoarsely. "I suppose it often is at three o'clock in the morning. I need warming up."

She put one arm round my chest and pulled me to her. Through my nightshirt I could feel her breasts. She was naked.

"You would be warmer if you had something on."

She ignored that. "Sorry if I disturbed you," she whispered. "But I really am freezing. I missed the last train from Nancy but I got a lift in a lorry bringing vegetables to Les Halles. I was grateful but the lorry had no heating and now I'm a block of ice."

She put one of her legs over my torso, trying to get closer, to soak up the warmth of my body. Max was dislodged and didn't like it. He growled briefly.

She ran a hand under the cloth of my nightshirt and pressed her cold palm to my warm stomach. Then she kissed the back of my neck.

Her skin was on mine in several places, cold but clean and, as it warmed, her body smell was released.

And suddenly I was turning, turning to face her, my mouth on hers and my stiffening penis scoring along her thigh. Her flesh was still cold but her mouth was warm and she rolled on to her back and opened her legs in one quick movement.

I cannot say that there was any tenderness between us that night. I didn't know what had happened between Justine and Gilles and I didn't ask. Her flesh was soon warm, and damp with the sweat of sexual exertion, her blood near the surface of her skin, the shadows playing in stripes over her legs and abdomen and neck, making of her a tiger of the night. She took little nips out of my skin, and dug her nails into my back. Her body shook and shuddered, and then collapsed.

Madeleine was in my thoughts. How could she not be? The ocean of grief is constantly shifting.

Justine and I didn't talk, not then. We slept eventually and the next thing I knew it was daylight and she was sitting on the edge of the bed, wearing a black sweater, Max on her lap, and she was handing me a cup of coffee.

"I split up with Gilles. That's why I was late — we had a terrible fight."

I nodded. "What we did felt a bit like a fight."

She smiled. "But we were both winners, yes?"

I laughed.

"I have never made love with an Englishman before."

I looked at her levelly. "You French are the experts, right?"

"Not experts, no. But . . . making love is half of life, *n'est-ce pas*? Today, and from now on, you and I will be different with each other, yes? Matthew, Colonel Hammond, you know when to take charge, when to surrender."

"You make our fight sound like a battle."

"I am paying you a compliment."

"Thank you."

"And how was I?"

"All that I imagined."

She sipped her coffee. "The second time we will be better, you will see. Now we know each other more. Maybe we should use some protection next time, no?"

This was moving a little fast for me. Last night had been what it was: sudden, unthought-through, full-blooded, loud. I had some thinking to do.

And it was time to change the subject.

"No news on Pforzheim, yet. I am spending today writing up my interim report. We don't need you in the office, if you have other things to do."

She nodded. "I need to see François, to give him Gilles's news, before the meeting tomorrow."

I drank some coffee. "Is there broad agreement on what the communists will say to de Gaulle?"

She bit her lip. "Everyone is united in their loathing for de Gaulle, but we must work together, Gilles says. Our strength is in what we have achieved in the Resistance — no communists have had their heads shaved, not one. We were here, when de Gaulle was in London. This is what the main plank of our election strategy will be. We are the nationalists more than de Gaulle. That is Gilles's message."

She gave me a look. "Which raises the question of Antoine Picard and Monique Brèger. Are they linked? Is that why Picard came to see you?"

"Yes."

"Was she a Gaullist spy in Avenue Foch?"

"Yes."

I told Justine the whole story.

"And Picard came to see you after we visited Claudine Petit?"

"Yes, a gesture of cooperation."

"So you are a Gaullist now?"

I laughed. "Are you worried you just made love with a Gaullist? Don't be. I'm not taking sides, Justine. I have a job to do and will use whatever help is offered."

I kissed her forehead. "Will it be a noisy meeting, do you think?"

She didn't reply straightaway, simmering down. Eventually, she said, "There will be fireworks, yes — flames, I am sure. But then we will settle down to work together to take on de Gaulle. If you come to the meeting you must promise me that you will not reveal what goes on inside the hall. No one must know of our divisions; all others must think we are united. Do you agree?"

I nodded and smiled. "Of course. I'm not on anyone's side, Justine. I promise." I kissed her forehead again.

I lay back in bed and closed my eyes. I couldn't be totally certain but I thought she had just given me an idea of how I might kill François Perrault and get away with it.

The Théâtre Stendhal, on the corner of the rue Beaubourg and the rue Pierre au Larde, was — like a lot of Parisian theatres — a creation of the 1920s. It was ornate, with art deco twists and twirls around its entrance doors, which were themselves composed of languid, flowery stained glass and shiny metal that must have taken hours to polish. Lights shaped like upside-down flower buds hung from the ceiling of the foyer, which had a dead bar at one end, all its bottles and glasses tidied away. Today's proceedings were not entertainment.

At the other end of the red-carpeted space — lined with framed posters of long-gone shows — Communist Party membership cards were being assiduously inspected, though Justine seemed to know all the guardians of the proceedings. I was allowed through, so long as I remained with her — that was made very plain.

Inside, the auditorium was small — there were no more than eight hundred seats, by my eye, and about half of those were occupied. The seats were like theatre seats everywhere — red velvet with gold trimmings, small ashtrays fixed to the backs of every other one.

For obvious reasons, I wanted to sit as far back as possible, while Justine, for reasons of her own, wanted to sit at the front. She won.

She had spent the previous day on party business, she said, which I assumed meant that she was helping to sort out today's agenda; and I had at least completed my interim report and sent it encrypted to Hilary in London.

In the theatre, Justine was all business, waving hello to several colleagues, and kissing — or nearly kissing — others. As the moment drew near for the meeting to begin, she climbed on to the stage, took a sheaf of papers from one of the three men sitting at a table, and started handing round the sheets to people in the "audience." That done, she came back and sat down next to me.

"Have you seen your man, Luc Lippens?"

I shook my head. "No, have you?"

"It's possible he's not coming — so from your point of view it's all a waste. Do you want to leave? Won't you be bored?"

"No, don't worry, I won't be bored. We've discussed this before. I'm interested to see how your meetings are run. Is Gilles here? Can I meet him?"

"No, he's not." She paused. "His mother's ill."

I nodded. "Who are the people on the stage?"

"On the left is Roger Clayard, general secretary of the party, in the middle is Daniel Wildmayer, head of the Paris Communist Party, and on the right, in the black sweater, is François Perrault, head of theory, intelligence, and communications."

So that was my target.

"Head of theory? What does that mean?"

"We are Marxist-Leninists here. François is well-read in all the classic communist literature. Since the war has been on, we haven't been able to keep up with our Russian colleagues, who normally lead communist thinking. So François does it instead. He will be the first into Russia as soon as it's possible for anyone to go, to renew friendships and discuss policy initiatives."

If François Perrault was that intent on going to Russia at the earliest opportunity, well, that made my task a little more . . . not easier, exactly, in a practical way, but somewhat easier morally. Not totally clean — the man *was* a Nobel Prize–winning scientist, after all. But her remarks had made it almost certain that if he *did* find out about the Manhattan Project and the atomic bomb, he would certainly tell the Russians about it, just as soon as he got the chance. And I accepted that he had to be stopped.

I was grateful for today's meeting in another way, too. Having a specific meeting to attend didn't make the solid mass in the pit of my stomach go away, but it did keep it from taking me over completely, as it did in bed in the early hours, or when I was in the office alone, or even just walking the streets of Paris. At one point I had searched the faces of passers-by, on the Paris pavements, looking for Madeleine. Now I couldn't even do that.

One of the men on the stage stood up and moved to a microphone. He tapped it, heard his taps reverberate around the theatre, and called the meeting to order.

I didn't follow the proceedings at all closely — a lot of people, including Justine, made a lot of speeches, many with references to Marx and Lenin. They were universally anti–de Gaulle.

After the speeches, there was a hiatus while people prepared the motions to be voted on, and I took the opportunity to tell Justine that I had seen and heard enough and would meet her later at the flat. I needed to escape before she did, of course, so that I could wait somewhere convenient and follow François Perrault when he came out.

She smiled and nodded, and I left.

Outside, it had started to rain.

The Café Beaubourg was about a hundred yards away, down the rue Beaubourg on the opposite side of the road. I bought a newspaper from a nearby tabac and sat inside the café, from where I could see the doors of the Théâtre Stendhal but couldn't myself be seen.

There I waited.

Buying the paper had reminded me — I still had to get Justine to take me to the Bibliothèque Nationale to consult the article with the archaeological report. Then I caught myself. What was the point now?

I drank my coffee and opened the paper, trying to concentrate. I had to hope that all the people at the meeting would come out through the main doors. There was a stage door to the theatre, on the side street, but the people on the stage were hardly actors — they would leave with everyone else.

I had no idea how long I would have to wait but Paris cafés were not normally nosey places. So long as you kept buying coffee, or a beer, no one would interfere. Other people were in the café sheltering from the rain, so I didn't stand out.

I did, however, pay straightaway. I didn't want to be delayed by a tardy waiter.

In the paper I read again that the Germans in St. Nazaire were still holding out — apparently they had seventy-three heavy guns with which to defend themselves. I read that Paris women had a new hairstyle, piled high in emulation of the Eiffel Tower, to mark the liberation. I read an interview with the new British ambassador to France, who was liaising with the provisional government, exhorting the Parisians to rejoice in the fact that, despite the occupation, the fabric of the city had been well respected by the Germans.

And then, after about forty minutes, I noticed a crowd of people spilling on to the pavement outside the theatre. The show was over.

I finished the coffee I was drinking, but kept on reading the paper, with one eye on the theatre.

More people came out and overflowed into the road. Four hundred people are a lot of people, and I realised that, from where I was sitting, I might not be able to see everyone as they left. Also, I could see that a few of the party members were heading straight for the very café where I was sitting. I got up and quickly — but not too quickly — crossed the road so that no one from the theatre would see me close up.

Then I ambled back towards the Stendhal.

This was tricky. Should I bump into Justine, she would rightly want to know what I was doing. I could say I had lost something and was retracing my steps, but would that work? I couldn't afford to look suspicious in any way.

I stood for a moment in the doorway of the tabac where I had bought the newspaper.

Then I saw Justine.

She was standing on the pavement outside the theatre, kissing people again — to say goodbye this time.

Then, behind her, François Perrault appeared. The black sweater he wore was very distinctive. He kissed Justine and she kissed him back. Then he walked off with another man.

And that was a problem.

To follow him, I would have to walk straight past where Justine was standing, still talking and kissing farewells. She showed no sign of moving on just yet.

What could I do? François Perrault was already a hundred and fifty yards away.

The only thing I *could* do, which was a risk, was to turn left into the small side street, the rue Pierre au Larde. I had seen that it curled round to the right and I had to hope it would lead back on to the rue Beaubourg further along.

I walked quickly into the side street, keeping my face averted so that Justine would hopefully not see me, should she look up at the wrong moment. I held my breath, but there was no shout of "Matt!," no alert of any kind. Twenty yards into the street I broke into a run. After another twenty yards the street began to curve and I was relieved to see that fifty yards further on there was a T junction with another street, which would lead me back to the rue Beaubourg.

I ran all the way, reaching the main street in a sweat, but slowing to a walk at the last moment. I turned the corner and looked to my left.

No sign of François Perrault.

A hundred yards along, though, I could see the wavy lines of a Métro station. And there, just disappearing down the steps was . . . not Perrault himself but a figure I thought I recognized; it was the man with whom Perrault had left the theatre. Had he gone on ahead? I assumed that he had, and I was already running again, towards the station.

I reached it and clattered down the steps without stopping.

Perrault and his companion were just going through the ticket barrier.

I turned and reached into my coat pocket, as if I were looking for my wallet, but actually so as to hide my face from them. When they had gone beyond the barrier, a rapid inspection of the Métro map established which line they were taking: the one to Porte de Lilas. I bought myself a ticket to the farthest destination on the line, just in case.

Then I followed Perrault and the other man on to the platform and stood a few yards from them.

This, I thought, would be the easy bit. Métro carriages had glass doors at the end of each coach. When the train came in, I got into the carriage next to theirs. I could watch them discreetly from there without arousing suspicion.

Perrault's companion got off after three stops, at Goncourt, and Perrault himself got off two stops later, at Jourdain.

I got out there, too, along with a dozen or so others.

I followed Perrault at a safe distance as he emerged above ground into the boulevard Jourdain. He walked along the boulevard, past a large church, a small *rondpoint,* with several streets leading off it, and turned into the rue Froissart. Halfway along this street was a small *place,* with a few trees growing in it.

I watched as Perrault crossed the *place* and stood outside the door to a narrow three-storey house, next to a small tabac. I watched as he opened the door. Inside was a staircase — he lived in what New Yorkers, at least in the movies, call a walk-up.

I waited.

A couple of minutes later a light went on at the first-floor level, immediately over the tabac. There was only one floor above that: was it a separate flat or part of Perrault's? I needed to know. Then the windows of the top floor lit up. Good.

509

I looked about me. There was a café in the square with a few tables and chairs on the pavement, and a small fountain by the trees in the middle.

I stepped across the square and entered the tabac, to be greeted by the welcoming tobacco smell that I loved. It was a small shop, what we in London called a lock-up, lined with wooden shelves. Cigars, cigarettes, tins of tobacco, cigarette papers, matches, lighters, tubes of lighter fuel, cigarette holders, and ashtrays were all on display. Behind the counter was a small pleasant-looking woman, in her forties, as I judged.

I bought two tins of tobacco and some cigarette papers. There was cellophane around the tins but I tore it off, as if I intended to roll a cigarette immediately. The woman smiled, took the cellophane from me, and dropped it into a waste bin behind the counter.

I left. I had seen all I needed to.

That evening as Justine and I lay in the striped half-light that fell across the bed, I tried hard to keep my mind off Madeleine — and failed. Justine's hair, though redder than Madeleine's, was an unruly reminder, as were the shadows that played over her skin, her unselfconscious nakedness.

I laid my hand on Justine's thigh and brought the conversation around to the other subject that was on my mind.

"Tell me, those three men on the stage, running your meeting, what's the pecking order?"

"What do you mean? What is a pecking order?"

I laughed. "Sorry." I switched back to French. "Who is the most important? Who is the top dog? Who runs things?"

She curled into me. "You want to talk politics, even now? Very well . . ."

She lay back. "Roger Clayard is a brilliant organiser — I think he will become the leader when the war is finally over. He has charisma, he has the rhetoric. But François Perrault is the thinker. He doesn't want the top job, he is the purist, the idealist. He will keep us clean, good communists. He gives a weekly seminar at the École Normale Superior, on communist philosophy."

"Is he married?"

"Why do you ask?"

Slow down! Careful. "You make him sound a bit of a monster, a dry zealot. Is he human?"

She didn't reply straightaway. "I think he may have been married once, but his wife died — he never talks about it. And I think he had a child who for some reason he never saw." She crossed her fingers. "He and I, we were like this, once, many months ago."

"It didn't work out? Why not?"

She shrugged. "He is — or was — a scientist, interested in abstract physics and mathematics. He has a great attention to detail and a passion for justice. He is in charge of *épuration* policy and is determined to ensure that people are not charged improperly. That's why I was so interested in the fact that you have seen Monique Brèger. Where does she live, by the way? François wants to know."

"I don't know," I lied. "We met in a café, by appointment."

"Does she go out, looking like you say she does?"

"We met at night," I lied again. "Tell me about François."

She curled a strand of hair in her fingers. "He is amazing. So many interests and abilities. He tries to keep up with science, though it's hard. He liaises with the Resistance all over France, keeps track of who has been arrested, interrogated, put in prison or hospital, or sent east. It is easy for people to be forgotten in war, he says, so he keeps an archive. And he says we must be more understanding about *épuration,* otherwise . . . otherwise what happened to Monique Brèger will happen to others — other heroes.

"But he is so wrapped up in Resistance work, I couldn't get close to him. I gave up."

"So he's not married now?"

"I don't think he's had a woman since me. And he didn't have me for very long. He lives alone in a flat on the Place Royère, which he shares with six thousand books. He's a great man in many ways, and he will do great things for France — he has *already* done great things for France. But I couldn't live with him."

Time to move on.

"And us, Justine. What are we doing?"

She curled back into me. "We are thrown together. What's happened is lovely. You are still . . . Madeleine is still in your head somewhere, in your heart — I think, of course she is. But who knows with us, we are doing what we are doing. One day at a time, yes? We are thrown together, *bricolage,* as we say in France, a *bric-à-brac* affair, yes? Let's not make it more than it is, not yet anyway."

That was her good answer to a fraudulent question. No one in Paris in those days expected anything to last. It suited me tactically — oh yes. But was she really over François Perrault? It didn't sound like it — and that made everything ahead of me that much harder.

25

The next morning I was at the café in the Place Royère at seven o'clock. It spilled out on to the pavement in the normal way of cafés. I sat inside, armed with two news-papers and a notebook so that I could see out but couldn't be easily identified by anyone across the *place,* where François Per-rault's flat was. I ordered two croissants and a café au lait, opened the first of my papers, and set about waiting.

I was there with a heavy heart, but I was there. My aim today was to study Perrault's movements and refine my plan as to how to kill him.

I had known this moment would come. That day in the prime minister's bunker, when I had agreed to the deal that had been proposed, I had not been blind, or blinkered, or unthinking. I was thirty-one, a full-grown man. Yes, I was at the time in love properly for only the second time, and love does change us. Perhaps my emotional state had clouded my judgement, or made me desperate. But I hadn't *felt* desperate. Yes, I was worried sick about Madeleine, but both my feet had been firmly on the ground when I had agreed to Hathaway's plan. He had made the task seem all-important and the PM himself had taken time out to lend weight to what Hathaway was proposing.

I had been let in on the war's biggest secret, perhaps a secret even bigger than the date and location of the invasion itself, which had dominated my thoughts for so long. And now I had to fulfill my part of the bargain. I had to close my mind to the dreadful details of the specific task I was about to carry out and consider the wider picture. The bigger picture.

At Ardlossan we trained people to kill. It was only the fact that Perrault was an ally that troubled me. But I had the prime minister's blessing. His *authority.* A soldier couldn't ask for more.

I opened the paper. Aachen had fallen, finally, after fierce hand-to-hand fighting in the streets. How terrifying that must have been. The paper had a page of small notices, paid for by individual families, giving news of sons lost in the war. I lifted my eyes, unable even to engage with the private torment those notices meant.

I looked out and surveyed the *place.* There were a couple of plane trees in the centre, a fountain, some iron benches, a patch of gravel where, on warm nights, the locals played boules. The houses were mainly narrow, three storeys high — all of them walk-ups. They weren't wide enough or the area plush enough to have lifts. They had steeply sloping slate roofs. The shutters on some were completely closed; on others lines of thin rope ran between them with washing hung out to dry. A few motorbikes were grouped in one corner, near some double doors, set back, and a taxi was parked nearby. But it wasn't waiting for anyone. Most likely the taxi driver himself lived in the square. This wasn't a location where taxis came and went, dropping people off or picking them up. It wasn't smart enough. I stared for a while at the double doors in the far corner.

Seven thirty came and went. By my calculation, and my understanding of Paris life, two croissants, two newspapers, and the second café au lait, which I would order in due course, would buy me a good two hours in that café before anyone became inquisitive.

Ten to eight. I opened the second paper. I read that Argentina had given the Allies a "definite assurance" that the country would be no safe haven for war criminals. Five hundred artworks were apparently missing from Florence following the Germans' retreat.

Twenty past eight. I was just thinking of

ordering my second café au lait when I saw the door to Perrault's walk-up — next to the tabac — open. There he was, wearing a raincoat today and carrying a briefcase, but with the same black sweater just showing at his throat. He started across the *place.* I had paid for my breakfast when I ordered it and so I now began to fold my papers and collect them together. But then I noticed that Perrault was heading straight towards the café where I was seated.

He was going to have his breakfast here too.
I had half anticipated this. I couldn't risk Perrault getting even a glimpse of my face. There was always a dim chance that he would recognise me from the meeting in the Théâtre Stendhal. We hadn't been introduced, or met face-to-face, but he knew Justine intimately and, according to her, they had had a fling in the distant past. It would have been natural for him to pay attention to whoever she was with.

I turned naturally so that I had my back to the entrance and opened one of my papers again and buried myself in it. Perrault swept into the café and stood at the bar, the way many French did. I heard him order a croissant and a black coffee. I heard a tall stool being scraped across the floor. Was he sitting down?

I studied my paper assiduously.

I felt pretty sure that he hadn't noticed me,

or recognised me, but obviously it was too risky for me to look up or turn and look at him. All I could do was wait and keep my back to him. Fortunately, I had some of my second croissant left, so I ate it slowly as I inspected the paper.

Ten minutes went by. I heard him order another black coffee. What was he *doing*? Reading the paper like I was? Smoking a cigarette? I kept calm and waited.

"Encore un café, monsieur?" The waiter was standing over me. This would surely draw Perrault's attention to me.

"Merci," I said, shaking my head.

Another ten minutes went by.

Then I heard Perrault say, softly but distinctly, *"L'addition, s'il vous plaît, Sylvaine."*

"Tout de suite," said the waitress at the cash register.

I sat stock-still, where I was. Would Perrault acknowledge me in any way, as he went out? Just to let me know nothing escaped him? I felt pretty sure he was oblivious to my presence but . . .

I heard money rattle on the counter. I heard a tall stool shift, scraping on the floor tiles of the café.

"À tout à l'heure," I heard him say.

And he went past me. No tap on the shoulder, no glance in my direction, no turn as he stepped outside, and no nod of recognition. He just buttoned his raincoat and kept on walking. As he fiddled with the buttons of his coat, I noticed a gold ring on one of his fingers as it caught the light. Was there a new woman in his life?

I allowed him to reach the edge of the square and then got up myself and followed him.

One thing I did know: I couldn't get too close. He might not have spotted me in the café — I mean he didn't seem to have linked me to the man who had been with Justine at the Communist Party meeting in the Théâtre Stendhal — but if he saw me in his vicinity, he would certainly recognize me as the man who had been in the café.

So I didn't get any closer than fifty yards, and even then I kept to the other side of the street. And I wore the flat cap I had brought from Ardlossan. That shielded part of my face.

But I soon saw where he was headed — it didn't take a genius.

He skipped down the steps of the Métro and I followed at a distance, lingering at the ticket barrier and not emerging on to the platform until a train was coming in. I knew this line from previous visits to Paris. As before, I entered the carriage next to the one he used.

He got off at Grands Boulevards.

I had no difficulty following him out of the station and along boulevard Haussmann. He turned in to rue Lafayette, crossed the street, and reached rue Taitbout. There he entered a large stone building where — I could see — a carved stone façade announced the PCF, the Communist Party of France. So this was their headquarters.

A few yards further along the street was a café — thank God Paris was a city of cafés. My plan was falling into place, but I had one more hurdle to clear before I could really start on the detailed reconnaissance.

I still had the newspapers with me, so I sat inside the café, ordered a *thé au citron* and a *pain au chocolat,* sufficient to keep me there for at least an hour.

I deliberately chose small drinks, to go easy on my system.

I read more about the bombing of Germany — Bremerhaven as well as Berlin this time. The south coast of Britain was being shelled, one or two people had been killed in Dover, where Madeleine and Philippe had . . .

I couldn't keep my mind off her.

Ten fifteen a.m. A second small tea bought me another forty minutes. After that I played on the pin table for twenty minutes, taking me to 11:15. Still no sign of Perrault.

Now I switched to a water and nursed that for more than another half an hour. I had a map of the Métro with me and brushed up on what I could remember. You never knew when such knowledge might come in handy.

Halfway through my second Perrier, by which time it had gone noon, I saw him. He walked swiftly out of the headquarters building, accompanied by another man. He had on his raincoat but was carrying no briefcase. They turned right and walked briskly down the street.

I followed. At the far end of the street, they turned right again, crossed a wide, busy boulevard and marched straight into a restaurant, Le Flandrin.

He had done exactly what I hoped he would do; he had gone for lunch. This was my chance. He would be in Le Flandrin for at least an hour and a half, maybe two.

I waved for a taxi and gave the driver an address about two city blocks from the Place Royère.

The journey between Place Royère and Communist Party headquarters had been thirty-five minutes by Métro; it was fifteen by cab. That meant I had an hour and a quarter at least.

There was a bench in the middle of the place and I sat on it.

I waited a few minutes, until there was a crowd of people in the tabac, and then moved quickly, but not too quickly, to Perrault's front door.

The lock was no problem. With all my years and training in SC2, I had more than sufficient unobtrusive equipment — and the skill

— to open the door.

I inserted the short arm of an L-shaped tension wrench into the keyhole and gently swiveled it. The difference in the resistance — more spongy to the right than the left — told me that the lock turned clockwise. Holding the wrench in place with one hand, with the other I slid the small hooked pick I had with me as far as it would go into the lock. Then I pulled it back towards me, pressing upwards, until I felt the first tumbler fall. Then the second, and third, until all five were dislodged. The door swung open.

I closed it behind me and stood for a moment at the foot of the stairs, listening, in case he should have someone else staying in his flat, or a cleaning woman had arrived. But all was quiet. I looked at my watch: 12:55. I still had a good hour to myself.

I climbed the stairs. They were steep, covered in brown linoleum.

On the first floor was a bathroom, a kitchen, and a living room. The bathroom was virtually empty, save for the bath and the lavatory, and the usual soaps, razors and combs.

The kitchen likewise was functional. This was not a man who liked to cook. I had guessed as much when I saw that he took breakfast at the café in the square. The shelves were tidy; there wasn't much in the way of food, no fresh fruit so far as I could see.

The kitchen was directly over the tabac — its floor was the tabac's ceiling. There was even a faint tabac smell in the room. Or did Perrault smoke? I didn't recall him doing so.

The living room had a fireplace but all it contained were matches and cigarette stubs — so maybe he did smoke. There were a few photographs on the mantelshelf, including one of Perrault and Justine. A new possibility suggested itself: She might be over their fling, but was he? There were other photographs, of people I didn't recognize, and one that I did: Perrault, in white tie and tails, receiving his Nobel Prize from the king of Sweden.

The furniture in the room was undistinctive, the carpets worn, the lamps uncared for, in that two of the bulbs didn't work when I tried them. There were one or two contemporary paintings on the walls, but none by a hand that I recognized.

I went upstairs.

The bedroom was on a par with the living room. A bed, a wardrobe, a chest of drawers, more pictures like those on the floor below. A stack of books by the bed, some scientific, some political, no novels or history. An alarm clock, three packs of cigarettes — so he did smoke — very few clothes in the wardrobe, some condoms in the chest of drawers. Some money rolled up in an elastic band, a set of spectacles, some candles for when the electricity failed.

A gun.

A revolver which, if I was not mistaken, was of Russian make. It wasn't loaded but a box of bullets was half hidden under some underwear in the same drawer.

Now why would François Perrault need a Russian gun?

I didn't stop to think but picked it up, with the bullets, and went through into the study.

This, clearly, was where Perrault lived, where he spent his time.

It was a large room, with one window on the square, a large desk in the middle, piled high with papers and what looked like scientific models. There was a sofa against one wall. There were no pictures on the walls here, for every available area of space was covered by bookshelves — there must have been thousands of books in this room. Science titles predominated, and politics was also well represented, but so too were modern French novels — Gide, Camus, Genet.

I moved to the desk. A bulky typewriter stood in pride of place, paper still in it. Scientific journals, typed pages, folders, cigarette packets, ashtrays, a candlestick, a camera, all competed for space here. There was a black folder with, in gold capitals, UNIVERSITAIRE DE BELFORT on the cover — his old place of employment. Next to the chair, papers were stacked on the floor — Perrault was clearly in the course of writing something. I cast my eye over what was in the typewriter, but it was mathematical and I could make neither head nor tail of it.

Next to the typewriter was what looked like a diary, open. I looked at the entries. There, in an entry for the very next day, were written four words followed by a large exclamation mark: *"Legros, soudain et enfin!"*

Perrault was meeting Legros tomorrow.

What I had to do, I had to do now, tonight.

Then I noticed something else.

Over the fireplace, on the mantelshelf, was a photograph, elaborately framed, as if a lot of thought had gone into it.

The photograph showed Perrault and this time he wasn't in white tie and tails but in a denim jacket and a hat with a peak. And next to him, smiling, with a broad bushy moustache, was none other than Iosif Dzhugashvili himself, better known as Stalin.

Later that afternoon I put in an appearance in the office. At the very least, Justine would want to know where I had been, and if I didn't turn up at all, she would be even more inquisitive.

"Hello, stranger," she said softly as I walked through the main room.

I smiled and gave her a half-wave. "Let me check my post," I said, "then we can talk."

I went into my office and closed the door behind me. There were telegrams from London, army communications about supplies, intelligence reports, bills to pay, requests for leave, and one small envelope, still sealed, marked TOP SECRET. I opened that first, fancying I knew what was in it.

I spread out the thin paper on my desk. I was not disappointed.

+WHAT·NEWS·OF·THE·WEDDING?·STOP+

It wasn't signed.

I screwed up the piece of paper in my hand and slipped it into my pocket, to be disposed of somewhere else. They would get their answer soon enough, I hoped.

I scanned the rest of the post, lingering on just one, from Hilary.

+MANY·THANKS·INTERIM·REPORT·STOP+MIN-ISTER·MOLLIFIED·FOR·NOW=HILARY+

That was something.

I got up, went round my desk, opened the door, and beckoned to Justine. I sat on the edge of my desk as she leaned against the jamb of the door.

"Are you having your own private war? Where have you been?"

She didn't say it aggressively; in a way, she wasn't so far off.

I showed her the empty envelope the "wedding" telegram had arrived in, the one with

TOP SECRET on the front.

"There *is* a war still on, Justine, and everyone can't be in on everything. I have orders I can't tell you about."

She raised her eyebrows so I made a tactical retreat.

"If you're very good, I'll tell you. Actually, this secret is nothing special. De Gaulle wants to know what we are up to and I had to brief his chief of staff, a man called Leclerc — know him?"

She shook her head. "And what did you tell him — I hope you didn't talk about the meeting in the theatre. You promised —"

"No, of course I didn't," I interrupted. "Of course not. I told him what we've been doing, our trip to La Santé, to Saarburg, the plan to visit Pforzheim. Just that. Is there any news on Pforzheim, by the way? What have you been doing?"

She played with the elastic band on her wrist. "Party business, mainly." She nodded to the outer office. "Roland knows about Pforzheim. Ask him."

"I will," I said, looking at my watch, to show I wanted to move on.

I stepped around my desk and gestured to the papers on it. "I've got all this to catch up with. Can you get by without me tonight? I've got to go to a dinner and intelligence briefing out near Versailles. I may have to stay the night."

She moved forward and gently stroked the lapel of my jacket.

"Of course. In fact, I hope you don't mind, but I'm having dinner with François tonight."

"Old flames getting together?"

I made light of it, but this was *not* good news. What if dinner turned into . . . more? What if she went back to his apartment, and stayed?

"We are old flames, as you say, but the flame went out long ago. The reason for the dinner is very different. What I am about to tell you is top secret too: François has been invited to Russia. It won't be easy for him to get there, but we are beginning to plan for after the war. He trusts me and he wants to discuss what might happen. There will be no sex."

This was riveting news. If Perrault was scheduled to meet Daniel Legros tomorrow, and going to Russia any time soon, then . . . then . . . everything fell into place.

But I needed to end this conversation on a different note, something personal, intimate, away from politics and war.

"I didn't see Max in the outer office. Is he all right? Will you look after him tonight? Or is Roland babysitting again?" I grinned.

She made one of her French faces. "No! Max is in disgrace. In the park today, for his walk, he chased after another dog, a bitch, and before I could do anything, he was . . .

you know, he was . . . he made sex with the bitch. It was embarrassing. He is locked in my apartment — you are *not* to let him out. He must learn he has done wrong — why are you laughing?"

"I'm not laughing, I'm smiling. Is what he did *really* so terrible?"

"Yes, yes, it was. I had to pull them apart. It was humiliating."

"I'd pay money to have seen that."

"*Ouf!* I am beginning to go off you, Englishman."

"Have lunch with me tomorrow and I'll make it up to you."

"We'll see," she said, curling a strand of hair around her finger. "I may not have forgiven you by then." But as she let go of her hair, and turned on her heel, she gave me a quick smile.

26

I was at the café in the Place Royère by eight thirty. I sat outside, because although it was fresh it was darker there, with fewer people. This time I had with me a French novel I had found on a shelf in Justine's flat, *L'Étranger* by a certain Albert Camus. I ordered — and paid for — a beer and a brandy. That should see me through for an hour and a half.

I had made a precise calculation. If François Perrault was having dinner with Justine, he would not be home before ten thirty and perhaps not even then. As I looked across the square, all the windows in his flat were dark. So too was the tabac, a blind drawn down its door, big cardboard cut-outs of cigarette packs in its windows. You couldn't see inside. That suited me.

I sipped my cognac and opened the novel. My plan was to remain in the café for an hour or so. I needed to be in the square just in case, for some reason or other, Justine's dinner with François ended prematurely. But then I would transfer to the more remote spot I had identified the day before — the double doors set back in a niche by the motorbikes. If I moved there too early, it would look suspicious, someone just lurking in the shadows. Later, there would be far fewer people around.

I couldn't concentrate too hard on the novel, of course. I could never take my eye off the square completely. Confident as I was that Perrault would not be home any time soon, I still couldn't be sure.

The waiter approached me.

"Another beer, please," I said before he could say anything.

"Encore un cognac aussi?"

I shook my head.

He went off and I scrutinised a man crossing the square. It wasn't Perrault.

I had the correct money for the beer on the table by the time the waiter came back, hoping he would just pick it up and leave. No.

"Would you like something to eat?" he said.

I shook my head. "No, thank you very much."

"Do you want to move inside? The lighting is better, if you want to read."

He was just trying to be friendly, and possibly hoping to add to his tips for the day, if I had dinner there.

I leaned forward. "I'm not hungry and I

suffer from asthma. I'm more comfortable outside — thank you."

I kept my head turned, so he couldn't look directly at my face.

"I understand, monsieur. Just say if you need some water."

I nodded without looking at him, and inspected *L'Étranger.*

He went away.

I was sure that, if what I planned for later came off, he would remember me. Of course he would. Whether he would link me to what I was going to do, I didn't know. If the police questioned him, and he mentioned me, I am sure they would attach some importance to it. But there was nothing inherently suspicious about asthma. It was not in itself remarkable.

He left me alone after that, and I went back to my joint task of keeping one eye on the square and reading my book.

I finished my beer, waited a few more moments, and then, without looking back at the waiter, I left the café, in the direction away from Perrault's apartment and the tabac.

I strolled around the square until I reached the double doorway I had noticed, by the stack of parked motorbikes, at the far corner. Up close, it looked as though it led into some sort of yard. The shadows there were deep and I quietly stepped into the murky gloom and stood still.

Ten o'clock came, 10:15, 10:25.

Then I saw them.

What *was* this? Was Justine going to spend the night with François? She had told me all that was over, but, well . . . people lie. But that was less important, I told myself, than how it affected my plan.

I had to kill Perrault tonight, here in this square.

But I couldn't kill Justine.

I watched as they paused at his front door, let themselves inside, and closed it behind them. A few moments later, the first-floor lights went on.

Then the lights went on at the *second*-floor level, where his bedroom and his study were. Were they still discussing politics? Or had Justine really lied to me, and were they preparing to spend the night together?

I waited, hoping that some idea would come to me.

It didn't.

At eleven o'clock the lights in the café were put out and the square grew a great deal darker.

Still no idea came to me.

About a quarter of an hour later, I saw the light in Perrault's study go out, though the one in his bedroom stayed on.

It looked very much as though Justine *had* lied to me, and was spending the night. What was I to do? I tried to whip up a hatred of

533

her that would justify what I was planning.

It didn't work. I had no hatred for Justine.

And then I heard a sound. Moments later, Perrault's front door opened and there were the two of them standing in the square, still talking. Justine was carrying something, a folder of some kind; she stood on tiptoe, kissed Perrault's cheek, and then half ran across the square, by herself. I looked at my watch and realised she was running to catch the last Métro.

The familiar sweating on my neck stopped, and I suddenly craved a cigarette. But I couldn't draw attention to myself by showing a light. Instead, I just watched as Perrault turned and went back through his front door.

Now it was just him and me.

The square was deserted. The sounds of the night — the whistles and clanking of shunting railway trains, ambulances on emergencies, all-night buses — reached me in my shadowy niche. Occasionally, a child cried somewhere in one of the houses lining the square; a cat called out. Now and then the wind got up. Litter lifted, and settled back down again.

All the lights had gone out in Perrault's flat about twenty minutes after Justine had left. It was now coming up to two o'clock. The square was dark and empty but I could only do what I planned to do when everyone was sound asleep and that, I judged, would be between two and four.

The sky was cloudy. That was a help — it meant there was no moon.

At ten minutes past two I made my move.

I had taken care to wear rubber-soled shoes so I made no sound as I walked slowly along the pavement.

I stopped first at Perrault's front door. I checked the handle. It was locked. I had with me a large tube of glue, the new kind that Duncan Kennaway had introduced to Ardlossan, the kind that hardened on contact with air. I unscrewed the lid, inserted the nozzle into the keyhole, and began to squeeze the glue into the key-slot. I kept squeezing until glue was oozing down the front of the door, sluicing everywhere. Then I put the tube back into my pocket, wiped the drips off the tube and the front door with my handkerchief, and waited.

After five minutes I tried to insert the key I had with me into the keyhole. The glue had hardened and the keyhole opening itself was blocked solid. The moving parts inside would also be congealed now into one mass — and it would be the same on the inside of the door.

Perrault was trapped. If he tried to get out through the door, he wouldn't be able to, not without breaking the door down. By which time . . .

I moved next door to the tabac.

My tension wrench and pick got me inside in no time. I shut the door behind me but didn't lock it.

Having reconnoitered the tabac, I knew exactly what I was going to do. On the right side, high up behind the serving counter, were boxes of lighter fuel. I took down as many boxes as I could hold. On the left, low down this time, was a display of pipes and cigarette holders, and a shelf of matches. I didn't need too many of them.

One by one, I unscrewed the bottles of lighter fuel and started sprinkling it over everything in the shop. The smell of alcohol rose to my nostrils — it was not unpleasant. I spread lighter fuel over boxes of cigars, packets of cigarettes, boxes of cigarette papers, over packets of tobacco, boxes of matches, all over the floor, all over the shelves, all over the serving counter. The atmosphere began to cloy.

Then I moved some metal cigar cutters and took down two tins of tobacco and tipped the contents into the waste bin behind the counter. I opened two packets of cigarette papers and threw them on to the tobacco.

Now I took out the other thing I had brought with me, all the way from London.

An incendiary device.

I heard voices — and froze.

I turned and, with a finger, moved the door

blind ever so slightly so that I could see out.

Two women were standing in the middle of the square, talking. They wore high-heeled shoes, tight skirts, plenty of make-up. Two ladies of the night comparing notes. I should have guessed — Pigalle, Paris's main red-light area, wasn't far away.

I watched them. The smell of lighter fuel was very strong now, scratching at my nostrils and throat. It wouldn't leak out into the night air, surely? The women were looking my way.

But they were a good fifty yards in the distance and it was a quarter to three in the morning. They couldn't see me.

Just then they kissed and moved off, in different directions.

I couldn't follow their movements so I had to assume they lived in the square. Therefore, I now had to wait another half an hour, to let them get into bed.

I waited, looking at my watch every so often, and kept easing the blind aside to see if anyone else was arriving home late.

No one was.

At ten past three I sprinkled yet more lighter fuel over the contents of the shop. Then I took the lighter Celestine had given me and lit some of the packets of cigarette papers I had earlier doused with fuel in the waste bin.

The fuel-soddened papers ignited straight-away with a "whoosh!," and the flames immediately began to spread.

I lit more cigarette papers and set fire to other parts of the shop that I had doused with lighter fuel. The flames were now spreading right across the fittings.

I lit the incendiary and laid it in the waste bin. It sizzled softly.

Now for what I hoped would be the clever bit. I took from my pocket two cigarette tins, the two I had bought on my first visit to the tabac. One by one I opened them to check that what I had put into the empty tins was still there.

Everything was in order.

I closed the tins and placed them just inside the door of the tabac.

I let myself out as the smell of burning began to scratch at my notsrils, not locking the door as I went. Then, without looking around me, I walked quickly back to my shadowy niche.

Reaching it, I turned and watched.

For a few moments, I could see and hear nothing.

Then I saw the blind on the door edged with flames. After that I saw the coloured red-white sparks of the incendiary. That was followed by the cardboard displays in the windows going up. One of the displays — an outsized cigarette packet, built of cardboard but bolstered with plywood slats — fell against the window, which shortly afterwards cracked with the heat and fell outwards. The rush of air that this must have generated blew out a great tongue of orange flame.

Roland had given me the idea when he nearly sent up the office with his hand-rolled cigarettes. And Justine had talked of "fireworks" at the party meeting in the Théâtre Stendhal.

Now the fire was raging through both windows — it would, I judged, have started to eat into the wooden joists supporting Perrault's kitchen.

I continued to wait. No one in the square seemed yet to have been awakened, though the fire was crackling now, its sound breaking into the night air.

All that changed suddenly when there was a series of explosions a few moments later.

I had taken the precaution of moving Perrault's gun and the box of bullets he kept with it from his bedroom to his kitchen, in a drawer close to the floor.

Almost immediately after that, I saw that the fire had reached his sitting room, on the other side of the flat.

A light went on in his bedroom, and then snapped off. Had the electricity been cut?

A few moments later I saw a figure silhouetted against the flames of the living room. He tried to open the window but his hands were scorched by the heat and he retreated.

Now people *were* hanging out of their

windows, pointing and shouting. A few ventured into the square, some in their pyjamas, others in raincoats over their night-clothes.

One looked up, then ran to Perrault's front door and pulled at it. It couldn't be budged.

The man kicked it. It was too sturdy for him.

He began shouting at the door. Was Perrault on the other side, trying to get out?

More people were gathering in the square. Now the flames were leaking from the top floor of Perrault's flat, his bedroom and his study.

I saw him at the window of his bedroom. He threw open the hinged frame. He looked down. Was he going to jump?

It was too high. He would seriously injure or kill himself.

He didn't jump.

A bell could be heard ringing a few streets away. Someone had telephoned for the fire service.

Perrault heard it too. He disappeared, only to reappear at the kitchen window. He must have decided the fire service was still too far away, that he had to escape by jumping from the first floor.

He disappeared again, then the window was suddenly shattered as he aimed a typewriter through it. He picked shards of glass from the frame, so that he could climb through.

Some of these were obviously hot and he scorched his fingers again, but he knew he was fighting for his life.

Intense orange-red flames raged all around him, smoke and shadows dancing across the face of the building.

The ringing bells of the fire service were getting closer.

Perrault had one leg on the windowsill.

Then there was a loud, cracking, crumbling, crashing sound, and the flames that were licking at the kitchen window were suddenly sucked inwards. Immediately afterwards, the flames in the tabac whooshed outwards, spitting into the square and destroying all that was left of the tabac's shopfront, save for the metal door frame.

As I had hoped.

I realised what had happened with grim satisfaction.

The floor of Perrault's kitchen, which was also the ceiling of the tabac, had collapsed. The exploding bullets had done more damage than was at first obvious.

But it meant that Perrault had fallen with the floor directly *into* the inferno I had created in the tabac. He would have been incinerated instantly.

I saw the fire engine pull into the square, slowly because it was a big contraption and the streets leading into the Place Royère were narrow. But it moved steadily towards the tabac, men getting down from the truck, unravelling fire hoses as they went, looking for hydrants.

The fire engine stopped about thirty yards from the conflagration, which was now raging throughout the entire building. Hydrants had been found and some of the locals were helping the firemen unwind the hoses. All eyes were on the flames and all thoughts were surely the same: How could anyone in that building survive such an immolation?

I judged it the right time to leave.

I stepped out of the shadow and turned and walked slowly out of the square. Other people were running in, hearing the commotion, but all their eyes were on the flames.

27

Next morning I was deliberately late getting into the office. Since I was supposed to have been in Versailles overnight, I thought a late arrival fitted with that cover story. In fact, I had walked from the Place Royère across Paris to Pigalle. At that hour the Métro was closed, I didn't understand the system of all-night buses, and I didn't want to take a taxi — the driver might, just might, remember the fare he had picked up near the square in the small hours.

I knew where I was headed. I picked up a girl, and she took me to a small establishment she knew. It was now gone five, I paid for four hours, she and I went through the motions, I gave her the money owed, she went home, or back to work, and I — believe it or not, given what I had just done — fell fast asleep. In fact, I slept for longer than I had paid for, but was happy to give the *maître de la maison,* the man who ran the place, extra cash when he came knocking on my door. I bought another hour.

Which meant I didn't hit the streets until 10:00 a.m.

I judged that the fire had occurred too late for the newspapers, so I didn't bother buying one.

When I reached the office, Roland looked at his watch, muttering, "Is today some public holiday in France that I don't know about?"

"What do you mean?"

"You're in late, Justine's not in at all. Have you two been — ?"

"Be very careful what you say next," I shot back quickly. "I spent the night in Versailles, at a conference. Yes, we went drinking afterwards, but Justine wasn't with us. Has she not phoned in?"

"Not a dickie bird," he said, looking puzzled.

"Well, let's get to it," I sighed. "Anything new this morning?"

"Yes," he said. "Your Pforzheim papers have come through. But I'm having a problem with transport."

"Oh yes?"

"It's a problem if you want a driver or a car —"

"You're not suggesting we take a train into Germany?"

"I was just looking into that —"

"Don't bother. It won't work, that I do

know. Keep trying to find me a car."

"Okay, will do. But don't expect a positive answer any time soon."

We broke off and I went into my office and closed the door.

When last night's fire reached the papers, if it *did* reach the papers, and the victim was named, my superiors in Churchill's bunker in King Charles Steps would draw the obvious conclusions. But I couldn't rely on the newspapers. I had to tell London right away. I should probably have done it already, but part of my orders were to make it look like an accident if possible and that meant I'd had to make my movements fit my cover story.

I sat down and drew my typewriter to me. I had to type this telegram myself, in code, and transmit it myself.

It didn't take long:

+HAVANA·SMOKING+

There was no need to sign it.

I was just folding the flimsy paper when the door to my office barged open, and there stood Justine.

Her face was red, her hair was all over the place, her blouse was pulled out of her slacks here and there, her hands were dirty, and one of her shoulder pads had disappeared.

I stood up and prepared to put on a performance.

"What is it? You look dreadful. Something's happened. What is it?"

She stepped forward and leaned on my desk, looking up at me.

"François is dead. He has been murdered."

I went cold, and I hope I showed it. What she said confirmed Perrault's death — but how did she know he had been murdered?

"What do you mean, murdered? You mean he's *dead*? How? Didn't you have dinner with him last night?"

I reached into the bottom drawer of my desk, where I kept half a bottle of Scotch I'd brought all the way from Ardlossan. There were two glasses on a shelf, and I poured us a shot each. I handed one to Justine.

She gulped at it, making a face but finishing it in one, so I gave her another. This one she nursed.

She slumped into the chair behind her and held the whisky glass to her forehead, steadying herself.

"Yes," she breathed softly, "I had dinner with François last night. Afterwards, we went back to his flat — he lives in a square called Place Royère, I think I told you that — it's not far from Pigalle. I didn't stay long but he wanted to give me some papers. I left about — oh, about eleven thirty and he told me he was going to bed straightaway."

546

She gulped some of the whisky.

"Then, so far as I can make out, according to what the local police told me, at about four o'clock this morning a fire started in the tabac that he lives above. It's a small shop — his kitchen is directly over it."

"How did the fire start?" I said.

"That's just it. The fire people said there were some cigarette papers in a waste bin that might have been where the fire started, but that an incendiary bomb had been used, to make the fire spread much more quickly, and that lighter fuel had been spread everywhere —"

"Hold on!" I leaned against my desk. "You're saying the fire was started in this tabac, under François's apartment?"

She nodded and sniffed. "The firemen, or the police — I forget which — found a tin, a tobacco tin, near the door of the tabac. The door had a metal frame — all the rest of the shop was lined with wood."

She sniffed again, close to tears.

"In this tin there were . . ." She looked up at me again, her nose wet.

"In the tin . . . were some German-made contraceptives — condoms. The police think the woman who owns the shop was —"

"What?" I did my best to look astounded. "You mean . . . you mean this was an *épuration,* payback for . . . what's it called . . . a *collaboration horizontale*? In that case, François wasn't the target —"

"No! *No!* That's just it!" Now Justine was crying. "Don't say that! That's what the firemen said, and the police, that it was an *épuration* that got out of hand, went too far —"

"It's happened before. Look at Monique Brèger —"

"Yes, but . . . the woman in the tabac was a member of the party, she was a communist —"

"Oh, come *on,*" I said, shaking my head. "Are you telling me no communist ever slept with a Nazi? How do you know she was a member of the Communist Party?"

She sniffed again. "I *told* you: the communists were and are the backbone of the Resistance. We do *not* sleep with the enemy. How do I know she was a communist? Because there is a café in the square and the waiter there is also a member of the party — and he told me. Didier something, that's his name. She is his . . . They are lovers. He says she never slept with *any* Germans."

"Justine! Would the waiter *know*? He might be the very last to know."

She said nothing.

"You really think François was the intended victim? How could whoever did this be sure the woman wasn't there?"

She nodded. "The tabac is a lock-up, as you say. The woman is never there at night. Someone must have watched François yesterday evening — and maybe me as well — after we had dinner. And . . . when everything was quiet, he set fire to the tabac. François had a gun with some bullets and they were exploded by the fire. The floor of his kitchen collapsed and he . . . he fell into a room of flames."

She was crying again now.

"And the police?"

She sniffled. "No. There have been so many cases of *épuration.* They think this is another that went too far."

I stepped around the desk and put my hand on her shoulder.

She wouldn't be comforted.

I sat back on the edge of the desk. "If François *was* the target — let's assume he was for the moment, despite what the police say — why do you think he was killed? Who would have wanted him dead?"

She sniffed. "Political opponents? De Gaulle's people? François was so talented, so popular."

I had been nervous at one stage. Now I was beginning to relax. This was a long way from me. But her words brought home the scale of what I had done.

"Would de Gaulle's people go that far? The war's still on."

"It's the perfect time." She sniffed again. "While there's so much chaos and uncertainty. Easy to make it look like *épuration.*"

"What are you going to do? What *can* you do?"

"I don't know." She looked distraught. "Well, I do know one thing. As I told you, I talked to the waiter in the café — Didier Roque, that's it, I remember his name now. He is a party member and knew François a little bit, and when I said to him that François and I used to be . . . close, he told me there had been one or two customers in the café recently who were strangers, sitting at the tables for hours on end, just reading newspapers or books and drinking coffee. He thinks they could have been sizing up François's flat ahead of time. I've asked the waiter to come with me tomorrow, or the day after, and we are going to wait outside the headquarters of de Gaulle's organisation and see if he recognizes anyone. It's a long-shot, I know, but it's something." She sniffed again. "I must do *something*."

This was an interesting development. It didn't feel immediately dangerous but . . . you never can tell. Something to keep an eye on.

She finished her second whisky, refused a third, and handed me the glass.

"You haven't shaved," she said suddenly, surprised.

"No. The conference was followed by drinks, followed by more drinks — we went on quite late, one bar after another. It was too late to come home, so I stayed in a hotel and, well, I was quite late getting up this morning. So I came straight into the office."

She nodded. "I know Versailles slightly. Where did you go drinking?"

Was she suspicious? Why would she be suspicious?

"We were fed in the conference, by the military. It was in one of those outbuildings by the Petit Trianon. I haven't a clue where we went drinking and as for the hotel . . . well, some of us picked up a group of . . . ladies, and they took us to, well, I think you French call them a *maison de passage*."

She looked at me dubiously, wiping her face with her sleeve.

"Do you have any more of these conferences planned?"

I shook my head. "But I can't rule it out."

She nodded. "Well, I want you to see a doctor and have yourself examined before you come anywhere near me!"

She was too busy being outraged to query my alibi.

I waved the piece of paper I was holding. "Justine, I have some things to do right now, following on from the conference last night. But we can still meet for dinner. I can try to cheer you up. Meanwhile, is there anything I can do for you, anything to help you?"

She stood up and tucked her shirt into her slacks. "Well, there *is* one thing. Will you come and look at the site of the fire, in the Place Royère? I'd like to know what you make of it — you told me you've got experience with incendiaries and explosives. You might have some ideas. And I'd like you to meet the waiter, see what you think of his story."

"I'm sorry, Mathieu, I can't eat. I'm too upset. Do you want my food?"

Justine pushed her plate towards me, but I shook my head.

"The chicken was good, but I've had enough. How did you hear about this restaurant? It's new, isn't it?"

She nodded glumly. Tears weren't far away.

"François told me. We should have come here last night — he had booked a table. But we worked late, so we had a bite near his office instead, just some soup and an omelette. I haven't eaten anything since then, so I should be hungry, but instead I feel sick."

"Have some bread, you must have something."

The restaurant we were in, Bistro Victoire, was on the Left Bank, near St. Germain de Prés, in a little side street. The tables were crowded together but there were only a few other people besides us in the restaurant. The walls were covered in posters, travel posters and Communist Party posters if I wasn't mistaken. The tablecloths were red, of course — red gingham.

I waved to the waiter to bring us another *pichet* of wine and I leaned towards Justine one more time.

"Shall I ask him to bring some bread? Will you eat that?"

"I'll try. No, don't waste your money. I'm really not hungry."

"Be careful what you drink, then. Don't drink too much on an empty stomach."

"You sound like a priest."

I made a face.

"When are you going to see a doctor?"

"What?" I was thrown for a moment.

She lit a cigarette. "Many women who find the man they are sleeping with has been with a prostitute, they would be more, much more . . ."

She glared at me. "How are we going to be tonight, in bed? François is dead, murdered. I want you to . . . to hold me, make me feel safe. We could have the oblivion of sex — except that we can't."

She blew cigarette smoke in my face. "I hate men!"

How long would Justine's grief last?

How long would mine?

The *pichet* arrived just then, and I thankfully busied myself refilling the glasses.

I still didn't know what I was going to do about visiting the devastation at Perrault's flat and the tabac, the scene of my crime. Trust that damned waiter to be a member of the Communist Party. He would surely remember me, and that I had been in the square on the night immediately preceding the fire. I had to worm my way out of my promise.

I tried to say something comforting to Justine.

"I'm sorry I didn't know François better. He was obviously a fascinating man."

She nodded and blew smoke in my face again.

"And a good one, too. I haven't had the chance to tell you yet, but after we finished work last night, as I told you, I went back to his flat. I went because he said he had a document he wanted to give me."

I nodded and sipped some wine.

She reached down into her bag on the floor and took some sheets of paper from it and put them on the table.

"And they are?"

"Remember that woman we interviewed in La Santé prison?"

"Claudine Petit?"

"That's right."

Justine shuffled the papers neatly. "Well, the *épuration* committee visited her in jail after we did. François was one of them — I think I told you that was one of his responsibilities."

I nodded. "And these pages are . . . ?"

"A complete list of people who passed

through the Gestapo offices in Paris from January 1 this year until it closed down at the end of July. And details of what happened to them. It was one of the last things the bureaucrats in Avenue Foch produced."

She sucked on her cigarette. "Claudine Petit had it all along. She stole it amid the chaos of the Gestapo's last days. She didn't tell us because you are a foreigner and I was too junior. She knew the *épuration* committee would visit her and that, if she produced it for them, it would help her cause . . . show how well-motivated she was. It worked — she has been released and gone back to her family."

"And?"

Justine turned the pages and pushed them across the table, leaving her hand on them. "When François told me he had the list, I took it so we could be certain, if we ever do get to Pforzheim, that we have full and accurate details of who was sent where. Claudine Petit's memory, Monique Brèger's, even Ulrich Kolbe's recollection, could be flawed. This list is official, the Gestapo's own."

She lifted her hand. "Read the lists for yourself."

I reached forward and spread the sheets of paper across the table, moving the *pichet* out of the way.

I scanned the list.

I scanned it a second time.

I read it more slowly a third time.

"I don't see . . . Madeleine's name. It's not . . . there."

She spoke through the cigarette still in her mouth.

"That's right."

"But Claudine Petit said that she remembered Madeleine's code name, Oak. So did the others, Monique, Kolbe —"

"No."

"They did!"

"No! I wasn't there when you saw Monique Brèger, but what Claudine Petit actually said — in French, remember — was that someone with the code name Chêne came through Gestapo headquarters. And so did Ulrich Kolbe."

"So? It amounts to the same thing."

"No it doesn't. Look down the list for the name Barbara Hapgood. César circuit, Auxerre."

I did as she said. "Yes, I see it."

"And what is the code word next to it?"

"Chain. So what?"

"Chain in French is *chain.*" She looked hard at me. "It is pronounced exactly the same as *chêne.* You speak French well but with a bit of an accent. I think that both Claudine Petit and Ulrich Kolbe may have misunderstood you. Maybe Monique Brèger did too."

Chêne . . . chain . . . chain . . . chêne.

Justine was right. Different meanings but they sounded the same. My heart was racing. My heart was ahead of my mind.

A thought struck me. "I wonder . . . Did you notice, in Saarburg, when we interviewed Kolbe, when we asked him a question about Chêne, he hesitated. I remember, he chewed his cheek as if he was going to say something, then thought better of it. Was he perhaps going to point out the possibility for misunderstanding, then dropped the idea?"

I was, of course, aware of another possibility, that Kolbe had been about to tell us that Madeleine — Oak, Chêne — was a German agent. But I wasn't about to tell Justine that. I wasn't sure what the situation was. The Gestapo lists told us Madeleine hadn't been captured, or executed. They didn't tell us whether she was alive, or where, or with whom.

Another thought struck me.

"And Monique Brèger commented on my accent, too. She asked me to repeat words, even code words."

Justine shrugged. "Maybe what you say is true. But the point is, your Madeleine never came through Paris. She was never sent to Pforzheim, or Ravensbruck, come to that."

She sat back.

"If she hasn't turned up, after . . . after more than four months, I am afraid to say that she must surely be dead. And the chances are — I'm sorry to say this, too — you may never find her grave."

She tapped ash into the ashtray.

"That's what I thought you should know. That's what these records confirm. I don't think there's any point in your going to Pforzheim, not if your main aim is to find your Madeleine."

Given what Justine knew, or thought that she knew, she was right. It had been four months, four long, eventful months — historic months — since we'd had word from Madeleine. Long enough — more than long enough — for her to have got in touch if she was alive and free, more than long enough if she had escaped via a ratline.

I gulped some wine.

Justine reached across the table and put her hand on mine. "I'm sorry if this is bad news. I know you were hoping to find her grave, to say goodbye. Now —"

I held up my free hand to stop her talking. "You may be right, but there's something you don't know, something I've never told you."

Taking a deep breath, I poured more wine into our glasses. I was — *of course* — not going to tell Justine about the bleak possibility of Madeleine being a German double agent. Instead, I began to explain about Philippe, his activities in the Resistance, his life in the caves, his marriage to Madeleine, his death, the newspaper cutting in *Limoges Matin*.

"So you see what's going through my head," I said when I had finished. "Maybe Philippe *isn't* dead, maybe that incomplete *Limoges Matin* article was about *him.* If he's alive and Madeleine — who was in that part of the world when the invasion took place — went looking for his grave, and found him instead, it could explain her silence. She . . . she has gone back to her first love."

Justine stared at me. "Don't put yourself through this. Don't think it — and don't go looking. Either way, if she's dead, or gone back to this Philippe person, you have lost her and are going to crucify yourself. You're not married to her — she's married to him. You've already made a break — you've been four months without her. Don't stir up your feelings again. Stay here. Stay here with me."

I didn't say anything for a while. I lit another cigarette and smoked it. I drank my wine.

I shook my head. "No. I can't. This changes things, Justine. I'm sorry. But you're French, you're a woman, you know what I'm going through. I really do need to settle this. And that means I need to go to the Bibliothèque Nationale immediately. Tomorrow."

She gripped my hand more firmly, and said softly. "Don't, please don't. I don't want to lose you, too. I am losing all the men I know and like, and all at once."

"I'm sorry." I shook my head again. "I'm sorry."

A long silence elapsed. I noticed a clock ticking somewhere.

Slowly, she disengaged her hands from mine. A tear coursed its silver trace down her cheek.

She sniffed again. "I think you are making a mistake. Some things are better left . . . alone. But I know a lot is happening in your head and it is not certain, is it, that this article is about the man you think? So yes, I will take you to the Bibliothèque tomorrow — after all, I can't stop you going by yourself. But, in return, I want you to come with me to see François's flat and the waiter. You owe me that."

My throat was dry.

"Of course."

That night, Justine took her time coming to bed. She ran a bath, so hot that steam leaked out from under the bathroom door. All was quiet from within the room, so she was obviously just lying there, soaking up the heat and whatever bath oil she had mixed in with the water.

I was sitting on the edge of the bed, in my undershorts, cleaning my shoes, just to make doubly sure they were free of any lighter fuel I might have spilled on them, when I had a disturbing thought that I should have had before. I got up quickly and knocked on the bathroom door.

"Yes?"

"You're very quiet. I was just checking."

"Checking what?"

"You know . . . what with François being killed . . . that you haven't done anything silly."

A pause. "The door's not locked. Come in."

She was lying there, the bath very full, foam covering her shoulders and breasts, just her head showing.

"I did think about . . . *alors* . . . doing something silly, as you say. *Fou.* But then I thought . . . to get all the way through this war, safely, and to . . . No. I'm miserable, but you have never misled me, so I don't complain. We had what we had. I had my first English lover, and maybe my last. You had . . . What did you have, Matt? What did I do for you — anything? Anything you haven't had or done before?"

I sat on the edge of the bath. "Let's not keep score, Justine. I just need to know what happened to Madeleine. It's partly duty and partly . . . Well, you know what else. There's still a possibility she was killed, a strong possibility. And she had a suicide pill if she wanted to avoid capture and the torture that would follow. Then . . . if that's the case . . ."

"You'll come back?"

"Would you want me to?"

She didn't answer. Instead, she sank under the water and, for a moment, disappeared. Then she stood up, naked except for the foam, her body glistening in the light, the hair between her legs dripping wet, succulent.

"Go back to bed," she said softly. "I'll dry off and be there soon."

I went back to my shoes. My mind wasn't on them, of course. My mind was on the waiter in the café in the Place Royère. How was I going to get out of meeting him?

I lay back on the bed with that day's paper. Death notices continued to fill the pages of *Le Monde.* The war was still on. From the accounts of the fighting in the east I could see that Pforzheim still hadn't fallen. There was now a small section in the paper headed *"Épuration."* There I found details of the death of François Perrault, described as an accident in an arson attack that had gone too far.

Justine came through in her dressing gown, drying her hair with a towel. She sat on the edge of the bed.

When she had finished she made no attempt to comb it but left it wild — red strands falling like rope all over her shoulders and down on to her breasts, leaking droplets of water. Then she took off her gown and got into bed.

I put aside my paper and got under the covers alongside her.

I turned towards her.

"I can tell you one thing," she said, sniffing.

"Yes?"

"I telephoned the Bibliothèque Nationale today, to check in which part of the library they keep the newspapers. When I was put through, the woman in the newspaper division was very helpful and asked which paper I wanted, and for which dates, so she could have it ready. But when I told her, she said that the papers for the dates you are interested in are at the binders, out at Massy, and can't be consulted until the binding is finished. I asked if *Limoges Matin* has a Paris office, but she said she didn't think so. It just uses agency copy."

Her eyes searched mine. "Does that make any difference? Are you still going?"

I paused. But not for long. "Yes."

She lay her head on the pillow, her eyes glistened, a tear nestled on the side of the bridge of her nose.

"Kiss me," she said softly.

"I thought — ?"

"Kiss me!"

Her mouth was wet. Her cheeks wet from the tears. Her hair wet from the bath.

As I kissed her, she pulled me to her and wrapped her legs around mine, the hair between her legs still wet.

I broke off kissing her and looked at her.

Her eyes were closed, then they opened.

563

"Get *into* me! I don't care where you were last night."

She pressed her wet pelvis against my upper thigh and her mouth closed over mine.

My body responded fully to her advances. But as I made love to her, I couldn't get out of my mind the fact that if she knew where I had really been the night before, she would care very much.

28

Breakfast the next morning was — well, difficult. Justine didn't touch her coffee and only picked at her croissant. At length, she said, "When will you leave? Tonight? Tomorrow?"

"Tonight, if there's a train."

If Madeleine was a German agent, I needed to know that quickly, too. London would need to track her mother, and any other people she'd had dealings with.

"I'm sorry. Last night was so . . . Sorry."

She was close to tears.

"Come to the square? You promised?"

I couldn't get out of it. In her current mood, what she felt for me could easily turn to loathing, and any suspicions she had of me would set like steel.

"Yes, I promised," I said. "But there are a couple of things I have to set in motion at the office. Can we meet *at* the square?" I looked at my watch. "It's now nine fifteen. Shall we meet there at, say, two?"

She nodded. "*D'accord.* Will you find it okay?"

"Place Royère? I'll come by taxi — how's that?"

She nodded, threw down her cigarette, and trod on it. "It will be a sad place for our last date. But perhaps fitting."

"Don't say that! I don't know how this story will end."

Justine only knew the half of it. How could she know more? But I didn't know the whole story myself. Not yet.

At the office I had three things to do. The first was to get a call put through to Blakeney in Norfolk. So far as I recalled, Madeleine's mother did not have a telephone, but I knew someone who did — the taxi firm just around the corner, the firm whose drivers had ferried me to and from King's Lynn railway station. I didn't have their number either, but I remembered their name — the King's Men — and I asked Colette to find their number through directory enquiries.

That would take a while, I knew, so in the meantime I asked one of the other secretaries to book me a ticket on that night's overnight train to Limoges, if there was one. Then I took down a copy of the Paris telephone directory and began a search that only I could do — for the café in the Place Royère.

I couldn't remember the exact name of the

café, but it was the only one in the square, so I took a chance that it was called the Café Royère.

It was.

I took a deep breath, wrapped my handkerchief around the mouthpiece, and dialed the number.

After a couple of rings, a voice answered.

Speaking in my singsong Lorraine-style French, as best I could, I asked if that was the Café Royère?"

"Oui, monsieur."

"You have a waiter there, one Didier Roque."

"Oui, monsieur."

"May I speak to him, please? This is the police."

"The Paris police? You don't sound Parisian?"

"I am not, madame, but that is not your concern. I wish to speak to Roque."

"He's done nothing wrong, I hope?"

"No, no. Nothing for you to worry about. But bring him to the phone, please, now."

"Of course. *Ne quittez pas.* Hold on."

A delay. Traffic noises, both outside the office and through the telephone receiver. Having spent time in Lorraine, it was the only French accent I was familiar with.

Then, "Hello, this is Didier Roque. Who is that?"

"This is Police Headquarters, sixteenth arrondissement. Inspector Ravenal here. I am investigating the fire in the Place Royère the other night. I understand that you have told more than one person that you noticed some strangers in your café before the fire."

"Ye-e-e-s."

"You sound doubtful. Yes or no?"

"Well, there was one person, yes, who was hanging round here on the day before the fire. He wasn't Parisian. He said he —"

"That's enough. I want you to come into headquarters. We have some photographs we would like you to see. It could be important. Can you come in . . . Let's see, can you be here at two o'clock?"

"Where is 'here,' as you put it?"

I gave him an address well away from the Place Royère.

"That's a long way. Why are you so far away?"

"Because, if we are right, our suspect lives in this arrondissement, where he is known for other crimes. Now, can you come? It's urgent, we may be talking about murder here — you realise that?"

"Yes, of course I do. That's why I mentioned my suspicions. Who told you, by the way?"

"That doesn't matter for the moment. We can talk about that when you get here. Answer my question — can you get here by two o'clock?"

"Hold on, let me ask the woman who owns

568

the café."

The line went dead again.

As I looked up, Colette was waving a piece of paper at me. She laid it on my desk. It was a phone number for the King's Men in Blakeney. I nodded my thanks.

"Monsieur?"

"Yes?"

"How long will the meeting take?"

"Oh, I don't know. Half an hour, forty-five minutes."

"Will you pay my fare?"

I exploded but tried not to show it.

"We'll pay your fare by public transport, and give you a ride back to the café in a police car, how's that?"

"Okay, I'll come. Two o'clock?"

"Two o'clock it is. Ask for me, Inspector Ravenal, Pierre Ravenal."

I rang off.

I picked up the phone again immediately and put through a call, via the international operator, to England. Since I had an army rank, it took only ten minutes.

The line wasn't good but it was good enough. Swishes and storms all over again.

"The King's Men, Blakeney," said a voice.

"I'm calling from Paris," I said loudly. "I hope you can help me."

"Paris? Paris in France? Oh my. It's a call from Paris," the voice said, obviously speaking for the benefit of everyone within earshot in his office. "You know this is a taxi office. Have you got the right number?"

"Yes, yes, I know who you are," I said. "And I want you to do me a favour, please."

"Oh, yes? What's that then?"

"I need urgently to talk to Mrs. Dirac, she's a good customer of yours —"

"Yes, she is. You want to talk to her?"

"Yes, please, can you go and get her? I'll hang on."

"Oh," said the voice. "Oh. I don't think . . . no. Don't go away, here's our Jeannie."

There was a short pause. Was Victoria Dirac still in Blakeney? I needed to know — it would tell me a lot. If she had moved out, that would point to Madeleine being . . . what I feared most. If not, had she heard from her daughter . . . ?

A voice broke in on my thoughts. "Jeannie Slater here. Are you wanting Victoria Dirac?"

"Yes, that's exactly who I *do* want. Can you go and get her for me, please? It's urgent."

"I can't get her, I'm afraid, because she's not here. I'm looking after Wellington, her dog."

"She's away? Where's she gone?"

This was not good news.

"I'm not sure. I mean I don't know."

"Oh? *Why* has she gone? Do you know that?"

"No, I don't. She was very private about it all. She left very suddenly, four days ago.

Took the train to London, left me three pounds to look after Wellington."

Had Mrs. Dirac told Jeannie Slater the truth? Had she disappeared, and sacrificed her dog?

I barked into the phone. "What else did she say?"

"Nothing, not to me anyway. Who *are* you?"

"I'm a friend of her daughter. She didn't mention her daughter?"

"No, no. She didn't mention her daughter, nothing like that —"

"Did she say how *long* she would be away?"

"Not exactly —"

"What does that mean? What did she say exactly? Please, it might be important, very important."

"It was as she was leaving, in one of our taxis, leaving for King's Lynn, I mean, to take the train to London. She said she didn't know when she would be back."

I paused. The swishing on the line was bad. "Is there anything else you can think of? Anything you can tell me about her departure?"

"Only . . . only . . ."

"Yes?"

"She took a bag of photographs with her. I know because I saw them slip out on to the back seat of the taxi as she was leaving."

The tabac in Place Royère was still smoking.

The smell of burned wood clogged the nostrils and even penetrated to the back of the throat. Blackened timbers lay everywhere, scorch marks disfigured the exterior brickwork, tiny fragments of glass caught the daylight. The shop was still giving off heat.

Justine and I stood together surveying the damage.

I looked up at what was left of François Perrault's building. "What a horrible way to die," I said softly, mentally crossing my fingers as I did so.

Justine nodded, but didn't say anything for a moment.

"It's not much of a shop, is it? I mean in terms of size."

"A tabac needn't take up much space, though. Cigarettes and matches are hardly bulky." She held up a Gitane, to make her point.

I shook my head. "Being here rubs it in: it was an incredible thing to do — set fire to the shop to kill the person living next door, above. Are you still convinced that's what happened?"

She nodded furiously.

A policeman walked by. He looked at us intently and Justine turned away.

"What do you think?" she said, gesturing with her hand to the fire site. "Any thoughts?"

I nodded decisively. "This is an incendiary-type fire, very much so. I recognize the configuration, the pattern of heat generation." I made a show of looking up and down the smoking remains. "And I can tell you that we in SC2 parachuted *thousands* of incendiaries to the Resistance. This is a Resistance job — make of that what you will. If the tobacconist *was* sleeping with —"

"But she wasn't!"

I shrugged. "Have you met the woman who runs the tabac? Do you really believe her when she says she never — ?"

"No, I haven't met the woman, but I've met her man — Didier, the waiter. Come on, the café's over here." She moved off towards it.

Here was the crunch. Had the waiter done as I had enticed him to do, and gone to police headquarters? If he hadn't . . .

Justine crossed the square and walked straight into the café, past the tables on the pavement and on inside.

My stomach was in a brawl with my other organs.

"Is Didier here?" she said to the woman behind the counter.

"No, he's been called to the police station," said the woman.

I relaxed.

"Oh? Why?" said Justine. She turned to me and said, "This is Matthew Hammond, a British colleague."

The woman held out her hand and I shook it. "Good afternoon," I said in French. "We

573

were hoping to see Didier."

"The police want him to look at some photographs, of people who might have been in this café on the night of the fire."

I suddenly realised with a start that the woman behind the bar was looking at me intently and the skin under my chin began sweating. She was, of course, the person I had spoken to when I had called the bar, pretending to be a policeman. Had I been too talkative and had she recognized my voice? She had remarked on it earlier.

"But how did the police know he had seen some suspicious-looking people? So far as I know, he had only mentioned it to me, and I certainly never told the police. I was going to but I haven't yet. We wanted to have some potential suspects first." Justine frowned at me.

The woman shrugged. "I don't know who Didier talks to. I'm his employer, not his confessor. He talked to lots of customers. The police telephoned here earlier today — I answered the call myself. Didier spoke to them and they fixed an appointment for two o'clock."

"What time was this call from the police?"

The woman shrugged again. "Eleven, eleven fifteen."

Justine looked at me quizzically. Did she suspect me? Was that behind her question over timing? She *couldn't* suspect me.

Could she?

"How long will he be gone?" Justine said to the woman.

She shrugged again. "He didn't say. But you're welcome to wait."

Justine looked at me.

"Sorry, Justine. I've done what you asked, but when I went back to the office today, I found out that Madeleine's mother has left her address in England. Something had happened suddenly, and that means —"

"I know what it means," she said softly but bitterly.

She didn't know everything it might mean, but I wasn't getting into that. Madeleine's mother might have been telling the truth to Jeannie Slater, or she might not have been.

What I did say was, "I'm going to Limoges tonight, on the overnight train. I'm sorry but . . ." I tailed off.

"When does the train leave?"

"Eight. But I need to go back to the office first. Loose ends to tie up."

"Shall I come to the station, to see you off?"

"I . . . Well, if you wish. Are you sure?"

"I'll be there at a quarter to, on the platform. For my last kiss."

I have always loved the smell and bustle of railway stations. The steam, the soot, the drama of arrival and departure, the hugs and tears — there is nowhere quite like a big station to make you feel quickened by ordinary events.

But this time I was apprehensive as well as excited. I had of course lied to Justine about having things to do in the office. I knew she would wait for Didier Roque, that he would arrive back at the café flustered and irritated, having found that there was *no* rendezvous with the police, and that he had been set up. At that point, when he and Justine were discussing what had happened, would the bar's owner recall that my voice was quite similar to the one she had heard on the telephone that morning? Both had remarked on my accent. Would Justine put it all together? She could have no understanding of why I would wish to kill François Perrault, but she might be suspicious enough to bring Didier with her to the Gare Montparnasse, to settle it once and for all.

I had thought this through while we were standing talking to the café owner, and that is why I had also lied about the departure time of the Limoges train. It left not at 8:00 but at 7:10 and I was banking on Justine's not doubting my word about that and not checking the timetable herself. If she *did* check the timetable and found out that I had misled her . . .

I was seated in a compartment now, at 7:05. I had no suitcase with me — I'd left my belongings in Justine's flat, so there was some ambiguity as to whether I would return — but I hoped I could buy the basics I would need in Limoges. The compartment was filling up — there was no officer's section for this journey, as we were too far from the front, and it was likely to be an uncomfortable night. But, so long as I got out of Gare Montparnasse without a confrontation with Justine, I could live with that.

7:06. I had had some time to digest the news from Blakeney, that Mrs. Dirac had gone to London and didn't know when she would be back. Or so she had told Jeannie Slater at the King's Men. And that she had taken a bag of photographs with her. Madeleine's mother's drawing room flashed into my mind, with its mantelshelf and the photographs on it, in particular the photograph of Philippe. And crowded in there, among the other thoughts, was the moment Madeleine's mother had told me that Madeleine had "unfinished business" with Philippe, when she had said that "you are never in love in quite the same way that you are in love the first time, when you are innocent in a way that you are never innocent again."

I remembered her words only too well.

She had told me that Madeleine would want, if she were able, to "wind up" that part of her life — to visit his grave, if there was one.

What if Madeleine had gone to Louzac

looking for his grave — and instead found the man himself, alive?

Or was I running on ahead, too fast? If Madeleine was a German agent, she could have been duping him as she had perhaps duped me. If she was a German agent, and her mother was too, the whole Philippe story could have been invented by them, but based on a real person, for verisimilitude. Her mother could have removed the photographs because, in some way, they identified who she and her daughter really were. The two of them could have invented his death, never imagining that I would stumble across him being alive.

Alternatively, Madeleine might have swallowed her suicide pill, soon after her last message had been interrupted. Something else that I simply didn't know about could have happened to her. The ambiguities hadn't gone away.

If Mrs. Dirac had spun Jeannie Slater a line, however, and that was certainly a possibility, if both she and Madeleine were German agents, then she could have left Blakeney for anywhere, anywhere at all.

Which would mean I had no hope of finding either of them.

But since Pforzheim had still to fall to our forces, finding out the exact truth about Philippe was my only way forward for now, blind alley or dead end that it might be.

I'd bought an evening newspaper at the station kiosk. I looked at it now. On the front page, at the foot, one particular item immediately caught my attention: a report that a German newspaper had published an account of Leni Riefenstahl's latest exploit. In a break from covering the front with her camera, she was making a film in Berlin of Hitler's favourite opera, *Tiefland.* In typical Hitler-Nuremberg-Riefenstahl style, the film had hundreds of extras.

7:09. I willed my watch to go faster. The compartment was full now. Sleep tonight, for me, would be out of the question. I had with me some sandwiches and a beer. Better to go easy on the beer — if I stood up I'd lose my seat. I studied the timetable and the route: Étampes, Pithiviers, Montargis, Gien, Briare . . . I gave up. It wasn't an express, and with so many stops, the journey was going to be interminable.

7:10. Wasn't the damn train supposed to leave now? What would I find when I got to Louzac? If Mrs. Dirac had been right, that Madeleine's first love was like no other, that in truth she had never got over Philippe, would Madeleine be there, and how would she feel about my turning up unannounced? Whatever had happened later, she hadn't made straight for Louzac. Had she behaved impeccably to deceive us still further, while she passed on information from France to Berlin?

7:12. I reminded myself one more time that I had only Madeleine's word, and her mother's, that there had ever been any connection with Philippe Sompre. Or that he existed.

7:14. I kept my eyes averted from the window, so that should Justine be on the platform, having worked out when the train actually was scheduled to leave, and was actively looking for me, I would be all the harder to spot.

My geography of that part of France was hazy but I thought Louzac was about 200 kilometers — 120 miles or so — from Le Gâvre, where Madeleine had been dropped. She could have cycled there, had she wanted to, in a few days.

7:16 and the bloody train still hadn't left. The biggest question, the most awkward question, was this: If Madeleine was still alive, why had she made no attempt to contact me? Did she not want to see me? If not, why not? Did the fact that she was reunited with Philippe mean that our life together counted for nothing? She had made no attempt to contact me, so far as I knew, or get information to me . . . Did *that* point to her being an enemy agent . . . ?

7:18. The carriage jolted into motion. My nervousness began to subside. But not completely. The train was packed; passengers were standing in the corridors. Justine, if she wanted, could have boarded the train further along, and I would never know. I wouldn't know, with certainty, until we got to Limoges tomorrow morning.

■ ■ ■ ■

LIMOGES

■ ■ ■ ■

29

Justine wasn't at Limoges. I took the first local train north and was in Louzac — changing twice, with hefty waits in between trains — by six o'clock on the evening of the following day. I used the waiting time to buy a small suitcase, a razor, a spare shirt, and other bits and pieces. When I reached Louzac, I found a hotel near the railway station, had dinner in a steamy brasserie almost next door, took care not to get involved in any conversations with curious waiters, and, having hardly slept on the overnight train from Paris, was in bed by ten o'clock. With any luck, tomorrow would be a crucial day.

■ ■ ■ ■

LOUZAC

■ ■ ■ ■

30

My first stop next morning was the university. The archaeology department would surely contain several people who knew about the cave discoveries.

I found the university easily enough, by asking people in the hotel, and tracked down the archaeology department, which occupied part of a barracks-type temporary building that must surely once have belonged to the army. A woman secretary, in what appeared to be the main office, had no idea what I was talking about, but then a small man came in, carrying what looked to me like a stone axe.

"Excuse me," I said in my best French. "Do you know a Philippe Sompre?" I had to bend the rules here and take some calculated risks. "I believe he is the man who has discovered the ancient painting of an ox in your local caves — I read about it in a newspaper in Paris. I believe he may be able to help me find my wife," I lied, or exaggerated. "She was an undercover agent near here about the time of the invasion — D-Day — and she has gone missing."

The man looked at me, hard. Had he been in the Resistance — or, worse, had he been a collaborator? All France was still deeply divided.

"I can tell you where the cave is. I don't know who or where Philippe Sompre is."

"Well, that's a start," I said. "Tell me, please."

"You go out of town, to the south, on the Cognac road. After about four kilometres, you come to an avenue of trees, poplar trees, on both sides of the road. At the far end of the poplars there is a bridge over a river, the Vienne. You walk upriver for about three kilometres until you come to a narrow gorge. There is a small path along the cliff on the left, the north side. After a few hundred metres you will come to a narrow slit in the cliff, with a small stream falling as a waterfall into the river. You climb up that stream — you will get very wet, I am afraid — and you will come to the cave."

I thanked him and retraced my steps to the railway station, where I had noticed a couple of taxis waiting for business.

The first man didn't want to take me to where I wanted to go, and wait for me there, but the second man didn't mind. In fact, as we were driving out of Louzac, he asked me why I was so interested in the cave.

"I'm not, really. I'm trying to locate someone called Philippe Sompre. I believe he's the man who found the cave and the ancient painting on its walls. If they are still excavating there, someone will know where he is. I need to contact him because I gather he's a Resistance hero, and he may be able to help me find my wife, who parachuted into France ahead of the invasion, and went missing."

"You mean you don't want to go to the cave at all, not really?"

"No, as I say, what I really want is to find Philippe Sompre."

"But I know where he is."

"You *do*?"

So he was alive! I had been right to have my suspicions all along. But why had he been reported dead? Had Madeleine misled me about that?

"How do you know he's alive? And where is he?"

"I was in the Resistance, we were in the Resistance together, in the caves. Do you want me to take you to him?"

"Yes, of course I do. Where is he? Is it far?"

"About forty-five minutes from here." The driver stopped his car, did a three-point turn, and went back the way we had come. "He's in a convent, St. Hilaire-en-Fôret."

"What's he doing there?" The name rang a bell.

"The convent is also a hospital. Many

people in the Resistance were injured — the convent is where they recovered. It was also the place where the Resistance kept records of collaborators. It is from there, now, that old scores are being settled, what we in France call —"

"*Épuration* — yes, I know."

He looked at me and nodded. "Now that the war is nearly over, France is a strange country, *n'est-ce pas*?"

"What do you mean?"

"Philippe is a communist — we are all communists in Louzac, we are anti-Gaullists. Yet we have our home in a convent, in the church. There will be elections soon and we will fight the Gaullists for the future of the country. Philippe has a wide following here. He will be elected."

We were leaving Louzac now, the country hilly and green, the cows chewing their way through lush fields, with no sign anywhere of the war: old buildings, lines of poplars, horse-drawn carts, men and women on bicycles, people carrying bread and fishing rods.

We headed north for about twenty-five minutes. The traffic was light, mainly rural — a few tractors with enormous rear wheels, cascading mud everywhere — and we had to wait at most bridges, which were too narrow for two-way traffic. We took our turn.

"Tell me about Philippe? He was injured — yes?"

He nodded. "He was shot in the leg and chest as he ran from a bridge he had blown up."

"But he has recovered now?"

"Well, he walks with a limp, but I don't think he's in pain any more. I haven't seen him for a few weeks."

"Is he married?"

"No. There was a rumour that he had an English girlfriend once, but it didn't work out. But I'm not the one to ask — I was injured myself and left the Resistance two years ago. I just acted as a messenger — a taxi driver can do that well, because he goes everywhere as part of his job."

We turned off the main road on to a lane. The countryside here was thick with trees and the lane was so narrow that twice we had to back up when we met a truck and a tractor coming the other way.

Then I saw some roofs among the trees, slate roofs, and stone walls.

"This is St. Hilaire," said the driver.

He drove off the lane into a gravel forecourt, and as he did so we nearly collided with a large black dog, which ran off at the last moment. The driver stopped the taxi in front of a stone-built porch with two huge wooden doors, into one of which was set a much smaller, human-scale door with a shiny brass knob. This was the door that was used most often.

"Shall I wait?" the driver said.

"I don't know. Let me pay you for so far. How much?"

He told me and I gave him the money.

"I don't know how long I'll be," I said. "I could be half an hour; I could be here for the rest of the day."

He made a gesture with his head. "Go in and see what there is to see. Then, when you know what the story is, come out and tell me. It's a slow day so I can wait here for a bit. Just don't forget me."

"Okay, good," I replied. "Let's do that. And don't worry, I won't forget."

I got out of the taxi and approached the convent door.

As I did so, it opened and a nun appeared. She was dressed in a pale grey habit, with white edging all the way down to the ground, and a white cloth enveloping her head. She looked surprised to see me, but managed a smile.

"May I help you?" she said.

"Thank you. I am looking for Philippe Sompre."

"When did you make the appointment?"

"I don't have one, but I have come all the way from England," I replied. "I only found out an hour ago where he is living."

She looked at me, inspecting my clothes, the state of my beard, the neatness of my hair. How plausible was I?

"Come with me, please," she said at length, turning and going back through the door-within-the-door.

I followed.

Inside was a cavernous hall, built of stone, with granite flags on the floor and two tall, narrow windows of stained glass, throwing a perpetual evening light over everything.

"Wait here, please," she said. "I won't be long."

I looked about me. The convent, I could now see, was mediaeval, with a large stone superstructure and elaborate heads tenoned into the walls at varying heights — heads of saints, heads of grotesques, shields and rosettes, angels blowing trumpets, lions' heads. A Christ on the cross but not one slumped in suffering, rather triumphant, radiant, his body arched in an act of bravado.

Ten minutes passed, twenty, twenty-five. She had said she wouldn't be long but she was.

A bird, a shiny coal-black crow of some kind, was suddenly flapping in the hallway. It had got in somewhere and was now desperate to get out. I opened the door-within-the-door, hoping that the light that streamed in would attract its attention and help it to freedom.

It didn't work. The bird continued to flap about in the higher reaches of the hall, far too high for me to be of any use.

More than half an hour had passed. The nun had disappeared through a solid-looking, brown wooden door and I thought it time I went after her.

But as I approached the door, it opened and a figure came through.

It wasn't the nun.

Its was Victoria Dirac.

"Colonel Hammond," she said softly. "So it *is* you. I thought as much."

My throat constricted. I swallowed. "If you are here, Madeleine is here." My heart seemed to swell and lighten all at the same time.

"Come," she said. "Sit down over here. I need to talk to you."

"No. I want to see Madeleine."

"Please. Let's sit. You'll see Madeleine, but we need to talk first."

So Madeleine *was* here; and alive. My heart had not been so spring-loaded in months.

"Why do we need to talk? I don't understand."

"Let's sit. Please. I promise you that when I tell you what I'm going to tell you, you'll understand."

Reluctantly, I sat down. I'd lived with doubt for weeks. It was time to end it. I didn't know what to think and I was in no mood to slow down.

She sat alongside me. She was wearing a cream blouse, I remember, and a tartan skirt, but not a kilt. There was rouge on her cheeks but she wore no lipstick. Odd, the details one remembers.

She spoke softly, hesitantly.

"When you came to see me in Blakeney, neither of us knew what had happened to Madeleine. You were in the dark almost as much as I was. What happened is that Madeleine did her job, as you know, until D-Day, the invasion. But then —"

"She came looking for Philippe's grave, but found him instead. Isn't that what happened? I know now that he's alive."

She shook her head. "No, it isn't, not at all, and you mustn't think it."

She fingered the pearls of her necklace. Her voice was weak.

"Shortly after D-Day, Madeleine made a mistake — she'll tell you herself what happened. But, as a result of her mistake, she was captured at a place called Nallies, just outside La Rochelle. She was taken to a holding hospital-cum-prison there and interrogated."

Victoria Dirac caught her breath.

"In fact, she was tortured — she won't say what exactly was done to her. But she held out well and, while she did so, the invasion proceeded. As you almost certainly must know, three places in France — three coastal cities with U-boat fleets — fought hard and became isolated pockets of resistance. Those areas were Brest, St. Nazaire, and —"

"La Rochelle. Yes, I know. You mean — ?"

She nodded. "As I have had it explained to me, the Gestapo's original plan would have been to ship Madeleine — once she had been captured — to Paris, interrogate her further there, and then transfer her even further eastwards, into Germany itself, where she would have been . . . executed."

"I don't understand," I said. "La Rochelle has still not fallen. If she was interned there, how did she get out?"

Mrs. Dirac had been holding a pack of cigarettes in her hand, and a lighter. She took out two cigarettes — just as Madeleine once had — and offered one to me, lighting both with her lighter.

"All in good time." She inhaled the smoke of her cigarette. "The Resistance in Paris intercepted Gestapo radio traffic, or they stole details at Gestapo headquarters in Paris — I'm not sure which. Among those details was the fact that a named British agent was being held in the Dompierre Secure Hospital in La Rochelle. These details were circulated to local Resistance groups in the area, in case they could help.

"Philippe saw those lists —"

I struck my fist on my knee and cried out, "I was right all along! But how can that be? Is that why — ?"

"Hold on, Matt! Hold on! I'm telling you

everything I know. I'll get to Philippe in a minute. But Madeleine first."

My insides were in turmoil, fighting one another. Where was all this going?

Victoria Dirac breathed out loudly, blowing cigarette smoke up into the air. "Now, as I know you know, Philippe is an expert on the caves in this region —"

"Yes," I said. "I read a report of his great discovery. I presume it was his. That's partly why I'm here, now."

She nodded.

"Well, it turns out that one of the caves hereabouts leads *into* La Rochelle. There is one cave, one cave at least, which starts here in free France and ends up inside that part of La Rochelle still occupied by the Germans. It's too small — and zigzags too much — to mount an assault through, but it has been used for intelligence purposes, or so I'm told.

"So Philippe mounted a rescue attempt —

"The rescue went well. The Resistance had people in the hospital, Madeleine was freed, and they reached the entrance of the cave inside La Rochelle . . ."

"But what . . . ? I can tell from your voice that —"

"Hold *on!*"

She drew on her cigarette.

"They got into the cave, some way inside. In fact, they were nearly out the other side, in free France, when the Germans, who had found out what had happened, and gave chase . . . Well, they found the entrance to the cave and exploded a bomb inside it."

I said nothing.

"The explosion sent a terrific blast of air, dust, and stones throughout the cave, collapsing part of it. Madeleine, as it happens, was half protected by a wall of rock but Philippe wasn't. Having a limp, he was slower than the rest, and he was deafened, blown off his feet, and hit his head on the stony ground. Rocks and stones fell on him and he was badly hurt. The others carried him to safety, and brought both of them here."

"Why not a proper hospital, now this part of France has been liberated?"

"This *is* a hospital. It has acted as a hospital, secretly, throughout the war. It has doctors — doctors everyone in the Resistance knows — and it has an operating theatre and a supply of medicines. The nuns are excellent nurses. It's as good as any other hospital in the area in the aftermath of occupation and the locals trust it."

I nodded.

"May I see her now? Where is Philippe now? Is he with her?"

"A few more details first. You'll see why."

She fingered her necklace again.

"That all happened about ten days ago." She eyed me levelly. "What you don't know, what she was frightened to tell you, in case

600

you stopped her being flown to France, is that Madeleine was pregnant —"

"What?"

Mrs. Dirac nodded. "I didn't know either, not until I got the call in Blakeney to come as soon as I could. And what you need to know is that, amid the excitement and danger of the escape, and the trauma of the explosion, Madeleine went into labour. Her daughter — your daughter — was born in a farmhouse between La Rochelle and here."

I had a daughter.

She smiled a sad smile. "The baby is doing fine —"

"What do you mean by that? What about Madeleine?"

She reached out gently, took my chin in her fingers, exactly as Madeleine used to do, and turned my head until it faced her. "First, you should know that I was sent for because no one knew how to contact you. Obviously, Madeleine's radio transmitter was confiscated when she was arrested. Like Madeleine, I had the number of Hamilton Place in London, but there was never any reply when I phoned. Since the organisation you work for is secret, no one knew how to contact you. Philippe had been told by his Resistance colleagues in Paris that SC2 had showed up there and he was about to try to contact your organisation when . . ."

"When what?"

She looked at me. "Philippe died of his wounds the day before yesterday."

I didn't know what to say. The taxi driver who had brought me obviously hadn't heard the latest news.

It was a long time before either Victoria Dirac or I said anything.

Then, still speaking softly, she murmured, "One other thing."

I shifted on the bench.

She pulled hard on her cigarette. "While Madeleine was imprisoned she was badly treated, and she caught typhus, either from the lice or the rats. Or . . . it's possible that the Nazi doctors experimented on her, gave her typhus deliberately to see if they could manipulate it. We don't know, but there are all sorts of rumours floating around."

She sniffed. "The important thing for you to know is that complications set in — kidney failure and pneumonia."

She looked up at me.

"The baby is doing well, Matt, but . . . Madeleine is not so good. Her kidney failure is quite advanced and the pneumonia . . . It's . . . it's not good."

Mrs. Dirac touched my knee. "Madeleine doesn't know it — but she hasn't got long to live."

I stopped breathing. My chest tightened.

"I'm sorry. We are all . . . it's terrible. It's a matter of days, hours even — she may not last the night. I brought some photographs for her to have near her bed, for comfort."

Stunned, I said nothing. I couldn't speak.

Then I tried. "How . . . how weak *is* she?"

"Even talking is an effort."

"Then let me put my questions to you."

"I'll do my best to answer."

"Why was Philippe reported dead when he wasn't?"

"Ah, yes. I know the answer, now. You speak very good French, Matthew, you have an accent, but your French is first-rate. But you are not French and so, perhaps, you can't understand.

"It was his mother. Philippe's mother always hated the fact that Madeleine was a Protestant, when her son was a Catholic. When Philippe was seriously injured and captured at the beginning of the war, and before he escaped, his mother got word to Madeleine that he was dead. She thought that would kill whatever there was between them. As it did. Without that, Matt, Madeleine would not have turned to you."

I swallowed.

"There's something else."

She picked up my hand and held it. "When Philippe rescued Madeleine, he knew she was pregnant. It was part of the intelligence he got from his Resistance colleagues in Paris." She squeezed my hand. "He went ahead anyway."

She squeezed my hand again. "And of course, he was present, at the farm, when Madeleine gave birth."

A farm, I registered, thinking back to that other farm, where it had all started.

"I talked to Philippe before he died. He was delighted for Madeleine that she has a daughter. His own mother is dead now, but he still blamed her for her deception. Had she not interfered, maybe Madeleine and he could have picked up where they left off when the war ended. But he went through a war like the rest of us, and he told me he'd seen enough to know that all manner of . . . that things like this happen. And, since he knew Madeleine was dying, he was happy for her that she has a child. It is the one thing that comforts her in her last days."

The cigarette she held in her fingers was shaking. A tear fell quickly down her cheek to her chin. She dropped the cigarette to the floor and crushed it with her shoe.

She wiped her face with the ball of her hand. "Now you know everything."

We sat, side by side, for a while, neither of us talking.

Then she whispered, "Let's go in."

I let the taxi driver go. Through the brown wooden door, the corridor seemed endless. It seemed at the time like the longest walk I had ever made. We passed several niches, in

604

each of which there was a marble bust, as I recall, and some landscape paintings of Mediterranean scenes. I have no idea why I registered these details. My mind felt numb.

At length, Victoria Dirac stopped and lightly touched my arm.

"She's very thin. Try not to look too shocked, when you see her."

We went through a door, where two nuns were sitting. They both stood up.

That room gave on to another, with windows high up in the wall, but covered with blinds.

This inner room was shady rather than dark. There was a bed in the corner with a figure in it.

Victoria Dirac was right. Madeleine was shockingly thin, her slight frame made her unruly hair seem more untamed than ever.

But it was her. Not quite the Madeleine of The Farm, or the beach at Ardlossan. Not the Madeleine of the Southwater meadow, that May night, in a blue cotton dress.

But nearly. The eyes, brown like whisky. The cleft in her chin. Her ballerina's neck.

Victoria left us.

Madeleine and I were alone.

"Hello," I said, bending down and kissing her cheek. My stomach was chopping and churning again. Tears did their best to break out over my cheeks but I wouldn't let them.

I kissed her again. "That's from Zola."

She closed her eyes and smiled. I could see that even that was an effort.

Then she opened them and, for a moment, they were bigger than ever.

Then she closed them again.

The truth was, she was weaker than I had expected.

I sat on the bed and held her hand.

"So . . . how are you feeling?"

"Weak," she said. "But I'll get stronger now you are here."

"We'll both get stronger, now."

"You have a daughter."

"*We* have a daughter. Where is she?"

"Being fed. I'm too weak. They will bring her in soon."

"What shall we call her?"

"You choose."

"No, let's choose together. How about your mother's name?"

"No, not that. Something . . . to remind you of me."

"What do you mean? Don't talk like that — you'll be getting stronger now that I'm here."

She closed her eyes again and nodded.

"Your mother has told me everything. About how Philippe came back from the dead, how he came to save you even though he knew you were pregnant. The injuries which . . . which ended his life."

She opened her eyes. "He was a good man.

You are a good man. I've been lucky."

Seeing her lying there, pitifully weak, thin, pale, save for the shadows under her eyes — how could she say that?

But she did.

I blinked back my tears again.

"Speaking of good men," she said, in barely more than a whisper, "I have a favour to ask."

The sound of the door opening interrupted us. It was the nursing sister bringing a little bundle into the room.

I stood up and took the bundle from the nurse.

She was so small she was barely there at all, but even so, as she wriggled, and as she squirmed, I could feel the energy coiled up in her tiny body. The strength of her minuscule fingers wrapping themselves round my thumb, the gummy lips that twisted into the first smile she would ever direct at me, her vivid whisky-brown eyes — just like her mother's — trying to focus and to work out what I was, holding her.

I kissed her forehead. How close to tears can you be and not actually cry?

"She's beautiful," I whispered, lowering her to Madeleine.

"Not yet," she replied. "Not yet, but if genes are all they are supposed to be, then, with yours and mine, she stands a good chance of being beautiful someday. If not, you'll love her anyway."

I laughed. "We'll both love her always."

Madeleine closed her eyes and nodded.

"I have an idea," I said softly.

"Yes?"

"Philippe rescued you, knowing you were pregnant with someone else's child. He gave this little bundle a chance to live. Let's call her Philippa."

Madeleine smiled. A radiant smile. Like that day in the Lagonda, with the top down, speeding down the Chiltern Hills.

"You wouldn't mind?"

"It will keep part of him alive."

"Philippa . . . Philippa Hammond. Will people call her Pippa, do you think?"

"Will you mind if they do?"

Still smiling, she shook her head. "With any luck, she'll never need a code name."

I laughed.

Looking down, I could see that Philippa was already fast asleep in Madeleine's arms. Totally content.

"What were you going to say? You mentioned a favour."

Madeleine nodded weakly. "I am alive — little Philippa is alive, we are both alive — because Philippe rescued us." She paused. "I thanked him — of course I thanked him."

She closed her eyes and waited for a moment, gathering her strength.

"But Philippe knew about my capture, and where to find me, because of the Resistance in Paris, one man in particular, their head of intelligence, who kept an archive and who was informed that I was captive in La Rochelle."

She breathed out, the air escaping from her lungs with difficulty.

"When you get the chance, when you eventually get back to Paris, I'd like you to thank him personally from me. From us, from all three of us, from Philippa in particular, who probably would not have lived but for him."

She coughed. Her whole body shook.

"His name, Philippe said, is François Perrault."

Moments before Madeleine spoke, I had anticipated what she was going to say. I could see the shape of the words forming on her lips and I wanted to cry out, "No! Don't say it, please don't say that name!"

My throat was dry, the palms of my hands were clammy. Suddenly I was burning up. The sunlight of Madeleine's radiant smile had disappeared.

I had to calm down, but that was easier said than done. Should I tell her straightaway that François Perrault was dead? That I had . . . ? No, she wasn't strong enough.

I took Madeleine's hand and squeezed it lightly.

"Of course, I'll do as you say."

The sound of the door opening made me

turn around. It was the nurse.

"That's long enough now, sir. Madeleine must rest."

But Madeleine was not playing ball.

"What time is it?"

I looked at my watch. "Nearly three."

"Come back at seven. I have dinner at six thirty. You can take me for a walk in the garden. There's a full moon tonight."

I stood by the entrance to Madeleine's room and watched the nurse wrap a shawl and a coat around her. What there was of her.

The nurse had warned me that a walk at night was not a good idea, that Madeleine wasn't strong enough, that her pneumonia was so far advanced that a little night air could tip her over the edge.

I hadn't insisted.

But Madeleine had. She was going to take a walk. There was a full moon that night and that was that.

The very sick have a moral authority that is hard to refuse.

Before she had put on her shawl and overcoat, she had sat on the bed and combed her hair, applied a touch of lipstick and rouge to her cheeks. She had a bit of colour. But she was undoubtedly weak.

She stepped into her slippers and pulled her belt tightly around her waist. Her hair fell about her shoulders as unruly as ever.

"Ready for take-off," she said softly.

I held out my arm and she slipped hers inside.

We went out into the corridor.

Several nuns were there, and her mother.

She looked at them but said nothing. We crossed the corridor and went out into the garden.

There were hedges and bushes, long arrays of roses, what looked like willow trees in the distance, a lawn directly in front of us, and the sound of running water somewhere.

"Look at that," she said. "Look at the light."

The moonlight bathed the garden in a white light, a light quite unlike any other form of light, casting indistinct shadows.

We looked up and the moon looked down.

Around the rim of the moon, the sky was indigo blue.

"When you took off that night in Sussex, I stood and watched your plane. It flew directly towards the moon, or it appeared to, a black silhouette getting smaller and smaller until it was no more. For ages I could hear the plane, but in the moonlight I couldn't see it."

We kept looking up.

"After you'd gone, I stopped in the pub in Southwater, the Black Prince. There was a soldier there who knew everything about movies. He was telling his friends that Leni Riefenstahl was nearly the star of *The Blue Angel,* but that Marlene Dietrich got the role instead. Did you know that?"

"Of course I did, silly."

"And I read the other day, in a Paris paper, that she is now filming Hitler's favourite opera. I forget what it's called but apparently it has *hundreds* of extras."

"She has had a better war than I have."

"She doesn't have a Philippa."

She squeezed my arm.

"Why didn't you tell me you were pregnant?"

"You know why. You'd have stopped me going. And . . . if, by some miracle, you'd allowed me to go, and I had been killed, you'd have grieved twice over. I would have killed your child. I didn't want that. That's why I talked about babies so much. I wasn't feeling well and I worried that you might put two and two together. But if I talked about having babies in the future — that day we went by the unexploded bomb, for example — I thought I might put you off the scent."

An intake of breath. "And before you ask, I thought that, when my tummy began to show, it would be the perfect cover. No one would imagine a pregnant woman being sent as an agent."

"And . . . when the nine months were up?"

"I'd cross that bridge when I came to it. A baby might be even better camouflage."

I said nothing for a long moment.

"Did they confiscate the acorn I gave you?"

"They confiscated everything."

As she spoke, the moonlight cast the tiniest of shadows along the cleft in her chin.

"I still have the cigarette case you gave me."

"I wonder where Erich is now. What happened to him?"

I shook my head. "I don't know."

"I thought . . . if I gave you his case, you might look for him, give it back, find out how he was. Was what he did so bad?"

"I thought so, at the time."

"And now?"

"I was given special duties, Madeleine. Things I can't tell you about. I couldn't go looking for Erich. I'm sorry."

"And the others — Ivan, Katrine?"

"Both captured. Both executed. I'm sorry about that too. The circuits they joined had been penetrated by the Gestapo — they walked into a trap. That would have happened to you, too, if you had contacted your circuit. You would have been dead by now. For weeks, I thought you *were* dead."

I leaned forward and kissed her cheek. "That day, by the Thames, by the Savoy, I gave you the most difficult assignment. You made the most of it, and you are still alive."

"I feel a long way from the Savoy," she said. "I don't think I could dance right now, but I would like to taste an American cocktail."

"They have wonderful names, some of them — old-fashioned, sidecar, screwdriver, white lady. That's you in the moonlight — a white lady."

She smiled. "I like that. But perhaps it's as close as I'll come, now."

I again thought of that day, months before, on the Embankment, when I had told Madeleine where she was being dropped.

"Was it what you expected — being in the field, I mean? Being an SC2 agent — did it live up to its billing?"

She hesitated and pulled her coat more closely to her.

"No." She tightened her belt. "You were right — the nerves get to you, everything is so uncertain. I was good in the field, I think, but no, I didn't enjoy it as I thought I would. I was silly ever to think that. A silly girl."

"How was it you got caught?"

She gave a short laugh. "It's embarrassing."

I said nothing but looked at the shadows.

"I was in a café, sitting outside in Nallies, about ten miles from La Rochelle. It was a convenient crossroads to watch traffic going either to La Rochelle harbour or to the beaches at Fôret de Longeville. One of the other customers had a West Highland terrier, just like Zola. Its owner let him — or her — wander in and out of the tables. I bent down and stroked it, and spoke to it — just a few words. I said 'You look just like Zola' — that's all, *but I said it in English.* Exactly what you told us to beware of in Ardlossan, but what I was always doing."

She coughed and laughed at the same time.

"I didn't think anyone had heard me but obviously some collaborator must have. They must have. They followed me, found out where I was living, watched me for a day or so. Found out where I was hiding my transmitter, then reported me. It was my own fault I was caught." She breathed out and coughed. "No one else's."

"It was an understandable mistake."

"You are being kind. I don't need that sort of kindness. It was a mistake I shouldn't have made. I would never have been promoted to SC1."

A cloud passed over the moon. For a moment all was shadow. Then the moon came out again.

I squeezed her arm. "There never was any SC1, Madeleine. It was a trick. We thought that if people in SC2 *thought* there was an SC1, they would try harder, in the hope of being promoted. That's why we called it SC2. It might also have confused the enemy."

She nodded, smiled, and again feebly squeezed my arm. "How many more tricks did you devise that I don't know about?"

"You were top of your class at Ardlossan, Madeleine. If anyone qualified for SC1, it would have been you."

She shook her head. "It was my one weakness that trapped me in the end."

I bit my lip. Her habit of breaking out of French and into English had been one of the things that had initially made me think she might be a German agent. Should I tell her that?

No.

She was too weak to know that I had ever doubted her.

I was ashamed of having doubted her myself.

"Madeleine, I have to ask you one thing. When you saw Philippe again, when he arrived at that hospital in La Rochelle, after you thought he was dead, what went through your mind, what did you think?"

She paused but squeezed my arm.

"Do you doubt my love for you?"

Doubt. There it was again.

"I went to see your mother in Blakeney —"

"Yes, she told me."

"She had a photo of you and Philippe on her mantelshelf . . . She said . . . she said Philippe was your first love, that a first love is like no other . . ."

"Mothers don't know everything, even if they think they do. When Philippe came for me, in La Rochelle, I couldn't believe it. Of course, I couldn't — I was amazed. Well . . . it was wonderful in its way, and it brought back all that we had been through. But . . . all that . . . it was *past,* it was *over.* I looked at him and he was the same Philippe, the same wonderful man, but . . . *but* . . . I had your child inside me, there was so much *more* between *us,* Matt, dear Matt, between you and me. Ardlossan, the sands, the standing stones, the bicycle rides, black-market whisky, London, all the lovemaking and conversations and training. You *formed* me. Right from that first meeting at The Farm, you were hard on me but fairly, for a good reason. You treated me as an adult, as an equal."

She looked up at the moon, then back to me.

"When I knew Philippe, he was a *boy.* Yes, we were innocent and in love, as my mother says, but we didn't know any better. Now I do. There's so much *more* to being an adult than to being a child."

It was my turn to squeeze her.

"I was worried . . . You know, that photograph of Philippe on your mother's mantelshelf . . . it was very prominent."

"Why believe my mother rather than me? Why can't men trust their women?"

"Did you always trust me?"

"Yes, I did."

"Did?"

"Do."

My gaze swept the garden. Lots of detail lost in the pale light. "Tell me . . . the interrogation . . . how bad was it?"

She didn't say anything for a moment.

"I wasn't tortured. Not with pain, anyway."

She looked up at me. "You were right, half right."

She breathed out. "I was humiliated."

She squeezed my arm. "Don't ask how. It was more than being stripped naked — much more. That's the point. It humiliates me to remember it, and to tell you — anyone — would be to revisit it. Just imagine the worst humiliation you could suffer, and that's what happened."

I didn't know what to say.

Then I whispered, "Did it work?"

She laughed. "Not as well as pain might have done. I kept thinking of The Farm, of you and those other men ogling my body, and I imagined that what the Germans were doing to me was a test. So yes, Colonel Hammond, your training helped me — a little bit anyway."

She took my hand and kissed it. "Even when I was . . . when I was completely degraded, when I was reduced to being an animal, a wild beast, I clung on."

And I had thought she was a German agent.

She laughed. "I remembered spitting at your people in Scotland so I tried that too. It helped a little."

She kissed my hand again. "I think I was in line for a more physical session when Philippe and his people intervened."

We had reached a bench.

I turned and looked down at her. "Let's sit here."

We sat down.

The moon was shining brilliantly again.

Her face was so very pale in the moonlight.

She didn't say anything but shortly afterwards she started to shiver.

I took off my jacket and put it round her.

"Shall we go in? Let's go and see Philippa sleeping."

Would I ever be able to be with my daughter without thinking of what I had done to Perrault?

Madeleine stood up. She squeezed my arm. What strength she had was waning.

She looked up. Her neck as white as moonlight allowed.

"Is this the last full moon I shall ever see, do you think?"

"Don't say that, Madeleine. Don't say that."

EPILOGUE

Madeleine died three days after I arrived at St. Hilaire, from liver failure brought on by typhus. Although she was a Protestant, she was buried there.

I don't know whether this account will ever be published: the Official Secrets Act forbids it for the moment. But I hope one day it will be deposited, perhaps, in the archive of the Imperial War Museum, in London, where Philippa at least might be given the chance to read it. I'd like her to know what happened.

For the record, I killed François Perrault on Tuesday, 24 October 1944. In the wider scheme of things — the Churchillian scheme of things — how useful was my action? As the world now knows, the German-British Soviet spy Klaus Fuchs, who worked on the Manhattan Project at Los Alamos, began passing information about the atom bomb to the Swiss-American Soviet agent Harry Gold at the end of 1945. So, arguably, I delayed the start of the Cold War arms race, which began in earnest in 1947, by twelve or thirteen months. Was it worth killing a good man for that?

No one ever found out that it was I who killed Perrault. The Paris police never quite believed Justine's idea and continued to maintain that it was an *épuration* that had gone too far: there were just too many similar incidents occurring all over France at the time. Monique Brèger's account was eventually published, including her role in helping SC2 — and she received the Croix de Guerre. The DSO that I received in the 1946 honours list simply said "For services in France during World War II," so less than nothing was published about Madeleine's heroism.

I never saw Justine again, and with good reason. The rogue agent within SC2 turned out to be — as you may have guessed — none other than Roland Kemp. Ulrich Kolbe had been correct in that Roland was neither solely a British SC2 agent nor a Gestapo agent — he was in fact a Soviet mole, playing each side off against the other.

The evidence against him was there, in a way. His circuit was one of two not compromised by the Gestapo. Like Monique Brèger, he knew that if his circuit had been the only one not infiltrated, it would have looked suspicious. So he didn't drop all of our people in the soup. Should I have registered that Roland had a shiny new lighter, and put that together with Monique's story that Kolbe had been given an English model which he hid away after she noticed it? I suppose I should have done — but I didn't.

And it was he, you will remember, who introduced Justine to me. Roland and François Perrault had instructed her to get to know me, and yes, to sleep with me, to pretend she loved me, all in the hope that eventually we would be married, and she would move to London as the wife of someone high up in British intelligence — the classic "sleeper," in fact. Gilles, her boyfriend in Nancy, didn't exist. She invented him so she could turn up later, after their "fight," and worm her way into my bed, to advance our relationship. When we were interviewing Kolbe, she had reacted with horror when she thought he was about to reveal the names of the double agents. Had he done so, the whole set of events would have blown up in her face. All the tears she shed in the restaurant where we had our last lunch were for Perrault, not for me.

Justine had never loved me, and Perrault wasn't quite so blameless as I thought. He wasn't aware of Madeleine's links to me, or to Philippe, when he had included her name on his intelligence lists as a captured SC2 agent. That was just as well. But he had been willing to use me in the communist cause, and that meant I didn't feel *quite* so badly about what I had done to him.

We found out all this only after Guy Burgess and Donald Maclean defected to Russia last year, and certain documents were discovered in what they left behind. Roland had been recruited, like all the other Cambridge spies, at university before the war. He's now in Parkhurst Prison on the Isle of Wight.

Kolbe had said there were two enemy agents in SC2, but that was probably mischief on his part, to make us waste time looking for someone who wasn't there, a trick much as the one I had devised about SC1 and SC2. There was no mention of a second spy in the Burgess and Maclean papers. Kolbe's trick certainly worked on me. On the strength of it, I doubted Madeleine for weeks.

Hilary got the knighthood he always wanted, but he didn't have much time to enjoy it. The headache he had complained about when I called him from Paris turned out to be not just a headache but the early warnings of the brain tumour that killed him in 1947. He left me a pair of his brogues in his will — dead men's shoes.

After the war I was promoted and transferred to a new outfit, but since that organization I became part of still exists, unlike SC2, I can't give its name.

I fell into the habit of taking Philippa (never Pippa) to see her grandmother in Blakeney, and it was on one of those occasions that I met Elizabeth, when we shared a taxi from King's Lynn in the rain. She is a headmistress at a school in Sussex, a few miles from the Southwater meadow from where Madeleine flew to France on the night of the last full moon before the invasion.

Elizabeth's job comes with a house and so we divide our time between my flat in Hamilton Place and her house in Sussex. Philippa, who is eight now, has just started at Elizabeth's school, where she is shaping up to be no less of a tomboy than her mother. She has her mother's unruly Botticelli hair and as I said, the same whisky-brown eyes.

Whisky is still my vice, more than ever.

All four of us (I'm not forgetting Zola) walk in that Southwater meadow from time to time. Elizabeth understands, and both Philippa and Zola — who are the best of friends — love it.

But not at night. Never by moonlight.

London, 1952

AFTERWORD

Madeleine's War is fiction: the plot and the characters have been invented. But the background — the context — is real.

SC2 is modeled on SOE, the Special Operations Executive, set up by Prime Minister Winston Churchill to parachute agents — male and female — behind enemy lines in occupied territories all over Europe, to carry out acts of sabotage and to prepare Resistance workers for an uprising when the invasion occurred. The existence of the organization — especially its use of women — was a closely guarded secret for several years.

The female agents were often recruited through FANY, and were trained in remote locations in Scotland and England, where they were taught sabotage techniques, communications skills, disguise, and how to resist interrogation because, as stated in the text, half of them were caught within six months of being dropped behind enemy lines. As part of their training, recruits were taught how to spot if they were being followed, and how to lose a tail when it was necessary. They were sent on exercises where they had to live off the land in the most inhospitable parts of the Highlands. As described, they were made to memorize a poem that could be used as the basis for code should their one-time pads be lost or used up. When they were parachuted into occupied territory, their silk one-time pads were sewn into their clothing. They were not sent out into the field until they could transmit Morse code signals of at least forty words per minute.

Carborundum powder — silicon carbide — *was* used to disable the axles of railway wagons, and cyanoacrylate *was* developed as a gunsight but found wider use as a powerful adhesive. All efforts were made to make training as realistic as possible, with recruits being duped at critical times.

The Paris Gestapo were headquartered in the avenue Foch, where they had several prison cells for interrogation purposes. The Gestapo did penetrate SOE security, and did break their codes. They announced this to SOE in a series of dramatic communiqués following D-Day and just before they withdrew from their locations in Paris and elsewhere in occupied France. This news was leaked to Members of Parliament, and this is how the existence of SOE was revealed.

The headquarters of SOE were near Baker

Street, much as were those of SC2, hidden behind a misleading "front" set-up. They did provide the BBC with its nightly broadcast of mysterious codes, many of which were made up.

There was a ten-mile coastal exclusion zone around the southern half of Britain throughout most of the war.

Winston Churchill did operate much of the time from a bunker below ground, under King Charles Steps, off Whitehall. These offices may now be visited as a tourist attraction.

The Manhattan Project — the Allies' top-secret operation to create an atomic bomb — employed hundreds of scientists of many nationalities in Los Alamos in the remote New Mexico desert, and French physicists were central to the success of the development of nuclear physics, winning Nobel Prizes for their efforts. The communists in France *were* at odds for most of the later months of the war with General de Gaulle, who worried about their links with Soviet Russia. He also tried to play up the role of French forces in the liberation of the country, and sought to minimize the role played by British and other Allied special forces.

After the invasion of 1944, when Allied forces swept south and then east through northern France towards Paris, German forces did hold out at three Atlantic ports where they had submarine bases: Brest, St. Nazaire, and La Rochelle. The latter two locations were in areas honeycombed with underground caves; and it was in one of these, at Lascaux, that during the war prehistoric paintings were discovered, showing many animals, some of which were extinct.

All the prisoner-of-war camps and concentration camps existed just as described in the text. Lysanders were one type of small aircraft used to drop agents into occupied territory and, most of the time, they flew when the moon was full.

ABOUT THE AUTHOR

Peter Watson is a well-known and respected historian whose books are published in twenty-five languages. He was educated at the Universities of Durham, London, and Rome, and his writing has appeared in the *New York Times,* the *Los Angeles Times,* and numerous publications in the United Kingdom. From 1997 to 2007 he was a research associate at the McDonald Institute for Archaeological Research at the University of Cambridge. He has written two previous novels, *Gifts of War* and *The Clouds Beneath the Sun,* under the pen name Mackenzie Ford.

The employees of Thorndike Press hope you have enjoyed this Large Print book. All our Thorndike, Wheeler, and Kennebec Large Print titles are designed for easy reading, and all our books are made to last. Other Thorndike Press Large Print books are available at your library, through selected bookstores, or directly from us.

For information about titles, please call:
(800) 223-1244

or visit our Web site at:
http://gale.cengage.com/thorndike

To share your comments, please write:
Publisher
Thorndike Press
10 Water St., Suite 310
Waterville, ME 04901